PRAISE FOR
METAL FROM HEAVEN

"*Metal from Heaven* is a work of feral and furious imagination. It's pulpy, bloody, sexy, gleefully seditious and seditiously gleeful. It's a battle cry of a book; read it, and rise up."

—**Alix E. Harrow**, Hugo Award winner and *New York Times* bestselling author of Reese's Book Club Pick *Starling House*

"Rich with lush prose, *Metal from Heaven* is a murderously good tale of highway robbery and sapphic revenge, that tackles important issues head on, and hits with a powerful ending that will stay with you long after the book is closed."

—**C. S. Pacat**, *New York Times* bestselling author of *Dark Rise*

"August Clarke is one of the most electrifying voices in genre fiction today. In *Metal from Heaven*, the volume is turned all the way up. This one will blow your hair back."

—**Sarah Gailey**, Hugo Award winner and bestselling author of *The Echo Wife*

"I know comfort books are in, and yes, they have their place, but there's nothing quite like reading something dangerous. Something rich with ideas, something challenging, something transgressive, and revelatory, something that feels like it's pushing the genre forward, something punk in the true meaning of the word, something that truly does not give a f**k what you think of it. This is that book. *Metal from Heaven* is a thunderous, visceral, Sapphic fever dream of a book, thick with religion, myth, and revolutionary ideologies. The prose seduces, the worldbuilding astounds, and the heart bleeds pure. This one goes on my best of 2024 lists for sure."

—**Rebecca Roanhorse**, *New York Times* bestselling and Lambda Literary Award–nominated author of *Black Sun*

"An ambitious, ferocious, sex-driven fever dream. Clarke's prose is ornate, enveloping, radiant."

—**Megan Whalen Turner**, *New York Times* bestselling author of *Thick as Thieves*

"Delicious, chaotic, and whip smart, *Metal from Heaven* will leave you with the burning urge to rise up and revolt against tyranny. What starts as a swashbuckling tale of horny, queer outlaws blooms into a mediation on otherworldly geopolitics and consciousness itself. August Clarke has written a freakishly original novel and I love it."

—**Annalee Newitz**, author of *The Terraformers* and *Stories Are Weapons*

"A sprawling, glorious, ichor-bright story that reads as both an ancient legend and an anti-capitalist howl of rage. Clarke's hope for a better world spills out onto every page. You're going to love this one."

—**Andrew Joseph White**, *New York Times* bestselling author of *Hell Followed with Us* and *The Spirit Bares Its Teeth*

"Hits like a piston, loves like an outlaw, and thinks like China Miéville. Made me want to cry, left me feeling like a giant. 'I read this book and I must shout.'"

—**Seth Dickinson**, author of *The Traitor Baru Cormorant*

"Surprising absolutely no one, *Metal from Heaven* is such an excellent book. I adored every heartbreak moment of *Metal from Heaven*. It's a bitter triumph with an oil-slick beauty. This one's for the dykes. It hits a lot of tender spots, beautifully done. If you trust me, read this book."

—**C. L. Clark**, author of *The Unbroken* and *The Faithless*

"This is industrial fantasy like you've never read before. With prose that drips like honey and burns like a forge, *Metal from Heaven* is all hungry revenge, human tenderness, and bloody political intrigue. August Clarke does something new here, and I can't wait for more!"

—**Bethany Jacobs**, Philip K. Dick Award–winning author of *These Burning Stars*

"Drenched in sex, blood, and hot-pink ichorite, *Metal from Heaven* is a high-octane revenge story that doubles as a rallying cry for a better future. It's the chant of a picket line, the glory of a highway robbery, the heat of a lover's flesh. Clarke shoves you headfirst into unapologetic dykery as praxis, and it's worth every battle scar."
—**Lauren Ring**, World Fantasy Award winner and Nebula finalist

"A queer, bloody love letter to rebellion that'll stick like a knife in your heart. At turns tender and violent, humming with tension, *Metal from Heaven* is immersive, rich, and an absolute joy to read."
—**Nino Cipri**, Hugo Award–nominated author of *Finna* and *Homesick*

"*Metal from Heaven* is a book you sink into like molasses, like the ichorite so revered and reviled in its pages. More than revenge, this is a love story—for the pasts that shape us, for the communities who nurture us, and for futures we might not live to see. Vivid, visceral, vicious: August Clarke takes no prisoners."
—**Naseem Jamnia**, Crawford–, Locus–, Astounding–, and World Fantasy Award–nominated author of *The Bruising of Qilwa*

"*Metal from Heaven* goes down gritty and gets stuck between your teeth. Come in for the glorious, breakneck, fuck-you-Fordism dyke revenge story and don't be surprised when Clarke handily devastates you as the dust settles."
—**Em X. Liu**, author of *The Death I Gave Him*

"A poignant and visceral tale of blood-soaked revenge, set in a harsh eco-fantasy world that feels lived-in and textured. August Clarke masterfully combines murderous thrills and political intrigue so that both elements hit you like a hammer made of ichorite right to the face."
—**Trevor Henderson**, author of *Scarewaves*, creator of Siren Head

METAL FROM HEAVEN

a confession at the end

AUGUST CLARKE

an imprint of Kensington Publishing Corp.
erewhonbooks.com

EREWHON BOOKS are published by:
Kensington Publishing Corp.
900 Third Avenue
New York, NY 10022
erewhonbooks.com

All Kensington titles, imprints, and distributed lines are available at special quantity discounts for bulk purchases for sales promotions, premiums, fundraising, educational, or institutional use.

Special book excerpts or customized printings can also be created to fit specific needs. For details, write or phone the office of the Kensington sales manager: Kensington Publishing Corp., 900 Third Avenue, New York, NY 10022, attn: Sales Department; phone 1-800-221-2647.

Erewhon and the Erewhon logo Reg. US Pat. & TM Off.

ISBN 978-1-64566-098-9 (hardcover)

First Erewhon hardcover printing: November 2024

10 9 8 7 6 5 4 3 2 1

Printed in the United States of America

Library of Congress Control Number: 2024932750

Electronic edition: ISBN 978-1-64566-099-6 (ebook)

Edited by Diana Pho
Interior design by Leah Marsh
Images courtesy of Adobe Stock

for workers everywhere,
and countless cicada broods

"The Copper Bosses killed you, Joe.
They shot you, Joe" says I.
"Takes more than guns to kill a man,"
Says Joe, "I didn't die."
Says Joe, "I didn't die."

—Alfred Hayes, *Joe Hill*

DRAMATIS PERSONAE

*most players, alive and otherwise, by initial geographic
and vocational association*

Ignavia City

Dalton Honeycutt

Linda Honeycutt

Edna Honeycutt

Poesy Honeycutt

Marney Honeycutt

Flox Gwyar

Etule zel Alchumena

Birdie James

Workers

Ramtha thu Ramtha XI

Ramtha thu Ramtha XII

Baron, Baron Apparent

Yann Industry Chauncey

Gossamer Dignity Chauncey

Tlesana thu Tlesana III

Easun thu Tlesana

Vikare zel Tlesana
Capitalists

Baird Steadfast Clay
Enforcer

Fallowlin
Brianna Beauty Lloyd
Prumathe thu Cerca
Teriasa zel Cerca
Betsy Sincerity Clune
Colton Gallantry Baker
Workers

Fingerbluffs
Mors Brandegor the Rancid
Tita zel Priumna
Mallory Valor Moore
Uthste thu Calaina
Reverend Amon Pierce
Jody Honesty Blake
Georgia Candor Blake
Sisphe thu Ecapa
Harlow of Delphinia
Thomas Fortitude Lockheart
Alcstei zel Prisis
Artumica thu Artumica Tanner
Dash Mercer
Wyatt Piety Stytt
Nero of Jira

Harriet Magnanimity Tanner
Benji Diligence Lockheart
Iodine of Trasa
Urusthe zel Achile
Nestur thu Urusthe
Olive zel Urusthe
Elisa Prosperity Jones
Pantasila Mahk Urphe
Clyde Lenience Barker
Bandits

Horace Veracity Loveday
Baby Loveday
Baron, Baron Apparent

Montrose
Helena Integrity Shane
Baronet

Glitslough
Abram Loomis
Susannah Loomis
Baron, Baron Apparent

Drustlands
Dunn Ygrainne
Strife Maiden

Laith Herzeloyde
Guard

Cisra

Alichsantre L
Countess

Royston

Miles Exemplar Vaughn
Perdita Perfection Vaughn
Prince, Princess

Crimson Archipelago

Hiram of Jira
Mir of Jira
Princes

Mago of Jira
Advisor

Tasmudan

Darya of North City
Hierophant

One

KNOW I ADORE YOU. LOOK OUT OVER THE glow. The cities sundered, their machines inverted, mountains split and prairies blazing, that long foreseen Hereafter crowning fast. This calamity is a promise made to you. A prayer to you, and to your shadow which has become my second self, tucked behind my eye and growing in tandem with me, pressing outwards through the pupil, the smarter, truer, almost bursting reason for our wrath. Do not doubt me. Just look. Watch us rise as the sun comes up over the beauty. The future stains the bleakness so pink. When my violence subsides, we will have nothing, and be champions. In the chasms wheat spikes and poppies will grow. Rarely is the future so immediate and tangible. Bless our triumph! How small you seem. How small you were. Remember?

That morning. Barely morning, still dark. A redness cast over the factory. I was freshly twelve. That meant I was a worker in earnest. A lustertouched worker, the oldest one so badly affected. Remember all of us, that's *all* of us (would-be scabs aside): my parents and my sisters and my uncles and my neighbors and everybody off the floor, my community that loved you, and you, darling you, chanting together in rings around the first and then-only Yann I. Chauncey Ichorite Foundry. I held your hand so tight. You wore the ring I made you and the feeling of its memory shimmered hot pink in my palm. It was proof that I existed. That I am real.

We had stood like this all night and now a gorgeous orange morning fell over Burn Street. Sunlight licked between bruisy limestone smokestacks and telegraphy spires, and the crumbling knuckled colonnades of an empire that's long gone. Stripes of yellow everywhere. Yann I. Chauncey himself was depicted in a stained glass window above the foundry door. He watched from above in flat candy colors.

The breeze melted on my tongue. Noxious and creamy. Far-off shops roasted cloves, quails, apricots, and wafting off the cobbles came a greasy wet animal petrichor and that citric bright *zing* of ichorite. Screaming birds unfurled from the eaves.

My family and I are Tullians. Dawns for us are holy. You were Flox Drustish and I wasn't sure what was holy for you. I hoped it was this.

For our health and dignity, we held vigil on this doorstep. Until our concerns were acted upon we'd let nobody enter. Ichorite would go unsplit and unsmelted. It'd molder raw in its fudgy sludge in the big crates in the foyer, and left unrefined as such, stock'd go unallocated, shipments would

2

stall, and materials demanded by various stuff-making processes all across Ignavia would fail to arrive, so that every
monied hand might share the stress. The whole twitching market machine, of which we were the nascent heart,
wrenched still. No grime under our nails. No fits out of me.

Cooperation, now! Hereafter, Hereafter!

We sang discordantly, but we were smiling. It was brisk
out, and the heat of our breath made mist above our heads.
The song was for morale. It keep us breathing together, collectivized our lungs, made us bellows. In unison we were
louder than one man alone could ever be. Them in unison,
that is. I couldn't remember the words. Despite my cen-
trality, I had somehow neglected to learn my part, so I just
mouthed the air and stomped along and let you be louder.
I pretended to be certain. Dumb kid. I had my family to do
proud and you to look after. You must know how precious
you are.

Usually speaking, Burn Street was swollen with carts
and day workers at this hour, sometimes enforcers on lurchers, and laborers in boots and boilers and long wool coats,
plus those girls you and I adored so much, the painted ones
working in big cinched silk dresses who leaned down from
the balconies where they smoked slim cigars, flicking their
ashes. Seeing, then, the bustling reverends and magistrates,
children running, otters and boars and cats, flower sellers
and meat barkers, who carried long hooked sticks from
which eels and sausage links hung with pepper and garlic
garlands, and beggars crying for alms. Everyone rushing,
rushing, all the world, yet that morning, nobody was on

Burn Street but us. We sang to nothing and no one. Dust floated in the air. Vacant. Funny.

When we'd practiced, we'd imagined this part happening before a gathered crowd.

You bounced on your toes and got paler. Tensed your jaw so tight I thought your freckles might pop off. *Told you you'd be nervous.* I swayed against you so that you'd sway against me. This was an alright kind of hypocrite to be, I reasoned. A useful kind. You pressed your nose into my arm.

My oldest sister Edna approached the crowd that wasn't there. I watched the breeze ruffle the wisps on her nape. Blonder than mine. She never could put her bonnet on right. Edna raised her hands, palms flat, fingers stretched, and the singing cut on cue. She tossed out her chin. "We address Yann Industry Chauncey as the staff who made him. It was you who found ichorite and devised the means of refining it, knowledge which has already refaced Ignavia, and soon'll change the whole world over. We applaud this, but knowledge not acted upon is nothing. We are the work. Our hands on the splitting belts, in the skimming, in the furnace—our hands are the engine that will cast tomorrow in luster. In the fifteen years of this foundry's operation, not once have you, Yann Chauncey, worked this floor. You have not seen what becomes of us. When pressed by the papers, you've denied knowledge of the lustertouched. You thus neglect us. This must change."

Hand on my shoulder. My father's, I knew his callouses. I fought the urge to lean against them, ducked forward. I wasn't a baby anymore.

In my ear, you whispered: "Marney."

Edna tipped back her head. "We work ceaselessly, through ail and injury, from bleed 'til bleed. I will never fish all the splinters from under my nails. I will wear these burns forever. My mother has been sweating here from the day you opened your doors. She carried my baby sister to term on the luster line, a line my sister's now old enough to work herself. I split your ore for you. I'm expectant. I'm afraid. We hardly know the properties of the material we work but we know— we know—that something is happening to us. Children borne of us suffer maladies of the mind. Hallucinations, vertigo, an acute sensitivity to touch such that handling any ichorite at all, even breathing furnace fumes, torments the afflicted. My baby sister succumbs daily to such fits. And still, she works your line! We know this factory whelps sickness. You must act upon this knowledge. We have demands for you to act upon before we walk that floor again. Until such a time you will see no profit, may dawn and dusk bear witness. Yann Chauncey, hear us. On one another we depend.

"Our first concern: we seek safer conditions, slimmer hours."

Harsher, higher: "Marney."

I stole my eyes off Edna's back. I wasn't close with Edna. It felt unfair to muddle this moment of her talking about me with unrelated chatter—then, I saw how your face looked wrong. You were sharper than me, cleverer, and whenever something occurred to you that'd occurred to nobody else it played around your eyes. Little muscles flexing, tensing. You'd figured something out.

You gnawed your bottom lip and I vaguely recalled moments spent crouching under the staircase with you between skimming shifts, knees against knees in the dark, you telling stories about the Drustlands that I pretended to believe while I rubbed the hurt from your wrists. You'd kissed me once under those stairs. We hadn't talked about it since.

You yanked my elbow and pressed your cheek against mine, pushed my face skyward, made us stare at the same spot. "Up on the roof!"

"Our second concern: a robust inquiry into the health of the lustertouched," Edna said.

I squinted against the light. The sun crowned behind the gables. I blinked and green-pink splotches smudged the backs of my eyelids. Second glance, still nothing. There was a chimney and a weather vane. I was unsure of what it was you wanted me to see.

"There's a man up there," you insisted.

I opened my mouth to negate you before I saw that you were right.

A man knelt on the roof with his back against the chimney. I'd missed him before, because the jacket he wore was a not dissimilar burgundy to the bricks behind him. Burgundy trousers, too, with wide blue stripes down either leg. So, an enforcer. I watched the enforcer watch us. Deftly, he loaded his gun.

"Our third condition is this—"

You bolted.

Edna hit the pavement with a crack.

My father threw himself down and he gathered up Edna, hid her with his shoulders, but her head lolled back like a doll's and I saw the gap between her eyes. Ranks broke. My family and everybody ran around and through me. I buffeted between people who sprang apart, tore down the alleys and the length of Burn Street while my brain boiled between my ears. I spun and I couldn't see you. My uncle or maybe one of his friends took my wrist and dragged me left, shouted instructions at me that I could not make out, said *Marney, Marney*. I lost traction. I fell out of his grasp and my body struck the ground and the wind clapped out of my lungs. My ribs closed on my chest like a fist. I sucked in. I couldn't get full. I crawled backwards on my elbows but got nowhere, the pavement was slippery and my shirt was drenched and hot and clung to me.

People tripped over me. Dirt caked under my nails. I propped myself up on my hands, and under my hands I felt—string. Hair. Long wet clumps of it. The heel of my hand ground long wet hair into the pavement, a half-unraveled tawny braid. My thumb pressed an inch below an ear. Little mole on the lobe. Poesy. I was crawling over Poesy's hair. Poesy, my middle sister. Her bonnet had come off. It rocked beside her, pleated ribbon ruined, the yellow straw brim smeared red. She'd always been the prettiest of us. I could see her teeth through a hole in her cheek. It had torn her tongue. I saw the inside of her tongue.

I jerked away from her and skittered back, flipped on my chest, hands flat, tried to get my feet underneath me. I couldn't tell gunshots apart. They echoed in my head and ate each other. I pushed up, I whipped my head around, I couldn't see you anywhere. I needed to find you. They killed my sisters. Where did you go?

Weight collapsed across my hips. My pelvis knocked the pavement and I heaved but could not scream. I wriggled. I kicked but it was pointless. Whoever had died on me had pinned me to the street.

Everyone was down. My limp neighbors, tangled, slack. The smell smothered me. It was everywhere, the muck and blood and *ichorite*, scalding sour bright ichorite. My mangled friends all glowed with it. It shimmered at the new edges of their bodies. I saw double. Venomous pink doubled everything, blurred everything. Edges waved. The sunlight that glistened on the blood from my family's bodies stung my eyes. The convulsions in my limbs started, slight but inescapable. The feeling unfurled: the first stages of a fit.

All of this was for us lustertouched. This whole demonstration was for the sake of my health.

I sank my nails into the meat of my hand, squeezed my fists so tight I thought my knuckles might stab through my skin. Stickier, chalkier, more impulsive than thought: *come come come come come.*

Time to make it worse.

A girl heaved herself up from underneath my mother. She pushed aside my mother's body, clawed over a knot of thighs and wrists and hauled herself upright. Only one standing. She clutched her head in her hands and gaped like she was howling. I saw her eye between her fingers. Animal

8

eye. Live mouse in a spring trap, pupil whirling, whirling. She staggered. Tripped, caught herself, swayed onward.

Bullet casings wormed out from under my friends.

The girl ragged a cough. She cleared her voice.

Over the spill, scraping and smearing, the bullet casings swarmed around my hands. They nudged against my knuckles like iridescent minnows. Pure ichorite, not a cut alloy. We made these. We'd picked and spliced and burned these, we'd cut them and beaten them with lead. Other people's anguishes on the line seized in the roof of my mouth. Mallet strikes on rhythm. Slimed metal kneaded into molds. Sweat and bleeding, that pounding sound, someone laughing, it tearing the lining of their throat. Someone's thumb catches the machinery's edge. Their nail lifts. Their nail is mine. Gluey blood strings and big bright pain. *Hallucinations*, Edna had said. Hand-me-down memories. Oh, Edna. Is this my fault?

The girl sang, "Unalone toward dawn we go, toward the glory of new morning."

An enforcer shot her belly, and when she did not fall, her head.

Bile in my mouth and my brain but I swallowed it. I closed my hands around the casings. They melted in my palms and I kneaded them, sculpted the mercurial ooze, thought *sharp sharp sharp sharp sharp*. The trembling got worse. My body shook apart under whoever's body was on top of me. I could not see. The world gushed greasy pink and vicious, and I wanted—my father. I wanted my father. I wanted my pa. The lustertouched fit came over me in waves. My blood was sparks and needles. I tasted that citric sour taste and stolen feelings *oomph*ed through my body and I was gone.

It was bright blue daytime now.

I did not move for a long time. I looked at the stained glass Yann I. Chauncey above us. My shirt was drying. The bodies above me went cold. Flies glittered around my head. Scintillating flies who changed colors when I blinked and left shiny streaks in the wake of their flight, pulsing zigzags. You always said you thought it must be pretty, how it gets when I'm like this. Mid-fit the world's a bubbling gem. It occurred to me that you had probably been shot.

Enforcers came down from the rooftops. Three of them. Just three. Two wore their rifles slung across their backs and the third, the man you saw, the one who killed Edna, kept his in hand. They squelched along the tangle's edge. Nudged someone over with a kick.

"Fuck, Baird. They're kids."

"Old enough to make property is old enough to break it." That one—Baird—propped his weapon against his shoulder. "Chauncey wants a count, and a clean curbside by sundown. Even he can't afford to keep Burn Street cordoned off longer than that. Get them in a line, mark them off, and I'll see about the wagons." Baird clicked his heels, then peeled off.

The other two mimicked Baird. One rubbed her nose. The other went for somebody's ankles.

Think think think think think. I couldn't move, couldn't wriggle out from under whoever crushed me. I couldn't

10

let them see me. If they saw me, they would kill me. I squeezed my hunk of ichorite and candy colors bubbled at the corners of my eyesight, warbled and acidic. I recalled unbidden kneading hot split ore on the skimming belts, wringing out the gooey luster from the fleshy clumps of dross. The pain of it. I gripped my knife. I tried to look dead. I could play dead. We were all playing dead.

The weight dragged off me. Smeared me against the pavement along with it before it was gone. Blood flow crashed back down my legs and vomit fluttered up my throat.

The enforcer walked beside my head. She stopped there. Her heels were a breath from my nose.

I slashed my new knife through the backs of her calves.

The cut sprayed my cheeks.

The enforcer screamed. She toppled and her rifle went off, cracked a window in the foundry.

I scrambled back. Stuck the knife in my waistband between brace buttons and clambered over bodies, bodies, bodies. I stumbled upright. I bounced on my toes. Where do I go? Where can I go? Pink whirling sizzling lights that were not real pulsed around my head. The other enforcer saw me. He pointed at me. I ran.

I ran down an alley away from Burn Street.

I left everybody behind me. I abandoned you, dead girl.

I swore this, I meant it.

Yann Chauncey, I will take your life.

Two

ENFORCERS WITH LEDGERS CROWDED THE front stoop of the tenement where my family had lived for all my life. I couldn't go in. Didn't try.

Ignavia City is the capitol. Forever ago the Bellonan empire tucked her on a hill between the Flip River and the Lueli River in the middle of the pines and in the centuries since, the swelling city has had no space to sprawl, so it built upwards. Every development plan here is a race to puncture the sun.

I climbed a rickety little staircase in an alley over some roof, then up an adjoining staircase, went five six seven stories high. The rails flinched when I stomped on them but they were old, so they weren't ichorite. Iron or whatever. I could touch them without exacerbating things. Things were bad. I could throw the knife away and not have ichorite touch me awhile, sometimes that calms me faster, but I needed to be safe.

My fit carried on. The sun fuzzed and I could not make my teeth stop chattering. I could hardly see past my fingertips. The rails rippled under my boots. If I slipped, that'd be curtains for me, I'd crack on the street like an egg, but I couldn't slow down, because if I did thinking and itinerant feeling would come and I would be destroyed. I went faster. Up another flight then over the street in a cage bridge meant for chimney sweeps and window washers. Perfect tube of knit iron rods. I could stand in it, but nobody much taller could. Flowering vines twined through the mesh. The flowers blurred together: unctuous, molten, purplish. I trampled them. Shouldered past a laborer with a kit over her shoulder. Her kit checked my chest and I reeled, knocked against the cage bridge's wall. The whole structure wobbled in the breeze. The laborer shot her arms out to balance. She blinked at me and said, "Are you hurt?"

I ducked under her arm. I got off the cage bridge and scampered down a staircase, ran longwise across the worker's walk that hugged the forum's vaulted roof and frightened the starlings, tore down a second cage bridge, this one forked, took the left finger. Underneath me a crowd churned. Merchants carts and commuters shouting, their boars bellowing, brass music muffled by the purr of lurcher engines, on which enforcers rode. Enforcers everywhere. The scene sparkled between the cage bridge rods, a mirage of drooling bayonets.

Down a staircase, and I was in an alley. It was humid and dark. I could smell myself. The clarity was suddenly

13

inescapable and I pawed at my chest, revolted and gasping, but my shirt was stiff and caked and blotched an awful rancid burgundy, enforcer uniform burgundy, and it kept sticking to my skin. Dried bits cracked and flaked. I wasn't a woman yet and didn't wear a bonnet, so when I touched my head, I felt my naked braids. I found a wet hunk. The Tull Shrine was beside me. It was a polished pink wall with a door. I took the iron ring knocker with my filthy wet hunk hand, but the door was heavy. I threw myself down, my weight screamed against my arm sockets and my hands burned and the door groaned and gave, just barely. I shouldered through the gap. It swung shut on my heels and the street sounds snuffed.

The Shrine theater was a square room. Horizon-facing windows, not that you get the horizon line in the city. Religion doesn't work here. Sloped ceiling. No adornments, polished walls aside. The floor was vacant. Well past dawn scene, that made sense. Cushions had been arranged in concentric rings for kneeling around the Shrine table. At this hour, the Idol wasn't out, so the table wore peonies and rye spikes and pale blue tapers that'd burn until sunset, when the Idol would be brought out for dusk bleed, after which these offerings would be swept and the Shrine would be dressed with black tapers and boletes and bread knots until dawn. The air smelled like pollen and dust. It was freezing.

I limped down an aisle and collapsed by the table and wept. I must've slept eventually. In dull flickers of wakefulness, the attendant Tull reverend stood over me with bread that I did not eat. He prayed aloud beside me.

14

I woke to pounding fists on the door that erupted and let in two enforcers on lurchers. They tore through the dark and seized the reverend by his smock. The squeal of rubber on tile was awful. From under the table where I was curled, I heard the reverend speak the bleed while the enforcers screamed nothing at him, they screamed wordlessly like animals, and I ran and crawled out a window and heard something shatter behind me but didn't investigate and climbed up the frigid molding and threw myself down on the roof and retched. There was nothing in my stomach to give. I heard the enforcers screech out of the Shrine, the panting machinery of their lurchers fade to silence. Perhaps they took the reverend with them.

Quiet stretched. I spat and I dug my fingers in my ribs and collapsed on my back. My shoulder blades scraped the rough shingles. The air was gritty. I didn't move. I watched lavender smokestack vapors choke the nearby moon. I couldn't see the far one. When I went back down the Shrine was empty and the table had been turned on its side, the offerings scattered and nibbled by rats. I didn't really sleep after that.

The next five days got cold. I wandered around. It got harsh out. Word was that the Yann I. Chauncey Ichorite Foundry had been beset by violent riots; that laborers had amassed to steal and destroy the refinement devices inside those walls. Rumors that they foamed with loathing toward Mr. Industry Chauncey, and jealousy of his great work, and frustration with their own smallness and the constrictions of their stupidity, and that generally Ignavia City must be growing calloused and ought be buffed. To soothe the propertied and nervous, Ramtha thu Ramtha, the baron of Ignavia City, signed writ for expediated inquiry into this calamity that bade enforcers to snatch and wring out all suspected riot affiliates within the week, in public, with standard-issue cherrywood batons.

The Foundry reopened. A host of new workers replaced my gone family in brand-new unstained boilers, having materialized from nowhere. Traitors.

Snow fell thinly. It smeared blackish on the street. I drank from a mermaid fountain and ate smashed stone fruits under the stalls in Market Street, stole scraps from collared boars, stayed hungry. I slept under the awning of Tlesana's Treasure, an expensive dress shop, and behind a butchery on Rake Street. The gore on my body faded brownish; perhaps people assumed I was caked with mud. Nobody looked at me. I made up my mind to leave.

Sixth dawn, I made for Flipcross Station. I'd never before had the means nor cause to go inside it. Not that I had the means as of now. I'd never been outside the city. Three generations of my family had moved to this city for work when the crops failed twenty years ago, a choice that had changed what it meant to be Tullian. If we had family in Glitslough or the smaller peasant baronies, I did not know them.

One thousand years ago, Flipcross Station was an imperial Bellonan forum. Presently it was a slab of marble and sleet. Few people milling about this hour. Trash dusted the gilded palm-and-knuckle-creased floors, and the air was sourcelessly breezy, lit by gas lamps that flickered like revenants. Knuckled columns dangled lacquered black-boards where departure times were marked in chalk. I could read numbers, but phrases were harder. I picked the platform that'd leave soonest with little care to its promised end. It was at the crown of a flight of stairs. I climbed them. The stairs had iridescent ichorite handrails that I could not suffer to touch. I walked in the middle and I kept my hands to myself. I chewed my tongue. At the top of the stairs, the floor stretched to a trench that held the waiting train. It was huge and wheezing. It looked like leashed-together rhinoceros beetles. I saw faces in the windows and felt a lunging horror that the train would leave without me. All of my bones chattered. I stumbled through the stragglers and up the little steps, and the warmth hit me, and I collapsed. I hit the floor.

The amber light was thick with pine resin and varnish. Molded mahogany ceilings and lush brocade curtains and brass hooks affixed with ichorite studs, from which dangled satchels, rolled over me, as did the backs of leather booths, the edges of skirts, a red rug that scraped my jaw as somebody lugged me upright. My arm was in a fist. I thought, enforcer. I sought my knife in my waistband before I blinked and saw properly the conductor, a broad and young Veltuni boy. His lip ring glinted. "Nasty spill," he said. "Are you alright?"

On my breath's edge I said, "Yessir."

"Do you have a ticket?"

Lying came so quick to you. You would've told him a story and saved me. "I don't," I said.

17

He adjusted his grip. With dripping kindness, he told me, "If you don't have a ticket, you cannot ride this train."

I saw every vein and sun fleck on this boy's face and divined in them that he was serious, that with ease he would guide me down the stairs and abandon me on the platform to wither. Futures unfurled in my head. I saw myself starve on the platform. I saw myself caught and killed. He was already forgetting my face. I could thrash and cut at him, but he would hail guards, and I had no saving charm nor rhetoric. I held my tongue.

"Young ma'am," he prompted. He took a step toward the door and gave my arm a tug, like he'd leashed me.

I dug in my heel.

"Fare," said a stranger. Molasses voice. A hand emerged from behind a leather booth and pinched between two long sharp nails was a crisp and gleaming bill. "For the girl."

The conductor let out a sound. He released me, and with a bashful glance used that hand to collect the offered cash. He flinched as he took it, but thanked the stranger curtly, and turned back to me looking wan. "Enjoy your trip," he said. Then he whisked himself down the carriage and was gone through a latched metal door.

There was an open booth diagonal to the one that housed my savior. I got myself there. The leather felt hot to the touch. There must be some heating apparatus beneath the cushion, and when I put my hands down the heat seeped up between my bones and revived the blood there, made it flow again. I thawed and regained needles of feeling. A sob bubbled but I mashed it. I could not risk making a fuss.

Dawn spilled through the window, red and vital, and I mouthed the words to the bleed. In my mind, I arranged wheat spikes on a square table. On either side of me, my sisters daubed their eyelids with morning paint and understood what I said; they were adults and had studied Tull scripts, they understood the necessity of our work and dutifully refused to let me in on the secret. Still, we knelt together. We folded our hands over the table's edge and wriggled our fingertips. The Idol of the Torn Child remained motionless, placated by our rigor and precision. I drifted in and out.

Outside, Ignavia City fell away from me. Dense conifers blurred into a shivering whirr of color, unbroken by streets or tall buildings. Executed criminals dangled shirtless from their ankles occasionally, tattoos sprawling, but they thinned out and vanished the further we got. I felt the numbness where my horror at the sight of them should be. I had no idea where we were going. I imagined some snow-capped lodge in Montrose Barony or a stone fruit orchard in Glitslough. Another country, maybe. Hallowed Cisra or chalky hungry Royston. The swamps of ancient Tasmudan, where everyone was rich, and nobody was allowed to leave. The Drustlands. You'd told me once you'd never go back. I felt a shock of anger that you'd been robbed the chance to change your mind.

The train sound was good on my nerves. I liked the engine's grind and purr. It occurred to me that this was the longest I'd gone since I could recall without a shift at the foundry. I'd never been left idle. Too much room for wandering thought. The mechanized constancy felt like home and I sank into the vibration, imagined the fast-churning marriage of gears that propelled the train forward, the slag burning in the furnace, the exhaust fumes twirling toward the sky. I had some vague sense that the rails beneath this train were cast ichorite, as with the bolts that held the windows and the doors in frame, but I pushed that away. I had to plan.

When I left this train, I needed to find a Tull Shrine and plead sanctuary long enough to scrub myself clean and orient myself to the new air. Then I'd find work and throw myself into it. Of course, I could commit myself to a mill, I'd done factory work all my life, but there were other options that might take me. I could become a miner. I could serve some farmer, a proper Tullian vocation, pick fruit or drive livestock, or I could apprentice myself to a cart driver, join a company of sailors. I could learn some trade. I'm good with my hands. I thought to myself, I have survived every fit I've suffered. I should have endured life at Yann Chauncey Ichorite Foundry without complaint. It would have spared my family the sympathy that'd spurred their deaths if I had just shut up. The magnitude of what I'd done dangled over me. I felt its breath on my neck. I stared out the window. I let my eyes go soft.

A warm sweet smell brought me back. A fruit tart had appeared on the cushion beside me. Hot dark cherries and azurine marmalade glimmering in a golden crust. My attention snapped toward the aisle but whomever had given it was gone. My gut twisted. I'm meticulous except where feeling good is concerned. I gathered the tart in my hands and drank in the smell and wolfed it in one swallow, sucked my fingers clean. Rich and bright and soursweet. It thawed something in me. Heat bloomed in my diaphragm and at once I was crying and I couldn't do anything about it. Tears dripped off my chin. I blinked until my eyes weren't blurry and I looked at my hands, shimmery with butter, then at the cushion where the tart had been left. There was a note scrawled on a ticket stub.

I picked it up, dully sorry for how my thumbs smeared on the paper. It'd been written with a quick, light hand. I could scarcely read it. I held it to my nose and sounded the letters aloud. Chewed over sounds for longer than it should've took, strung them together, tried to make words from the pieces. I stumbled with a vowel, made it too small and properly round, then gave up and let it hang low in my mouth and then understanding struck me. I read the whole note to myself with dire certainty:

KEEP TO THE WINDOW. YOU WILL BE JUST FINE.

Gunshots blasted across from me.

I dropped the note and skittered back, flattened myself against the narrow plate windowsill. I seized my knife from my waistband and clutched it beside my thigh. My heart beat my breastbone, my pulse banged my teeth. The train screamed down the rails with impossible speed, there was nowhere to go, surely if I jumped, I'd splatter. My knife squirmed against my palm. I squeezed it harder. The edges

21

of my vision smeared pinkish. I glanced around without moving my head.

A woman stood diagonally from me. Big frame in black suede, brimmed hat tipped low so that just her red mouth showed. She held a rifle in her bejeweled magician's hands. I remembered her hands. She'd given the fare that saved me. She was not standing alone. A short slim bald woman stood at the car's far end, revolver in one hand, open satchel in the other. She walked down the aisle toward my savior and me. As she passed, she whistled, and stricken well-to-dos in seersucker suits dropped their wallets and their watches in the bag. It was quick, compulsive, like their valuables were hot to the touch. I saw a man shiver as he surrendered his golden rings and prayer pearls, but he didn't protest, didn't so much as blink. Nobody breathed. Hands floated beside stretched faces, palms empty, helplessness fully displayed. They acted like this woman was a revenant. Surely, she would suffer no lip.

My savior grinned. Her teeth were long and yellow. Another gunshot sounded, distant, the carriage behind ours. I wondered if it was another warning shot. The big woman plucked a slug from thin air, rolled her wrist, made a show of loading her gun. She curved her mouth. "Good morning! What educated stock we've got. Good little pigeons give and live to see tomorrow." Her molasses voice echoed off the walls. She could've been an opera diva with those lungs.

Slowly, with fluid ease, she dipped her rifle over the booth before her and kissed its muzzle to a weeping woman's head. The metal glinted in the woman's ringlets. I felt a phantom chill on my scalp.

The short slim bald woman whistled past me. I didn't dare move but watched her, tried to memorize her. Furrowed brow over hooded eyes, gaunt cheeks, thin pierced mouth pinched around her ringing note. She didn't look at me, stopped beside my savior. They stood side by side. The weeping woman covered her face with one gloved hand. She was Stellarine, wore a dozen pearl bracelets that clacked when her shoulders heaved. Then she went still. I feared for her mortality.

My savior flicked her tongue between her teeth. Her big red grin flipped.

Something was wrong.

The latched metal door swung wide, and snow gusted shrilly inwards as an enforcer jumped the gap. His shoulders filled the threshold. He snapped his weapon shut and took aim at the bandits, barked an order that nobody heard. I tore my eyes off the enforcer to watch my savior die, but caught the weeping woman, whose fingers had suddenly splayed. Between her knuckles her eyes were dry and burning. A gunshot smacked and my ears whined, and I saw the pistol hooked in the weeping woman's free hand, saw smoke drift from its barrel. She brought it to her lips and blew.

The enforcer howled as he fell.

The spell broke. Passengers screamed and lurched and hurled themselves against the windows or dove for the thrumming floor. A man scrambled from his booth and threw himself across the gap, but the train lurched, his ankle twisted, he slipped and was caught just before gravity stole him by a second enforcer, who tossed him down in the second car, strode across him as she advanced on the bandits, but she'd lowered her weapon to catch him and had no time to ready it again. The shot cracked. Her shoulder opened, her maroon jacket soaked black, she collapsed against the wall and panted. It was like the shot had nailed her in place. She writhed without falling and her good arm dangled limply. Her fingers loosed and her gun clattered to the floor. She spat blood at the bandits. She said, "There are more of us coming, Rancid. You aren't getting off this train."

The short slim bald woman went rigid. She stopped whistling. Her eyes fixed. "Tita," she said.

The far latched metal door swung. It banged against its frame, then rattled inwards, knocked the wood paneled wall where the shot enforcer leaned. The next carriage's door had been propped open. I could see inside it. There was a woman on the ground. Edna. She could not have been Edna but she was Edna, the dead woman was Edna. I saw her yellow hair. My bones vibrated under my skin. I squeezed my knife and the ichorite warmed and swelled between my fingers, that citric zing coated my tongue. It cloyed down my throat. My gums and lips felt puffy. I put my boots on the booth and crouched, fighting some impossible animal desire to scurry up the wall. Blood foamed in my temples. I was going to bust out of my skin.

The three bandits sprang apart from each other. The short slim bald woman sprinted across the carriage, cleared the first enforcer's body with one stride, and booked over the gap into the second carriage. The weeping woman sprang after her. The big woman spat something in a language I didn't recognize and whirled around, seized the near door's painted latch. She heaved and the metal squealed but didn't budge. She snarled, harsh and dripping sweet, "Open up, Etule! Open this door or widow your wife! Don't cross the Choir! We've taken care of you!"

The weeping woman shouted, "That's the fork, the bridge's nearing—Uthste, Tita is *dead*, you have to get up—"

Uthste gathered dead Tita to her chest. She cradled her neck like a baby's.

The big woman slammed her fist against the slim frosted window. She called, "Etule zel Alchumena! Open the fucking door!"

The bleeding enforcer laughed.

The weeping woman took her hands off Uthste's shoulders and faced the second carriage's far door. Aimed from her hip as it opened.

I crawled to the booth's edge and slipped into the aisle. Quick little steps. I trod so lightly that even the train couldn't feel me as I crossed it, and I made for the woman who'd saved me, no thoughts in my whirring rattling head. I put my twitching knife back in my waistband and held up my empty hands. My blood was froth and brine and spun sugar. My tongue was dry, it hurt when I spoke.

Soft I said, "Pardon, ma'am." She paid me no mind. She pounded harder. Her great shoulders worked under her black suede coat.

Louder I said, "Pardon me, ma'am."

She slammed her fist against the door and held it still, like she'd pinned a fly. She turned her head. She glowered down at me. It felt like sunlight through a curved lens on paper. If there was anything left in me to burn it would've caught. I averted my eyes and bowed my head and made my movements as obvious as I could muster. I tucked myself beside the metal door and I flattened my hands over the ichorite bolts in the hinges. I mouthed, prayed, *loose loose loose loose loose*. My eyes buzzed beneath the lids. I saw iridescent double. My gums were throbbing and I wondered vaguely if they'd surrender my teeth. The cast ichorite got pinker. It yielded to my touch. The hinges sloughed off the wall that'd held them and oozed between my fingers, dripped thickly like honey or tar, and the metal puddles on the floor stiffened into awful little drizzled coins. In my head I huffed furnace fumes and felt my hammer hand go raw. I heard the hammer slam. I felt it pull in my back. The hingeless door went slack in its frame. With a scrape, it fell. It clattered into the bright cold and crunched under the train's wheels. The vibration felt sick in my shins.

My savior stared at me in a new way. Hatred melted down to bewilderment.

Gunshot in the second carriage.

She snapped out of it. The big woman crossed the gap, kicked open the opposing door in that same stride. The carriage we'd opened was the engine room. The engine driver, young Etule, the man who had nearly thrown me off this train, looked back at us with dread. Us! The bandit stood over him. She took him by his lapels and shook him hard, then shoved him aside, took up the steering levers herself.

I looked over my shoulder and moved before I comprehended. I saw the weeping woman holding the second carriage's far door shut with the strength of her back; I saw it buck against her. I had wet ichorite in my hands. I crossed the carriage and didn't look at the panicking passengers, I stepped over the enforcer and shouldered open the flapping door, swallowed a sour lump of uncertainty about the gap and jumped it.

Ache flowered up my calves as I landed. It was a grounding sting. I dashed past limp Edna in the bandit's arms and I sidled up to the weeping woman, who watched me coming and did nothing to stop me, and I smeared my gooey hand down the seam of the door and the frame. I felt delirious. My mouth itched. I squeezed my eyes shut so tightly and I thought, *solder solder solder solder solder*, and opened my eyes to see the ichorite slime drip off my fingers and slither into place. It glued the door in crazy strings. My hand tingled. It was going numb.

The weeping woman said, "What are you doing?"

I swayed in my boots. I suddenly felt extremely unwell. I shouldn't be upright. I scrubbed my hand on my thigh, but the ichorite feeling wouldn't come off. I imagined the enforcer still battering the door was Baird and that he was here to bottle my blood. I imagined him with a monstrous face, a bestial face. I imagined him with a snout and horns. I tried to look the weeping woman in the eye, but her face swam, her features blurred, the whole of her shimmered lusterlike. Her prayer beads sizzled. "Take me with you," I said. "I'll be useful. Please."

The train lurched. I fell, the weeping woman caught me. She held my shoulders in her hands. The sides of her pistols pressed against the meat of my upper arms. Steel felt like nothing at all. The train was slowing down, I think. My blood rushed like it wasn't, but I was aware of the pine trees individuating outside the frosty windows. Needles came into focus. It was so cold. I saw my breath. I rolled with sour sweat.

"She'll ride with me," said the big woman, who emerged in the second carriage with us to the passengers' chagrin. Someone cried nearby, someone grown. Someone whispered, *Rancid, Rancid*. I wanted to retch. The big woman ghosted her talons over Uthste's scalp, and Uthste stood, held Edna in her arms like a bride. My savior then reached toward me. She smiled again, red and wide.

I took her hand. I couldn't breathe. The weeping woman holstered her weapons and slung the loot satchel over her shoulder. She stood before the sliding passenger doors and pried them apart with her hands, prayer beads clicking, held them wide to reveal ancient conifers rolling slow. Without a backwards glance at us, she stepped into the morning. Uthste followed wordlessly, Edna nodding in her arms, and then my savior brought me to the carriage's edge. The wind scraped my face. She pushed me square in the back. My boots touched nothing and briefly, I flew.

Three

WE STOMPED ON DEAD BLOND FERNS ALONG the railroad going south. A murmuration of cranes flew above us. Their song was throaty, discordant. The forest was thick, the trunks broad as I was tall, and moss fuzzed the undergrowth, barbed flowers opened, crinoline mushrooms fruited in rings. The air was crisp and delicious. It felt alien on my exposed skin. I savored every lungful. It's better to be grateful than get wretched over sores. The excitement was leaving my body and exhaustion felt close. I tried to outpace it. I sped ahead of Uthste and the dead girl, kept pace with the woman who'd saved me.

I did not yet know that I belonged with them. I didn't know that they would be mothers to me. That I'd be their heir and squire, then come of age, that I'd be the Whip Spider and that the gentle and monied would weep to hear my name.

Dirt crunched under my heels. Pines swung low and touched my hair. It occurred to me how filthy I was, and that I hadn't taken out my braids since *it* had happened. My braids had stayed pinned in a wreath above my brow, revealed to heaven, gathering violence's grime, and I feared what they'd feel like when I finally took them down. I imagined finding a piece of someone tucked inside a curl. I felt faint. Wild dogs yelped out of sight.

None of us spoke, but Uthste whistled. Pretty name. Oo-*thess*-tea, it should be said, but in my mouth I felt it slur into uh-*thez*-dee. Damn a Tullian drawl. My teeth chattered. I scratched the gooseflesh on my arms. I didn't know how to ask the other women their names or offer mine without potential rudeness. What did I know about bandit propriety?

Uthste was Veltuni, she had the name and the lip piercing to show for it, and the weeping woman who hadn't ever been weeping was clearly Stellarine, made obvious in her pearls and her posture. In Stellarine temple school, they made you walk with books on your head. Women from the smelt line told me that. I couldn't begin to guess about my savior's faith. Religious heritage was important in Ignavia but she wore none of its markers. I tried to focus on nothing. Peered into the vivid tangle and searched for enforcers that weren't there.

The ground dipped, and we diverged from the rails and edged down the slope, which opened to an expanse of fast black water. Stringy algae clung to the bank. Smashed glass sparkled green between small flat stones. The water teemed with thumb-sized fish and broke into bubbles over jutting rocks, and I watched the churn and thought abstractly about lace skirts. A wooden bridge comprised of splintered and grayish and seemingly structurally dubious planks skated above the water. Could scarcely be fit for freight. The bandits trudged down beneath the tunnel bridge into a shady muddy crevice, and I kept close behind them. I put my stinging hands under my arms.

The weeping woman strolled up to a misshapen lump of sediment, and she hooked a nail under some hidden edge. With a rattle, it became the corner of a tarp. She yanked it free, sent dirt and debris scattering, and revealed a set of four lurchers. I'd never seen one up close. Their metal frames looked dull, gunmetal matte. Leather cushions on the saddles looked finely made, and I traced the treads on the big rubber wheels, the horn curve of the dark notched handles. They were expensive and skeletal. I recoiled from them. I couldn't reconcile what I saw with my company. Bile tickled in my throat, and I scanned the creek, expecting enforcer bodies to surface and bob along like apples.

"They're ours," said the big woman. She took off her hat, pulled a comb from her twist, and let down thick waves of black hair. She had dark, proud features, wore long mink lashes that cast shadows on her cheeks. She looked me over. "When's the last time you've eaten?"

"When you fed me," I said.

A smile twitched on the weeping woman's mouth.

The big woman squared her shoulders. Her height was incredible. She must've had inches on my father. I wanted

31

to shrink from her but I couldn't make myself move. She said in her smooth voice, "You've come into the custody of the Highwayman's Choir. I'm Mors Brandegor. I ride with Uthste thu Calaina and Mallory Valor Moore, and lately Tita zel Priumna, our sweet undone girl."

"She wasn't sweet," Uthste said. She had knelt beside the creek bed and pulled the dead woman across her lap, and she took her head between her palms, rubbed her thumbs in the hinges of Tita's jaw. The tenderness made my belly ache. Tita's eyelids looked bluish. I saw little veins inside them. Uthste smoothed the little whisps along her hairline and said, "Don't you soften her now."

Mallory Valor Moore looked at the water. Her smile was still there. It looked waxy, frozen.

Mors Brandegor stiffened. Her name was inscrutable to me, revealed nothing of her origin, but I had some implacable sense that I had heard that lilt in her accent before. She twisted her heavy-looking rings, then jabbed a long nail at the corpse on Uthste's thighs. The corpse looked less like Edna from this angle. She hardly looked like Edna at all. Mors Brandegor flashed her teeth. "If you come with us, you'll end up like this. The Choir courts death, kid. Misery will hound you. You can part with us here and be rid of the risk. You aided our stunt, so some portion of this loot is yours, it'll help you on your way if you barter right. Follow the tracks south for Ignavia City and north for Kimball or Montrose. You can have a fresh life for yourself."

"No matter." I smiled back. It felt deranged and it made my face hurt, but I couldn't stop, and it kept the screaming at bay. I dimpled. I felt my chapped lip split. "Where are we going?"

"Is that blood on your shirt?" Mallory Valor kicked a rock into the water. Under her delicate ruffle-edged dress, she wore work boots with round steel toes. The current swallowed the ripples.

I couldn't blink. "Yes'm."

She kicked another rock. Feigned interest in the insects that squirmed beneath it. Long leggy pale things. "How's a girl your age wear that much blood?" Then, sharply: "Explain that door trick."

"Valor," Uthste warned.

"Those are factory-issue double-knee canvas trousers she's wearing," Valor said, uncowed. "She's not a common urchin. She was under someone's employ recently enough to look strong, and if she's old enough to labor, she can speak on her own. Talk to me, girl. Explain to me what you've done."

I panted. I looked to Mors Brandegor, who was looking down at Tita. I looked at Uthste, whose eyes had shut. I looked at the useless sky.

"Be prompt," Valor said.

I opened my mouth and tried to say the foundry's name. It caught in my throat. I wrapped my hands around my neck and kneaded but I tasted sour, I opened my eyes until my lashes brushed my skin. I was going to sob. I was going to hurl up my own ghost. I tried again and worked my lips but sound didn't come. I managed a thin moan. My vision freckled. Something twinged funny in my knees.

33

"She'll talk in time." Mors Brandegor folded her arms. "Tita'd have company if the kid didn't do whatever that was. Now. Are we bringing her body back bluffways?"

"No," Uthste said. She covered Tita's empty ears, then covered her shut eyes, her still nose. "She's with her hand in ancestry. The body's becoming ground again, and she'd hate her remains to be hauled around like cargo. Let's bury her here. Regroup at Beauty and Prumathe's and go home when morning comes. Girl?"

I slid my hands from my throat to my collar.

Uthste said, "What do we call you?"

"Marney Honeycutt." My voice was coarse and small.

"What Virtue?"

"None," I said. "I'm Tullian."

Uthste furrowed her brow. "Are you well enough to help us dig?"

I nodded vigorously.

Uthste laid Tita's head on the ground. Her yellow hair fell across her face. Uthste turned Tita's cheek, spared her the sight of this work, then set to digging without ceremony, found a flat stone with a sharp edge and carved open the ground. Valor joined her after a moment, tied her lovely skirts high on her hips and stood in the mud in her boots and pale stockings. I crouched beside Valor. I used my hands first, but the open ground stung with frost, so I scraped up dirt like Uthste, with slippery creek bed rocks. Mors Brandegor stood over us. I heard a lighter click, and a sigh. She blew perfumed smoke above our heads. I liked the smell. Then she knelt, her cigar dangling from her long teeth, and dug alongside us, and the four of us in tandem bore a hole into the ground, made it long and deep, then deeper. I jumped in the hole and emptied it with my hands again, I had worked my body warm and relished the chill against my knuckles.

I could not bear the questions that were always squirming under the next fistful of dirt. What had been done with my family? Where are you? Is the place marked? Did they bury you or burn you? Did they toss you in the Flip River? Did they hang you by the ankles for display like murderers in the spring? Tullians are meant to be given to the ground. I asked you once and you told me you'd never die, so what's the use in planning.

I handed a rock up to Uthste and she did not ask why I was crying. The hole was deep enough that standing, my eyes hovered just above the grass. Snails slimed between wildflower petals. I traced their spiral shells. I reached up, and Mors Brandegor and Valor grabbed me and pulled me out.

Uthste stripped Tita of her jacket and her boots. She pulled off her trousers, untied her shirt. It fell translucent to her thighs. She took off her jewelry, unhooked the golden ring from her bottom lip, a mark of Veltuni adulthood, a vow to join the ranks of watchful ancestors. She put the lip ring under her tongue and closed her mouth. Tita's body glowed with tattoos. I'd never seen tattoos like this, whenever I passed the executioner's garden, I'd always hid my eyes. Drawings of chains and ships and girls and knives covered her hard arms and the curves of her legs and her unmoving concave belly, dark lines on her hip bones and on her ribs, I saw fish bones down her sternum, wilting lilies where her clavicle met her throat, her whole body done up in art. Tita had been beautiful. Her body was beautiful. Her chest had upside-down writing above the swell of her breast, I could count the letters through her shirt. Big square letters for simple eyes like mine. TITA ZEL PRIUMNA, they spelled. I must've stared too hard, because Mors Brandegor's purpled smoke curled across my cheek, and above my ear she purred, "So they know our names if we dangle."

I folded my hand over the toe of Tita's hollow boot. I felt a sudden surety. It pulsed through my body, quicker than blood. I looked up at Mors Brandegor's broad face. "When will I be tattooed like this?"

Her brows shot high and her smile hooked huge, too stark for life, like it'd been illustrated. "You want it?"

"When I'm got, nobody will mistake me." I fought an insane urge to embrace her. I rubbed the boot lacing with my thumb. "I want my name marked plainly and unremovably across me. When can I have it done?"

Still smiling, Mors Brandegor flicked cinders in the hole. I watched the cherry smolder in the dirt. "Before you go on your first run alone. Depends on you."

Uthste gathered Tita up. She leapt in the grave with Tita in her arms and arranged her in the dirt, arranged her hair around her shoulders, arranged her hands across her chest. Valor handed down her things, and Uthste placed them folded at her feet. Tita looked like a doll from this distance. Again, I allowed myself to mistake her for Edna.

Edna, unpregnant and older. Uthste crawled out of the grave, and together we pushed the ground back over Edna Honeycutt. We hid her from heaven. You did not cross my mind. You're in my head unburied. We pushed the soil flat, laid speckled stones across her plot, and Mors Brandegor plucked the cigar from her lips and threaded it through one of her thick gold rings. She lay the gilded cigar down, said something in that language I didn't know, then something in Cisran that I recognized but only half understood.

"Sleep well, sister," Valor said.

"Sleep forever," Mors Brandegor said.

"Keep at my heel," said Uthste.

I rubbed my eyes. "Work no longer."

Mors Brandegor put an arm around Uthste's body. She caressed the nape of her neck. "Past midday," she said. "We ought to be off to Beauty's."

"Prumathe will be heartbroken," Valor said. "We ought to pick up a bottle of rye."

"Looking like we do? No side trips," Uthste said. "Straight there."

"Decided," said Mors Brandegor. She took up a lurcher, mounted it. A flick of her wrist and the engine purred to life. She was a sight on the lurcher's back. Enforcers rode so stiffly. Mors Brandegor leaned into the machine like it was some beast she'd tamed from the woods. Like it knew her touch and would obey it. She jerked her head. "Marney. Come."

I started walking, but Uthste caught my shoulder. She draped black suede over me, guided my arms into sleeves. It smelled like cigars and lilac perfume. Tita's, I understood. I looked back at Uthste, who pointedly looked elsewhere, but said to me, "Riding gets cold. Go to."

The jacket moved with the breeze. I buttoned it, hallucinated a pulse in the soft leather. I stood beside Mors Brandegor, and at her prompting climbed on behind her, wrapped my arms around her middle. She was a broad, fat woman. My fingertips didn't touch. I held her coat, and I pressed my cheek against her back, and I let my body fall into the machine that held me upright. I watched Uthste start her engine. I watched Valor throw the spare lurcher into the creek. Mors Brandegor didn't wait for her to join us. She kicked off, the tires whirled, and we shot ahead along the creek's edge.

I imagined something running beastlike beside us. A boar or a dog. A lynx. A girl. As the dirt became a road I imagined the chimeric Tita Honeycutt bounding along the pavement, leaping between pines, flickering half moth half revenant. I pictured her face turned toward me, her eyes keeping pace with mine, her veiny blue eyelids drooping low over her irises, which were sightless and as black as Edna's were in life. She said nothing, she was not a thing that could speak, but I knew what'd slake her, and that it was my new purpose to fetch it for her when I could. My knife glittered through my shirt against my skin. Keep at my heel, low creature! Let me not forgive nor forget.

THE DAY WAS late when we reached town. Fallowlin, I learned later. Thatched straw roofs crowned long white buildings. There was a mill of some kind, an enormous dark wood waterwheel turning beside it, and a Stellarine temple to a Virtue whose painted likeness wore a bird's-foot garland and a translucent bluish dress. We drove along side streets, avoided the square, but still I caught glimpses of the fountains, which sported some fantastical mixed-up animals that'd been carved out of veiny marble. The jets weren't intricate but fell neatly without sound. We kept going. I had no idea where we'd found ourselves, but the bandits seemed sure of it. I had nothing to do except trust them.

We pulled beside a stable. Oxen slept there. Someone had tied bells and silk ribbons around their horns. I got off Mors Brandegor's lurcher and staggered, my legs had jellied during the ride, and I swayed toward the stalls with a palm outstretched. I touched an ox's soft black nose. It allowed this, assuming it noticed. The bandits spoke to each other in terse Cisran. Cisran was almost like Ignavian, when Cisra and Ignavia were one nation, that short-lived Rasenna, they'd shared the same post-Bellonan bastard tongue, once. Two hundred years ago Ignavian revolutionaries had decided it was unjust to have a class-based truth tense and hearsay tense, that is, it was a moral injury for the poor not to be taught truth's grammar, for everything a working man said to be assumed to be half figment, for the privileged to be the authority on all things. So they stopped teaching the truth tense entirely in Ignavia, and then the languages drifted apart, and the barons regained dominion and cordoned the senate from the rest of the populace by requiring aristocratic merit for entry and anyway, I knew maybe half of the words the bandits said. Something about sharing and paying. I pulled an ox's big spoon of an ear. What long lashes it had!

"Girl," called Mors Brandegor.

I snapped my head back.

The bandits had leaned their lurchers in a line. They lingered outside a red door, and Mors Brandegor beckoned me over, so quickly I came with my hands in Tita's jacket's pockets. Valor opened the red door, and Uthste shouldered inside, Mors Brandegor just behind her. I slipped in after them. I wondered if I should've offered to hold the door, but my wondering cut short.

The room fell over me. There were purple damask walls strung with loosely painted portraits and fearsome bearskins, deep green plush velvet couches beside mahogany tables strewn with wine glasses, clamshell ashtrays and ceramic hands from which prayer beads dangled, trays of rouge and perfume bottles, atomizers sparkling, an open book with illustrations that made me dizzy, legs over shoulders, long hair in fists, a brass bowl where cinnamon and myrrh and rosebuds burned, knucklebone throwing lots, lemon peel curls, purpling azurine rinds.

I looked up to exclaim to the sky but saw myself. The high ceiling was mirrored. Upside-down Marney was a horror. I pulled my gaze back down. The lanterns wore colored glass. Dim light flickered pink and crimson. It was like a fit without the fit, the overwhelming splendor without the accompanying loss of my edges. I stood transfixed. I forgot for a moment what had happened to me.

A gramophone leaned in the gallery's corner; it played low brass music. Melodic but wandering, harsh and soft. Who made this place? Whose work was it, painting paradise? I felt a deep ache, something more selfish and sharper than grief. I coveted. I wanted to keep this room. I wanted to trap it in a locket and carry it with me, I wanted to dwell here in secret, I wanted to have it to myself. I wanted to feel every gorgeous texture with my hands and my lips and flip through all the unmarked books, I wanted to memorize the lines of that illustration, the way they traced the screaming girl's braid. Palaces must be like this. This must be the lair of some lost princess. I held my jacket close to me, felt suddenly sure that it was mine, and I marveled at my heartbeat under my fingertips. Some panic feels so good.

A tapestry moved, and from behind the woven manticore came a woman. She wore a long cream slip. It rippled in the light as she walked, hid and revealed the shape of her thighs with every forward step. The woman's hair fell to her waist, it rippled like her dress did, and dragging my eyes up I saw the rouge blurred on her bowed lips and the peaks of her high cheeks, across the bridge of her bony nose, over the darkness on her top and bottom eyelids. Her brows were penciled black. She wore pearls in her ears and around her neck, they vanished beneath the cream silk's low neckline. I saw the shape of pearls down to her belly, saw the little shadows they cast as they nudged against the fabric. I blinked. I looked her in her face. She wore thin black paint around her eyes that swept sharply toward her temples. Her bottom eyelashes joined in angled points. She was so artfully painted that it looked natural, as a songbird's colors are their birthright, but what a slight it'd be to deny such craft!

The woman walked toward me. She outstretched her hands, her bracelets danced and glittered madly in the candy-tinted lights, and her face contorted, her brows lifted, her dark eyes went suddenly glassy, her mouth curved into the saddest smile I'd ever seen. She took my face in her hands (touched me!) and tilted my chin upwards, left then right, examined me with an intensity that frightened me. Then she tossed an arm around my shoulders and pulled me close. My cheek pressed her chest. I felt her prayer pearls roll against my ear. I heard her heartbeat through the silk. Her perfume was implacable, it smelled warm like blood or sugar. "Poor little fawn," she said. "No child should have eyes like yours. You look at me like you've known the end. Brandegor, did you hear about the massacre? What a heinous week we've had, a stain on our shared morality."

I couldn't think. Little fawn, she'd said. *That's me.*

"The work riots?" Uthste's voice, maybe. Or perhaps it was Valor's. Who's to say. My tension was such that I couldn't even muster a scalding hatred for the word riot signifying the action my community had planned for near six months. I listened to this woman's breathing. I never wanted to be anywhere else ever again.

"Prumathe's boy Svutaf union salts for steel mills, he was hanging around the Chauncey scene for organization intel I understand, there's been whispers of a serious movement among the ichorite workers, and the story he's told

Prumathe doesn't match the papers a lick! There was no violence at all from the foundrymen, and even if there had been, I cannot fathom what violence could be done to the side of a brick building that'd warrant even one single drop of blood on the pavement, much less the outright annihilation of an entire labor cohort. Industry Chauncey is a blight. Not that he deserves a Virtue so high as that! *Yann.* I'd poison him myself if I had the man in reach. Trust of course that Baron Ramtha took the given story as an excuse to furnish her enforcement with new little uniforms. May her beating brigade be spiffy! I feared for all your lives! Knowing you four rode in Ignavia City while the security theater thrashed the streets, having no sure way to telegram you or send word, oh I worried myself into a fever! I denied clients for days. Shame on you all, not fleeing at once. Oh, Tita. What a good woman she was." The woman pulled me a little tighter. She muffled the sob I loosened. "Little fawn wears her jacket. What's happened to you three? What happened to Tita zel Priumna?"

"Hello, Beauty." Mors Brandegor took a seat on one of the green couches. Valor and Uthste leaned against opposing walls, ready to take flight, but Mors Brandegor leaned back, wrapped her great arms along the couch's sculpted backboard. "The conductor betrayed us. Etule. He's young, but his family's cooperated with the Choir for years. The train was crawling with enforcers." Mors Brandegor's voice rang off the walls. "We let Tita alone in a carriage. I'll take full fall for that. She'd wanted to scout, and I didn't think better of it. We didn't see the violence that took her, but we got her killer good. We buried her under a covered bridge down south. I'll show you where if it'd please you."

Valor coughed. Uthste worried her hands together.

"Little fawn," Mors Brandegor said, "is called Marney Honeycutt. Etule didn't slow the train at our designated stop. He locked the way to the engine room, trapped us with the advancing enforcers, and Miss Honeycutt dove under my arm and ripped the door off its hinges. It was the damndest thing. She bounced over to help Valor, sealed the far door, made it impenetrable. If I wasn't wiser, I'd say it looked like she'd welded it shut. Or smeared it with the walls. She helped us bury Tita. She earned the jacket, I'd say."

Beauty took my face in her hands again. She held me at arm's length, re-examined me. My body pulsed where it'd been against hers. She looked at my mouth, tugged down a lip to glance at my gums, then slid her thumb up my left cheek and nudged down my bottom eyelid, scrutinized the undercurve of my eye. She folded her hand over my hair. Said gently, "Marney, are you lustertouched?"

I sniffed. My tongue felt gluey, my blood all taffy thick. Tears fell in random bursts. I bit my big lip and I nodded, looked up at Beauty, at the mirror above our heads. "Yes'm," I managed. How funny we looked together.

Beauty covered her mouth. She pulled me back against her. I was happy to think about nothing but the nearness. She said to one of the women around me, whose silence made clear a certain understanding, "Will you be taking her back to the Fingerbluffs?"

"Unless she tells us otherwise," Mors Brandegor said. "She'll make a fine Choir girl."

"Let's draw you a bath," Beauty said to me. She drummed her nails on the part of my hair. "We'll all have supper, and you can stay in the attic. I've got a full night ahead of me, I might be sparse, but you'll be well met." Over my head, she said, "This is not an inn."

"We'll make it up to you," Valor said. "You've always been too good to us."

"That's true." Beauty made a thin throaty sound. "Prumathe's out. When she gets in, she'll coordinate something for you in Tita's memory. She always liked Tita. Sunny?"

"Yes miss?" Smaller voice, youngish. A girl peeked from behind the manticore tapestry. She wore her hair in two braids and a pleated pinafore, cheek rouge in unblended circles. She looked eager to impress Beauty, which seemed only natural, but little impressed by myself and the bandits behind me. She flickered between earnest sweetness and sour scrutiny. She reminded me a little bit of you. Prettier than you, but just as pokey.

"Take Marney upstairs. She needs a hot bath and fresh clothes. If you give her something of yours, I'll buy you something new next near gibbous. She's had the worst week in the world. Be kind to her." Beauty gave Sunny a smile that told me kindness was not always Sunny's style. "Now, please."

"Yes, miss!" Sunny bowed her head. She did not walk, but skipped beside me, and reached past my hand, took my sleeve. She held onto me hard. Curtseyed to the bandits, then dragged me toward the unicorn tapestry, pulled me beneath it without ceremony. The light was cherry red here. There was a stairwell and a set of doors that I did not have time to look over, because Sunny hauled me up the stairs with a strength that made no sense for her shrimpy little frame. Surely, she was younger than me. Sunny was absolutely eleven.

We reached a landing, Sunny unlocked a door, and I was shoved into a cozy little room. The walls were painted with tall vivid flowers. The bed was frilly and neatly made. There was a doll arranged on a mint feather pillow, and a little rag rabbit. "You're filthy. Touch nothing," Sunny said. She opened a door that led to a little washroom, and I heard her pump water for the bath.

"I can help," I called after her. "You don't have to do that for me."

"You can't help. Take off your boots! Leave them by my door. You're covered in muck." Sunny looked over her shoulder at me, whipped her braids around. They were tied with little ribbons. Now I knew who'd decorated the oxen outside. "Okay, come here. Carefully!"

Unlacing my boots sapped whatever animal survival strength I had in me. My fingers hurt, my feet hurt, I didn't want to think about what I'd look like underneath my clothes. I didn't rib Sunny for being prissy. She was right. I was vile. I peeled my boots down, and my open blisters screamed in my stockings, and once again I felt so *bad*. Aching and disgusting. I took off Tita's nice suede jacket, I draped it on the back of Sunny's doily-covered chair. I tip-toed across her bedroom. I'd never had a room this nice. I'd shared my room with both my sisters, and it was half this size. No painted flowers, certainly. Frilly had not been Edna's style, even as Poesy would've loved it, and what's the youngest girl to do? I smiled a little, despite myself. I'd never been in another girl's room before. You never let me visit you at the sanatorium. I wondered vaguely what Beauty's room looked like.

Sunny climbed up on the sink. She faced the claw-foot bathtub, pointed at the steamy swirling water. "Get in!"

I frowned. "Are you going to sit there the whole time?"

Sunny smiled.

I had no energy left to feel prohibitively shy. I turned my back to her, pulled down my suspenders. I took out my knife. I balanced it on the tub's edge. Sunny breathed in sharply, but she didn't ask about it. I wondered what she'd seen living in a place like this. I peeled off the stiff clothes, cringed when they crinkled, stripped to my skin. My clothes retained my shape on the floor. I felt along my head and pulled the pins. Each pin was long as my mid-dle finger, wicked sharp and hooked on the end. I found seven of the eight. One must've dropped at some point. I put the pins in a little pile, took down my braids. They knocked the back of my knees. My scalp howled. I kneaded my fingers against it. I had no crying left in me, but my lip trembled once.

I stepped into the bath. Too hot, I thought, or maybe I was too cold. It hurt. I sat anyway. I pulled my knees to my chest, glanced over my shoulder at Sunny. Sunny looked stricken. I cleared my throat and said, "Have you got a rag?"

She threw one at me. I caught it, barely. Soaped it and started scrubbing. The water turned reddish. I fought a wave of nausea, thought helplessly that I'd been carrying my family for days. Random stretches of pinkish skin looked greenish, though I had no memory of acquiring half the bruises. I looked heinous. I tried unraveling one of my braids and found, with horror, that blood or mud or heaven knows what had clumped it inseparably together. I yanked hard. Something ripped.

"Stop," said Sunny. She hopped off the sink and rummaged through a little basket, withdrew a pair of scissors. "Don't pull on it, that'll hurt too much. Want me to cut them?"

I'd grown them all my life. It's what Tullian girls did. We only cut our hair when we got married. I felt a flutter of fear, but I mashed it down, physically pressed on my breastbone until it felt like I'd pop my heart with my blunt little nails like an overripe fruit. "Yes," I said. "You may."

She crouched beside the tub. Took my left braid in her hand, pulled it taut. The snipping sound made me dizzy. She cut until the braid gave, then she took the second, cut from my ear to my nape. She pulled the wet braids out of the bath and draped them over the sink. They looked like snake skins. She ruffled my hair, then snipped some more, pinched it between her fingers and clipped along the seam of her knuckles. I didn't watch. It was off my neck, and my head had never felt so light.

"Get out of the bath," she said. "We should give you a second scrub up here. I think the heat loosened everything up. Needs another go." I felt numb and bendable, I let her guide me upright, swayed against her when I saw gnarly black splotches in thin air. She drained the tub, pumped fresh water, soaped up a clean rag. I didn't look at the one I'd used. She took my wrist and held it away from my body, swept the rag in little circles up and down my arm. She scrubbed down my back, down my legs. I lifted my foot for her when she wanted to get at my heels. I didn't complain about the blisters. When the fresh water was drawn, I let her guide me down into it, let her pour water over my head and wash my shorn hair. Her hands on my skull felt nice. I wasn't sure if I was crying. She poured more water over my head and I guess it wouldn't matter either way.

When she got me out of the bath, Sunny toweled me off rigorously. I wondered if she'd ever had little pets. She shut the door on the washroom's horror scene, and she took me back into her room, arranged me on the foot of her bed. She opened her wardrobe and leafed through it. She had no less than four dresses, which to my mind was luxury's height, each a different taffy shade. She didn't pick any of them. She found a white button shirt and tall white stockings, grayish button suspenders, and a pair of pleated wool trousers. I wonder if she'd picked the closest thing to what I'd been wearing. Sweet of her. I didn't need help getting dressed, but Sunny didn't ask and I didn't protest, was pliable when she moved my arms and my legs and repositioned me, buttoned the shirt up to my throat, adjusted the suspenders over my shoulders, smoothed the well-pressed pleats. I glanced at the doll on her pillow, smiled a little. She thrust Tita's jacket, my jacket, back at me. I caught it and donned it.

"These were Prumathe's clothes. I never wear them. What happened to you?" Sunny sat on the edge of the bed beside me. She fiddled with my cufflinks. "The welts."

I shrugged one shoulder. "Is Beauty your mother?"

"No. My older sister is Beauty's partner. They own this place together. I help with chores." She gave me a warning look. "Housekeeping chores. Nothing else until I'm older. Are you going with the Choir girls?"

"Yes." I pawed my short wet hair. It felt alien. I tugged a stray strand, wrapped it around my finger. The ringlets would be crazy when they dried. There'd be no weight to force them flat. I wondered if I should ask about the Choir. I didn't know why they called it that, or anything beyond the fact that they stole from strangers. Thing was, I didn't care just then. They could do whatever, and I'd be theirs. I had nothing else. I already had Marney written upside down on my chest in my mind. I'd see it realized. "Sunny? Could you show me your doll?"

"Why?" She pulled one knee to her chest, scowled at me, or maybe her face was just like that. "If you make fun of it I'll pinch your cuts in your sleep."

"I want to play with it," I said. I wanted to pretend I was still little. Little fawn, Beauty'd said. I would never feel little again.

Sunny gave me a long look. "Fine," she said eventually. "Her name is Velma, but you're not playing with her. I am. You can be the rag rabbit."

I lay back on her bed, lifted her toys as gently as I could, like they were alive. I didn't want to bruise them. I set them on my chest, smoothed the little frilly skirt and the stiff felt ears. I tried to smile at Sunny. I said, "I'm more like a rag rabbit anyway."

Sunny lay down beside me. She reached out and touched my hair.

Four

IN SOME DEEP PURPLE CHAMBER IN THE BASE-
ment of this house, I sat at a table with the bandits and
Sunny and Beauty and a host of painted women in loose
velvet and silk, who spoke fluidly, laughed and fanned
themselves, ate olives and cherries and cheese scraped on
rye, little silver fishes from the tin, ribbons of peppered
dried meat. The proper meal, a roasted swan that one of
Beauty's girls had placed steaming between us, was bones
now. I sucked the marrow from a rib. The creaminess
in my mouth tasted prayerful, like saying the bleed after
a cold solstice sermon, the words that usher the longest
night of the year. Syllabic revery. Unctuous and thick. I
kissed my fingertips, fanned them over the table's edge,
pretended the scraps were an Idol. I would be grateful to
these women so long as I lived. Nothing would pass that
would harm them and they'd have abundance and golden
frivolities gathered at their fingertips, forever. Praise our

work, the mystery's maintenance, and praise the Torn Child half-dead beneath us, who feigns sleep and thereby abets us. Amen.

Mors Brandegor purred in Beauty's ear. Sunny spoke with Valor, they discussed the new fashions in Ignavia City, and it was strange to see Valor speak so crisply and sweetly, not that I knew her well enough to say whether she was otherwise usually. I saw her distressed, on her shift, after a failure. Did bandits structure their days thusly? Did they have clocks in their head like I did? Uthste stared at the open swan body. She didn't blink, looked at the greasy spine half-lidded, her whole face slack. A noble skull showed through her translucent bruisy skin. She sat across from me. She caught my looking, looked at me. Her eyes were liquid black and long-lashed, downturned at the edges. I saw myself across them.

Uthste said, "I like your hair. Very crawly."

That word—crawly—was not kind. Uthste didn't seem cruel, that is, she could be cruel, but this didn't seem like a curse from the revenant woman whose glance compelled the rich to part with their wealth. She just looked at me.

Unsure of what else to say, skin burning, I said, "Thank you, ma'am."

A woman with glossy black ringlets draped herself across Uthste, whispered something in her ear, then leaned her cheek against Uthste's temple, looked at me with a wide magenta smile. "No sighs! We're crawling with crawlies around here. This right here's a greenhouse. Don't tell the clientele."

"I'll drink to that," said Mors Brandegor, who cleared her glass and flipped the cup, slammed it rim down on the table. "Who's that I see, darkening Beauty's doorway?"

"The crawly of the house," said somebody behind me.

Beauty stood. She'd wrapped a thick fur stole around her, and she hugged it to herself, looked past me with such open fondness that I wondered if I ought avert my eyes. I didn't. I turned in my chair, and I saw the woman who I'd guessed was Prumathe. She looked like Sunny, just taller, sharper, with her hair cut short and slicked back. She wore an open coat and pleated trousers. Her lip ring was yellow gold. She'd lately been crying, she had maroon splotches around her eyes, but she beamed, a little lopsided, and she rounded the table and took Beauty by the waist, swept her close, and kissed her.

I felt a plunge inside me. I pressed my hands against my thighs and took fistfuls of my trousers and squeezed. I thought uselessly about you. Kissing you wasn't like this. It was quick, and as you reminded me, common and natural for girls enjoying one another's company. There were no implications to be had, we weren't—*insects*. We weren't no creepy crawlies, we weren't bugs, that is, we weren't girls turned boyish by impulses toward *buggery*, my mother and all the older kids on the line were wrong about me, when I asked you about it you always told me not to worry, these things sort themselves with maturity. We'd outgrow it. It meant nothing. You weren't a crawly. Of course, I'd seen crawlies, or women who were called such, they worked the furnace alongside my father and my uncles, but that's a rumor anyway, and it's unfair to say that work masculinizes you, Tullians devote ourselves to work and consequently our femininity is strong and broad sometimes, that grace ought to be extended toward Stellarine and Veltuni women too, anyway I'd never seen a woman take a woman in her arms like that. Seen a woman go slack and glow against another woman's chest, look up at her with such perfect open sweetness. I wanted to be Prumathe. I wanted to wear her skin. I was strangling the fabric of her trousers, I was wearing *her* clothes I realized with a start, I thought about dead Tita on Uthste's lap and how tenderly she'd handled her corpse and I thought, *oh bleed above me, I have crawly hair!*

Prumathe sat Beauty back in her chair. She tucked her into the table, bent to kiss her shoulder, then straightened, took the swan's tray off the table. She set it aside, and in the space where the swan had been, she lay down a deck of cards, a ripe azurine, and a handful of dainty little forks. This got gasps and groans out of everybody, but I couldn't parse why, I was trying to make my lungs work normally. Prumathe surveyed the table. Deliberately, she stabbed the azurine with each little fork, one by one, until the pinkish purplish pulp showed through the baby blue rind and all the forks jutted out at odd angles, like spokes on a wheel. She said, "Pardon my lateness. When I was told, I had to step out. Ancestors should not be made so young." Prumathe left Beauty's side and circled the table, bent to whisper in each woman's ear, lingered for a quick exchange by some of the painted girls, and with Valor, whose knuckles Prumathe kissed. When she passed Sunny, she kissed the top of her head, and when she passed Mors Brandegor, they both grinned like devils, big and toothy and mean. When she reached me, I thought I'd die, and could scarcely meet her eye when she bowed her head to greet me.

"Hello, ma'am," I breathed. I sounded reedy and horrible.

"Oh, never ma'am." Prumathe looked at me seriously. Her brows came together, her mouth pulled sharply left. "I'm Prumathe thu Cerca, it's a pleasure. Welcome to my home. Call me Pru. Or Scrawny, that was my mortal name. 'Yes sir' me if you must. Are you the lustertouched bandit baby?"

"Yessir."

"Have you been in my closet, bandit baby?"

I couldn't unclench my fists in my, her, trousers. I tried but I couldn't. I couldn't blink.

Prumathe shook her head. She stood up, put her hands on the back of my chair, and said to the room, "Round of teatime before we send the kids up. Bandit baby deals." Then, in my ear: "Do you know how to play?"

My parents didn't approve of cards. Gambling was fine by night, but in ill taste. My quiet must've been enough.

"There are five suits of eleven cards each, that's mothers, fathers, sons, daughters, and thieves, they're numbered in the top corner. You shuffle the deck, then deal everyone five cards. You keep the excess by your right hand. What you want is a hand of matches, all the fives, all the sixes, anything like that. You're the dealer. Top of each turn, you pull one card from the excess, and you pick a card to pass

along, face down, to the girl beside you. She'll do the same.
It'll go fast. Do you follow?"

I did. I had a good head for quick figures and moving
parts. "If I get a hand of matches?"

"You take one of those forks in the fruit in the middle.
You'll be quiet about it, and subtle. You don't want anybody
to see that you did it. You put it in your lap, discreet as you
can, and you keep passing cards, keeping your perfect hand
intact. Once anybody sees that a fork is gone, they'll damn
their cards and dive for a fork. There's one less fork than
there are people. Somebody fails to grab one, they buy everyone a round. Or, in our case, let themselves be laughed
on. That all clear?"

"Yessir." I reached for the cards to prove it, tried to shuffle like the boys in the packing line did, in quick choppy
shakes. I couldn't quite get my hands around them right.
I was afraid to bend them. I shook them lightly through
themselves and dealt, felt a tug inside me, liked the repeti-
tive motion and the attention on my hands. I put the excess
in a pile beside me.

Prumathe sat to my right. A woman whose name I didn't
know sat to my left. We all picked up our cards. Father six,
mother nine, mother five, daughter five, thief one. I pulled a
son ten and passed the father six. It moved slow, then faster.
I found a rhythm to my movements that I liked, liked how
the cards felt between my thumbs and forefingers, liked the
intensity of focus around me, the pretending everybody was
doing like we weren't all deadly serious. I had three fives. I
tried to keep my attention between the cards in my hands

and the teaspoons sparkling where my Torn Child swan had been. Pretty little doll forks. Good silver. You'd have tried to snake them and sell them to orderlies for cash.

When the cards moved fast it was like their figures danced. They wore Old Bellonan garb, wrapped and translucent, like they'd been caught in an unraveled bolt of fabric. The father was bearded, the son was shaved and shorn. The mother's dress revealed one breast, the daughter wore her long hair loose. The thieves were all hung upside down. I had four fives.

I glanced over my hand. Mors Brandegor and Uthste and Valor had all adopted the same expressions they'd worn on the train, the wolf smile and frightful cool and misery. Beauty moved languidly, I suspected she wasn't too pressed, but many of her friends, or coworkers maybe, seemed dire. I eyed Sunny, who I suppose was properly Sunny zel Cerca, assuming she and Prumathe shared a mother and there weren't other siblings in the mix, and noticed that she was hardly looking at her hand. She took her new card, wove it between her existing cards, and passed it along without so much as frowning at it.

I looked at the milky white forks in the glossy purple pulp. The pith showed like bone. I counted us, and counted them, and reached for the middle of the table.

Prumathe shot her hand beside mine, and as I closed my hand around a fork in the fruit I looked to my right to tell her something quick and gracious, but the table squealed and shoved sideways and I fell under somebody's body, somebody laughing, because everyone had climbed onto the table and scrambled for forks, crawled over each other, wrestled and squirmed and laughed and wheezed. Dresses slithered over dresses, the fabrics gleamed over each other, elbows shot and hairpins clinked against porcelain plaits and high-heeled slippers swam through the air. The fruit was a smashed-up mess. It smelled tart and soursweet as ichorite. I felt a flutter in my chest and thought I might shout, it was too much pressing in on me, I slipped under the table and shivered with my fork in my fist.

Sunny crouched under the table. She smiled serenely with her sharp little cat teeth. She reached out a hand, showed me her fork, and unsure of what else I should do, I took it with mine. Our forks clattered together. She wrinkled her nose but gave me a tug, pulled me out from under the table and snuck me out of the room, where Beauty and Valor were strangling each other with the stole. Sunny took me down a hall and up the stairs. We went higher and higher, up the eerie red stairs to her bedroom, and she shut the door behind us and the quiet poured over me.

I panted and sat on her floor.

Sunny took the forks out of my hand. She put them on her bedside table, fetched the frilly quilt off her bed and Velma and the rag rabbit, and she flounced on the floor beside me, threw the quilt over our heads, bathed the four of us in darkness. We breathed with our knees pressed together. She skittered her hands over my shins, looking for something, so I gave her my hands and she squeezed them.

"Marney," she breathed, "I cheated."

My tongue was clumsy. "What?"

"I didn't have a perfect hand, I was just impatient for the fun part," she said. I could hear her smiling. It fluttered at the edges of her voice. "Did you see Brandy? I thought she'd kill Uthste! The way she had her pinned!"

I felt dizzy. I smiled at nothing, marveled over my heartrate. All that chaos over a little trick. I liked Sunny, I realized. With a sudden boldness I took the hands I held, and I brought them to my lips, ghosted a kiss over her knuckles. "Seems in the spirit of the game," I said, then dropped her hands, suddenly petrified.

She pushed me. I opened my mouth to apologize, but then she pushed me again, hard enough to knock me flat. She lay down beside me and tucked into my side, pressed her nose against my cheek. She said, "When you join the Choir down in the Fingerbluffs, they're going to give you a lurcher, and you must ride back up here and spend time with me sometimes. Not too often, or I'll get sick of you, but sometimes, so that I can upkeep your haircut and show you what I've picked out at the market. You've got to swear!"

"Yes ma'am," I said. "I swear."

I WOKE ALONE in Sunny's bed. Sunny's side was neatly made up, her toys arranged on the big squashy pillow, and I saw the clothes she'd picked yesterday folded at the foot of the bed. Fresh stockings, kind of her. It was well past dawn, I felt a stab of guilt about missing the bleed, but it seemed an unproductive feeling, one I could take to a reverend in the Fingerbluffs, assuming there were Tull Shrines there.

I knew the Fingerbluffs barony only by name, had no real idea what it was like. It was on the coast, I thought. Nearer to Tasmudan than Royston.

I climbed out of bed. I smoothed the quilt, tried to make my side as neat as hers. I wore one of her nightgowns, it was ruffled and dripping with little bows, and I folded it after I pulled it over my shoulders, replaced the laid-out clothes with it. I pulled up my suspenders and buttoned my shirt most of the way. I didn't like the tightness on my throat. I put on my boots, my bloody filthy boots, and Tita's jacket. I tucked my knife in my waistband. I left her room. I closed the door carefully, imagined somehow that the frame would bruise if I shut it wrong.

Mors Brandegor smoked in the stairwell. She stood in the landing in a long slip dress, like one of the dresses the women here wore, with her hair down her back. She faced away from me. She flicked ash in a sconce. "I can hear you breathing," she said. "Come down and join me."

I touched the wallpaper as I descended. The pattern was felted. The texture twinged. I stopped a step above her and tensed.

"Beauty loves a story. She told one about you. Later last night, she recounted to us that the workers at that big ichorite foundry keep having magic children. That the magic children are sick and insane, that those factory fumes their mothers sucked all through their gestations produced a certain sensitivity to the stuff. Lustertouched children. Beauty says Industry's burned good money hushing the press. Wouldn't want rumors about freak babies sullying

the reputation he's building for the empire of his brand."
She took a drag. "Beauty says, and Prumathe agrees, that
last week's massacre wasn't a riot, nor a standard union bid,
but a plea for Industry to ease their children's suffering. He
cut them down to protect his profits and cull insubordi-
nates, and to snuff noise about the lustertouched before a
public discourse spread. Beauty says you're one such child.
She says the stray I've collected survived one of the worst
strikebreaking slaughters on record, and that she is, that is
you are, magic. Squares with what I've seen. You agreed last
night when she asked you, but Beauty's an easy woman to
offer a yes to. Tell me, now. Are you lustertouched?"

I pressed harder on the wall. I didn't run up the stairs
but I entertained the thought. "Yes ma'am, I am lustertouched," I said. "I wouldn't call that magic."

"Magic is abundant where I'm from. Luck. Weather.
Drugs. Grief. Magic's crammed in the walls and stitched
into skirts. It's in the blood. It's dull to me, the Ignavian
insistence that knowing better changes things. A nation ob-
sessed with religion but shy about superstition is impotent
and sour. If Yann Industry Chauncey gets his hands on the
free Drustlands, slaps factories beside our Halls, our lustertouched babies will be magic. We'll invent some sprite to
inhabit you and hide pendants and heather in your cribs to
trap it."

"How do the Drustish tend to their dead?"

Mors Brandegor turned her head. The gloss daubed on
her eyelids caught the candlelight. She said, "Do you see
death's hand on me?"

"No ma'am," I said, "I meant no disrespect. My friend Gwyar is dead."

"Gwyar," Mors Brandegor repeated. She rolled your name off the back of her tongue with an ease I couldn't, a slickness. "Last week?"

I nodded. I couldn't feel my hands. You were dead. How dare you.

"What was Gwyar's Hall?" She searched me. "Mine was Mors. I belong to Mors Hall, if such a thing still exists. That's why it's formal to call me Mors before my name."

"She's Flox Drustish," I said. You told me tales about the Drustlands, but not about your family, never nothing about a Hall.

"Flox Hall." She put her cigar in her teeth, showed me her palm. She traced a line with her long nail, stopped at the meat under her little finger. "Is here. Northeast, past the badlands, in the mires. The Flip River cuts by it. Floods it sometimes. It's a hard Hall. No feuds, at least when I left. They cleared all they provoked. Your dead friend, was she here with family?"

"No," I said. I didn't like you called that. Hearing you called dead abraded me. I resented you for being it. "She lives in Crellin Sanatorium. She's sick. She works with me to pay for her bed there."

"*Blodfagra*." She closed her hand in a fist. "Don't worry over how Flox Hall would've tended the corpse of your girl."

"I need to do right by her," I said too fast. I averted my eyes. "I don't mean to intrude."

"I'll get you good with a gun." Mors Brandegor, just Brandegor, grinned at me. "You should go on down. Uthste and Valor are ready to leave. They'll be gone soon. The Fingerbluffs are calling."

"Won't you come?" I wanted her to come. The lurch in my belly was childish, stupid, but absolute. I didn't want her to be far from me. It made me worry.

"I'm the Choir's girl. I'll be back. I've got some favors to pay with Beauty and Prumathe, and I'll stay until they're attended. Shouldn't be long."

"How long?"

"Don't start, Miss Marney. Don't count on your fingers and jinx me. I could be dead by dinner, or I could be back in four days' time, or two months'. You'll see me when I come. Understand me?"

I wanted to bite my hand. I felt a jolt of sizzling energy, like I'd had too many sweets and made myself sick. My skin buzzed. I set my jaw and nodded, eyes down, fixed on the hem of her silk dress. There were tattoos on her arms, on the proud expanse of her chest. MORS BRANDEGOR upside down beneath her collarbones. She looked like a tapestry. She was beautiful. "Yes ma'am."

"Scamper off," she said, an order.

I passed her on the stairs and panted on the landing. I pushed the manticore aside. The beautiful room was empty of people, brimming with treasures that I tried not to drool over. I wanted to hold onto my fear. I slapped my chest, beat over my heart, and breathed on a work song rhythm. Lungs empty on hammer strikes. My fear grew, it bubbled up my throat and pushed the backs of my eyes. I shook all over. I walked through the beautiful room and its beautiful things and pushed open the big red door, stepped out into a grayish chilly day.

Valor and Uthste leaned their backs against the wall. Uthste glanced my way when I emerged, gave me a curt nod. She and Valor smoked cigarettes with blue paper, like the ones the shipping boys Edna sulked around used to smoke. Stellarine boys. One of those boys had been *her* boy, maybe. I didn't know who'd made her pregnant. She never said. In my memory they all looked the same. I saw the straps on their shoulders and the skin of their necks. Pearls in their ears, cheaper and more stylish than full prayer strings. Mother had been furious. *Collective bargaining ain't good Tullian orthopraxy neither*, Edna would say. *Organizing is a feat of secular reverendship. Hate my folly, go on and hate all of it. I am laid low in wickedness and will speak no more. Surrender the movement for your pride.* So bold! Had mother hit her? My memory fuzzed. Uthste said, "With us?"

I nodded. I thought about asking after Sunny but thought better of it. I ran my hands through my shorn hair. The curls sprang between my knuckles. I wondered if I'd recognize myself.

Valor dashed her cigarette on the wall. Sparks fell and disappeared. She took up her lurcher, climbed across it, squeezed it to life. She looked at me.

Uthste took another drag. She jerked her chin at Valor. I was scared of Valor, slightly. I'd been hoping for Uthste. Still, I don't deny hospitality. I walked away from Beauty's house and climbed on the back of Valor's lurcher, held her waist. She breathed against the crooks of my arms and I squeezed my eyes shut. I heard Uthste's lurcher scrape the gravel. Then Valor kicked off, and we were gone.

FOR HOURS WE chased the pines. The pines opened into cities; we blazed through them. Places I'd never seen before melted into the air. Colors rushed over my head. The day warmed as it passed. I sweat under my jacket. The pines bled into maize and rye fields, I watched farmers with their skirts tied at their hips reap with long white sickles. There were mills and plants but they got scarcer the closer we came to the coast. Under-industrialized, I think it'd be figured. Yet-to-be-paved. I wasn't sure where one barony became the next. Edna said the work would come this way once the provincial barons bent to the new economy's glow. She said this with an ambivalence that could've been approval as easily as it could've been loathing. Edna called me crawly with that tone sometimes. *Crawly little pest.* The back of Valor's dress was done up from her tail to her nape in little covered buttons, and I rubbed my cheek against them.

We stopped by the Flip River. Fast water, murky green cut with silver bubbles, heavy with algae and eels. There was a narrow dock with a ferry, and as Uthste dismounted to speak with the ferryman, Valor and I went to a vendor stall beside. She bought hot fried okra and buttered bread with azurine marmalade, gave the paper parcels to me to carry. She walked her lurcher onto the ferry, where Uthste waited, sitting beside her machine with her head in her hands.

I sat beside her and opened the parcels. I liked the battered smell. Valor's lurcher cast a weird shadow over us. She joined us on the ferry floor, and the three of us ate. The ferryman took us from the shore. The sway and bob of water underneath me made my ribs feel tight. Hadn't ever occurred that boats aren't still on the inside. I wasn't too sure about that. Without much effort I managed to ignore the unease, hunger was a greater power. I licked my fingers. I watched the sunlight glance off the broken water. We passed a grand riverboat with musicians and dancing, and I watched a woman spin backwards with her skirts in her hands. The bright sharp ichorite taste of the azurine marmalade clung to my hard palate. I watched the clouds churn above us. It'd be the bleed soon.

"Thank you," I said.

Valor pulled a compact from her bodice. She checked her rouge. "The Choir cares for its own."

Uthste rubbed the corner of her mouth. "I'm going to share the truth with you. Once you have it, you'll be bound to it, on pain of death. Do I make the stakes clear, Marney?"

"Yes'm," I said. I folded my hands in my lap. "On pain of death."

Uthste said, "All outlaws aren't in the Choir. The Choir's got a code of ethics, and our grace extends to all those, but only those, who uphold it. Fifteen years ago, Baron

Fingerbluffs, that's Horace Veracity Loveday, got *got* by his servants. Those servants are insurgent Hereafterist partisans. The partisans reached out to the Choir, and to the pirates who've long gathered in the Fingerbluffs, and offered community." She spread her hands, then clasped them. "The Fingerbluffs are the Choir's home, Loveday Mansion our open hostel. A third of our spoils, that's a third minimum, belongs to the Fingerbluffs and her children. We don't hold property there, we live together in shared trust, and we are rich, and unalone, and beautiful. Everyone in the Fingerbluffs is wealthy. The poorest man's a king. Everyone in the Fingerbluffs vows to keep the charade that Baron Loveday still lives. We take turns writing letters for him, making excuses for him not to attend the baron's senate, and the villagers protect knowledge of us, stave off our certain annihilation at the hands of the law. Cooperation and collaboration are sacred. Without each other, we'd be damned."

I've never known nobody rich. Beauty's house was the finest thing I'd ever seen, plusher and more luxurious than the Tull Shrine had been, and the grand tone Uthste took made me shiver. "What's the code?"

"Do right." Valor snapped her compact shut.

Do right seemed frightful vague for a code of ethics. I looked between them and the shifting water. "Do right on pain of death?"

"Mhm." Uthste turned her collar up against the wind. "Do you swear to do right?"

I chewed on the fact that stealing was plainly and obviously wrong, as was frightening people and threatening people and killing them and so on. We'd taken a hard turn from right. I stretched my legs out in front of me and looked at the week-old violence on my boots. Dried down like this, it looked like peat in my laces. "I can swear to try."

Valor smiled. I had no idea how old she was. "Right's a star by which to navigate. You'll have to make hard choices in this work, you'll worry about them when they arise. Worry now about composure. Be smart about yourself. Conduct yourself with dignity. Don't be cruel for the sake of it. Be generous. Don't leech from the Fingerbluffs or act against her people or we'll beat you bloodless and kick you off a cliff." She lifted her chin like she was scenting the air. "Almost across."

We stood. The ferryman sang to himself. A tattoo's frayed edge peeked under his sleeve. I watched the ripples change as the vessel slowed. The grass on the other side was thicker and bluish in this light. It looked like fur. Valor put her hands on my waist and hoisted me on her lurcher, my lungs quit and my head fizzled, and she arranged herself behind me. She was enormously strong, despite not look- ing it. Solid, dense. She radiated heat. She reached around me, closed her fists around the sloped horn handles. She squeezed a lever there, and the engine purred below us. She moved her hand. I put mine there, tried. The vibrations shook the bones in my fist. I looked over my shoulder at her, and she jutted her chin forward, pointed toward the road that adjoined the dock now ahead of us. "Go," she said. "If you crash us you'll carry me the rest of the way."

Uthste snorted, then clipped past us.

Valor held her hand over mine, not touching me. She shifted her wrist. I followed her motion like she puppeteered me, and the lurcher lurched, and we flew forward. The sky flew fast around my face. I didn't say the sunset bleed, but I felt it, held that kneeling feeling in my chest while road unfurled ahead of us, suddenly existing where only hills had been. I imagined it frothing my blood up. Valor was driving properly, when we teetered she put a hand on my arm and pressed the pads of her fingers down, and the tendons under my skin obeyed her will in ways my head didn't. I moved how she showed me. When I turned too subtly, she leaned and I followed her weight. It felt good. I hardly thought. My curls flew around. They were *curls* now. They whipped and whispered against my neck.

There wasn't a town for a long time. No settlements aside from the stray hut and goat herds. Big twists of horns capped with little bells. The whole scene got bluer, then bluer still. Azurine clouds that melted into azurine fields, then azurine *orchards*, acres upon acres of gnarled trees with leather bark and spined feathery leaves and heavy drooping fistfuls of glistening fruit. The soursweet fragrance was sticky on the breeze. I prickled all over. My gums swelled puffy soft around my teeth. Uthste stood up on the lurcher's stirrups, plucked one from a branch as she rushed past it. The whole tree shivered in recoil. Dewdrops bounced from it. I didn't dare take my hands off Valor's lurcher, but I let myself steal my eyes from the road and gaze at the abundance suddenly everywhere. The fruit hardly looked real. They looked like smudges that come after one rubs one's

eyes too hard. The rinds illusorily luminous. Nothing was
so powder blue, besides some flowers maybe, and fabric nobody I knew could afford. I tried to wonder if there was
a Tull Shrine around and an attendant community, we're
an agricultural people, or were once, but I couldn't imagine past the aliveness everywhere. It smelled so bright.
Breathing was sweet and hurt slightly.

I wanted to show you. It did not feel like you were dead.
I wanted to pick an azurine and split it with you. I wanted
to peel the rind with my thumb and watch my thumb turn
red with you. You'd pinch the tip and say, *does that hurt?*
How about now? You love the stingy favors, don't you?

And I'd say nothing in particular and do it again. That's
the ritual. I missed you.

The orchard went on a long time. Then there were
lights through it.

Valor reached a hand into the advancing shadows as
though someone would take it. The lights flashed at the
ends of her fingertips, glowed through her nails in slivers of
mean dark pink. The Fingerbluffs waited there. Gulls flew
above them. Behind them was nothing, a drop over the sea.
I'd never heard the sea before. The rushing was so loud. Salt
cut the azurine smell and my heart inverted and I wanted to
tear my hands off the lurcher and slide them under my shirt
and touch my belly and my breastbone. I throbbed there.

Into the Fingerbluffs we rode, the gorgeous, heaving
Fingerbluffs, whose dingy narrow mews peeled out from
the brick streets and held children who played there in the
darkness, chasing each other and shouting, twisting, braids

71

floating behind them in deference to their speed, not working, not governed, unafraid. The buildings slumped against each other, hipped rooves embracing, shrouding those pink lights that seeped through the red papered windows onto the pavement like a hand cupped around a lighter in a breeze. People danced inside. Naked tattooed arms tangled, foreheads rested on shoulders, hands cupped the napes of marked necks.

We rode past looming skinny temples and triple gallery shotguns with deep shady overhangs painted bottle green, fountains, freestanding archways strung up with beads, gaslit stalls with blinkering festival games. Knives juggled and swallowed and hurled through azurines balanced on the outstretched hands of smokers who lounged along broken knuckled Bellonan column hunks, lichened over like boulders, who gestured with long pipes and fanned themselves, shouted when the knives knocked the balanced fruit down and yawned laughter that swirled and swelled with brass music and low chatter and more laughter, deeper sourceless ceaseless laughter whose component voices were indistinct and crested and ebbed like the sea does. The crowd churned. People hailed Valor and Uthste by name from balconies above us. They tossed down fistfuls of petals. We rolled through the molten golden languid city, and strangers waved to me, and I shook the little white petals from my hair. We rode to the mansion at the cliff's edge. Its silhouette was enormous and darker than the surrounding sky.

"We all live here together," Valor said. "This is home, Marney."

I slumped backwards against her chest and she took the handles. I watched the mansion envelope the sky. Its corners covered both moons. Its big roof was the whole heaven. Forgive me that another place could so quickly become my home. Forgive me for loving twice. I'll do it again. I'll fall in love again. It doesn't diminish you. It was for you, in its way. We fell in love together, the shard of you in my brain and me. We devoted ourselves to the Choir and chose to continue living.

Five

THE FINGERBLUFFS BECAME MY HOME, AND
Mors Brandegor the Rancid was gone for years.

Those of us too young to serve the Choir outright didn't
work as such, but we had our chores. We woke at sunup,
the seven or nine of us that shared a room on Loveday
Mansion's third floor (me a bit beforehand to say the bleed
when I was good). We made our beds and beat each other
with pillows and play smothered each other and put on
our trousers and washed our faces and stretched until our
blood moved right. There were other kids elsewhere but I
don't know when they got up. We, the kids from the corner room, slid down the grand mahogany banisters and
clambered into the tapestried dining room with its sea glass
chandelier and scary mosaic floor. Its smashed tiles showed
the beasts of Below: the Stellarine understanding of the
Bellonan understanding of the Tullian understanding that
something is alive and awake and in pain underground.

We got our bowls, then split off. I was no good in the kitchen. After we ate I went around back and chopped wood with a few boys younger than me. Sometimes I sat on the edge of the cliffs and looked over the edge at the rough green water. The whitecaps looked like skirts on dancing girls. Sometimes I would watch the ships come in, and I'd scramble down to the jagged unsafe lovely pier where the smugglers brought their big blond crates and helped sort and haul them ashore. Only pirates around here. All the Choir.

Other times I'd just watch until my heart felt wrong, I didn't know what to do with my free hands, I'd go busy them with something. I'd go into town. I'd help the sellers put out their wares, arrange cockles on ice or belts on hooks by the buckle. I'd sort units in spoils and help pack moving goods. I'd let myself be swept into rooms with younger rougher sweeter kids and pretend to learn my letters. I'd be assistant dealer in the dance halls, I've got a good head for counting and liked being around the glorious robber warriors, who'd tell stories while they gambled of what they'd done. Everyone is rich in the Fingerbluffs. When bands came home they'd proffer up a portion of their spoils, at least a third, or an honest handful we'd say, often more. Selling was for fun and pride, not to stave off starvation. For the good stuff the pirates brought in before it was ushered down to Tasmudan or up toward Cisra. For special favors.

I liked the way cards felt in my hands and liked how the light glanced off the sticky cosmetic gloss gamblers wore on their lips and eyelids. I liked when women who won reached across the bar and mussed up my curls. I ran around and gathered up bits and pieces from the road, there was a man who lived above the cobbler who'd reward gathered trash with thimbles full of laudanum and thumbprint cookies, and I cleaned 'til I earned my treats.

I kept to myself and was friendly in no specific way. I danced with girls in alleys beside lounges where we could hear the music, older girls mostly, but I didn't ask for names, and I played games with the other kids around the Fingerbluffs but rarely spent time with anybody alone. After dusk bleed I'd keep to myself. I didn't keep track of what was and wasn't folly. I became a worse and less rigorous Tullian, I guess. I saw Valor sometimes. Uthste more rarely. I wondered if she'd gone where Brandegor went. I had the suspicion they were lovers. The thought would flicker around my head sometimes. I wondered about how they would look astride each other.

I wept constantly but felt little. I suppose I felt hollow, something different but not dissimilar to hunger. I wanted for nothing and everything was lovely. I learned to tie and climb ropes. I learned to scale buildings for sake of sneaking out when called upon to do so. I watched the bandits return from their raids and fantasized about getting my first tattoo done, but in the Fingerbluffs coming of age meant Veltuni coming of age, age-wise, not until somebody hits sixteen seventeen eighteenish, not the Tullian thirteen. At some point I hit the Tullian thirteen but I didn't feel it happen, then passed it. I didn't have the ceremony, anyway. I never learned the full burden of Tullian worship. Maybe I was stuck a kid forever. I never got myself a bonnet to wear. There were Tullians around, a few of them, but I felt odd about acquainting myself. Most of them were locals, Choir protectorates, not bandits. I'd picked something else. A bandit future felt mutually exclusive with my heritage's faith. I was too shy for my own good.

I wondered about Beauty's house. I wondered if Sunny remembered me. She'd been so sweet to me. I wondered about Ignavia City and the Industry Foundry. I wondered about Yann Chauncey. I wondered how he walked. I wondered if he was a breathing, bleeding thing like any man. In my head he was a block of ice. In my head he was a viper. I wondered about where the pirates went when they left the Fingerbluffs.

The Fingerbluffs are called such because the bluffs themselves are these massive rain-gray pillars, basalt columns someone told me, with knuckles and nails carved a thousand years ago along each shaft. Hands of something giant reaching out of the water, holding our city up. Cradling it or shoving it off itself. Birds nested in the knuckle crevices. I balanced along the rough rock cuticles. I wondered sometimes about falling off. Whether it'd kill me, what it'd feel like if it didn't. It was a steep drop. The water underneath was very pretty. I watched it all the time. It was easy not to think about Burn Street, looking down. Otherwise I sometimes faltered, and I wondered about Burn Street. I wondered about what we'd looked like from above.

Bandits died often. They'd return like kings to calamitous applause with sacks of stolen gold to toss among their gathered comrades, or they'd come limp on the backs of lurchers, or they wouldn't come at all. There weren't funerals, I learned. There was just the party. The party never ended and was always in celebration of, memorial of, the Choir that kept dying all the time. Dying young, at that. Fresh bandits with tattoos still scabbing would fall their first outing. People wept all the time. They drank and danced and clung to each other and wept. They feasted and wept. They bejeweled themselves and wore elaborate brocade and rich creamy silk and linen so fine that light shone through it, and they watched the sunset sea kiss the basalt hands that held them, and they'd weep themselves into a stupor. I wasn't so unusual. I didn't tell anyone what happened and for a while nobody asked.

Again, I rarely saw my saviors, they were constantly out raiding, though they were kind when they were briefly home. When I was found weeping by Choir strangers I'd be given a little sip of whiskey and I'd hate it and suffer and everyone would laugh, then I'd laugh, and we all carried on. I did my chores. I assumed Brandegor was dead. I didn't think or feel a thing about it. If I did for even a moment my chin started shaking and I felt I'd cough up all the organs inside me and turn into paper mush and gravel. I hoped she wasn't dead. I sat sometimes on the steps of the mansion and waited for her to come home.

I gave you a tour. Why I fixated on you more than my family wasn't clear to me, but I was so devotedly not thinking or feeling that I didn't press the strangeness. I buried Edna Honeycutt under the covered bridge. I didn't bury you. I didn't see your corpse. There was a daydream future I could build for you. Your death was so mercifully ambiguous.

I showed you the ring where pirates and train robbers boxed. Everybody loved land against sea. I showed you the tailor's shop; you'd always liked Tlesana's Treasure, that dress shop where the gowns looked like divine substance made real and spun and draped. The tailors in the Fingerbluffs made garments from fabric so luxurious it made my ribs hurt to touch them and sold them cheap enough that everybody wore them. You liked fashion's craft, you'd said. I liked the craft too. I liked imagining how it'd lie on the women who wore them.

I showed you the mansion, lush and gilded and busting at the seams with Choir members initially too numerous for me to name, who felt fewer and more discrete as some died and I got to know the currently living. In the mansion, all the Veltuni bandits hooked their cast ancestral hands on the same wall, so the ballroom became the ancestral parlor, where every Veltuni bandit might watch and guide the house when they themselves had died. It was a gorgeous sight. The bandits who came of age here, or had some money around when they took their ancestral name, had polished bronze hands, and the poor ones from beyond the Fingerbluffs had clay ones, fired black. All the reaching was reassuring to me. It must be a comfort, being Veltuni, the dead so able to touch you.

Tullian death is like this: when you die, your spirit returns to heaven, men to day and women to night, and your body returns to the Torn Child below, who knows flesh is androgynous and inescapable, a part of its vast material nothingness. You're distinct and individual in life alone. The burden of selfhood is abandoned once you're gone. Unless you're a revenant, you as you don't exist anymore. You're unhewn. The closeness I wanted with you and my family would rob you all of restful edgelessness. Asking you to haunt me is cruel to you.

I showed you the bathhouse. I showed you the orchards and the theater. I took you down to the base of the fingers, on the little stretches of salt white beach, and let the water sweep over the backs of my knees.

I met Tricksy that way.

I was on a jutting broken finger column throwing little finger chips down at the water. The water was rough and splashed high enough to get at my face. Cold and clingy. I had been there for a long time. I'd chopped firewood all morning and my hands were raw and red. I squeezed them and pinched at them. The pain was low and dull under the milky heavy calluses. I pinched harder. Tingly. Experimentally, I rolled the skin of my palm between my opposing thumb and forefinger and twisted. Feeling slipped up my wrist toward my elbow. Whole beams of life between my bones. I tossed more pebbles into the water. I liked watching them be swallowed up.

Then Tricksy said, "How many flips can you do?"

I turned around and there was a girl. Tricksy. I didn't know that yet. She wore a gingham pinafore and her knees were skinned. Her bangs were in her eyes. She crossed her arms and showed me her teeth.

I'd never seen her before, or if I had, just in passing. She wasn't in my bedroom of seven or nine kids.

I didn't say anything fast enough, so she tossed her hands up toward heaven, took a running stride, and spun through the air four five six times in a row. She stuck her landing, missed a step, caught herself, then set off in the other direction. Three more flips. One of her stockings fell down around her ankle. She hopped on one foot while she yanked it back up over her calf. She spat on the sand. She glowered at me. She put her foot down and smoothed her dress and shimmied her shoulders like, *ta-da*. "Could you beat that? Could you do more flips than that?"

"No ma'am," I said. I put my chin on my knee and hugged my arms around my shin. "I don't think I could."

"That's boring. D'you know how to do them?" She smiled again, bigger. She looked me right in the eye when she smiled, which made her look crazy. She had very thick eyelashes on her lower lash line. They touched the freckles. She had so many freckles. "I can show you how. You should know how to do flips. I love doing flips."

"I don't know if I know how," I said. I'd never tried. "What are you called?"

"Tricksy thu Ecapa." She kicked sand. "Answer!"

"I did," I said.

"D'you want me to show you how!"

I got off the rock and waded to the beach and stood next to her, sopping. I hugged my arms around my ribs. "Hi."

"We're past that. Are you Stellarine? Your posture is lousy."

"Tullian," I said.

She looked at my hair. "Okay," she said, "You look like a babydoll. Did your mother drink a lot when she was expecting you? It makes you look like a babydoll in the face when that happens."

I blinked at her, taken aback.

"I'm being cute," she said. "I'm saying you look like a babydoll because I like babydolls. Also it's true. Did you like it when I did all the flips?"

"Yeah," I said, in awe. My jaw worked over nothing. "Yes'm."

"It's all about momentum and being sure about things. You decide you're going upside down and you throw yourself forward really hard and the motion just goes. It's fun. It's easy. You'll be really good at it." She stuck out her hand for me to shake. "Hi."

I took her hand. I examined it. Rough, which surprised me. She didn't skimp on chores. "Thought we were past that."

"What's your name? How are you doing today?" She flipped my hand and pecked my knuckles.

I stared at her.

"If you don't have a name, I'll make one up!"

"Marney," I said somehow.

"Hi Marney." She beamed. "Tumble with me?"

I looked at my hand in hers. I felt an enormous and ridiculous urge to cry. I pulled my hand away and flexed my fingers, and before she could look sad I took a long stride and stuck my hands out like she had, I threw my body up, my shoulders hit the sand, then my tailbone, then my legs in a pile. Sand smudged up against my cheek. The water rushed in and got in my nose.

She laughed and clapped and helped me up. She dusted me off to no avail. "Again! Like this!"

She flipped and I followed her. Eventually, I got it. It was like we had won a war.

I followed her up to the mansion. It was dark now, I said the bleed as we went. She asked what it meant and I told her I couldn't tell her, on account of she wasn't Tullian, but my version of saying that, which was, "Pardon. Wish I could."

She didn't press and instead took us to the kitchens, we were served our bowls, and we found a space on the steps to eat together. Another girl joined us, a friend of hers who immediately became a friend of *ours*, a tall quiet girl called Georgia Candor Blake. She preferred her Virtue, so we called her just Candor. She wore her pearls around her wrist and sucked on them when she was nervous. She shared her bread with me when I finished before her.

The two of them were in the same bedroom on the floor below me. There weren't so many kids in the mansion, all things considered, and they told me I hadn't known them because I was shy, not because they were elusive. Candor and Tricksy were legacy bandits. Both of them were orphans. Candor maybe had a father around, given that who her father was wasn't a certain thing, there were a few men who'd been around her mother, and they all tended to Candor where they could, given that her mother died on a raid about a month ago. Her mother had been important to the Choir, a strategist. Still hard.

Meanwhile, Tricksy's parents were a pirate and a Hereafterist. The Hereafterist, she told me, was executed in Cisra when she was very small. Her father had been the one to smuggle her mother across the sea to refuge here, but her mother was proud and loved the cause, and went on and continued her work north until it was taken from her. Her pirate father died as pirates sometimes did. She spoke about this lightly. They were part of the ancestral congress. They were downstairs with their hands in the ballroom. Then Candor and Tricksy looked at me like, *so do you have parents, or what?*

I told them about the massacre and you.

Neither of them said anything. It was a good silence, a serious one. Then they asked if I had met the butler.

We put our bowls away and they took me to a part of the mansion where kids generally weren't invited, not by edict, but by custom so clear that nobody dared question it. It was the part of the mansion where bandits discussed the already inevitable end of the charade, when the baron's senate would vote unanimously to send great military force to the impostor barony of iniquity and theft and destroy everything that'd been built here with deadly force. Old-school Ignavian revolutionary total warfare. It was certain. It was just a time game. Not a place for flipping around and impressing girls. I tried to conduct myself with the dignity and solemnity I would if I walked through a Tull Shrine with the Idol out. Tiptoe with my shoulders back, not ogling any of the luxury that studded the walls and ceiling. Someone was getting tattooed on a fine settee while we passed. He watched us without turning his head, just a roll of the pupil from tear duct to lash point. The ship etched on his shoulder sported beautiful sails.

Tricksy and Candor stood outside a tall door and knocked twice. Tricksy subdued a little, but bounced on her toes. Candor looked ashen. I put my hands behind my back and felt vaguely ill.

"Come," said someone on the other side.

The door slung open. None of us touched it.

Sitting around a table were a few stern bandits with diagrams and unfolded telegram sheets and big leatherbound volumes laid wide open. They had been speaking tersely, the flavor of what'd been said hung in the air, but they stopped talking abruptly when they saw us. One tried for a smile. Across from the door, facing me, was an elder. He wore his hair long. There was a smudge of pink paint in the middle of his eyelids, like someone had swept their thumb through rouge and pressed the pigmented pads in a line from his brows down to his cheekbones. He had a lean face and a slim jaw under his beard. He was Tullian, clearly, but the paint should be blue. Tullian men wear blue paint, women wear black. He was one of the only bandits I'd seen this old. He looked at me.

I tried to fix my posture.

"Candor. Tricksy." He inclined his head. I could see myself reflected on his eyes. Hollow-eyed babydoll revenant under his lashes. The pink paint made me dizzy. "What can I do for you, little one?"

"Pardon. Hello sir. My friends said I oughta meet you."
I spoke barely above my breath. I moved my hand across my
chest, hand stretched down and backwards, wrist toward the
sky. Gesture of morning deference. "Are you the butler?"

The other bandits around the table snickered. One
closed a book.

He said, "You're Tullian?"

I felt my age and that I was shorn. I wanted to fall down
and cough up my insides. My knees locked instead. "Yessir."

"Come sit at the table," he said. "When we're done I'd
love to talk with you."

I looked over my shoulder at Tricksy and Candor and
they looked in equal measure elated and very nervous.
Then they both darted off, and I was alone in the doorway.
I looked back at the table. I loped to a vacant chair there
and sat. There was a map in front of me, the full stretch
of continent, the Crimson Archipelago in the Amandine
Sea, far-off Delphinia and Raphnia and Laodamia warring
across the water. I looked at the hook promontory of the
Fingerbluffs, our mean perfect part of the coast, and the
seam with Tasmudan and Cisra, at Royston above us, at
the Drustlands' sharp diagonal. I looked at the little script I
couldn't read. The hand was too sprawling. I looked at the
sea monsters woven between the islands and wondered if
any of them were real. I didn't look at the bandits for shame
of drawing attention. I'd love to talk with him too.

There was a hearth behind the Tullian man. It crackled
and cast warm shadows on the walls. Someone at the table
called the man Amon, which I took to be his given name,

and as they spoke about the contents of a telegram—an ask from Baron Glitslough if Horace Veracity Loveday's daughter was going to Wilton School in Cisra, some academy for aristocratic brats around Loveday's daughter's age—and degrees of urgency that might be alive behind it. "Of course," said a bandit to Amon, "Horace's agoraphobia only gets us so far. The girl will come of age eventually. It'll be suspect, even if he's possessive and cruel, for nobody to ever glimpse her. We'll need to produce the girl. Candor's not ready for that."

"I could be," said Candor very softly from behind me.

"Letters are so much easier to leave unscrutinized than a girl in the flesh in the room with you," said another. "Too much risk to our own. I'm sorry about your mother, Candor. I say we kill the girl and spare us all the trouble."

"Baron Glitslough and Baron Montrose would insist upon funerary gifts," said a third, "and making the trip to see those gifts received. We'd be fucked. Baby Loveday needs to be alive and skittish. She could have her father's condition. Delay the necessity of Candor's charade for a decade or so and minimize the demands of the song and dance. Doesn't need to show face in social scenes if she's inherited the family weirdness."

"Not appearing at all stretches belief," the first said. "Surely the girl Loveday would show her face eventually. She's the only heir. She'll need a spouse and offspring. She can't just cloister herself away."

"Or we could proceed per Jody Honesty Blake's wishes, rest her spirit. Let little Candor do her work. We send baby

Loveday off to school and plan an affliction like her father's first week. Big show that proves her inherited madness. Then we have her shipped back home, so that the kid is seen and known to be real, and the longer performance is put off 'til Candor's grown," said a bandit who hadn't spoken up yet. He had a pad of tobacco in his lip that lisped his voice. "What do you say, sugar? Do you feel ready?"

Glancing at her, Candor looked worried. If she repeated that she was ready, everybody would know better. Her chin wobbled. I wondered what her dead mother Honesty had intended for her. If Candor wanted it. Doesn't always matter what the kid wants. Wasn't like I'd wanted to work. Beside her, Tricksy scuffed her toe. This distribution of attention was neither of their preference. Why couldn't Tricksy do whatever it was instead?

The adult bandits caught the silence's tone. They looked at each other, grim and certain. Someone spoke up. "She could stay here for the duration of her schooling. Horace could educate her personally. He's a paranoid man and an unkind one, mistrustful of his only daughter in some other teacher's hands."

"Or we can admit to ourselves that the charade's not sustainable and plan for war."

"The homeschooling story would get us a decade. After that, if the story fits, it could last a good long time! It's not like provincial aristocrats are important anymore, it's all about liquid cash now, which the Lovedays sorely lack. The charade works. It's lasted us so far! Have faith in our tricks."

"That's right. We jump right to war and we're smithereens, understand? We'll be like a border town up in the Drustlands. Candor's not ready. That's fine. We're not ready either. We make preparation for a fistful of futures and keep our heads clear."

"Baby Loveday will be a debutante afterward that decade's up. Someone will seek her hand for land's sake, even if she's crazy. We've got a stretch of the sea. Someone will want it. If anything, she might seem easy pickings, insane and isolated out here with her tyrant father. They'll come here. They'll find out."

"I can do it," Candor said, but nobody seemed to hear her.

Aiming to be helpful, I said, "Where's the real daughter?"

Amon looked at me kindly. "I threw her off the bluffs some years back."

My jaw dangled. I breathed through my open mouth.

"A plan for the next decade gives us a decade to plan," Amon said. "That'll mark a predictable end. We'll be decisive when we must be about the Loveday charade and our aims against annihilation. Write the letter back. I think curt is best. Short, cold, formal. Wilton decadence won't serve our daughter. She'll remain home where her duties demand her. Give you more time to mourn, Candor. I regret we've put this on you."

Two of the bandits started scribbling. They compared when they wrote. They snipped about preposition placement. I thought I heard Candor sniff.

"What's your name?" Amon still looked at me. "How'd you find your way to us?"

"Marney Honeycutt," I managed. "How little was the daughter?"

"Little," he said. He deliberately opened his hands and laid them palm up. "An ugliness that demanded doing."

I felt a swell of ghastly nothing. It was a slimy lump in my chest.

Bandits around the room started standing. They had reached some consensus over our heads, the script for the telegram they ought to send in response. Delayed decision was the decision. Quickly the room just held Amon and me and my two friends.

Amon spoke. "You're a good daughter, Candor Blake. Your mother would be proud of your resolve, but she's dead, and you're nigh a woman. You can chose for yourself if you're up for the charade."

Candor grunted. I got the sense she disagreed. Borrowed grief hit me and my head swam. I fought bile back down my throat. Hands on the arms of my chair, squeezing hard.

"Let's talk about it," Tricksy said, then whispered not-so-quietly, "*Come on!*"

"I'll think on it, sir," said Candor. "Appreciate the time."

There was a noisy shuffling behind me, hissing and pleading, then the door shut. I was alone with Amon.

The fire glow behind Amon tinged his hair pink. His lined face fell slack, solemn. He flipped one hand over, put his thumb on his opposing palm. It was a day gesture, but not one whose particular meaning I knew. Tull Shrine

reverends have a whole choreography of poses around the
table, and only adult Tullians are burdened with knowing the moves and their meanings. I didn't know what he
wanted. I didn't know what to do.

Hoarsely, "How old are you? Why are you here?"

"Dunno. Fourteen I think," I managed. Fifteen, maybe?
Surely not sixteen. I hadn't had my menses yet. Without the
wage clock looming above my head time had lost all texture. I
put my hands on the table the only way I'd been taught how.
"Mors Brandegor and Uthste thu Calaina and Mallory Valor
Moore brought me here. Everybody else I know is dead."

"Uthste's a good woman," he said. "Dead how?"

"By strikebreakers outside the ichorite foundry in
Ignavia City. We worked there."

"I remember word of that." Amon pressed his thumb
harder, rotated his hand like he was snuffing something.
"Are you in the faith?"

"I don't know how I'd leave it." My hair wasn't covered.
I felt stupid, underdressed. "I am. It's hard."

"Your parents were murdered at dawn that day. Or was
that journalistic dramatics?" He inclined his head. There
were shadows in triangles under his eyes. He seemed bigger
than he was. Head stooped, shoulders braced against the
ceiling. Every breath pulled the whole air from the room. I
wanted to bolt. I held still.

"Yessir," I got out. "Dawn."

"Tell me what happened."

"My sister was preaching to nobody that we deserved
more than what we got. She was talking about how I'm

91

sick. Then they shot us from the rooftops. It wasn't dawn by the time it was done. It was," I watched the woman climb out from under my mother and remembered the way her hair looked, the fern shadows it cast on her jaw and her neck, but couldn't remember if it was brown or bruise pink, it couldn't have been pink, it must've been the light, like with Amon's hair, but I couldn't remember how my mother looked aside from lying down, or otherwise being on the street, I couldn't be sure it was my mother, I didn't see her face, which maybe meant she was alive, but I am not so stupid, and suddenly my mouth was dry and my insides pinched and flipped. I felt vile. "It was awful," I said. "It was awful. It was awful. I ran away."

"Your survival should make you proud," he said. "It was no cowardice."

I hadn't realized it could've been. I was suddenly too sour for the grave. The ground would spurn me or else I'd kill the crops.

"You cut your hair unwed."

"I let it be cut."

"Are you Torn given?"

I didn't know what that meant. I looked at him help-lessly. His edges blurred.

"Our myth, Marney. There was substance which was nothing in the dark. Call it god. Eternities turned over and uterine god nothing started thinking. The contemplation was unbearable. It could not understand or be understood. So the uterine god nothing split itself, made a baby to be its equivalent, so that it had a partner to see and be seen by, so that there was something to know, and something that could behold the uterine god nothing's glory in becoming a *something*, minded and dignified, distinct from the other it had made, and be impressed. With this creation disharmony brewed. The second thinking thing was repulsed by having been made, rather than having been the maker. Jealous and inferior, it became luminous to distinguish and exalt itself above the other. Day and Night," he said, moving his hands.

"While Day claimed superiority it was clear they depended on one another. Without each other, they'd be alone, which Night knew and Day believed to be unbearable, but so long as there were two, there'd be strife. So together they made a baby. Their child would decide which god was stronger, better, and bow before the victor. The child did not want to bow. It loved Day and Night with perfect symmetry and by the force of this love it would not kneel. Day and Night couldn't bear it. If the child wouldn't yield to one, they'd fight to dominate it. They each took a limb and yanked," he parted his palms, "and ripped the child in twain.

"The Torn bled enormously, ceaselessly. The bleeds of dawn and dusk overcame Day and Night, wed them, gated them, defined them and bound them in place. They saw their own tyranny, that their want for control required subjugation and was therefore worthless. They produced dirt to cover the child and hid its brokenness from their sight. We awoke on the dirt to tend the shroud over the body. We work in the day and we rest in the night, to suit the governance of the Father and Mother, to appease them in their grief. Men are Day given, they come of age and devote themselves to the toils the Day entails, and women are Night given, with their own attendant responsibilities. So goes the gospels."

There was a hymn about Night and Day burying the body that I had sung at the Shrine for an equinox bleed. Simple, pretty. *Lamentations for the little one!* They dressed me in a floaty shroud and crowned me with wheat spikes and poppies. Only time I was ever picked for a solo. My family's rigor with spiritual teaching had softened with each successive daughter, such that at the time I'd hardly understood what I was singing.

Something changed in Amon's shoulders. He sloped nearer to me. It was like his head had grown heavier. When he spoke again, he rasped.

"What hideous violence has been visited on you. What incomprehensible pain you've endured. As you mourn and rage and grow up, you do so *here* in this house where I was servant. It was my Day-given duty. I served Horace from the time he and I were boys. He became a man and inflicted himself on this barony. The bad telling of our myth, the version we use to hurt each other, says that trying for *more* ruins everything. That change leads to carnage. We are forbidden conflict. When we hurt each other, it is assumed we are like Day and Night, but the only reading of our myth worth telling is that we tend the Torn not to placate the warring weeping heavens, but because we are like the *Torn.* We endure the many hurts that power demands imposing on others in order to become itself. The Torn is alive. It wakes beneath the ground, otherwise there'd be no bleed. The blood comes from a still-beating body. The story isn't done, it ends in a yet-to-come vengeance with the Torn awake and wrathful, striking its gruesome twin parents from the sky."

He slammed down his hands. His knucklebones strained against his translucent skin, I thought they'd burst through into the air. "I'm Torn given, Marney Honeycutt. Neither Day nor Night. I killed Horace and his family and those servants who'd stand against the creation of our home, where the Choir now rests, and poverty is gone, property and the scarcity it makes replaced with abundance. Luxury for all. I struck down my tyrant. You, Marney. You're old enough to give. Do you want to strike down yours?"

I gasped and pressed my hands down. I could've bent the table. "Yes," I said. "I need to kill Yann Chauncey."

"I'll guide you through the rite," he said. "You'll be Torn given. Old enough to help us plan around the Fingerbluffs and to decide how you're going to kill Yann Chauncey."

I brought my head low. I was shaking.

"Look at me. None of that," Amon said. "The Torn demands no deference of us so we needn't give it to each other. Our respect can be proved in better ways." He stood. "We'll prepare the table for evening bleed. You'll set it to honor the Torn, you'll tell me why, you'll vow to kill Yann Chauncey. When the table is set, I'll unwrap the Idol, and we'll speak the bleed. Then you'll be an adult. Be back before."

Out of shame, I couldn't embrace him, so I snatched my hands off the table and knotted my fists in the front of my shirt. I turned and ran. I got the door open somehow, my blood foamed in my face and scalp, and I whipped my head around in the comparative coolness of the hallway until I saw Tricksy and Candor clearly listening. Candor looked worried. Tricksy looked rapt.

"I need to find things," I said too softly and too quickly. "I need to find gifts."

"Gifts for Amon? What gifts do you get for somebody who doesn't believe in owning stuff?" Tricksy thrust her hands in the pockets of her dress and rocked back on her heels. "Fruit, I guess. Does a body own the stuff it eats?"

"For religion," I said vaguely. I looked between the two of them, suddenly sure that I needed help, not because I needed assistance, but because I didn't want to be alone. "Will you come with me?"

They looked at each other.

"Yes," said Candor. I wondered if she'd decided something about the charade. I wondered if I would be right to ask. She caught my look and sniffed. "Soon."

"Duh," said Tricksy. "I love something to do."

So I took their wrists and dragged them through the mahogany halls, and I brought them outside, we clambered down the big luxurious steps of Loveday Mansion and onto the overgrown lawn, through the pale whisps of flower and brush, toward the dark pink shivering city. I kept a hold of them. Candor held me by the wrist and Tricksy hooked her pinkie in mine. Gulls flew above us and screamed and Tricksy screamed too. We peeled down an alley. Candor rubbed my wrist with her thumb, which was so kind of her.

She was so precious. If I understood right, she would pretend to be the dead heir to the dead baron when she was older and I couldn't imagine a baron looking so kind as her. We'd only just met and I felt so sure about her.

Around a corner, Tricksy laughing now, the three of us going so fast that her skirt flew around her knees. I wasn't sure what we were trying to find. Not grain, that was cultivation work, Day work; not mushrooms, that was foraging work, Night work. What was Bleed work?

"Where are we going?" Candor's voice was small. She was taller than me, her strides were longer, it was funny for her to trail behind me. "Can I help look?"

"We're looking for something that's just for pleasure. Not work, something given. Or taken." I spun once, tried to take in the whole city at once. I felt heartsick and nauseous and like I might fall apart. I could blow to bits in the breeze. Like a dandelion. "A symbol of resistance having been made."

Bandits flew by us on lurchers, hollering, revving and standing with one hand thrown back. Their fingers and the smiles on their faces were blurs. We huddled close while the engines roared past. I felt Candor and Tricksy breathing against me, bellies swelling. I watched the lurchers vanish.

"Marney," said Tricksy.

"Yeah," I said. "We should steal a lurcher."

"Seems risky," said Candor.

"We'll give it back," I said.

"Yeah," Tricksy said, clearly more eager for the doing of a scheme than its outcome. "Nobody will notice it's gone."

"Nothing elaborate," I said. "Quick and true."

Candor breathed shallowly. "Like that one?"

A lurcher had been leaned against a wall. Music pounded inside, the swell of brass and rhythmic stomping. It could belong to anybody. I could see my face reflected in its polished body, distorted into ripples. Something shifted in my belly. Tricksy and I sprang for it, I watched her braid swing out of the corner of my eye, and we put our hands on the horns and the body, it was cold and deliciously solid, it sang under my palms, and Candor covering us, she was broadest of us, she turned her back to us and faced the moving street to keep us safe, and thus protected we walked the lurcher down the street toward the mansion with our heads ducked low. Candor tucked in behind us, followed us close at heel, whistled along to the raucous music an octave above. Tricksy was trying so hard not to laugh. Her shoulders worked under her dress. I felt very sure that I was alive. I liked the weight of air on my tongue. It was humid, substantive.

We struggled with the lurcher up the stairs. It was frightfully heavy and the wheels only went so far. Candor pushed from the back and Tricksy and I pulled from the handles, and when that made little progress, I joined Candor and put my hands on the deep purple tire.

I jerked back like I'd been bitten.

The tingles started. The prickling of a fit.

I looked at my throbbing palms, then at the tires, which seemed closer to leather than metal. I hadn't had a fit in years. Ichorite doesn't make its way to the Fingerbluffs often. The trade had legitimate passage along the Flip

98

River, its smuggling routes ran north toward the Drustlands and south toward Tasmudan, the barony here hadn't been touched by the ichorite industry. The feeling gushed up with bile and a scream that miscarried, I stood there panting, I could hardly breathe. I scrubbed my hands together. I looked at the tire helplessly, murderously.

"The tread is smudged," said Candor carefully. "That's funny."

"Push! What's the holdup!" Tricksy screwed her face up and gave the handles a fruitless yank.

"S'ichorite in the tires," I slurred. My tongue felt fat. I gnawed on it and tried to force it back to normal. "Allergic."

"To ichorite? You can't be allergic to ichorite. That's like being allergic to wood. Or water. You'd be fucked," said Tricksy.

"I am," I said. The tingles were fading. It was just a brush, after all, and this wasn't pure ichorite. This felt muddy. I didn't get a glimpse of its making, and usually ichorite always carries its memories with it. Maybe I was outgrowing it? I reached forward again, put the heel of my hand against the tire. I pressed and thought, *move move move move move.*

The tire swelled like a blister. It pressed back against my hand, ballooned between my fingers. It moved. It oozed up the stairs, Tricksy yelped and leaped to the wayside as I pushed it higher, aware of its weight but unaffected by it. It rolled toward, then through, the mansion door. The world shimmered. Pink motes globbed across the foyer, dripped from ceiling and up from the floor. Every edge broke the light. I tongued my soft gums, and I noticed but couldn't parse the hands on my back. I went toward the room where I'd met Amon. The gallery where fun was forbidden. The mansion undulated around me. It was like being underwater. Somewhere, in the back of my mind, I felt the distant factory sounds. Rhythmic thudding, squealing. The cyclical clacking noises of some obscene device. Lots of tinny clicks and one heavy thud in a circuit. I felt like I was being scraped into ribbons. I felt like I was lying down on an oily leather belt while the ceiling rolled real slow above me. Chugging, chugging. I watched the rafters move like ribs on some snake.

The door shut behind me. Amon made a sound of concern. The pink marks on his eyelids looked gorgeous. I dropped the lurcher and my whole hand twitched at its absence. I shook it like the fit would come off. "For the Torn," I said.

"We'll sit 'til dawn," said Amon. "What's wrong? You look faint."

"She's allergic to ichorite," said Tricksy behind me. "There's ichorite in tires."

"Are you okay?" Candor, so I assumed, touched my arm, then my waist. "Marney?"

"It'll get better," I said. I watched Amon's face shimmer. "Just takes a while."

Amon took the lurcher and heaved it onto the table. He groaned but otherwise showed no strain. He twisted the handles, pressed the whole machine as flat as it could go, and then he waved his hands and Candor helped me into a chair, where Tricksy soon joined me. She perched on my lap. Candor sat on the floor beside the chair and leaned her head back, sucked the pearls on her wrist. I blinked fast.

"There's no formal ministry around the Torn. It's fringe, what I'm giving you. Traditionalists in the faith would call it illegitimate." He folded his hands, I watched the shadows they made flutter over the lurcher on the table. Stunning pulsing birdlike shapes. I scrubbed my palms on my trousers and then held out my hands, mirrored him. "The Father," he moves his wrists, "under the Mother's heel," he spreads his fingers, "with the Torn in his fist."

I closed my hand. I felt so sick.

The door opened. Amon didn't look up. His eyes were on me. Candor tucked herself under the chair and Tricksy whipped around and said, "Hi Rancid!"

I looked at the lurcher. Reflected on the lurcher in ripples over my shoulder was an oil-paint impression of Mors Brandegor. She got bigger. Her face became distinct across the steel, I saw her wide mouth and her black brows. She put her hands on my shoulders. She squeezed, I heard her glove leather squeak, and I looked up at my savior and felt twelve again.

"You stole my fucking lurcher," Brandegor said.

"Yes ma'am," I said.

Brandegor was drunk. She had a slowness, a deliberateness I didn't remember her having. Plus the smell. She peered down at me, wiggled her jaw. "Little fawn's not so little anymore. I'd beat you for it."

"I'm coming of age," I said to her. "After dawn it'll be yours again."

"Mine now," she said. "You're funny, Honeycutt."

"You've been gone," I said. "You've been gone for a very long time."

"Don't fight in the home," said Amon. "Have some propriety about you."

Brandegor barked a laugh.

"Pretty fingernails," said Tricksy, admiring the claws by my neck.

"We helped, Tricksy and I," said Candor from under the chair. "You'd have to fight all three of us."

"Little gang." Brandegor released me. She walked around the table's edge, leaned over Amon and kissed his temple. She left a smear of rouge there. She whispered something, and Amon made some low sound. His hands didn't stop moving. He had elegant knobby knuckles. All reverends I'd known did. Brandegor took a fistful of his shirt now, dripped something low and poisonous in his ear. She was bigger than him. If they came to blows I suspected Amon would fall. I thought about the knife. I still carried the knife, always wrapped in leather now so that the metal didn't touch me. I put my hand at the small of my back. I felt the handle. Then Brandegor straightened. She folded her arms across her broad chest. "Precious. When you're done growing up, I'll show you how to shoot and knock you upside the head for taking what's mine. You'll be good for the Choir. You'll be baby Loveday's valet. Proceed."

Then she left, and she dragged Tricksy and Candor with her without touching them, propelling them through force of will alone.

I stayed alone with Amon.

He put his hands on the table with the lurcher.

Shaking, so did I.

PRAISE THE TORN Child. I have nothing to offer you besides what I'm always offering you, my breath, not the fruit
of my thievery but the practice of it, the gesture which is an
object in and of itself. I give my love, my grief, my cut red
hands. Praise be the blur you leave in your wake. The smear
between dignity and indignity, kindness and unkindness,
the prefix and its root. There is no religion about you but
I will loyally and devotedly pretend. I grow up, my band
goes out, we pillage together and bring home our spoils, and
I recite the story of your torture and of mine. I say your
name every time I'm tattooed, when I'm branded, when my
wounds are sewn shut and patched over. We go out on our
lurchers under the enormous skies, we wear your redness
on our backs, and with my comrades at my shoulder I praise
you. By the pulse in my neck I praise you. I wear the rouge
on my eyelids not always, forgive me, but when I seek qui-
etude, and contemplation of your pain which is our pain, I
prick my thumbs and daub my eyes and I remember you. I
remember you, Gwyar. Forever gone from heaven, you fury
of the earth, I lay my cheek upon the ground and hear you
screaming. It is a low hum through all the rocks. It sounds
like an oncoming train.

Six

A YEAR OR TWO LATER I WAS NORTH WITH
Brandegor's gang. I was a Choir bandit now. Not a member of the gang, but a pupil of it. I endured their tutelage
and glutted myself on their attention. It made missing the
bluffs nearly bearable. I practiced my Cisran as we edged
the gulches. The land rose, the air thinned. We scaled the
viny mountain jags at Montrose Barony's legal edge, the
place where land was and wasn't Ignavia, Royston, and
Drustland alike. There was a border but it was diffuse and
hallucinatory, even more so than most. On legal papers and
state maps there were harsh lines that squashed topography
and sanded down the mountains into even hills in planter's
rows, but here among the jutting rocks and craggy heather,
the ground was lineless.

Roystonian claims that this land was theirs, or for some
reason Ignavia's, all felt flimsy, given that the Drustlands
themselves recognized no borders, and championed free

movement for all except their exiles. Traditionally, this land was Drustish. Drustish people lived here and spoke one of many Drustish dialects. A Drustish Hall was near. That's what was relevant. It was why we traveled so defensively, and walked our lurchers half the time to obscure their snarling mechanical loudness. Mors Brandegor did not give a consistent story of her exile. She just kept it clear that she was not welcome back.

The night previous we'd held up a private bathhouse in upper Montrose. The ornate grayish edifice had been built over a natural hot spring, and was not nearly as old as Bellona, but tried hard to pretend otherwise. The bathhouse was a massive granite dome, carved with deep exaggerated lines to suggest the stone was cupped hands over the spring. The doorway was tucked beneath two fingertips. Inside the ceiling was decorated with the gilded creases of its palms. It was ghastly, shell-like, not my kind of lush. I felt like a caught bug. We'd cleared out the bathhouse of all its fine perfumes and linens, the coins from its safe, the best possessions patrons had brought, and the hatchet the squirrely attendant kept beneath the counter, which Uthste now wore on her hip. I conjugated stupid phrases, *I loved her, I had loved her, I love her, I will love her, I've always loved her, I'll always have loved her*, and watched the dusk bleed glint off the hatchet's crooked beak.

I was set to be Candor's valet when she was young Baron Loveday, whenever that may be. Loveday's valet would've spoken Cisran. She would've known all the names of the major baron families and all the names of the

105

revolutionaries in the war that split Ignavia and Cisra out of Rasenna, and she would care about Rasenna, and its complicated legacy as the non-expansionist heir to the Bellonan empire. She would care about the proportion of baronies with political ambitions compared to those weaker baronies without strong enough economic or cultural output to care about much more than their relationships, who generally deferred opinion-making to their neighbors. She would care about the Senate and its continuation. The currents around Ignavia City, where a movement helmed by the young Chauncey heir argued that polities ought elect their own representatives, that baron blood as a pre-qualification for senatorship was tyrannical and antiquated, that the people clamor for industrial progress and its promises of individual freedom, rags to riches, grime to shine. It was difficult to imagine caring about these things. I'd figure out how. It was my duty to trick the wildly invested that I, the help, was competent and knowledgeable and wanted what was best for them. Help that wants to help is a cog that makes the right kind of ticking sound inside the machine and by harmony becomes invisible. I wanted to be invisible. How easy it'd be a shadow to gruesomely murder Yann Chauncey. We'd be grown up soon.

Valor sang. Her voice had a high clear quality, fluttered at the edges of each phrase. It was more fluid than either factory chants or stompy slurry Fingerbluffs dancing songs, intricate and intimidatingly delicate, the sort of song one had to be taught and keep pink lungs to sing. Like a hymn. Birds liked it. Big fat bald-headed birds with sickle beaks

and hooks for toes. There were lots of them. They crowded
the slouchy trees. We didn't speak, mostly so as not to interrupt her. That and Brandegor's queer mood. I understood
it, I'd be tense like that if I'd been near Ignavia City. Didn't
like rubbing up with ghosts.

You're from here. Or somewhere nearer here than home
was. I wondered if you had family somewhere. I wondered
if they knew what became of you. I hoped they didn't. I
couldn't bear the thought of explaining how inside of me
you remained alive.

I threw my attention under the lurcher's inexplica-
bly ichorite treads. Chevron trenches in the sooty mud,
displaced thumb-shaped gravel. Pleasant crunch accompanying Valor's singing. I walked Brandegor's lurcher and she
walked ahead, didn't look at us. Having destroyed them to
come of age, I'd replaced these tires recently with my spoils.
When we first left the Fingerbluffs we'd discussed money
for it. I'd balked at the price. Month's wages for just one!
Thieves' wage doesn't exist, I was told, I should be clever. I
should see what I need and take it. So I took it.

About seven months before now, down in Kimball, an
enforcer intervened in a raid of ours. He put a gun in my
face. I put my hand on his gun, it went flaccid as taffy, I
pushed it backwards toward his head. It folded like a goose's
neck. He spent a minute fussing with it while we ran, went
red-faced trying to bend it straight. Huffing and growling
and strangling the thing. He pulled the trigger for some
fucking reason. It blew up. It cleaved the nose from his
face. I spat up oily rainbow fluid and couldn't see or stand

touch for hours after but somewhere in that time, I crawled to his lurcher, and by grace of ancestral instinct I unscrewed the lug nuts and stole the dead man's tires. I brought the tires to Brandegor. She considered us square and told me I was so smart, such a smart girl, I was so stupid. Could've just stolen the lurcher itself. Lurcher's just as good.

I'd killed two men and a woman since leaving the Fingerbluffs. All enforcers. That first was an accident but the next two weren't. Funny timing, I was assured. Usually it wasn't so much so fast. Forgive me that I felt nothing about it. I felt nothing at all. I felt no rain and no chill. Just nausea. I bit my nails bloody and cringed from myself.

What a world I crawled across! I'd seen so much in the past months that it felt like my head had no edges. Images swam over me and I hardly parsed them. I drowned in texture and sound. I'd seen the backs of tangled serpents in the Flip River delta and the trunks of ancient redwoods, the spotted long-toothed tigers in the poppy fields, the beached skeleton of an old wrecked ship. I learned how to disassemble and reassemble a rifle. I stuffed candy in gas tanks and vats of raw concrete and memorized code phrases whose meanings evaded me. I'd seen the dull flat roof of a prison, inside which workers were made to weave rope from bleed 'til bleed without the removal of their manacles, and to dangle posts where a man squirmed alive from his ankles, bound in that rope of his labor, bare-chested, not Choir, half-insane. We cut him down and he slithered on his belly through the woods with the bread and gold we gave him. I learned how to string a bow. I learned

the meanings of Choir tattoo patterns. I got MARNEY
HONEYCUTT done under my collar bones. It itched
like mad when it scabbed and flaked. I felt across my chest
and became myself, committed to being the dead union's
daughter, the Torn-given crawly rat whom my dead community would've reviled if they'd been alive to see me, my
role in this fatal work. I learned to read, which was torture.
I bought my first cock in secret but didn't dare wear it. I
sometimes rubbed the leather straps against my cheek. I
asked a girl in a parlor to snuff her cigarette on my wrist and
she did; the scar shows like a cufflink. I learned arithmetic
and more ways to gamble. I learned the Histories, which
were Bellonan mythologies some roundabout bastard called
Tarpeia wrote down to punish me. I slammed my hand
in a door in a fit of sudden unstoppable anger and broke
two knuckles, which healed poorly in shades of yellow and
green. I got my menses. I stopped getting taller. For some
reason my voice never dropped.

Alarming number of birds, now. Too many roosting all
at once. The weight of their congregation bent the trees
they flocked upon. I didn't like the looks of them and Valor's
song was over. The tires and our boots crunched arrhyth-
mically. The scratchy cloudy sky hung low. I buttoned the
topmost button of Tita's, my own, jacket. My pulse beat
fast for no reason. My insides smashed together and my
brain was electrified pulp. Looking at slumped trees and
their meaty umbrella-shaped vultures hurt. I turned over
conversations we'd had across my tutelage for something to
say. The back of my skull gave me a fistful of words without

order: *pluperfect, artillery, cartilage, saltpeter, daffodil, bartering, lipstick*. Nothing worth its own isolated utterance. I thought the word *utterance*. I thought about Tricksy and Candor. I considered doing a flip. Cartwheeling down the mountainside as a one-man avalanche. My body in smithereens across the forest floor, feasted on by foxes and minks. I said to nobody, for something to say: "What's Hereafter mean exactly? I've said it all my life without knowing what it means." My mentors kept walking. Valor held her skirts up in one fist. The ruffles stirred like gills.

Uthste said, "Who're you asking, Marney?"

"You, ma'am," I sniffed.

"That so?" Uthste made a sound in her throat. She felt along her head. It'd been weeks since she shaved it, and a dark fuzz blurred the usually showy seams between her bones. "Why did Yann Industry Chauncey commission the slaughter of your friends and loved ones?"

My guts slugged with poison. I gnawed my tongue so hard it bled.

"The why's twofold. Intertwined and simultaneous. The first why is that Yann the man is evil. He claims ownership of the tools and the fruits of other people's work and smashes those who ask for scraps beneath his heel. His actions stain the earth. The remedy to this is your little knife. You kill him, he'll butcher no more workers. Second reason why," Uthste said, "is why the first emperor of Bellona sacked the patchwork city-states before he sewed them together into one imperial outfit, and why the kings of Rasenna always executed the village elders in the serfdom over from where the peasant revolt took place. When few rule the many, they must use force to take what they want, and demonstrate force not just to keep it, but to snuff the fires of contradiction from the collective. People above *must* do this. This is a quality of being above. Someone must be below, and to be below is to be bereft and suffer.

"The scripts of history show the above how to remake what's been made, and the way to do that's violence. Killing Yann will not prevent the ascent of his successor. It must be done to rid the world of Yann, but it is one piece to the solution. Hereafterists are champions of faith in all. We know that this evil is a machine made of history, it is created, it can be dismantled. We can try something else. We can make a way to be together without being above each other. Everyone can use everything. No one can keep the devices used to make the world to themselves. No borders, no punishment for movement. No wage clock, no work as a method for managing the masses 'til they're too exhausted to rise up and kill you. No enforcers. No rules besides the Choir's one.

"Being a Hereafterist is a commitment to creating a brand-new world all the time. It is the method of making a new world, it does not stop, we are never there yet. We have never arrived at a restful Hereafter, we must keep making. We will become a liberated collective, a plague will roll over us, and a famine, and fifty thousand bullets, and we will need to make choices. We will need to change. We must resist the ossification of precedent. We march toward Hereafter, not tomorrow, we march past tomorrow, we know tomorrow will be hard. Hereafterists raid prisons and free prisoners. Hereafterists kill bosses and hierophants and the hereditary rulers of the world. Hereafterists farm and teach and dance and die often. We have revolutions all the time. They fail. My brother and my father, they are Cisran Hereafterist partisans, they are in the ancestral congress and guide me toward that better future. They were put against the wall when the last Cisran uprising failed. That was decades ago now. Across the Amandine sea, there's a Hereafterist revolution in Delphinia, they've held their victory for three months and have collectivized all industries in their capital city. They're distributing food rations and have carried the grand oil paintings out of the royal palace, filled the public houses with that art. So long as the whispers that Tasmudan has armed the royalists are wrong, they might hold this glimpse of Hereafter for a good long while. We've held ours in the Fingerbluffs for over a decade and a half. When we are found out, we will call other Hereafterists to us, and together we will fight to defend our nearness to the future until we are dead."

"Thank you ma'am," I said. It was beautiful, the pursuit of Hereafter. It was beautiful knowing that my work would aid the bigger project of future-making. It was horrible to think of Yann in sequence. It was horrible, wonderful, unthinkable that I wanted to be closer to Uthste because her family had been killed. I wanted to embrace her. I wanted to slip underneath her skin. I wanted to vomit. Honor, real honor. I rubbed my hands together. Picked my chapped knuckles. Night had fallen, and with it cold. Brandegor struck a match against her boot and lit a lantern. She held it by her jaw. The birds beat their slashed-umbrella wings against the orange light but didn't fly off. Shadows flickered across the trail. No insect song. There was a smell in the darkness that I recognized, sweet and vile. The air tasted like the smell. I thought for a moment the smell might be wafting off my own nerves, an elaboration of my bad memories, but I saw Valor's painted lip twist. She peered over my head. Utshte touched the hatchet.

Brandegor stopped.

All of us stopped with her.

"Slow," said Brandegor.

I took a step nearer to her, spied under the crook of her elbow.

The lantern light fell in fingers over a depression in the trail. Scorched plants leaned away from it. Trees had been stripped of their lowermost rungs of branches. They looked plucked. The depression opened, and revealed within the exposed hollow were the burned out shells of low, sprawling wooden structures. The beams had fallen. Doors torn down, the frames still standing, veiling nothing from nothing. Long tables blackened, broken. Parts of a chair.

Horror. I sank my wrist in my teeth to blunt the scream.

Brandegor lowered her lantern arm to keep me back. The light swung, and illuminated the ruptured shapes on the salted ground. Hands, just hands. Nails, knuckles. Hands without their bodies, then the bodies. It must've been weeks. It'd rained since. I could not remember in that

113

moment how to do anything else but pray. I prayed like a child, without form or coherence. *Please sky, please night, enough.* I watched but did not follow Mors Brandegor as she walked down along the corpses in the rubble of this Hall. I watched her count aloud the people, and examine the burn marks on the fragments of what had once been grand. There were sixty-four people here, fourteen bodies small. Bullets glinted on the ground but they were lead. I could not move them.

A bayonet had punctured the skull of someone's hog, and the blade had lodged in the bone, so the wielder had abandoned their gun inside its body. Brandegor wrapped the weapon in a kerchief and put her boot against the pig's soft purple back, which seeped and crawled with little life. She snarled, yanked, and the bayonet screeched loose. Its blade spiraled like a unicorn horn. Brandegor carried it with her as she walked through the next structure, smaller, a cottage. There was less of it left. She used the bayonet to shift through debris.

As Brandegor turned her back to us, I looked at the body nearest me, the embroidery on his tunic. Neat thread flowers and slanting geese. I looked at the patches in the knees of his trousers. I looked at the braid in his hair, the cord still tied by the nape of his neck. I looked at the gun in his hand. Ancient. Hadn't never seen one like that before, but I could guess that it wasn't Ignavian. All our shit is mixed with ichorite now. At his waist was a ring of keys, a silvery bell instrument, a small neat utility knife, and spare ammunition. He looked well-fed. Youngish. There were

114

many people around him. They'd fallen close together. Or they'd been arranged. Their feet, stripped of boots, lay all in a line.

Brandegor waded through the rubble. She walked slowly, swiveled her head back and forth, and the lantern bobbed. The ruins and the incomprehensible totality of what had been done here slipped in and out of the light she carried. The people revealed by lantern light were flat past bloat and teemed with fleck-sized animals. Some were bone. Birds worked fast. In the cottages they did not lay in even rows. I assumed they had collapsed where they had been killed. The quick lantern-light flashes in which I witnessed them showed me nothing about who the people had been to each other and what lives they'd been leading. The fact of their bodies had been undone, the personal effects that marked them had loosened and faded with sun and rain and scavenger hunger. Just dead. I failed them as a witness. Nothing here was ichorite and I could ask the debris nothing. The scene was inert. Whoever had done this and whomever had survived this had moved on.

Brandegor knelt. She gathered something in her lantern hand, stood up. She turned back to us. I had never seen her cry. It was unfathomable. She was the vitality and bravado of our calling made manifest. Here she was, a mortal woman weeping. She looked older. Her eyes burned, she spat at the mud. She trudged back through the nothing and stood in front of us. Her breathing made no sound, nor did her footsteps. She looked down at me, with that look cut through me, then over my head at her companions.

"It was Laith Hall," she said eventually. She closed her fist on whatever evidence she'd chosen then shook the putrid weapon. "This is a Roystonian gun."

Nobody spoke. Nobody dared break the vigil.

"We should go. Pick up the fucking lurcher, Marney."

I must've dropped it. I jolted, I knelt, I could not feel my hands as I fit my fists around the lurcher's body and heaved it upright. I saw, I smelled, the pattern in the air. I did not breathe as Brandegor jerked the lurcher from my hands, hit the ignition and revved it, grabbed me by the scruff of my neck and pulled me across the machine in front of her. She put the Roystonian rifle across my thighs. I felt her ribs flutter behind me, I felt her choke and wheeze. I replaced her hands with mine, and behind me Valor and Uthste must've mounted, I heard a pair of engines roar. I kicked off, I turned us around, and I led us past Laith Hall.

GRIEF CHANGED BRANDEGOR after that. It made her mean. She got thinner, the bones showed in her face. She took Uthste as a lover, or maybe they'd always been lovers, and quarreled with Valor for sport. Her molasses voice harshened. She spoke less to me, but she looked at me with a surety that I understood. We had something new in common. She smoked perpetually, a poisonous cloud wreathed her brow, and she and I would spend hours drinking then tying up the empty glass bottles with twine, taking fifty paces back, and shooting them to dust. She didn't talk to me about Laith Hall.

I got the sense from Uthste and Valor's hushed conversations that border skirmishes between Royston and the Drustlands were habitual, but they were *skirmishes*, soldiers beating soldiers to death in the badlands further east. Laith Hall's desolation was not that. Laith Hall was burned-out nothing. Many Drustish people didn't have permanent settlements, from what I gathered. Only a few religious sites were constant. Most traveled with their livestock in summertime, built a Hall in autumn where they lived in winter, which they set ablaze in spring as an offering to the harvest cycle. A burnt Hall had a standard presentation. The wood was raked, scattered. The frames were scraped down, and the once-interior was seeded with grasses and moss. There was a deliberate wrongness, a cultural desecration in what had been inflicted on Laith Hall. Raw contempt. This was a stanza in a declaration of war.

I didn't know if Ignavia had a standing army. There hadn't been war on this continent since the Ignavian barons' revolution centuries ago. So far as I knew, our enforcement was strictly domestic. Ignavia only carved up carnage like this at home. Perhaps it'd extend elsewhere, if Royston successfully escalated the conflict from scraps to battles. I couldn't fathom why. The pattern was clear, but not its aim. Nobody fucking cared about Royston. Royston was a land of chalk-faced aged aristocrats with fluffy cows and lousy industrialization. Rich in rotting palaces, poor in usable cash. It'd been part of Bellona once, a point of pride quickly dampened by having not been a part of its successor, Rasenna. I thought of ample-bosomed pastel milkmaids with bayonetted rifles pushing a whole village populace into a town hall, bolting the doors, and torching the thatch. But then, that was not fair. The ample-bosomed pastel milkmaids who appeared in novels and pornography were often rural Hereafterist bands, who'd defend with their brothers their commons against the king, and be executed en masse for treason. Our fight was with the above and those below who'd betray their comrades to get higher.

It'd been months since the Hall, much longer since we'd left the Fingerbluffs. Rest never felt like rest out on raids. Eventually, we pretended to sleep in a dusty loft above a bar in the rye seas of Glitslough. I shook out my hands. Brandegor and Uthste lay in one bed, Valor in another, and I did push-ups on the floor. I worked myself until I was worn and drenched, and I collapsed, held my cheek against the chilly tavern floor. We were homeward bound, now. We had one last stop along the way.

I SAT OUTSIDE Beauty's brothel with the oxen for a while. One of the workers must have had an otter who must've had pups. They squealed in a basin on the back doorstep, splashing over the corrugated tin sides. I watched them nip each other. I wrung out my hands. Brandegor and Uthste and Valor had been inside for a while already. Music bled through the door, and laughter, jagged drunken chatting, the occasional heave like someone was moving furniture. I hadn't been back here since joining the Choir. I worried abstractly about having grown out past little fawn into something gruesome and lanky with horns. I worried about whether it'd been too long since I'd seen Sunny, if she'd remember me at all, or if she scorned my long absence. It'd been years. I was something like seventeen.

The door opened. Gathered violet skirts flowed through the gap. Then came the grasping hand, the ankle and buckled shoe, the narrow shoulders, the deep sleeves drifting, full at the elbows and cinched at the wrists, and the mass of unbound straight black hair. It fell around her thighs. She wore a ribbon around her neck and dappled rouge. She walked into the courtyard, frowning. She peered around, her earrings jingled, and then she saw me. Brooding crease between her eyebrows melted. Liquid black eyes fixed.

"Hi, Sunny," I got out. But she wasn't Sunny now. She wore a thin gold lip ring. She was an adult, she'd have an immortal Veltuni name. Calling her Sunny was an intimacy I might not be afforded.

"Are you avoiding me? Are you going to sleep in the stables like a cow? You'll catch your death out here." She balled her hands up, pressed them against her waist. Dramatic boning on her bodice. I examined a trampled dandelion in the mud. Above me, nearer to me, she said, "Marney Honeycutt, I'm talking to you."

"I've missed you." I tried for a smile. "You look well."

She put a hand in front of my face. Lots of rings, nails buffed to pearliness. No scars. "Come on. This is ridiculous. It's been forever. Greet me properly."

I took her hand with care not to smudge it and held her knuckles to my brow. "It's good to see you. What's your name now?"

"Teriasa zel Cerca." She frowned again. Rubbed her thumb against mine. "What's wrong?"

I stood up. Kept her hand in mine, held it aloft to the side, like I'd seen Candor practice for her baby Loveday charade. "We should go in. I worry about mud on your shoes."

She smiled, remembered she was mad, then frowned again.

We went inside through the parlor's impossible grandeur and pushed aside the manticore tapestry. Teriasa was a pretty choice, an uncommon one. We were grown up. She was taller than me. Older, probably. Her complexion was warm and clear, her stride so practiced it looked like gliding. Her dress shimmered around her body like a fit without the pain. Her flowing skirts as she climbed the stairs ahead of me had the hypnotic effect of high tide.

She still had her attic room. Deep blue linens on the bed and a cream lace canopy, tall tapered candles on her dresser, a mirror on the far wall with a woven wicker frame. I took off my boots where I had when they'd been gore-mucked. I sat on the floor.

Teriasa sat across from me. She took a brush off her nightstand, smoothed her hair. "You're a proper bandit now."

I nodded, pulled my shirt's neckline down enough to show the edges of my tattoo. "Yes ma'am." I fought for something to say that wouldn't have been hasty. "Are you working?"

She blinked. "Not tonight."

Stupid. I gnawed the skin off of my bottom lip. "Have you been happy?"

Teriasa put her hairbrush down. She pat the bed beside her.

Obediently, I rose and joined her on the bed's edge. I kept my hands in my lap. The angles of this room were different now. Maybe it was the lighting more than my height. In my daydreams the wallpaper was a bluer shade. The music downstairs was hazy through the floorboards. I tapped my toe.

"I've fallen in love," she said.

She turned toward me slightly. Her calf brushed mine. There was intricate stitching along the hem, which was bunched in her hands above her knees, she worried the little thread diamonds under her nail.

"You don't sound happy."

"I am," she said. "His name is Colton Gallantry. He writes partisan pamphlets about renewing the commons and village gardens. Illustrates them too. There's one on the mantle, see?" Yes, and on the windowsill as well. Flimsy folded paper and dark green ink. "Lovely prose."

Copper. My tongue stung, I jammed the bleeding tip in my cheek. Uselessly, I nodded. The illustrated edge of a rye spike fluttered gently with the window's draft.

"We're saving money to leave. We want to start a family," she said. "I've only been working for a few months, and the lumber mill where he works gives him dust for a wage. He wants to quit. I can't support us both and he doesn't want to work here."

"In the Fingerbluffs you wouldn't have to save to have a family," I said. "Lots of Hereafterists shelter there."

"We want to go to Cisra."

I stared at her floorboards until I saw faces in the wood grain. I looked up at her. Her cheek was turned, attention on the pamphlets across the room. I said, "Do Beauty and Prumathe—"

"They think I'm too young to make these kinds of decisions for myself."

"Tell me about Colton."

"He's tall. Beautiful hands," she said. "He's not built to be a laborer. He's not so rough as that. He lives by the mill with his comrades, they run the press together. You can see the fountain in the square from his room. He's sweet to me, Marney."

Belly breaths. I lay back on her bed, looked up through the lace at her ceiling. "It's good to see you again."

"It's good to see you too," she said. She lay on the bed beside me. She stretched her arms above her and looked at the backs of her hands.

WANDERED THROUGH FOUR dark houses before I found the right one.

Shabby gabled three-story wedged between the square and the temple of the bird-foot garland Virtue. The mill

122

groaned in earshot. The waterwheel spun round. I scaled
the building's edge along the gutter, pack and prybar on
my back, but didn't need to snake the window open. It was
cracked. Curtains danced inside with the breeze. I put my
hands through the gap, pulled upwards. The glass lifted
with a whisper. I slipped my body through the gap.

Dim room. A willowy sad-eyed boy hunched at a low
desk with a beaded lamp. Ink stained his palms and fore-
arms. His nose hovered over the paper, his hair hung in
his face. He didn't notice me, so engrossed was he in his
linework. His pen nib barely scratched the paper. His
bed was unmade, pillows strewn across the floor, mattress askew from its frame. Above his bed he'd nailed a
dry thyme-and-peony bouquet. Symbolic of something
Stellarine, wasn't sure what. A gramophone played in the
corner. The needle skipped; it'd reached the leather record's
end, and repeated a faint concluding breath, the sound of
instruments fading.

I took the needle off.

Colton twitched. He straightened, his ridiculous height
made suddenly evident. He turned his head. He saw me in
the corner of his eye. I saw my reflection grow as he peeled
his eyelids back.

I clapped my hand over his nose and mouth. I pinched.
He gasped, he squeezed his pen like he intended to brandish
it, I held him still. "Easy, Gallantry," I said against his hair.
"Be smart."

His face went red. His eyes popped. I let my hand
go slack on his face, and he sucked in, panted, was good

enough not to scream. His rib bones poked through even his vest. I didn't try to understand. He kept his eyes forward now, did his best imitation of a brave face. He adjusted his posture. He must have had head and shoulders on me. He was too long for this chair.

"I'll renounce nothing. I'll bear the torch of a better to-morrow until I die. Unalone toward dawn we go." His voice trembled. He looked like such a kid. Colton said, "Are you an enforcer?"

"No. Choir."

"Choir?" A vein kicked in his jaw. "I have nothing of value to offer the Choir and what I have I'd give freely to—"

"I ain't robbing you." I walked around him, looked at his wet pamphlets. He'd been drawing an azurine tree. Careful crosshatching along the twiglets. I picked them up, took care not to smudge them, set them to the side. I sat on the desk. I faced him. I searched his face. He was trying to fig-ure this out. He lifted and lowered his eyebrows like they were the pump on the engine of his brains. He made no move to fight me but he strangled that pen like he could. He was delicate, I guessed. His snappable wrists made him precious. He was not coarse. He was not reactive. He was ready for political martyrdom and had a steady hand, though I failed to see their particular beauty. They were un-calloused. Bitten nails and of course, all that acrid green. I tried, for the first and only time of my life, to feel something below my navel for a man. I imagined him on his back. I imagined his skinny thighs against his chest. I imagined his eyes from above.

"If I scream, my comrades will come." He tilted his head back. "There are enough of us to overpower you."

I lifted my shirt and showed him my gun. He made the right face. I dropped the fabric and flexed my hand. Pawed at the bag beside me, heaved it onto his lap. I picked up one of his pamphlets while he collected himself. He looked inside the bag, mouth dangling, and I blew on the ink to dry it faster.

"This is—"

"If you do wrong by Teriasa zel Cerca, I'll kill you. I will carry you to the train tracks and bind you to the rails, and I will stand beside you and wait with you until the freight train comes. I will watch you get ripped asunder." I sniffed. "Be good to her."

He stirred my spoils with his hands. I heard the rivery sound of coins sliding over each other, cold and bright. He just sat there, churning gold. He seemed unsure how to turn the feeling into thought. He pulled up his hands, watched the coins roll between his fingers. "I would never let harm come to Sunny," he managed at last. "She is the love of my life."

Sunny panged. My tongue hurt again. I left the bigger half with her. She'd see it when she woke up. It was my portion of our gains, I could give it how I'd like. My tithe to my home had been made. I gathered myself and I said to this man, "Thrive and be happy. If things fall apart, come to the Choir. We'll take care of you so long as you've taken care of her. You can make a press at home and us bandits will go around and tack your pamphlets to every post in the world."

"I won't feed my bride and children with stolen money," he started, but we both knew he was lying, and he dropped whatever clause he'd meant to append to his point. His brows were going up and down again. Thoughts flickering. He'd get eaten alive at a gambling table. He'd get eaten alive by woodpeckers if he didn't watch himself. He touched the gold again. He studied its intaglio texture against his palm. So many little ridges.

"Remember," I said, and got up. I imagined myself putting a hand on his thin shoulder, the lightest touch through his shirt bruising his unbroken skin. My breath could dissolve him like foam. Eyes down, hands to myself. I took one of his pamphlets, I wasn't sure if he noticed, I tucked it into my breast pocket. It moved in the night breeze as I climbed out of his window. I never saw the man again. This was the day before we got word that the Hereafterist revolution in Delphinia was over. The royalist insurgents had crushed the partisans and installed a brand-new King. Glory to the day after tomorrow, prophesied by our brief yesterday. Glory, glory. We stagger under the hilarity of grief.

Seven

I STOOD ON THE BRIDGE. DAWN, MIDSUMMER.
It was early. I pulled the lace mask down, it fully hooded
my head, and turned my collar against the thick breeze. It'd
be too hot in an hour. The mosquitoes were out. Frogs and
katydids still hollered unseen but larks joined them, and
birds that sounded mythic and bizarre, too much like little
kids. Something burbled. Something panted. We were in
the wetlands down near Tasmudan, and even this early the
heat seeped upwards through the soil, warmed the bridge
from below, teased the torture that'd be the air once the
sun came overhead. The lace didn't obscure my vision
much. Through the swirling dotwork flowers, I saw the
trees wigged with gauzy moss, their gnarly naked roots,
the standing water blackness on either side of the railroad tracks, matte and dull as tar. Lumps of animal swam
through it without ripples.

The rails were pure ichorite. The faintly rainbow luster glinted in two slim slashes through the muck. Ichorite rails are lighter than steel, and aren't so easily swallowed into the gluttonous swamp mud. The logic doesn't hold when cargo trains, profoundly heavy, roll over those pretty ichorite rails, but tracks weren't submerged too regularly, and from what I understood, the hold that Industry had over the papers was considerable, and safety concerns were kept mum.

Hereafterists around Loveday Manor lamented the lack of a free press all the time. They measured each other's scars and talked about Delphinia. Then they'd hate each other and hate the sky and talk domestically, bicker about how the free press would outline the standstill between the force of Chaunceyco, Yann's enormously powerful and constantly expanding business empire, against the ancient wall of the surrounding aristocratic class, the only legal landowners in all of Ignavia. The Hereafterists talked about how their free press would decry the hunting of Hereafterists globally, and the aggressions of Royston against Drustlandish disputed territories, which perhaps weren't disputed at all, rather were properly Drustish. They'd heard about Laith Hall, it was one of six comparable Halls. A free press might even discuss the plight of the lustertouched. More of us had been born to all those scabs after my community was slaughtered on Burn Street. How old would the new lustertouched babies be? Seven, now? Nine?

The actual press mostly discussed Gossamer Dignity Chauncey, young heir and political maverick. She wanted the Senate opened up, wanted citizens without a lick of

baron blood to be electable as mouthpiece of a barony's populace. She wanted a cap of six hours per working day to
be the new labor norm. She wanted to build housing for
Delphinian refugees and offer them factory jobs. I thought
about paper pulp and the waterwheel on that mill where
Teriasa zel Cerca's man used to languish for his daily bread.
I thought about Teriasa brushing her long black hair to
satin.

Here comes the train.

I stood alone. I had ropes hanging from my belt and my
rifle on my back and carefully, already anguished, I peeled
off my gloves.

The air stung against my nail beds. I flexed my fingers.
Stiff, tingling.

The train screamed under the bridge. No stops around
here, but it moved slowly, some theory about weight distribution and the hungry sucking swamp. The wind sucked
at my lace mask. The mask was deep red, the likeness of a
whip spider painted across it in bird's-egg blue. It tinged the
light. I breathed hard, I forced air down into my belly, and
I stepped off the bridge.

The roof slammed against my boots. Vibrations shocked
up my shins and I spat and made myself small, flattened my
weight down against the curved shell of ichorite alloy. Ugly
evil slope. Nearness brought the suffering on before the fit
even started. I ground my teeth, slapped my palms down,
and jerked my hands backwards. The roof of the train clung
to my palms. It peeled back like a blanket. Colors clapped,
the world undulated and jellied around me, my tongue

swelled, my gums went soft, my guts rigid, the sky was a whirl of orange and magenta molten poisonous candy pressing hard against my face. The world seethed around my body. A horrible delusion took me, and I imagined for a moment, imagined so concretely that my body responded with jitters and gooseflesh and appropriate recoil, that the ichorite roof had squeezed my hands, touched me like hands would touch me, or like how a sea anemone might wriggle around its little prey. Fucking ridiculous.

Mechanically, I got the ropes into my hands, felt along the iron weights woven through the fibers until I got the ends, which I plunged into the slurry wet ichorite train top. Active ripples, not passive. Something pulling, sucking, swallowing. My burning head. I threw the length down over the sides of the train. I could not see or hear but trusted that Candor and Harlow were close by in hot pursuit. I sensed their spectral lurcher below and beside me. It was not intuition, it was insanity and faith. I had done my big part. I breach. I breach, Harlow intimidates, Candor gets us out, and Sisphe, well.

I slumped through the hole I wrought. There was already screaming. Hurt my head. I slung the rifle off my back and fit my hands around it, I filed my action to match my grip exactly, and I brandished as I looked around. My vision sloshed. Passenger carriage. That was the style now, a few passenger carriages before the big cargo stripe, then more passenger carriages behind, so as to maximally segregate the shiny patrons from the dingy ones. Handy organization. Meant we seldom scared the dingy ones. The carpet

squelched. It licked at my boots. I rolled my shoulders and
tried to focus. My coat fabric bubbled against my skin.
Light pulsed. Lots of motion but no running, more like
people flattening sideways against the windows. Their edges
blurred and mixed. Someone cried out, *WHIP SPIDER!*

Once there's one *WHIP SPIDER* everybody went
WHIP SPIDER or *DEVILCHILD* or *MURDERER
MURDERER GIRL SNATCHER KILLER
THIEFTHIEFTHIEF!* Then the whole train fell in sham-
bles. Everyone got loud at once. Their limbs kaleidoscoped
in pastel wool and linen. Pleats whirled like notches on a
circle saw. I said, I slurred, "Pardon, please," but I was too
quiet, and that's for the best, I shouldn't be the one to intro-
duce us.

Then, my guiding star, the perfect scream. It's clear and
high, tremulous, sparkling. I went to the scream and with
magnetic compulsion, I thrusted a hand into the fray and I
seized the glossy braid of one stunning hysterical Sisphe thu
Ecapa, our own Tricksy, whom I dragged from her booth
with my off hand and displayed in the center aisle. I looped
her braid around the back of my hand. I pulled her taut.
Her hair was my rope, none could look upon her and imagine she'd ever escape.

Everyone imagined what might happen to her. Some
imagined with lurid detail. I've heard there were books
about us. Unbound books sold in cartons by the docks.
Schlock smut filth deliciousness with chains and hooks and
paddles stuck with nails. I hauled her shaking body against
my body, lifted her just slightly off the floor, and with great

flourish she kicked her little feet. Her satin slippers glittered ecstatically in the haze of my fit. She panted, her ribs fought against her bodice, chest heaving, top curves of her breasts glinting with sweat below her collarbone, and uselessly she writhed against my hands, pink tongue showing, cat teeth flashing behind her wonderful sob-swollen lips. Her year-old lip ring sparkled. It bruised the backs of my eyelids like it was a little band of sun. I walked her forward, to the center of the carriage, and presented her to the passengers. What a lovely girl. She put on such a show.

Sisphe tossed a wrist across her brow and cried out, "Ah! The Whip Spider's Gang!"

I hoisted her up a little higher, shook her to prove my cruelty. Sisphe yelped. She swooned against my shoulder, huffing, fluttering her eyelashes against the exposed skin strip of my throat below the lace mask. She tickled. I pushed down the impulses we'd trained so hard against—I didn't console her, didn't laugh, didn't break my immovable posture. Hard not to be a gentleman. Hard not to be kind. I pinned Sisphe against a booth's edge and tried to keep my balance. They kept putting more ichorite in these fucking trains. Making my job easier made it so much harder.

A clatter up the wall, a thud on the ceiling, then a figure dropped through the hole I'd torn to a fresh round of screams from the increasingly frantic passengers. They looked like a school of fish in colored water. I couldn't make out distinguishing details of their bodies. The figure, Harlow, my newest dear friend, our Delphinian Hereafterist boxing champion jackass nightmare, proud crawly, prouder than me, with a lace hood obscuring the shit-eating grin she always wore on her stupid handsome dimpled face. The centipede on her mask looked like a snake. I needed to sit down. I needed to get my head back. I bit down on my tongue hard, pain jolted, clean sharp pain and its companion copper taste.

Harlow swept out a hand and barked, "G'morning! Picked the wrong train! Backs to the windows, hands on your faces, yield and everybody gets to go home!"

For how recently I'd met her, I trusted Harlow fast. She'd been a revolutionary in Delphinia whom pirates had smuggled across the Amandine Sea. Here she was, my friend, my rival. I'd know her voice in a cacophony of thousands.

My body moved for me. A bad illusion, me being separate from my body. Spiritual separation of mind from corporeal apparatus had no place in my faith, it was stupid and Stellarine, but notions like these are clingy. I pushed Sisphe to her knees. I walked her along, braid leash pleasantly smooth in my hand, and offered her to Harlow. Sisphe wept at Harlow's feet. Harlow nudged her toe against Sisphe's belly, and Sisphe flew back, sputtered as though she'd been winded, like the nudge had been a sternum-snapping kick. Sisphe rocked back on her knees, looked up at me under her long lashes, lashes like a baby deer's, and she gasped, "Please don't hurt me with your magic, please don't hurt me, please don't hurt these people!"

The ripples went around again. Whip Spider, the devilchild bandit who pillaged banks and trains and riverboats and fine establishments that I didn't properly know the name for but sold armaments and aged brandy, was magic. Pulling the roof off this train was a feat of magic. Plainly so. It was devilry, atavistic and potent, and its function was another mystery of nature's tantrums. Whip Spider was very famous. She ripped through vaults like candy floss and tied enforcers to the train tracks with the tracks themselves. She melted armored cars into ooze pits with a touch. She summoned fallen bullet shells through the smoke and hurled them through the lawmen who shot them with a flick of her wrist, lightning fast and lethal. She and her crawlies, all of them crawlies, filthy rotten repulsive vile violent wicked depraved little crawlies, menaced upright women and harrowed polite society. Whip Spider's credited for destroying the nascent Ignavian commercial lurcher and motor carriage market, given that she'd so publicly melted tires into the pavement, vaulting the enforcers who rode them over the horns at great skull-destroying speeds, liquifying engines, sealing armored doors shut and trapping their riders irretrievably inside before shoving the whole machines off cliffs. The Whip Spider was a blight. A parasitic stain on society's moral fabric, sucking the pigment of good conduct and leaving fray and disillusion in her wake. She was a nightmare drawn from the breath of the new rich and condensed into a dew that became a flesh that became a woman, if such a creature can be called a woman, if any crawly can be considered more than a maimed in-between. Dread sight, the Whip Spider's lace! Terror! Terror!

"So long as all these people comply in a timely fashion," Harlow the Centipede sweetly said with a boot stomped on Sisphe's thigh, "we'll let you live, my dove."

Somehow, Sisphe managed to flinch in such a way that she yanked one sleeve over her shoulder. Exposed the precious little freckles there. Valor never had so much fun when she played victim-orchestrator. Sisphe batted her lashes up at Harlow, tears heavy at the tips, and exclaimed, "What will you do to me, Centipede?"

Harlow pulled her gun from her belt and pressed it against Sisphe's bottom lip.

Sisphe trembled, panted. She gave the dull metal a lick.

Harlow laughed. She made a show of swinging her head around. "Who's the jeweler? We've seen your ticket, best to let us know who you are."

Sisphe moved against my hand, bumped the gun against her chin. She angled her panting toward a thin man hyperventilating against the back of his seat. Harlow withdrew from her, approached the man, and took his bag from him. She opened it, grunted, shut it. She took it back a few paces and tossed it up through the hole I'd made in the roof. Beautiful morning blueness rushed above. I thought, *hold hold hold hold hold*, felt a gruesome flush of furnace heat and a squeal of steam through a notched valve, the valve spat white hot between my ears, and I was sure the bag had stuck. The ichorite flecks that'd glued themselves to my palms fizzled and stung. Such a dirty feeling. I widened my stance. I forced my knees not to buckle. Sisphe leaned against my shin and impossibly bore my weight. I'd be so dead without her.

Harlow leaned over the man, purred something harshly in his ear, and he stammered what I assumed was a storage number. This particular train hauled this jeweler's stock, see. Not so much stock as to warrant an armored car, but armored cars were hardly worth the investment, given that I could pull them in half like taffy if I was willing to spasm for hours afterwards.

Harlow put a hand on the man's head, a friendly pat, then strode past me, whistled as she unlatched the far door and vanished into a cargo carriage. This was a smallish raid, modest haul, but we'd had a good season in the redwoods and the moors. I shifted through our spoils in my head. Sorted out which share went to the Fingerbluffs' common wealth, a hearty half, and which would adorn Loveday Mansion. We gave more than was required and boasted about it. What good fathers to our people were we! Took deliberation, distributing riches appropriately. Everybody in the Fingerbluffs should want for nothing. Everybody in the Fingerbluffs should be prosperous and lush, well spoiled. Took deliberation to move all those goods, too, as much as recovering goods demanded, securely moving those goods across all of Ignavia was no small feat. Take what you can carry, they say.

I looked down at Sisphe. Darling Sisphe. Her posture had changed. Under her dress, I saw the ready shape of her stance. Sisphe was crouched, not kneeling. Primed to spring.

Harlow whistled as she came back. *Unalone toward dawn we go!* She had a lacquered box on her shoulder, cumbersome and double-locked, and she heaved it up through the hole with a groan. I heard it hit the top, I chanted in my head, it didn't clatter and slide away. I imagined vaguely what'd happen if we passed under a low stone bridge. Our spoils smashed and crumpled like confetti. Funny.

With that, I relinquished Sisphe, and she flung herself through the air. Apples bouncing. My skull ached. Harlow caught her, boosted her up through the hole, her skirts snapped around her like a banner and I watched her boots vanish into the sky. Numbly, I snatched a few satchels, a coat I liked, and a parcel, fit them all under my arm, and went to sweet Harlow, who knelt and put her hands under my heel. She sprung me up, I twisted my body, hooked my free elbow on the edge of the hole. Wind screamed over my hair and pulled the air from my mouth. The twisted ichorite alloy burned. I slammed the goods up and they obediently stuck, and hauled myself up the rest of the way, reached down to assist Harlow up. Her hand pressed the metal flecks against my skin. Felt electric up to my arm sockets.

On the roof I cabled the parcels together. Little rainbow scrap metal mesh. It broke the light into crazy iridescent ripples, made the spoils an enormous freshwater pearl. I worked my hands over the metal so mechanically and only cried a little. My ears dripped, my nose, but it was a thin stream. That ichorite taste was slippery on my bottom lip. I was drooling the stuff. I didn't know what it was. Serum, Amon called it. It looked like oil on water. It was wet under my ears. I wanted to scrub myself. I wanted to pull off my skin.

Sisphe called down to Candor.

Candor flew beside us on a tandem lurcher. Huge, gloating, sexed-up freak of a ride, with back wheels as tall as my hip, and an exposed engine that coiled around like guts. It was meant to sit three, a driver and two shooters, and carry a thick cache. Sisphe and Harlow took the pearly bundle from me and attached it to the weighted ropes I'd hooked earlier, I chanted *slow slow slow slow slow slow* at the backs of my front teeth, it glided down the cables, it was caught by handsome Candor, who had pulled her lace mask over her nose and mouth and gnawed a long slim cigarette. She put one boot on the gas, the other on the handle's central crux to keep it steady, had both hands on the enormous parcel which she lovingly detached and slipped into the back seat before twisting around, easing her hips back down in the seat, sliding her palms over the lurcher's horns and guiding it closer to the train.

Sisphe slung her body down the ropes. Her skirt rode up, the bullets belted around her garter reflected the sun. Brassy, pretty. Could hardly see the evil iridescence underneath. Harlow put a hand on my shoulder, said something I didn't hear over the howling wind, and gathered me up, swung me onto her back. I clung to her. She smelled like salt and suede and cedar. I pressed my face into the darkness between her shoulders, and she shimmied down after Sisphe, pulled us both onto the lurcher. I chanted in my head, I yanked the ropes, they oozed off the ichorite roof and flew into my hands in a heavy, stingy knot. I shoved them off my lap. I was sitting now.

Harlow had arranged me in the seat where the parcel had been, the parcel Sisphe now safely secured in the back of the humming lurcher. I scrubbed my hands on my trousers, tried to get the ichorite off. The knife, my special knife, sheathed and not touching me, pulsed through the leather, through the fabric, into the meat of my pelvis. I felt it in my tailbone. My mask itched. I pulled it off, smoothed it over one of my knees. Touched the baby blue whip spider with its careful, nervous fingers.

Sisphe clapped my back. "Drinks on me!"

"How was that for you?" Harlow eased into the seat beside me, pulled Sisphe onto her lap. She slung an arm around Sisphe's waist, pressed an open-mouthed kiss against her jugular. "Kick alright?"

"Easy crowd," Sisphe said with a shrug. She shimmed her shoulders once, then leaned forward so far she nearly fell off the lurcher, pawed around Candor's thighs for her cigarette tin. "No heroism. Pathetic, boring, yawn! That's that. Oh, you two were dreamy, that was fine. Marney's dripping everywhere."

I smudged my nose with the back of my wrist.

Years ago now, before she was Sisphe, we'd followed a widow downstairs. It was late and she'd swayed out of her bedroom like a revenant, the light shone through her flimsy nightgown, we saw the shadows of her shoulders and her thighs moving. She looked half-alive and loose with pain, like the muscles on her body were tense past tension.

Beads on a string. Her hair was unbound. I didn't know her. Her tattoos shifted under the dress like fish in murky water. Tricksy and I had been playing marbles in the hallway, Candor had had a fever that night, we were outside the sickroom listening to her cough, but she'd drifted off to sleep, and the woman had moved through perfect silence, she didn't even stir the air as she passed us. Underwater glossy movements. A red marble rolled, stopped.

We followed the widow downstairs. We hadn't discussed it, but we saw her in the dim light of the hallway, how she floated an inch above the carpet runner, and we looked at each other and something prickled between us. We felt a wind that wasn't there. We plucked up our marbles and tucked them in our pockets, it was such a fearsome secret suddenly that we were awake, I heard Tricksy's clothes whisper and heard the grandfather clock ticking and my blood fluttered under my skin. We tiptoed after her. We blew kisses at Candor's door, we'd never done that before and it made me twitchy, I was so vividly awake I could yelp, and we followed the woman down the stairs, hid behind Virtue statues and suits of fish-scale plate armor and hunks of still-gilded Bellonan column, we covered each other's mouths, Tricksy looked at me with insane rabbit eyes.

The woman drifted soundlessly into the ballroom. She swept across the floor, barely walking, and lifted her eyes. She came before the wall of cast hands, the Veltuni ancestral council, an endless sea of outstretched sculpted fingers reaching down. She untied the front of her dress. It slipped over her shoulders, was caught by her elbows. It draped at the small of her back. I looked at the dimples at either side of the base of her spine. I felt Tricksy looking at me. The widow woman reached for a hand on the wall. With a scrape of brass on marble, she pulled one hand off its stud. She held the hand against her cheek. She traced her jaw with it. She slipped its finger in her mouth, pushed it down to the knuckle. Tricksy looked at me. She reached for my wrist. I looked at my wrist in her hand and felt watery. I tucked myself closer to her in the shadow of our little nook. She lifted my hand up. She put my finger in her mouth.

"*I'm a special girl,*" Sisphe had told me. No husband of hers could die the way I planned to die. We weren't lovers anymore. We weren't getting married. It'd been discussed.

I accepted the bottle that Harlow passed to me. I pulled the cork with my teeth. I spat it to the side. I expected water, which was stupid of me. I swished the liquor around my mouth. It screamed against my raw tongue and swollen gums, but the sting was good. I swallowed, grimaced. Serum slipped down the back of my throat. It was thinner now, just a greasy trickle. I squeezed my eyes hard, then opened them wide. It was fucking hot out. My jacket was wet. I shrugged my shoulders, rid myself of it, shook out my sweat-soaked shirt. I traced the edge of a fish tattoo on my wrist with my eye. The fish was monstrous and toothed; there were myths about them that pirates had told me. Fish that hatched out of the far moon and crashed down like hail in hurricanes. I had an earring made of one's ivory. I took another sip.

We roared through denser swamp. Moss gauze teeming with humming bugs swept over our heads. Reptiles slithered through brackish sludge. The mud squelched and rippled under the lurcher. If we got stuck, it'd be me and Candor and Harlow up to our knees in muck, shoving, cursing every god in every faith, and Sisphe intently filing her nails until she was sick of waiting, then she'd strip herself naked to spare her dress and plunge into the mud and with impossible and infuriating ease would haul the lurcher into the air one-handed, leave us all to the adders as she swan dove a triple aerial over the tall back tires, landing standing on the horns, laughing and stretching and steering without movement through pure force of will.

We didn't get stuck.

"We had big lizards like these in the Bitters, that's south Delphinia, deep south, blue and fat and lazy, we'd tame 'em to lie around in the boxing rings, but of course they weren't ever tame, just too tired to get you. Beasts are good luck. They're a thousand years old," Harlow said. She combed her hair, mussed from the mask, and re-sculpted her pompadour in the mirror adjoined to Sisphe's clamshell powder puff. Her hair was jet black, stiff with pomade. She swept it back from her temple and pressed the little hairs in a curve beside her ear. "There was a Hereafterist guerilla band a bit before my time who called themselves after the lizards, they hunted them for cash beforehand see, and wore their skin on their hands. They were so smart, real sharp girls the lot of them, and brazen too. They'd sabotage supply lines by blowing up bridges, made a big show of their work. They slowed occupation a full few months just the five of them. Shame about the drowning. Bring your little ass back here, where are you going?"

"Candor," Sisphe sang, halfway off Harlow's lap again. "You're pouting. How come you're pouting?"

"They drowned?" Candor worried her lip with her teeth. She still wore her mask half-on. Her cigarette was all ash and filter. She wasn't supposed to do stunts with us. Being baby Loveday was too important. Not so important that the Choir would forbid a bandit their work, but enough that everyone would be mad at her if she put herself in the line of fire. Being driver was all she did. If it was me, I would've hated it. She didn't. Not a shred of resentment in her golden boozy heart.

"They did," said Harlow, a little quieter. "I was young then. Tough when it's an accident. Martyrdom's an honor. It was just a mistake. They mistimed an explosion and two of them were gone in an instant, two more got caught under debris, sank to the bottom of the river, got caught up in rebar and concrete. Bobbed just under the surface. Last one just swept away. Swept far, down into town, that's where I saw her. Didn't get to see the brief Hereafter. Bad luck, huh?"

Candor prayed. Not a Stellarine prayer, not even a prayer to the Oneness, the faith that held all of Tasmudan, the Crimson Archipelago (which was and wasn't Tasmudan) and the far continent (which also was and wasn't Tasmudan). She added the Hereafterist flip of that prayer, which made Oneness not an authority innately alive in and in command of all things, but a liveliness that came from togetherness that was immortal and unconquerable. Solidarity as god. Candor's accent was a little funny, but it made Harlow smile.

Sisphe shook a hand through her hair. It held so much sunlight. If she wrung it out, it'd drench the seats with gold. She leaned close to me now, put her chin on my shoulder, pressed her nose against my cheek. Held my arm above my elbow, fit her thumb in the ditch. "Marney."

"Yes'm?"

She fluttered her eyelashes against my cheek. "Speak. You look dead. Prove me wrong."

"I'm not dead."

"You could be rotting over here and we wouldn't know." She kissed my cheekbone. "Blooming mushrooms under your shirt."

"You can check if you'd like," I said.

"When they dangle the four of us, Marney won't rot. They'll put her bloodless body in the ground and she'll burrow out like a worm and walk barefoot to Ignavia City to put Industry's throat in her teeth." Harlow beamed.

"Not good luck to talk about us dead," said Candor softly. She held her palm under her lip and snuffed her cigarette against the base of her thumb, then pulled the filter from her lips, slipped it in her breast pocket. She was soft about throwing down smoke trash. Said she'd seen a bird eat a butt once and had nightmares about it choking for weeks.

I took another swig and shut my eyes.

I OPENED THEM on a porch of some gambling house in a town too small to call a town. Fishing shanties and grayish slats of wood over still water, lurching music, Harlow and

Candor boozing and boxing to great applause on the roof, other bandits whose names I halfway knew playing cards, I dealt for them earlier, but not now. Now I watched the dirty mirror water. Shapes moved underneath it. I watched one that watched me back. Through the propped-wide door, out of the corner of my eye, I watched the scene with Sisphe, who was hunting people alive. Strictly speaking Sisphe sat on the bar with a bar worker's hands in her hair, chatting idly, paying for nothing, and the bar worker was just enthralled with her, worshipped her breath in the air, had an expression I recognized because I'd worn it. Jaw slack, eyes on fire, tongue pressed between the teeth. Tight little nods, *mhm*s. The politeness behind which one dulls a desire to rip her in half. Sisphe swayed as she spoke, pretending drunkenness. She looked at the worker with her eyes half-shut. Cooed something that looked like, *you'd love that, wouldn't you?*

A big ugly fish breached the water. It was all mouth.

I tossed a knob of bread at it. There was bread beside me. I'd eaten. Had I eaten?

It swallowed with a flop and was gone. I watched the fish turn into nothing in the algae.

"Are you the Whip Spider?" A woman leaned on the wall behind where I sat. She had a thin face and bobbed hair, the long feathery eyelashes of a working girl. She smiled at me. "When I asked upstairs, they said it was you."

"Yes ma'am." My gut felt watery.

She came and sat on the arm of my chair. Wrapped an arm around the back, touched my shoulder, then my hair.

145

Her perfume rolled over me. "Could you show me the magic?"

My belly said no. I leaned my cheek against her hip, took another glance over the marbled black-green murk, then looked up at her. I looked at her looking at me. She wasn't wearing any ichorite. It was fashionable now, from what I understand. They make fabric out of it. Hands numb, I reached around to my waistband, felt around to the small of my back, where the knife lived. I winced when I touched it. The bones in my hand hurt. I fought down the nausea and laid the knife on my lap, blade away from her. Its shape was getting long. I added the bullets from all the enforcers we felled. Not so many, but more than most bandits. I saw that man who killed Edna in all of them. I snuffed down all the echoed thoughts inside the metal. I tried to swallow. Took my thumb along the edge and minutely, enough to show her, pulled the tip a little longer, a little thinner. It shimmered in the evening air.

"Oh, it's lovely," she said. She reached down, traipsed her fingers up the knife's edge. Her nails were bitten down. She tested the new tip I'd pulled, gasped when it pricked her finger. Blood welled up there, a little bead.

I took her hand and brought it to my lips. Put the finger between my lips, kissed her first knuckle.

She dragged her skirts over her knees. The underlayers were the same lace as my mask. Frothy burgundy, blood on milk. She pulled my mouth closer, her finger hooked behind my teeth, beneath my tongue, then slipped the finger out, reached for my hair. She closed her fist against my scalp. The pain was good. It brought me back to myself. She brought me close to her body, under her skirts, and I leaned my cheek against her thigh, let myself relax in the darkness inside her dress. I loved the smell of her. I pressed a kiss against her curls, then her clit. She sighed above me. Rocked against my mouth. I lapped at her wetness, soft and lazy, reached a hand around her hips, held the small of her back, pulled her against my mouth. I don't know how much time passed. She was soft and slick and dripped down my chin and when she came she vised her thighs around my neck. I did my best to hold her upright, I kept going past the point where she couldn't stand it, just a second, just three, then eased off her. I kissed her thigh, then her knee. I swayed out from under her skirts. It was darker now, the sky was dusty. I smoothed the lace. I put away the knife. It hadn't fallen, somehow. Touching it hurt.

She slipped off the chair and stood, ruffled my hair. She wandered inside.

I rubbed the edge of my mouth.

I wanted her to come back.

I stood up. I walked to the edge of the porch, leaned my hip bones against the rickety railing. It buckled but bore my weight. I sniffed. My rib hurt, I noticed now. I lifted my shirt and looked down at my chest, past MARNEY HONEYCUTT and the sea serpent and the azurine sprigs and the railroad spikes, above my navel to the left, where a welt bloomed so dark that it showed through the evening gloom. Pine green and furious. I watched my ribs press against the bruise when I sucked in. Wasn't sure how I got it. Climbing through the hole in the roof maybe. It looked like it was moving. I put my shirt down and went inside.

Tension by the bar. Taut and itchy, nobody killing each other, everybody yearning. The flavor made me think everyone was going on about global Hereafterist revolution and our chances after Delphinia had been lost. Hope and futility and bloodshed talk. Child soldier talk. Good way to split a room of even the proudest in the Choir. Me, I believed the Hereafter would dawn, beyond which tyranny would be over and humans would stand shoulder to shoulder, in steadfast togetherness, ungoverned, beyond domination, in the age of play and trust. Not in my lifetime, but eventually. It was either that or the same and the same was unbearable. But, cried the nervous and desolate, Delphinia was the most successful Hereafterist revolution there'd ever been. Similar actions had failed five times in Cisra and twice in Royston. The martyrs were endless. How young had Harlow been when she took up her gun? Younger than I'd been when you were shot. Or they were talking about the coming war against the Drustish, who had committed the crime of having land that Royston wanted as a remedy to its national identity's autocannibalism, or they were talking about baby Chauncey the reformist, who made the factories safer, who made the work days shorter, who made the process seem salvageable, who couldn't be trusted because she was young, because she was a slut, because she was a crawly who besmirched the reputation of good aristocratic girls, because the rich could not be trusted, but she was a woman, but she was an advocate for the workers in her employ, but she was a trailblazer, we need freaks like her. But compromise, but progress! But tomorrow by any means possible!

It wasn't work talk.

When I crossed the threshold, I saw Candor. Candor saw me, that is. She saw me and touched Sisphe's arm, and Sisphe, speaking animatedly without blinking, a horrible smile on her face, stopped smiling. Harlow threw a dart at the wall. It sprung there, little feathers twitching. She threw another. They thunked in a canary yellow line. A woman across the bar, facing Sisphe, drummed her nails on the side of her glass. Her jacket was buttoned to her jaw, her hair pulled tightly back, and each tap displaced the condensation. Drops fell and pooled like quicksilver on the bar.

I stood beside Candor. Put my hands on the back of a scuzzy blond chair. To the woman I said, "You alright, ma'am?"

"Just fine," the stranger said. She shook off her hand. "Seem to have ruffled some feathers is all. You've got sensitive friends."

It just wasn't so.

"Perhaps I could be helpful," I said.

"I want her to roll up her sleeve," Sisphe said brightly. "Easy as that!"

"I'm not showing my skin to nobody," the woman said. She had a peculiar diction. Precise, all upright. Like she'd wanted to say *anybody* instead. "I'm just trying to be friendly. Haven't been around these parts much."

I rubbed my thumb around a swirl in the woodwork. Fit my nail in a groove. "What's your name?"

"Casey Courtesy Miller."

"Courtesy," Candor repeated. "Where are you from, Courtesy?"

"Montrose," she said.

"Here I thought Montrose houses the Virtue Lady Righteousness. Heard plenty of the names Honor and Integrity and Steadfast and Probity out of Montrose, even a Solidarity out of Montrose, never a Courtesy." Candor carefully buttoned and unbuttoned Sisphe's sleeve, kept her eyes down, her voice soft. I was enormously proud of her. Boldness didn't come easy. "Lord Propriety's housed out in Glitslough and Geistmouth. Did your parents carry you all those miles coastward? Long trip for a baby."

"Aren't we clever. I was born in Geistmouth. Moved to Montrose with my folks for work. What's it to you? Where are you from?" She took a small sip of her full stein. Mouthed the foam. "Around here?" To me, "Where's the Whip Spider sleep?"

"We're from home," Candor said.

"That's quaint. Where's that?"

Sisphe reached for her gun.

She drew and Candor drew and Harlow spun, hurled a yellow dart into the back of Casey's hand just as Casey shoved the table hard, rammed the corner into Sisphe's solar plexus. Sisphe gasped. Her gun went off, smashed a hole through the ceiling with a rain of splinters and dust. The sound clapped. Casey Courtesy drew her gun. I knew the make. Only issued to enforcers. The yellow dart in her hand bobbed with gravity. Red flecked the feather fluff. I didn't have my gun on me. I dove across the table, and the yellow dart bounced, and in the emerging allergic haze I saw the enforcer turn her gaze on me. Move her gun toward me. My lips mashed, I mouthed *jam jam jam jam jam* as one smeared sound, I slammed my boot on her sternum and shoved her chest backwards hard and she tumbled as the gun went off, a pop of nothing, the oozy ichorite insides blobbed out from what was once buckshot and had not been expelled, then she fired again, and the gun tore. It was a pop of sound and sulfur. A long twist of metal jutted from a nearby stool. Through the smoke I saw bandits ebb and flow, rise up on counters and dive for cover, because it was enforcers, not just Casey, a third of the room stood and brandished, and I dropped under the table, scrambled for my knife, cringed as I found the throbbing handle.

Around me got loud.

Someone fell. An enforcer or a stranger, I wasn't sure, but they crashed to the floor and spilled blood from a hole in their shoulder, and I dragged them under the table, clapped my hands around them, hunted for a gun. The bloody mucky denim bore nothing. Nothing down their thighs or under their armpits, nothing at the small of their back. I saw the edge of a tattoo on their chest but it wasn't a name. With mechanical numbness I squinted through the horrible pink whirring that wasn't real at the blood that was, and I touched it, I balked at its texture, I swiped my thumbs over my eyelids, prayed wordlessly, and darted out from under the table. Someone else had fallen there, I took a gun from their hand, I loaded it. My pulse in my tongue, in my scalp, was sludgy and loud. The air cloyed. A floorboard beside me exploded into powder like a kiss from a cosmetic puff and got on my trousers, got in between my teeth. Someone came over me, a stranger, I saw the swish of their coat and a long yellow baton at their belt and their advancing light brown boots and I shot them. They didn't make a sound. They spun and fell. I scrambled back, got my legs under me, hopped a counter, into another room. It was identical, different reddish curtains. A long billiards table and fewer people. It was so loud but it wasn't as hot. The bodies in the other room had been sweltering. A fucking sting. Where was my band?

I thought of Burn Street and the thought engulfed me. I saw the pattern seething in the air.

I was behind a bar somehow, there were bottles behind me in rainbow-colored glass, infinite bottles stacked past the far moon on a shelf that accordioned upwards forever, and my knees were underneath my chin. I crouched with my hands inside of Candor's jacket. I was holding Candor's belly in my hands. Sweet Candor. *Don't you soften her now.* Ah, but she was *soft*, she was a perpetual drunk and self-pitying and forever tense and loved us, she was kind, she was such a kind girl. Quiet and thoughtful girl. I touched her harshly. I was holding her belly together, the skin was open underneath. We were sopping wet with sweat and the red of her body. I pressed down hard but I didn't weigh anything at all. I was hollow and made out of air. With such devotion I pushed down on Candor, pushed

harder, so hard I was afraid I'd hurt her, but I couldn't hurt
her. I brought my body low over her body. She looked at the
ceiling. Her eyes were a clear cold blue. She had all these
spots on her face that she picked at, right now they looked
like embroidery stitches. Little red dashes where her fingernails had been.

"Whip Spider," someone said.

I whirled around and fired a shot at whoever had spoken
because anyone who loved me would've called me Marney,
then had a glacial terror that I'd killed the working girl
who'd sat on the arm of my chair earlier, which became
nothing, because it was Casey Courtesy the enforcer standing above me, and my gun had not fired. There was nothing
inside it. I threw it at her, she grunted and batted it aside.
I pawed behind me for my knife. My hand was slippery
with Candor's blood. Candor was bleeding. What the fuck
could she possibly want? My fit swirled, electricity pulsed
through the inside seams of my skin, and Courtesy kicked
me in the jaw.

Pain clapped up the side of my head. Drool spilled, I
raised my hands without my knife somehow, I threw my
hands over my face. I was on my back. She'd kicked me onto
my back. She took my ankles and dragged me away from
Candor, pulled me around a corner into a stock closet, there
were infinite bottles in deep blue and pine green and bluish misty white on shelves. The elixirs inside them swished
when she kicked me again, this time in my ribs. The glasses
clinked. She held my chest down, stomped on my free wrist,
and I kicked my feet and tried to twist but she strained

and something in my wrist popped. I screamed. It rattled through my jaw.

"Your band," Courtesy sneered, "will *never* kill another enforcer again. You will never disrespect us again. Your stain on the force and the industry is over." She shifted her weight, I felt like my fingers might burst. "I'm scraping you off this floor and dragging you behind my lurcher to IC, and you'll be strung by the ankles, and everyone will look upon your little girl corpse and rejoice the end of superstition. Whatever is wrong with you won't be wrong with you anymore. I'll fix it. You killed my partner, you bitch."

Could've been any of a good few. A glimpse of the uniform stripped me of my mercy. I didn't think about it much. A spasmic laugh fluttered in my gut but couldn't come out. I turned my cheek and spat blood. "Good riddance."

"You're a blight," she said. "You're a smear." She unbuttoned her long coat with her dart-stabbed hand, showed her untattooed throat to me, her clean tailored shirt, the baton at her hip. She took it. She cranked it back, and slammed down on my chest. I heard the rib break. It was a funny sound. I thrashed again and a screaming, hysterical pain overtook me, a roiling pain in the back of my throat, in my palms, in the arches of my feet.

I opened my mouth to say something. To curse her. To scream so that someone might hear me.

She pressed the baton against my mouth. Into my mouth. Nudged it against my bottom teeth. My jaw pulsed, something was wrong with it. She pushed the baton deeper, over my tongue, jammed it against my hard palate. It had a greasy, laminated taste. My gut turned to jelly. She forced it deeper, skimmed my gag reflex, I convulsed but she kept her hand steady. She pressed the back of my throat. I couldn't get in air. She twisted her wrist, something vile scraped off the baton and onto my teeth. I thought she'd break through the membrane of my throat to bludgeon my spine. There were tears in the twists of my ear. I looked up at her, I saw the expression on her face, the venomous gloat, and I tore my eyes away. Such a fuzzy ugly molded feeling. I wouldn't fucking look up at her. I knew how this worked.

She straightened up abruptly, yanked the baton and one of my teeth from my mouth, and about-faced. My stomach flipped but nothing came. She took a step away from me. Gunshot. I rolled, pressed myself into bottles and bottles and bottles, and she collapsed beside me, moaning, very much alive. I saw her face in ballooned distortion across a bottle's neck. Thousands of her warped face moaning.

I coughed, spat blood, there was so much blood in my mouth, and rolled on top of her. I didn't reach for my knife, it appeared in my hand. Off hand, my good one felt stiff and wrong. I cut her. One long sawing cut from her hip bone up toward her clavicle. Then I stood up, panting. The woman was alive. I turned my back on her and collapsed against Harlow, who half carried me away from the room. I didn't feel my feet move across the floor. I could see Sisphe over Candor in the stance that I'd taken and I looked at Harlow's earrings, she wore so many golden hoops, fourteen in this ear. They looked like beams of light through a cloud, immaterial somehow in their brightness. They swayed as she carried me. I tried to apologize for the drool on her shirt. No sound came out at all.

OPIUM'S A BAD habit. I mostly avoided it. The jaw healed fine but it took two months in which time I spoke little and ate scarcely anything at all. My body wasted and became nothing. I stretched and cringed at the hollows in my shirt where my strength should be. I cringed at my hands, at the way the lurcher's handles felt, then retreated into feeling little. I recoiled from my own lividity. I prayed more. I planned a route with Sisphe. Sisphe talked through stops and I worked out the general shape, what'd be safest, most efficient, least likely to get us followed. We needed to be clean and purposeful. No dalliance. No wandering. Lurchers were a liability because we clearly weren't their intended riders but they were expensive to replace, which is to say, a pain to steal, and we had our haul to bring back home. A haul. How wretched of me.

We hid the lurcher on a boxcar, and slept in that boxcar, and undisturbed except by rain we rode north, nearly toward Montrose beside the border to the Drustlands. While the pines spun by and the earth broke and rose in jagged snowcaps, I thought about war, and the smoldering ruins of Laith Hall, and I thought about Mors Brandegor the Rancid, and I thought about you. Remembered, or tried to remember, your face. The exact proportions of your face down to the pore and follicle. I remembered your hair, it was hard to forget your hair. I remembered your smile. You smiled like you knew something about me that I didn't. I remembered us making a game when we were very small where we fashioned marbles out of smelt scraps and dropped them down a slanting surface, it was the belly of some device whose exact function I never learned, and they'd clink between the bolts in the device and smash, or fail to smash, little piles of rubble we'd stacked diligently on the floor. I remembered your determination that if you got bored, you'd die. I always found it wrong to rib you about it. You were dying, at least that's what Poesy said.

You were, I heard in Brandegor's voice, *blodfagra*. It made you pale and bruise in mad blue splashes. Your legs were always a mess. Like peacock feathers, you bragged to anyone who'd listen. When had you ever seen a pea-cock feather? I'd kissed you. You were my best friend, it wasn't meant to mean nothing. I know now what I am. It's straightforwardly clear that I'd loved you in that warm and easy way kids love, but it'd been love for real. I adored you.

I remember us in one of our hiding spots, a sweltering damp dark monster mouth of a nook behind a machine that'd burn us if we touched it, and I'd take down my braids and let you play with my hair. You plaited differently than my mother did. She always noticed and the tongue lashings she could give! But you touched my hair with such atten-tion. It was wonderful to have your attention. I would've broken any rule you'd asked me to break. How long had it been since I thought of my mother?

Once we'd gone sufficiently north we went coastward, on lurchers, but without raiding. We moved light. We slept in Hereafterist safe houses, brothels and salons and the odd radical Shrine, and boardinghouses above crawly bars. Crawly bars were easy to spot for those who sought them. They put flowers in the signs. Odd flowers, not the sort that anyone might use to decorate a border. Big hollyhocks and foxgloves, blue chicory and fleabane, thorn apple, creeping thistles, dandelions.

I sat at the bar sipping brown liquor with great care while an older girlcrawly, of the generation who said girl-crawly and boycrawly, of which I'd be a boycrawly, cut my hair. Gorgeous woman with snow-white braids swept back, her makeup done like illustrations that we hung on the walls of our rooms in the Mansion now. Big sweeps of green or blue eyeshadow, thin brows and drawn-on bottom eyelashes, high blush, black or purple painted little lips. She razored the fluff at the nape of my neck. With a kindness I didn't deserve, she gently bent down the gauze looped around my head that held my jaw shut, so as to clip the sweaty curls there accordingly. She cut it shorter than I usually wore it. Each ringlet was only one twist around. She ruffled it and offered me snuff from a porcelain clutch.

Across from me in a curved leather booth, Sisphe and Harlow grieved in each other's arms. Harlow, righteous and braggadocious, the most religious of our band, told Sisphe about dying for Hereafter and what martyrdom can bring. When a body is destroyed something else replaces it, an afterimage of that vitality that becomes part of the total, absolute, essential and incalculable Oneness; the collective projected specter of a hundred thousand human beings crying up to the sky for more. *Unalone toward dawn we go*, etc. But of course, to be a martyr you needed a purpose. Why did Candor die?

Sisphe looked younger when she wept. She looked like Tricksy again. The girl who built a slingshot out of her stocking to wage war on a boy who'd taken the fruit she wanted at breakfast and in the barrage broke a trophy stag somehow, just smashed its taxidermized head and flattened its broad boneless nose. The girl who was uninvited from needlepoint circles as soon as she joined because she'd sew FUCK ME! FUCK ME MORE! FUCK ME MOST! in baby blue loops across the hems of her skirts. The girl I thought I'd marry for years. I thought about her head in my lap. Her mapping out the bank we were soon to rob with her nail across my kneecap. She sat on Harlow's lap at the bar, her hair unbound, a dark curtain over Harlow's white shirt, and Harlow rocked her, looped a lock of hair around her trigger finger, told her about the future that did not yet exist.

Candor being dead would be ruinous for our plans. We needed sweet Candor to be baby Loveday. We needed our heir to pretend like tyranny still existed in the Fingerbluffs. Need wouldn't make her come back.

I drank slowly. Itchy little twists of my hair floated around like feathers. I kept to myself and thought about Edna. What would Edna think of Harlow? I thought about what you'd look like now. You were slightly older than me, though it hadn't shown. I had been tall for my age, you were built like a baby bird. Splinters for bones. I wasn't tall anymore, my height was nondescript, and maybe you'd have grown tremendously once adolescence hit you. I smiled at a woman who approached me. I nodded at her and answered her questions with all due politeness. No ma'am, I wasn't here alone. Yes ma'am, I'd buy her a drink. Yes ma'am. I closed my eyes and counted backwards in my head.

We passed through Beauty's. Strange feeling. That treasure box still held all my hope and love. Its perfume and perpetual saltsour sweat smell came over me and my resolve was gone. I saw Beauty, I hadn't last time. She had silver in her hair. She embraced me and I felt small again, I collapsed against her and wept. She didn't call me little fawn. I wanted her to call me little fawn, but the thought of such a ridiculous kiddish vulnerability frightened me, it was a hot coal dropped in my stomach, it blistered and burned its way out through my pelvis. Where was Prumathe? Out. Pouring sugar in the wet concrete foundations of a prison being built in Geistmouth. Putting the word union in the mouths of rural mill workers, who had the will and the might, but not always the script, to bargain collectively toward their mutual betterment. She was gone. Where was Brandegor? Where were Valor and Uthste? Far off. I knew that. I wept until I was heaving.

I rented a room, I didn't share the one split by Sisphe and Harlow, I paid for the companionship of a worker called Sincerity. I didn't let her touch me and she didn't talk back about it. When she stopped shaking, I pulled my hand out of her, I cleaned her up, and I lay beside her, one arm loose around her, the two of us breathing and looking

at the mirrored ceiling. I licked my fingers, I looked at
Marney Honeycutt, my crop of curls, not funny with gauze
anymore, my hollow crooked babydoll face, bruisy eyelids
and upturned nose, my mouth ichorite fit forever swollen
red and beestung, jaw finally unfractured, gone tooth replaced with a hunk of silver, the pink indentations where
my harness had rubbed against my skin and the map of
tattoos from my jaw to my ankles, my needled-on tapestry,
and the places where the tattoos were broken by cuts that'd
healed wrong. I had stopped bothering to count the marks.
They didn't matter individually. They were little patches
in a quilt that would tell whoever'd find my body exactly
what I was. A bad crawly. A Torn-given Choir wraith. An
overgrown baby rabbit. The wrong one to have survived the
strikebreaking massacre, no doubt. I looked at Sincerity,
who was looking at me, and tried to smile for her. Marney
in the mirror didn't move. Sincerity pulled herself upright.
She slipped off the bed, I watched her walk across the ceiling and pull a shawl across her shoulders. Its fringe kissed
the backs of her speckled thighs.

"Is Sunny here?"

She pulled her hair out from beneath the shawl, shook it
out. It fell in dark waves to her navel. She had a scar there,
pink and raised, maybe as long as my thumb. I wanted my
hands back inside her. Her voice was low, had that smoker's
honeyed sound. "Who?"

"Teriasa zel Cerca, pardon. Prumathe's little sister," I
said. "She's a friend of mine."

"Teriasa zel Cerca," Sincerity said, "isn't here."

Promising. They could be established up north by now. They could have a little screaming suckling baby. For assurance's sake, "Does she still work here?"

"No. D'you want a smoke?"

I watched her roll her pipe at the ends of her fingers. Graceful. I bet she'd be a fantastic pickpocket. I accepted a puff. I wanted to pull off my skin. I wanted to strip it in streamers and hang my skin up on a clothesline and let the breeze get at my insides. The muscle pulp needed some light. Something in this room was ichorite but I didn't know what it was. I itched down to the bone. I was wet, I felt it against my thigh, but I couldn't bear to touch myself, let alone let her touch me. I scarcely even let Sisphe touch me. My own pleasure horrified me. I couldn't afford to feel soft.

Sincerity took a long drag. She wasn't putting on a show, she'd dropped the posture. I felt a rush of fondness about her precision and its release. I watched her shoulder blades move inside her back, the shawl slipped, her hair parted, I could see the links of her back down to her waist. The flare of her hips, the dimples at either side of her tailbone, her smattering of tattoos, only enough to mark Choir affiliation, no further ornaments. She hung her head and the top vertebra showed. I wanted to lick it. I chewed a strip of skin off my thumb. I wanted my resin, the solid perfume we filled hollowed-out pocket watches and lockets with that made our bodies slip away when we huffed it. My resin watch was in my trousers, far from me, over in a pile with my harness and my cock.

"What would you like to do, Daddy?"

I skimmed my tongue over my teeth. Rubbed at the silver one. "I want to kill Yann Industry Chauncey."

"I want to be the queen of Cisra," she said. "I meant, do you want my tongue on that little slit of yours?"

"I mean it. I'm gonna kill him."

"Sure," she said. "How do you figure?"

"I'm going to case his house for weeks. I'll stalk his guards and staff. Anticipate their shifts. I'll kill the guards quick and quiet, then I'll go inside. I'll go to the room where he sleeps, and I'll drag him from his bed. I'll beat him awake then let him go, I'll pursue him to the stairs, I imagine he's got a sweeping staircase, and I'll cut his throat with this knife and push him over the banister. Watch the blood go up like ribbons. Watch him crack on the floor." I gestured to the knife. I still wore it. I rolled to show her. "It's why I'm alive. I'm going to kill him. I'm not being crass. I'm going to murder Industry."

"That's elaborate," she said. "Why not just slit his throat?"

"It can't be quick, like livestock." I gnawed my bottom lip. "I want it to matter."

"What he'd do to you?"

"Killed my parents."

"Personally?"

"No. He hired enforcers. A sniper team."

"Why not kill the enforcers then?"

"I do often." I reached toward her, she gave me her pipe, I felt gracious that I didn't need to ask for it, but thanking

163

her felt clumsy. I closed my eyes, I took a drag. I pushed the smoke to the bottom of my lungs, inflated my belly. Itchy, noxious. I liked the prickling. I sighed, the smoke left me, and I passed the pipe back to her. "They acted on his command. I'll kill him extravagantly for it."

"They'll arrest you. That is, if they don't shoot you on the spot. He owns the force. They're his property defenders. Not like the barons have sway anymore, at least not in IC. There won't be a trial. You won't have the chance to run. They'll kill you. They'll make a show of you." Sincerity sat on the bed and dropped the shawl. I watched her cross and uncross her legs. "You're stupid, Marney Honeycutt."

"So long as I get my turn." I got up. Slithered into my trousers but didn't bother with my shirt, pulled my suspenders over my shoulders, held onto the straps. I felt skittery. "Thank you, Sincerity."

"Mhm," she said.

I wandered out of her room. We were at the bottom of the dark pink stairway, and I climbed and despite myself I listened for Sunny's—Teriasa's—voice. She used a special voice for Velma, the doll. I remembered the melodrama of the rabbit and the doll. So much heartbreak. Heartbreak at the time had been so light and gushy. I'd seen so much. I wanted froth and peril without injury. Funny to think of myself as having been young enough that I hadn't understood heartbreak as injury yet. I hadn't felt it, I hadn't known it, I hadn't seen it put welts on paradise. Not that welts were always wrong. Often I liked mine. Still it wasn't

quite slaughter. I stood outside Teriasa's door. I cleared my
throat. My voice still felt small after disuse. I knocked. I
said, "Sunny?"

Nothing. There was no light under the door.

I went outside. I stepped into the night air, it was freezing, snow fell in bolts. A porcelain layer broke underfoot. I
wore no boots, hadn't thought to put them back on, and the
cold slipped between my tarsals and up my ankles and hurt.
There were still ribbons on the bulls, none sleeping but
silent, only swishing their tails. Different bulls, different
ribbons, and little seashell bells, but I found the continuity
a comfort. I went to our lurcher, Candor's lurcher, thrust
my hands under the tarp that held the ichorite mesh bundle. I pulled the mesh apart. It stung against the grooves
of my hands. The snow reflected the burning magenta that
floated through the air, and clearly, more clearly than the
hallucinations usually came, was the image of the ground
opening above me. Darkness cracked, and I was lifted, and
it was agony. The drills made such a dull percussion. It
was too arrhythmic to find beautiful. I was so tired. I was
still raw. I pawed over the bags, we hadn't touched them
in months, only I could break the mesh and neither Sisphe
nor Harlow had asked it of me. These spoils were drenched
with Candor's blood. Or her breath, the stuff her ghost is
made of. I hope she rested. I hope she didn't walk. Fuck.
Poor baby. I opened a bag, thumbed through clothes, shut
it. I opened another, then a third. Third bag had slim cedar
boxes, the painted kinds that hold a single cigar, wrapped
in a bundle with ribbon like dynamite. I pulled a box from

the bundle and opened it. Evil green beads glinted inside it.
A malachite string. The lurid stripes of dark green rippled
through the light green and spun off into wood-grain loops.
Shiny and faintly reflective, though I wasn't sure of what
light. I closed the box, swept a hand back over the mesh,
and put my tongue between my teeth to stop the chattering.

I went back upstairs. I knocked on Teriasa's door again.
Sunny still wasn't there. I didn't write well, besides which,
I had no idea where I'd find a scrap of paper lying around. I
knelt and slipped the box under the crack in the door. It fit
just barely. I thought about looking for Beauty, asking her
to pass along that I'd been here, that I'd been eager to see
her, but I couldn't bear the thought of waking her. If she
wasn't working, she was sleeping, and I had a hunch Beauty
seldom slept. My toes were blue. Sincerity was so smart. I
was stupid. I was tired. I went and found the room where
Sisphe and Harlow slept tangled, Harlow snoring gently,
her face in Sisphe's chest, lips by the mole under Sisphe's
left breast, her arm around Sisphe's waist, Sisphe's hands in
Harlow's for once fucked-up hair, a scene of perfect repose.
The room looked like an intaglio bedroom pressed from a
beetle shell. Everything was the same silky iridescent, iridescent in some way that I could touch. It wasn't ichorite.
A better, baser kind of lustrous. The fabric over everything
had a stunning red-green shift. I laid on the floor by the
foot of their bed. It was hot in here, it smelled like sex and
smoke and sweat plus Sisphe's too-sweet perfume. I shut my
eyes. I said my prayers. I waited for you. I thought about
killing Industry for you. I thought about you standing

beside me in the snow outside, snowflakes in your lank red hair. I thought about you standing at the bottom of a staircase. I thought about what Industry'd look like, throat cut, face abstracted and made fleshy from the stained glass portraiture that haunted my working childhood now struck vivid with pain, his arms windmilling backwards when I shoved him, then falling so slowly. Like how a feather falls. Him collapsing into a pile of laundry at your feet and you cupping your hands around your mouth and yelling up to me, *what's taken you so long? You've been out adventuring. What about your dear old friend? You love me, Marney, don't you?*

Eight

THERE WAS A PARTY ON A RIVERBOAT. THE BOAT was strung with little lights, like fireflies on leashes. A triple-story boat, ornately carved from wood in the style of the little gazebo Shrines where Stellarine worshippers stood perfectly still to let their sovereign star, a living essential Virtue that rose above the world to guide and preside over it without besmirching itself with terrestrial baseness, to shine over them and fill them with its frothy metaphysical beams. Fancy ornamental lattice full of curls and splits. The party shouldn't have been on the riverboat, because it overwhelmingly wasn't a passenger vessel, it had the slope and girth of a cargo hauler, with pretty affectations to hold those few who had reason to go with their materials. The riverboat wasn't made of ichorite. Past year, the subtle but palpable shift toward transporting sharply valuable goods on vessels that weren't an ichorite shell on wheels was something my friends and I had noticed. I was making a mark.

Sisphe was on the riverboat. Harlow pointed her out. She served a tray of purple drinks in a stolen pleated dress to a small crowd of glistening merchants. Glistening luminously. Lustrously. Even from this distance, Harlow and I standing shadowed underneath a boardwalk that jutted over the Flip, up to our thighs in cold water, I could see the air bruise around their heads. It was like looking at the sun, the green-pinks they burned on my eyelids. The silhouettes laughing stiffly up above me were drenched in ichorite. Coated in it. Once I'd driven by an ichorite ore mine, not gotten near, too fucking dangerous what with the enforcers dripping off every twist in the chain link, but the workers I'd seen all sparkled with ichorite, sparkled darkly, every part of them. They'd swirled with made-up colors. It was like they'd been smeared with diamond dust. These merchants above me shone brighter than those miners had. It was hypnotic. A girl whose slim green dress hurt to look at leaned against the stern, accepted a drink from Sisphe, then poured the purple drink over the rails into the water.

I licked my gums, not hugely swollen yet, and felt horrible. I looked at Harlow. She had little moles scattered across her square brown face. Thin brows and a full bottom lip. Very handsome. I thought for a moment about kissing Harlow. I thought about pushing her down into the water. Harlow's a boxer and stronger than me, she would've wrung me dry in a fair fight, but in my head I wanted to lose. I wanted my tongue in her mouth and her shirt collar in my fists. I wanted us to grab each other and scream until our throats tore. I wanted things I didn't allow myself to want. She'd understand the mess inside me. I smiled at her. She flicked her gaze over to me and smiled back, lopsided and toothy, then without a word we both sprang forward.

The riverboat had swept near the boardwalk in the time I'd been staring at Harlow. We moved now, ducked under the algae-fuzzed beams that held up the structure above us, and seized the ropes that Sisphe had arranged for us. Wet boots on the wood. We climbed in lockstep to a loading dock, boarded. There were enforcers posted there. Armed but not brandishing. They spoke lightly and looked out over the water, almost wistful. One was younger, scruffy, and the other was older, salt and pepper with a thin jaw and tough mouth. His eyes were heavily bagged, his nose reddish, pored like a strawberry. Deep vertical lines on either side of his mouth. He was armed differently than most enforcers were, with a hunting rifle on his back fashioned with a bayonet as long as a femur. He scratched his chin. Spoke less than the younger enforcer, didn't move his upper lip when he did. I knew this man. I knew this fucking man. I had seen this man on the backs of my eyelids when the misery got bad. I knew this man. I knew him.

Harlow climbed the rope at a studied angle, kept herself just past their periphery. She was silent and moved smoothly. The sound of her pant legs dripping was swallowed by the motor's hum. She dipped out of sight, into the alcove where the server's staircase joined the compact kitchen suite, as the plan mandated, and meanwhile I looked up at Baird.

Edna's butcher stood at ease above me. Swaying. Breathing. So alive.

Gone was the Flip River. Gone the music, the distant chatter, the moan of the steam engine and the heavy turning wheel. Gone theft and glory. Gone obligations, gone priority, gone my head. Gone Honeycutt.

In the darkness were crates lashed with heavy chains. Ichorite alloy chains, I could smell it. Thought of briars and railroad spikes. I thought *prick prick prick prick prick.* I twisted my hands on the rope. Distantly, the chains stirred. The links crawled like worms. The sound caught the younger one's attention. He turned his head. He watched then as the chains streamed forward hard and fast and sharp like needles, sharp like sea urchin spines, across the bodiless gap of shadow, then an inch deep in his back. He jumped away, tumbled forward, fell past me with a yelp, splashed into the water. Catfish teemed around him. He clapped his hands through the water, and the big whiskered mouths opened and shut in the murk around his weeping back.

The wet red tips of ichorite dripped. They glittered in midair where the young one had been. Baird held still. They had punctured all the way through Baird. They were nudging against the front of his jacket, tenting the fabric. It looked like he'd been gored by some elk.

Baird watched me. He could see me on the rope now. I wept, but not tears. I leaked from my nose and my ears, it was slippery and thin, like rubbing alcohol. I was dripping serum down to my collarbone. I looked up at him looking down at me. I had questions for him. Screaming accusations and vinegar. I wanted to beat my fists into him and holler in his ears. I wanted to break his teeth under my boots. I wanted him to hold me. My grip got slack on the rope. I wasn't sure what kept me upright.

Baird said wetly, "Whip Spider."

He wriggled the fingers of his bloody hand. There was a spike through that wrist, but the spikes were slackening. It didn't hurt to hold the ichorite taut like this, it barely felt like anything at all. It was like a summer storm under the surface of my skin. My blood washed around and overwhelmed all other sensation. I got the sense that this could kill me. This was killing me. I didn't stop.

I opened my mouth and out came with a spill of iridescent sweetsour drool, "Where did you put my pa?"

He curled his lip. He had dog teeth, long and yellow. His lungs must be a mess. "No fucking idea."

"The Yann Chauncey Ichorite Foundry massacre. Ten years ago. Where did you put the bodies?" I was shocked at my voice. I sounded so small. I recoiled from myself and spat serum on the boat's side.

Baird looked at me blankly, then laughed. He laughed deep in his belly, and it rumbled through all of him, rumbled above the motor. It drove the spikes through the fabric in his enforcer's jacket. He knocked his head back and bellowed, pulled one wrist off its spike to scrub his hand over his face. He was crying, he laughed so hard. He spat up thick black pudding. "That's rich," he said. "That's precious. Lustertouched factory brat, huh? No, sweet girl. I don't know where they put your pa. Some hole with the rest. Nobody bothered to write it down."

The hand on his face slid behind him. He touched his gun.

I screamed.

The spikes fanned out, went rigid.

Baird made a horrible sound. His chest rattled. I'd ripped something inside there. He held his rifle, its barrel brushed the curls at the top of my head. I twisted my hands on the rope. The spikes twisted above me. Then I let go, hugged my body flush against the hull, and felt the spikes soften. They sloughed off like mercury. They splattered the floor, and they released Baird, and he fell. He fell into the gaping catfish. They slopped over him, flopped and tangled across his body, and I felt like there was nothing inside me at all.

I climbed into the cargo hold.

Big blocks in the shadow. Bolts of luxury fabric waited, crammed like fish in a tin, inside those shapes. I lurched past them. I felt enormously dizzy, I felt around my face and was horrified by how much I dripped. I wasn't sure what I was bleeding. I looked at my hands, at the oil-on-water prismatic rainbow ugliness I'd been leaking. It'd never been this bad. I scrubbed my hands on my thighs. I pulled on my lace mask halfway, kept my mouth free. I thought I'd hyperventilate otherwise. I felt around for a door, gripped a handle, twisted. I stumbled into the music and light.

We had a plan at some point. We had a good plan.

The plan went like, Harlow and I apprehend the captain, we kill the motor, we wait for the others—Brandegor's gang, Brandegor was nearby, she and Uthste and Valor, or maybe it was just her and Uthste right now—to help us move product off this vessel onto the one they'd snaked for us. When I killed Baird there'd been nobody behind us. Where were they? Was Harlow with the captain?

Heads turned toward the sound. Casually then sharply. Sisphe poured a glass of bubbly. She looked over her shoulder at me. Her eyes flashed, a manic smile flickered at the corner of her mouth, a question mark.

I moved.

I seized Sisphe around the waist and hauled her backwards, and she shouted, dropped the tray with dramatic flourish. The elegant little glasses smashed to glitter. Liquor glistened across the polished blond wood floor. I hauled her backwards, found my dummy gun, fit it under her jaw. In her ear I slurred, *wherezarlow?*

"The Whip Spider's gang!" Sisphe yelped. She writhed against my hand, exerting no force. She was holding us both up. Without moving her lips she breathed, "Marney, you look fucking awful."

"I am," I said. Little voice again. I ground my molars and adjusted my grip on her, clutched her like a plush toy.

The music hadn't stopped playing. We weren't in the band's eyeline. The scattered patrons held very still, took calculated steps backwards, or held their ground. They had been mingling around an oil portrait of a severe and androgynous ginger girl who wore furs over her tailored suit and a cane across her lap. The oil-portrait girl leered at us. Unimpressed, maybe a little bit into it. The patrons were exquisitely dressed, mostly older than me, stone-faced with wide stances. Not combatants but not delicate. Someone showed me their hands. Lots of skinny rings stacked on their thumbs and pinky fingers. Someone else deliberately finished their drink.

"Everyone to the bow!" Harlow barked from a balcony above us. She sounded winded, less cocksure than usual. I felt with disgusting confidence that Brandegor the Rancid wasn't here. I wondered if she would be. Could've gotten got. "Move, now!"

I shoved Sisphe away from me, toward the group. She was good at herding. She looked over her shoulder at me, looked livid for a moment, then fell into a long stride, grabbed the two men ahead of us as she went and dragged them with her around the displayed oil-portrait ginger toward the bow. She clung to the men, gasped something scarcely coherent about everyone joining them, about her safety, oh she was *sooo frightened*, and the men peeled their focus off me, looked at her in her polished hysteria with awe and pity. People came when called. The band stopped playing, stood, and they and the staff wandered toward her, hunched around her in semicircles. She pulled them to her with the might of her big pearly tears.

I limped back into the cargo hold. Felt the portrait's flat eyes follow me, but I ignored that. Beyond the crates I saw the second boat and could've wept. Brandegor's, certainly. I felt so woozy. The ichorite ooze gummed against my boots and pulled like strings of taffy, and I felt sticky with it. The cargo wasn't lashed in place with chains anymore, and the crates themselves were fixed to dull wheels, I unlocked one with a kick. I heaved, it moved, splinters drove under my nails and I winced and shoved harder. Moving hurt. Everything hurt. Everything was glowing and lovely. I pushed the crate to the edge of the loading dock, pawed the open air for a hook, and found one. I hooked the strap across the top of the crate.

Mors Brandegor the Rancid stood on the bow with her cigar in her teeth. She waved the crate down with her big purple nails. Smoke coiled around her head. I took the rope that held the hook, marveled that every new object in my line of sight felt like it'd condensed out of breath and shadow and could melt and be gone, nothing was heavy or permanent, and lowered the crate. I was not nearly fucking strong enough to do this on my own. Harlow, probably. Candor, without a doubt.

The crate fell in ugly jerks, but Brandegor caught it, lugged it aboard.

I let go of the rope. My hands stung. I winced, stuck my most aching finger in my mouth and sucked a splinter loose. I spat it out. I worked my jaw. I turned around to fetch another and behind me was a passenger. The girl in the slim green dress.

She was a tall, lean girl. Hair blacker than the shadows surrounding swayed around her hip bones and was slicked back from a sharp face, all bone and diagonal angles save for her watery downturned eyes, long-lashed and burning, and her full painted lips twisted in a horrible smile, or grimace, or leer, I didn't know. I watched her move her lips soundlessly. She walked like she was Veltuni but wore no lip ring. She held a keen clip-point knife. The girl didn't blink. She looked like she might cry. She toed off her delicate high-heeled shoes, stood barefoot on the luster-splattered floor, widened her stance. I saw the tension in her thighs and core and shoulders through the dress, saw it release. She pounced knife-first.

I threw my body to the side but the knife clipped my collar. Bright slippery pain flowered under the bone. She cut forward again, I stepped back, I closed my hand and found my knife inside it. Behind my eyes pink bubbled. I slashed back, she drove a cut upwards, would've knocked my knife from my hand if its metal hadn't seeped into my skin. This girl was—better. She moved with a viciousness just past efficiency, a studied meanness. Sport dueler, though this— she slashed my upper arm, the cut flowed thickly—was not the restraint and acclaimed elegance of an aristocratic knife duel. She was a cat and I was a finch whose wing she'd already torn. Lots of light cuts to watch me bleed because she could. And she *could*. I chanted in my head, kneaded the ichorite pools underfoot into wires into snares to trip her, but she tore through them like they were nothing before they solidified. The ichorite strings snapped and drooped and became solid again. She seized a fistful of my jacket, fit her knife under my chin, and leaned me over the cargo bay's edge, balls of my feet on the floor, heels in open air above the drop to the whirling catfish.

"You wretch," she purred through her teeth. "You slime. You're a carnival barker. You're a road magician. You're not a devil, you lack the dignity demanded by a symbol so rich. You're nothing and nobody. How dare you frighten that girl like that? How dare you interrupt us?"

I panted. I didn't dare move.

"You are a stain on our age. You are a blemish on progress." She leaned over me. Her hair swayed against my slit jacket. Strands clung to where I bled. I felt her breath on my cheek, the sweet liquor on her snarl. Her eyes were enormous. I saw my horror mirrored across the little pink veins there. "You little freak. You little sadist. The look on that server's face. The disruption you've caused, the disrespect you've showed my staff, is repulsive. You don't deserve the air in your lungs. You don't deserve the blood in your body."

I willed the ichorite off the ground and felt my vision flicker. The world bruised. It bubbled, I saw the metal effervescing in my periphery, but I couldn't will it to shape. Yann Chauncey lived. I could not die while Industry lived. That man didn't even know where my father was. I couldn't die. I looked into the eyes of this girl, her liquid black eyes, and did not know how to kill her.

"Drop the knife," said Sisphe thu Ecapa, her gun nestled at the nape of the stranger's neck. "This is *my* little freak."

The stranger's face rippled. She looked furious, then exasperated, then fell into a sullen humor. Her eyebrows danced under her fringe. Her lip twitched. She threw down the knife. It *thwunk*ed into the scuffed plank floor. I breathed in sharply. She released me.

I felt gravity win.

The sky flew up in pink and orange slashes, and the Flip River slapped me, grabbed me with a thousand flapping catfish mouths. My head slipped under. The writhing fish bodies covered the boat above me. They whirred around my body, slimy and muscular, and I clawed at the nothing between their bodies. I saw long algae like hair and a limp, drifting hand.

Then fists closed around my upper arms and pulled me upright. I gasped, the evening burned against the lining of my throat and I spat up murky water, and collapsed against Brandegor the Rancid, who clapped me firmly between the shoulder blades so hard that something knocked loose. I shivered. I coughed up a laugh, I laughed so hard I cried, I sobbed into Brandegor's shoulder. She mussed my curls. The orange darkness behind my eyelids spasmed with luster luster luster.

SOMETIME LATER WE triumphed around the Fingerbluffs. We leaned off our lurchers and gave luxurious silks and fine jewels to everyone who gathered to watch us pass, and the crooked teeth they showed us were beautiful, and the air was perfumed with marmalade and tobacco flowers, and Harlow and Sisphe and I reclined on the cliffs like natural princes, eating fruit and sunning ourselves, adorned with scrapes and bruises. We looked at the place where Candor should be lying and I told Sisphe and Harlow about you. That time you stole raspberries for us. The day I made that ring for you. Pinched it from conveyor belt scraps and kneaded it for your littlest finger. I contemplated and then forbade the contemplation of whether your body wore that ring in whatever unmarked grave Chauncey's goons had planted you in. Was your body dissolved into my family's body? Had you fused with Edna and Poesy and the boys who chased you when you were smaller? Were you dissolved into flora? Had you been transformed into endless flying things? I thought about cicadas, underfoot for ages until maturity comes. Screaming flight.

It's easy when it's hazy to imagine that there is something moving underneath these rocks. Moving gently, breathing. Something deep asleep. It's easy to imagine a watchful slumber. My old religion has its merits. I rolled my cheek to the side, pressed it flush against the basalt and the forget-me-not sprays, and listened to a heartbeat I could not explain to my friends. My tongue itched. I scraped it with my teeth. I was eager again to eat the guts of Industry Chauncey. I gnashed my molars and yearned.

Uthste came and found me. She looked older, her eyebrows were dusted with gray. She stood over us on the rocks, where we passed a bottle between us, some rosy fizzy tonic edged with coca leaves, and her shadow interrupted our murmuring. The sun behind her shaved head looked crownlike. She frowned gently. Her boots glistened by my ear. She said, "It's the end. Marney. Come along with me, please. Amon's asked for you."

"Just Marney?" Sisphe put her elbows under her.

"Never just Marney," said Harlow, dragging a comb through her glossy black hair.

Uthste nodded curtly. "Marney by name. Come as you'd like. Be quick."

I found my feet. Harlow followed me, and we both took one of Sisphe's clever faux-limp hands, hauled her upright, whisked her off to Loveday Mansion. I felt small following Uthste. I wondered if she knew what she symbolized to me, herself and Valor and Brandegor, my saviors and bandit-makers. The thought of telling her seemed a repulsive imposition. I reckon she'd know when I showed her. I'd have to demonstrate it in deed.

The four of us gathered in the ballroom. Settees and wingback armchairs had been dragged in and arranged around the broad room's perimeter, and Choir-goers, not full membership but more than I usually saw in one place, flocked among the velvet furniture in corduroy and rough leather, features hard against the plushness. Younger kids lay on animal-pelt rugs and pulled the tufts of fur. A boy near me braided down a dead bear's back. He looked eight, maybe. Truly eight. He'd never seen hard labor and it kept him babyish. The abundance that the bandits brought humbled me. I felt grateful and young, but tired.

Uthste went and sat on the floor in front of Brandegor's chair, leaned back against her shin. Valor perched on the chair's arm, one of Brandegor's big arms around her waist. I scarcely knew what to do with myself. I looked back to Harlow and Sisphe, ached for Candor, then Sisphe turned my chin with her knuckles and pointed my attention at the room's far end. Amon sat on the floor with letters and telegrams and newspaper clippings fanned in front of him. Behind him, the Veltuni ancestral congress's cast hands kneaded and stretched. I leaned my cheek against Sisphe's hand, felt an old flicker of something I couldn't entertain, then crossed the cream-and-amber room and knelt beside Amon.

Amon smiled but did not look at me. He moved his hands, I moved mine back, an acknowledgement of our mutual faith.

Amon said, to the room itself, "Thank you, assembly. I'll be brief. Our masquerade has always been finite. Twenty years in glorious harmony will imminently meet its abrupt end. I believe this because the heir to Loveday Mansion is of age, and has been summoned to Yann Industry Chauncey's estate. His ward has a debutante showing. The Loveday heir has been invited by three separate parties, the Montrose barony, the Glitslough barony, and the Chauncey family itself. If we decline, our only option, they will come here. They will send their emissaries. Lately, we had plans for this. But our sweet girl Candor is dead.

"The barons of Ignavia alone supposedly own land. Before my friends killed him, Horace Veracity Loveday claimed to own this land. All the people who worked this land rented their homes from him, owed him the fruits of their labor, and the tools with which it was performed, and were subjected to his whim as law. The Baron's Senate is firm about land ownership remaining in their few fists, but the Baron's Senate is poor, and the money is in Industry

Chauncey's industry. Chauncey can't own land. All ichorite refinement centers are clustered around IC, as Baron
Ramtha has been enormously lenient with allowing
Chauncey's growth, but Chauncey wants to expand his en-
terprise. He needs land and lots of it, land for mining, land
for processing plants, land for the workers who labor in
those pits to sleep on.

"Chauncey is asking after us because he wants a
baron-class spouse for his ward. He wants this because he
wants to mine here, or thinks he can. We can refuse. We
can put it off. But the emissaries to be sent won't only ask
after the Loveday heir, they'll scout the Fingerbluffs for
mining. The blurring between the capitalists and the barons is already happening. This marriage, whatever it might
be, will mean that Chauncey will come to conquer us. He
funds the Enforcer Corps. They will come with force and
we will battle until we are dead, and then our home will be
maimed and stripped for parts."

Gray faces around the room. Nobody blinked. Murmurs
rumbled but I caught no words. I put my hands on the
floor. I looked at my hands. My fingers were blurring.

"We prepare for the war," said Brandegor. Valor beside
her looked stricken but sure. They'd go down blazing.

"We leave. Be reasonable," said a bandit called Alcstei
zel Prisis.

Alcstei's man, whose name I did not know, said, "The
Choir claim a new home. This place has served us for
twenty good years, but the Choir must be preserved. We
find a new stronghold."

"We serve this place. Not the reverse. Have pride," snapped a bandit called Artumica thu Artumica Tanner. "Do you imagine we will take with us the community who has defended us and nurtured us for decades? Beg the displacement of thousands upon thousands? Tell them to carry with them their histories on their backs and be dispossessed of all else, we've surrendered their home to the slaughterhouse? Or do you suppose we abandon them?"

"I was born on the Bluffs," said Valor. "Here's where I'll die."

"We will not suffer the indignity of surrender. We won't show belly, we won't scurry under some rock. Be righteous, Alcstei." Brangedor pulled attention like gravity. She strained against her clothes, against her skin. She held Valor's waist and Utshte's shoulder to keep herself seated. I thought she'd kill Alcstei with her hands. "We lost five this month. Five of us. Young Thomas Fortitude shot off the roof of a train, his body caught and brought home by his boys, buried by hand in the fruit grove. Cristhia's twins, gone. Dash Mercer, dangling up in Geistmouth. Wyatt Piety Stytt, dangling down in the Achrum prairies. We commit ourselves to death when we mark our names across our breasts. We will die for this. I am the last bull rider of Mors Hall. I will die for this place."

Alcstei's man stood up.

"Be fierce and proud for our Hereafter. To die for tomorrow is to die for our children's rich harvest," Harlow said.

"You don't have children," said Alcstei's man. "We do."

I stood up. My hands shook, I rooted them in my hair.
My ribs beat against my jacket. I spread my elbows, looked
across the room at nobody in particular, at everybody, at
Sisphe. She gave me a sharp nod. Her eyes flashed. I looked
down at the papers fanned around Amon, the array of bluish
and cream off-whites. I couldn't read the sinuous handwriting. The ink on the pages still looked wet. "The Loveday heir
should say yes. I'll be the Loveday heir. I'm not Stellarine but
I can fake it. I studied to be Candor's valet."

Amon looked up at me. He looked relieved. At last, I'd
said it.

"Pardon," I said. I looked to my peers and fixed my tone.
"Gentle Choir. I propose that I go feign being Loveday
heir."

A bandit whose name I didn't know said, "Would the
charade be worth it? It pushes back war only so far."

"It's worth it because I'm gonna kill Yann Industry
Chauncey," I said.

"That's true," said Brandegor the Rancid. "She is gonna
kill Yann Industry Chauncey."

"If Marney takes up the role," Sisphe said, vibrating
with such glee that I thought her hairpins might fall, "and
I accompanied her as her secretary or her valet, think of the
recon! I could squirrel away as many documents as I can.
Muddle things up for them. If we're to have a war, killing
Chauncey is a triumphant first blow. Let's not be passive.
Let's not wait like lambs."

"When Marney takes up the role," said Harlow, "we'll
have bought ourselves another month or two to strategize.

We'll know what their plans are, we could maybe even shape them, arrange the conditions of our discovery on our own terms. Be keen and ruthless against them, having studied their intentions and so on. Let her take on Candor's work. Let her be our girl's remembrance."

"Yes, and it'd be funny," said Magnanimity, the oldest bandit in the room, who'd served the Choir for forty-seven years, and been present for Horace Veracity Loveday's execution. She rolled her wrist, clanged her bangles together, and smiled at me. "That's as good a reason as any."

"Marney deserves to kill Chauncey," said Uthste. "And we deserve him dead for the threat he poses."

Magnanimity clapped her hands. "Those who want to flee, flee. Take a civilian's portion of treasure and be gone from our graces. Show of hands. Marney as Loveday heir to kill Yann Industry Chauncey?" Hands drifted up. The ancestral congress stretched their fingers behind my head. It felt like dusk bleed when I was small, all the floating palms. Such pride I had for the whole world. Such pride I had in my own survival. Such love for the Fingerbluffs, for the Choir, for my families, for you. My blood was thick and vibrant. Cut me and find grenadine. Cut me and find white hot light.

Nine

BARON APPARENT VELMA TRUTH LOVEDAY EX-
isted. She was real and twenty-something years old.
Visually speaking, she managed a delicate balance between
anachronistic Rasennese conservatism and the trappings
of a boardwalk pimp. She wore a bottle green jacket that
billowed by her ankles when she walked, luxurious and
melodramatic with an upturned collar and wide sharp
lapels, a military fashion barely softened for aristocratic con-
sumption that'd been a fashionable look twenty years ago
but never since. Beneath this slightly moth-eaten extravagance she wore sturdy boots, neat black canvas trousers, and
riding gloves that were not stolen, exposed leather braces
over her linen shirt. She wore her shirt buttoned to her jaw.
No skin showing, not one stripe, itchiness be damned. One
dangly pearl earring, a string of pearls for the resin watch
tucked in her back pocket, a modest showing of Stellarine
piety and, to the learned, the habits of resin enjoyers. Sex!

Sleep! Numbed-out brawls! She looked like a lamb turned rake. I wore Baron Apparent Velma Truth Loveday uncomfortably. My skin itched. It was war and brutal torture standing without a slouch.

Candor had worked so hard at this. She would've made our heir such a regular girl.

Sisphe, playing the role of charming Sisphe, normal secretary, thumbed through the invitations again. Her gloves looked so starkly black against the heavy cream paper. I watched her fingers move and wished the words she rubbed were larger. "Glitslough: Baron Abram Loomis is concerned for the health of dear old Veracity. They were school friends before Veracity's agoraphobia advanced. He wants Veracity's heir present to repair Veracity's reputation and reintegrate him into the senatorial social strata. His daughter will be attending. Adorable. They're Tullian, do you think that'll be a problem in spotting you? Montrose: Baronet Helena Integrity Shane has written you a novel imploring you to attend the festivities for sake of contributing an unaffected voice to, I quote, 'the claustrophobic and incestuous sprawl that is the Wilton School Lunarist Society' in hopes that you can be a 'dissenting voice with the strength of provincial pride' and that you and her may act as 'comrades and peers' who 'stand together for that which demands doing in service of the coming dawn.' Hereafterist talk. Double adorable. Would that I could see Harlow's face, that talk from a baronet. Last invitation is from the debutante herself. The whole note says, *Loveday, Come join the fun. I might fall in love with you. Big money if so. Cordially, Goss Dignity Chauncey, written in her own hand."*

Tullian could be a problem. Once I would've liked to meet the Tullian baron family, when I was young and naïve enough to strive beyond what was immediately in front of me. I'd avoid the Loomis girl. I wouldn't avoid the rich Hereafterist, who felt impossible, and thus must be proven with the naked eye. I toyed with my pearl earring. "It says 'written in her own hand'?"

"She wrote the words written in her own hand, yes." Sisphe folded the invitations crisply. She wore her disguise like she'd been born at it. She looked smart and quick. Aside from the fact that she was conspicuously covered, her presence on the drive up toward the estate would seem abundantly natural, even necessary. She had been theorizing and executing the aesthetics of her own subjugation for years. All her kidnappings were her choreography; where I excelled in mechanical logistics, she thrived where performance called. Even now, in the shadow of the Chauncey estate wrought ichorite gates, where I remained half Marney, she was immersed. Her body became discreet and orderly, excessive femininity reigned in, only suggested, briefly flashed; she walked with clean clicks, made direct eye contact, and didn't bounce at all. Her largess hung around her in the air, but it was implacable in her posture. Unimpeachable. She should be walking a prissy exotic dog. "They're all crawlies, miss."

"Miss is awful," I said. Them being crawlies was bizarre. A mercy for me, I wasn't sure how I could sustain tactical interest in a young man, but odd. Stellarine law, and Tullian law for that matter, were particular about gender and its function. That function was fixed. Women with men in closed pairs. No fucking outside of those closed pairs. Fucking extraneously made your gender sticky and complicated. Veltuni law less so, Veltuni coming of age allowed for self-determination in all things, gender included, but the religious weight on reproduction and continuation of the ancestral congress meant usually that demonstration of fertility was necessary for accruing any sort of power, even if that meant fucking once for the purpose of pregnancy and then returning to whatever one pleased. The Oneness didn't care at all. Actual Ignavian legal code was vague. It allowed for interfaith marriage and adjacent consolidation of debt and possession, an enormously progressive move by the revolutionary barons when Ignavia became itself two hundred years ago. Women could marry women in Ignavia under this code. They just didn't. If they did, that'd be crawly of them, and being crawly was vile. "D'you think they're more boy-crawly or girlcrawly?"

"How about ma'am? Revenge for you saying yes ma'am to me at five times an hour every hour each day for a decade. I would guess girlcrawly. I would be delighted to be wrong." She adjusted her stride and trailed behind me at a respectful distance. "You can be insane. Veracity is famously insane. Just commit to the kind of insane you are and I'll wingman it. Are you thinking big insane or little insane?"

I looked at her. I looked at the grass.

"Medium insane." She clucked her tongue. "What about sir?"

"Sir's better."

Faux Bellonan estate. High pitched roof and fingered columns, a broad veranda, a hulking squareness that suggested a garden courtyard in the belly of the house. It looked polished and smelled new. Behind us, the spires of Ignavia City broke the horizon in the otherwise endless pines. I forbade myself from looking at Ignavia City. Cataract clouds above us, a brisk southern breeze. I stared down the building that contained Yann Industry Chauncey. I could taste my own heartbeat. It was salty between my gums.

Barely moving my mouth I managed, "Do we knock?"

"Surely not." Sisphe cleared her throat, then called into the evening air: "Baron Apparent Velma Truth Loveday is here!"

I wanted my mask. I widened my stance.

The door opened. Tullian girl, younger than me. She wore a bonnet and what would've been a standard maid's uniform if the fabric didn't gleam like that. It looked like a polished shell, skintight where it wasn't billowing, so skintight I could see the slant of her ribs. She bowed her head. "Baron Apparent Velma Truth Loveday?"

"Yes ma'am." I stood as rigidly as I knew how to stand. "With secretary."

"With secretary," the girl said. She didn't lift her gaze. She had a pinkish complexion, I could see the lilac veins in her eyelids. "I'll inform Mister Chauncey, thank you. Come inside if you please."

"Mister Chauncey," I repeated.

"Yes, Mister Chauncey is entertaining the other guests. Or will be shortly. She hasn't come downstairs yet."

She? I clenched my diagram. "What may I call you?"

"Oh. Birdie." She took a backwards step that wedged the door wider.

"Thank you, Birdie," I said. Without a backwards glance, clinging to a desperate faith that Sisphe was nearby and retained her cunning under duress, I walked past Birdie, through the chilly monochrome foyer, into the frondy garden courtyard where a party unfolded slowly, as though the scene was underwater, or the honeyed air had gone tar thick.

Bodies stretched on elongated metal chairs. Women, mostly, all within a few years of me in age. Service workers dressed identically to Birdie swept around the garden's perimeter, strange shiny fabric crinkling against itself, and a smattering of dancers with corset strings drenched in glitz waved feather fans and whispered low witty nothings to whomever sat beside them. By my estimation there were nine guests, or seven, two with plus-ones, and none of them were Industry Chauncey.

Nearest to me was a lovely dark girl in a brilliant blue evening gown in that same stitchless fabric the maids wore who laughed from her belly with her head tipped back, and directly beside her on the luminous color-shifting abject little bench sat a sallow girl with an eye patch who did not laugh and looked aggrieved to be breathing. The sallow girl wore a silk sash across her chest embroidered with fifty bronze hands reaching for nothing. Cisran nobility. The happy girl's accent sounded conspicuously familiar. Ignavia City, I'd guess.

Near the loathsome metal bench was a loathsome metal chair that held a Tullian girl who must be the Glitslough Loomis heir, whose comportment was so flawlessly Tullian that I felt like I might hyperventilate. Like any flawless Tullian girl, she did not speak unless called upon, and as nobody called upon her, she remained silent. She watched the galleries on the floor above us with acute focus. She had fresh lilies tucked in the straw of her bonnet. Somehow I tore my eyes off her.

Across the courtyard lounged a trio that watched the Tullian girl with open interest. They didn't touch any of the horrible furniture. Most demanding of visual attention was a perky Roystonian woman. *Clearly* Roystonian. She wore gloves cut from an ocelot and a smattering of silk ribbons in her rigorously sculpted yellow hair. Her face was powdered white, and her features small, without any edges. She smiled unendingly. That's Royston for you.

Beside her was a man. The man was a pirate. That is, the man was a prince warlord from the Crimson Archipelago. I wasn't sure which prince currently held power on Jira, the archipelago's federal center, but I wagered it was him, or would be him beyond year's end. He wore gold and coral jewelry and his heavy brocade military dress coat dangled off his shoulders like a cape, arms free, the impossibly delicate fabric of his shirt sleeves shoved thoughtlessly over his elbows. He would need a new shirt in the morning. His arms were tan, scarred. He'd earned his place. Behind him, fussing over a bead on his epaulettes, was a man so pretty I nearly mistook him for a crawly. He looked stern, had a dart between his beautiful brows, more delicate bone than hair. An advisor, maybe? The princess and the pirate whispered loudly. She snorted when she laughed.

To my right, one dark woman sprawled across a metal bench, glorious with gold leaf in her straight-back braids, with proud round features and a studied ease, adorned in the flowing robes of a Tasmudani hierophant. I had never met a hierophant. I'd seen illustrations. She looked enormously comfortable, happy to be stretched out, and mouthed things slowly at the woman who swayed against the bench's wicked back. The woman above her was tall and whippet thin, I could see the bone through the bridge of her nose, and wore a heavy stole over her slinky beaded dress. She had a frenetic air that peeked through the scene's boozy languidity. She never stopped moving. The tall woman was stunning. She and the hierophant were rapt in one another.

Above, leaning from the second story gallery, was the girl on the riverboat who'd nearly killed me. She wore a dress that looked like poured quicksilver. She smoked a long cigarette and flicked ash down on the garden. She radiated displeasure. She didn't seem to see me.

I recalled the sensation of her knife.

My blood foamed. I turned to Sisphe but Sisphe was gone. She'd floated over to the bench to my left, spoke brightly with secretarial crispness with the laughing woman in blue. The woman in blue seemed thrilled to talk to Sisphe, offered a stretch of the evil couch. Sisphe sat. She crossed her ankles and cozied into conversation. I wasn't sure if she'd seen the girl on the balcony. During that raid, I'd been wearing a mask. Sisphe had not. Recognizing Sisphe seemed extremely feasible. Sisphe is hypnotic. Who'd forget Sisphe? Not the girl who'd nearly murdered me in her defense, surely.

Music drifted from nowhere. I glanced around for Birdie, desperate for anyone with a name I knew.

The sallow girl with the Cisran silk sash touched her glass with open contempt. She brought it close to her face, examined the lines of the stem, the breadth of the belly of the bowl, the tannins streaking a rim around the inside. She pinched the stem between her thumb and middle finger, held her trigger finger and her pinky at stiff, exaggerated angles. Agonizing, nonsensical way to hold something. She said aloud to the happy girl in blue, "Murky crystal, thicker than phlegm. My mother cannot drink from a crystal heavier than a calligraphy quill or her fingers will bruise."

"Bubbly?" I flinched away and threw a hand behind me, touched where my rifle usually lived. Nothing. With effort I forced my lungs back into their pattern, and found the voice's source. Standing beside me, head inclined, was the tall angular woman with the stole. She gave me a slow smile, flicked her attention from me to Sisphe then back. Deep-set eyes, dark and rimmed with pink. She looked like she never slept. This close she smelled like sweet

cloves and yellowed paper. "You're Veracity's heir apparent, yes?"

I nodded sharply. Managed, "Yes ma'am," then kicked
myself.

"Helena Integrity Shane," she said. She spoke with a
low, smooth intensity, enunciated clearly but with more
breath than required. "Montrose's third baronet. I'm glad
you came. May I show you around?"

"Yes ma'am," I somehow said again. "Much obliged."

"Are you going to offer me your arm?"

I couldn't tell whether she was joking. Her inflection
didn't change. I offered my arm.

She quirked a brow, parted her lips in a little *ah*. Then
she took it, touched me so lightly that it didn't rumple the
fabric. "Forgive me that I've entreated you to join me in the
viper pit and don't even know your given name and Virtue.
I confess in advance that if your politics mirror your father's, if we consider your father's absenteeism a politic, you
and I will be enemies come morning. Until then I would
love to catch up. It's a treat to be in the company of someone who hasn't made themselves the pariah of even a single
Lunarist dinner party." She inclined her head toward me.
The dark waves she had pinned around her head shifted. A
loose curl fell free, bounced by the spoon of her collarbone.
"In order, there in blue is Ignavia City Baron Apparent
Ramtha thu Ramtha, that's Ramtha XII. Wonderful girl,
compulsively loveable, not here to woo Goss. They're old
friends and abstractly cousins, and already business partners beyond the point where marriage would bring further

advantage. Beside her is the Cisran Countess Alichsantre thu Alichsantre, that's Alichsantre L. If she smiles, leave the room. Flee. I could not begin to tell you what she wants. Sitting alone is Baron Apparent Susannah Loomis, whom I imagine wants to talk to you. She is about to inherit the Flip River delta. Besides that, she runs a literary magazine. Be kind, please. In the corner is Princess Perdita Perfection Vaughn. We call her Dita. She's a hereditary military commander in Royston. She is personally, on an individual level, the most reprehensibly violent person I have ever met. She's here seeking conquest cash. Beside her is Prince Mir of the Crimson Archipelago, fresh from usurping his older brother Hiram. He's a shipping magnate. He wants the keys to Susannah's house, so to speak. That's Mago with him, his man. From what I understand, Mago was Hiram's man until the hour of his death. Finally, there's darling Darya, High Hierophant from North City, Tasmudan. She's not here for Goss. She's here for the negotiation circus. Now. What ought I call you?"

"Thank you. Loveday. Pardon, if you please, what do *you* want in this, Helena Integrity? And who," my riverboat fighter dangled her wrists over the railing, her hair floating in a breeze that otherwise did not exist, "is that?"

"I want to prevent this continent's auto-cannibalism." She licked the corner of her mouth. "Why, that's little Miss Ichorite herself. I suppose you wouldn't have seen her before, I understand that your father has been obstinate about keeping the ichorite industry out of the Fingerbluffs. She's everywhere in IC. They're calling it Luster City now. It's tongue-in-cheek but I've heard the formal proposal's in motion. She's Vikare zel Tlesana, of the Tlesana fashion empire. She's Dignity's dearest friend and the face of the Luster Revolution. Everything is faced in iridescent chrome in the shape of her famously perfect body. The past three years, they've managed to worm their way into every major industry operating out of IC. People eat food from ichorite cans with ichorite spoons wearing ichorite clothing, sitting upon their ichorite chairs in their ichorite homes beside the fabulous ichorite railway. Chaunceyco has an emergent monopoly on the building blocks of daily life. That's largely on Dignity and Vikare."

Different story than young Chauncey, labor champion. My birthplace would be poisonous to me. I wondered about the new lustertouched. I wondered if any of them had died by living in the city. It'd be an endless fit for life.

Helena Integrity paused. Without applying more pressure, she whisked me beneath a potted palm, and before my horror about the immensity of things I could no longer safely touch sank in, Helena said, "Loveday, forgive me my intensity. I am going to be frank with you."

"Please," I said.

"When Dignity picks her lucky victim, the world will immediately change. Dignity is enormously rich in liquid capital. Whomever she marries will immediately become the wealthiest aristocrat in the world. If that person is Dita, Alichsantre, Mir, or maybe Susannah, war will claim millions of lives. Darya can't marry Dignity, her office doesn't allow it. Dignity has no reason to marry Ramtha. That leaves me and you. Everyone here, Mir and Darya aside, went to school together. Wilton is a special place that mutilates the human spirit. It is a machine that produces baby tyrants. We were horrible to each other. Unspeakable to each other. Alichsantre looks so sour because she, like you, has seen Vikare reclining above us. Vikare took Alichsantre's eye out. So. All the delicate indirect dancing negotiations that will determine the arrangement of wealth and power on the precipice of the ugliest war this side of the world has seen in centuries are being colored by years of hazing and hurt feelings. It doesn't help that, being the astrologists we are, most of us have been tangled at some point or the next."

"Astrologists," I repeated.

"Lunarists. The astrology club." She pursed her lips. "The society for women who prefer the company of women. Thus the overrepresentation of women, here. Poor Mir must not have been informed. That or he's the most arrogant man alive, which could be fun."

"Oh," I said. "You're crawlies."

Helena Integrity Shane went very still.

"That's alright," I said. She still held my arm, I put my hand over hers, scarcely brushing her knuckles. "I'm a boy-crawly. Real old-fashioned. I just haven't ever called it by that name before. What's astronomy got to do with it?"

She breathed hard between her teeth, gave me a wary smile. "This goes to my point. You are an eligible stranger, truly a stranger. Be aware that some girls here might get . . . touchy, hearing that word. The Lunarist Society does considerable legwork to impress upon outside observers that we

199

aren't the things crawlies are assumed to be. For respectability's sake." She said the word *crawlies* with great care, like she'd bitten into a pepper, and didn't want the sting to touch more than the tip of her tongue. Like she was surprised to have enjoyed the burn. "Tell me, Loveday. Do you want to see war in the Drustlands?"

"No," I said. "I don't want to see war in the Drustlands."

"Then my dear, I will do my very best to make sure that Goss Dignity Chauncey falls madly in love with you. Darya will collaborate with me on this project." She jerked her chin down. "Your beauty may well save the world."

Something fluttered in my gut. The spit was gone from my tongue. I glued my molars and twisted my wrist, made a quick gesture of gratitude, two fingers curled, two spread, thumb jutted wide from the index. Helena Integrity didn't notice. In my periphery, Susannah did. Quietly, I said, "Is Industry here?"

"Yann? No. He's in IC I imagine. He'll come around when Goss has made her choice." She cocked her head to the side, listened with her right ear scooped toward heaven, then straightened up. "She'll be here in a moment. Go look handsome. I'll sow seeds."

Industry wasn't here? Tough. I widened my stance and forced myself to focus. *Go look handsome* was a difficult command to follow. I felt grateful for Helena, and a cloying tension. I was here with an express purpose, the fulfillment of which would kill me. I had to avenge you. Preventing the conquest of your homeland seemed not unrelated to avenging you. It would be a moral imperative regardless of your

heritage. But understand that by this point my religion had
been retrofitted to center you. I venerated you constantly.
Discreetly but compulsively. I was possessed by you. In life
you owned nothing, in death you are pledged every morsel
in my mouth, every electric ripple in my skin, all the intensities of survival and destructive frivolity I experience. Every
breath in my lungs is yours. You are the Torn Child, I am
given to you, and my devotion to your memory is absolute.
You are the abstraction of hundreds of workers smashed
to gore and thousands of workers who bend and go brittle
before and after your death's blunt violence. Some of my
memories of you are probably stories I told myself. I don't
know if you really swindled the foreman for his silver lighter
and pawned it to buy us fresh fruit and hard cheese. I don't
know if your advice was always so crystalline, if you were
always keen and clever, if you were as small as I remember
you being. Nevertheless you had become inextricable from
my sense of self. Your ghost lived in the meat of me. I was
going to kill Yann Chauncey. I was going to kill him for you.
Would it be deceitful to promise this other thing, this thing
that I had not pledged to you, as a priority of mine? You told
such fantastic stories about the Drustlands. You told me
about the elkhinds, whose antlers grew from every part of
their body, more thorn bush than animal, and the maiden
wells where the souls of unmarried women would collect and
pollute the water so that anyone who drank it became fertile
but would bear children that were not their own. I could in-
corporate this into my project, couldn't I? I remembered the
smear made of Laith Hall.

Yes. No. I'd tell Sisphe. Harlow and Brandegor planned for war at home. Could that war have dual purpose? If we were victorious over Chaunceyco, would that not eliminate the funding source upon which this war depends?

Helena Integrity was no longer beside me. I hadn't noticed her move.

I turned on my heel, and in the middle of the room stood the woman in the oil portrait. Gossamer Dignity Chauncey, in the flesh.

Gossamer Dignity Chauncey looked ill. She was a boyish, reedy, violently redheaded woman, who wore her hair bluntly cut and slicked back behind her ears. Glacial eyes under bruised eyelids, a lopsided grin too big for her face, long limbs and long neck. One slim ichorite hoop in her left ear. She wore a fur coat over a herringbone suit. The cane she walked with glinted like black licorice. She was not a tall woman, but she filled the entire room with her huge whirring vitality. The air sucked out of my mouth and floated around her. Plants bent to face her. The sky hung lower and the ground lurched up. She strode into the middle of the courtyard, up to a statute I hadn't previously noticed in the haze of aristocrats, and struck it with the cane. She hit it like she intended to break it, a mean overhead swing, the kind I'd use to crush bone.

The statue shuddered, then coughed. It was a fountain. A trickle spilled from the serpentine urn's mouth, flowed down to the shallow bowl of its base.

Goss stepped back. She threw out her hands. "Dinner!"

Immediately a stream of servants in identical ichorite dresses, Birdie among them, carried out a round ichorite table, hollowed in the middle, which they carefully placed over the fountain. In a synchronized flurry, the maids rushed past each other, returning seemingly without having left bearing ichorite platers of veal and lamb, braised peacock, blanched lamprey, a jewel box of sliced fruits and vividly green spiraled vegetables, a barrage of roots and sculptural loaves of bread and sweets on intricate racks, and milks, lots of little pitchers of milk, which were arranged around plates that they shuffled and dealt with a speed any gambler in the Fingerbluffs might've admired. The feast unfurled in one continuous motion, and Goss collapsed in a bigger, even more horrible ichorite chair, one that looked like a splash of water suspended in space.

This feast was a nightmare. I could touch nothing. I should eat nothing. The fit intensified just being near it. It was an elaborate array of poison, all of it was poison, all of it would make my gums swell until my teeth popped like buttons. My throat would shut and my heart would stop, I would seep the iridescent serum from every hole in my body and flood this courtyard and kill everyone. I stood perfectly still. I panicked.

Goss hooked one hand around the back of her chair, swung her knee up and hooked it on the spindly metallic arm rest. I didn't have any illusion that I understood expected aristocratic conduct, but I sensed it wasn't this. This wasn't even expected Stellarine conduct. I stared in open awe and horror while heirs and performers swirled around me, took seats together around the table.

Someone's feathers brushed me.

I jumped, my heart lurched up between my teeth, and the performer who'd brushed me spun and took my wrists. She looked at me, and in my peril I allowed myself to look back, and under the blunt bangs and full face of makeup was a scowl I recognized. My stomach flipped. "Teriasa?"

Sunny's eyes shot wide. Her mouth popped open. She seized my big lapels and pulled me into a deep kiss, her tongue flicked between my teeth, my vision whirred and my breath caught and Sunny pressed against me, she fit her hands behind my head, pulled her lips up my jaw, took my earlobe in her teeth and hissed, "Marney, what the *fuck* are you doing here, you suicidal idiot!"

"I'm Velma Truth Loveday and I'm here to marry that redhead so I can kill Industry Chauncey," I managed. Where was her skinny boy? Where was her family in Cisra? I doubted I made a sound, my lungs hung limp in my chest, but she responded against my chest like she heard me. She curled her fingers in my ringlets, yanked them, *tsk*ed as they sprung back into place.

"Like my doll? You're insane. I hate you. I'm here to rob that redhead," she murmured. "Okay. We're a team. Play along."

"Yes ma'am. Yes'm." I'd missed her. Oh, sky.

She pulled back and slapped me. She wore the malachite bracelet. Its greenness traced an arc through the air.

Quick bright pain. I took it. After the ringing she caught my chin, jerked my head up, and said loudly enough for the room to hear, "You can't just take something that good away from me, Loveday!" Her face was a knot of fury and, startlingly, shyness. She looked flush, on the magenta edge of tears. "You can't show me paradise then abandon me!"

"I didn't abandon you, sugar." I dropped my voice low, felt protective of the vulnerability she wore. I knew it was a show, but I hadn't braced for fake reactions, so everything I had came from my gut. I took a step toward her, angled my shoulders between her and the clearly keen aristocrats. "I did everything you asked of me, and then it was done. I've hurt you, though. I'm sorry about that hurt."

"I'm a good girl, Loveday. I'm the best girl in the game. Don't you forget it." She sounded heartbroken. I couldn't stand it. She broke away from me before I got my arms around her, and I took a step after her, but kept my arms down, in sight, lest they move against her wishes. "My heart is not a toy."

"I'd cut down anybody who ever accuse it of being such," I said. Why the fuck was she here to rob Gossamer Dignity Chauncey? Had her man wronged her? Had something gone wrong? "You're brilliant, Teriasa. Knowing you made me richer. I—"

"That's enough," she said. She reached out, stroked my cheek with the back of her knuckles, then stormed away, collapsed into a chair beside Sisphe, who was happier than any human being had ever previously been.

I stood still, blinking.

Goss, Mir, and Dita zealously clapped their hands.

I sat. The only empty chair was between Dita and Alichsantre, and I stared straight ahead, looked at neither of them. I especially did not look at Helena Integrity. I wasn't sure what her appraisal of the show might be. Oh, Sunny. Why are you here? The chair hummed underneath me. The clothes were thick enough that I didn't immediately fall into a fit, but a fit felt inevitable. Conversation struck up immediately. Largely not about me. The aristocrats spoke avidly and quickly about nothing, about weather and the taste of the food I hadn't touched. More laughter. Mir and Darya were in tears over something I couldn't parse. Susannah was talking to Sisphe now, and she was smiling to herself with ideal Tullian demure, eyes downcast, hands fluttering between slight shapes. Curiosity, gratitude, more please, yes please. Ramtha spoke animatedly with a performer and Alichsantre, who contributed monosyllabic responses and didn't take her eyes off her plate, occasionally elaborating on her opinions of the meal—wet, over-spiced, cheap, too lean, too experimental, sans technique. Dita caught my hand.

I looked at my hand in Dita's hand.

Dita beamed. She was all scrunched nose and dimples, too cute for all her powder, then her big bright smile flipped, and she pouted at me. She stamped her slippered foot under the table. The sound was louder than a slipper ought make. Alichsantre jumped. "How come we haven't met before? You're pretty. You've been keeping yourself from me. That's not very sweet of you."

"I don't leave the Fingerbluffs," I said too curtly.

Her smile returned. Very curved. "Stern. I like that. What did you do to that whore?"

I took a moment. Turned to look at Dita properly and willed myself not to strangle her. "Exactly what she asked of me."

"And what was that? I don't know anything about these things." She thickened her accent, made the *th*'s into lispy *z*'s. "I'm a student of the world and I would love to learn everything about you and your magic whoreslaying powers. I'm Princess Perdita Perfection, by the way. Aren't you gonna kiss my knuckles?"

I broke her hold and caught her wrist, twisted it. Discomfort, not hard enough to bruise. "Probably not. Pardon."

She grinned *wider*. The corners of her mouth went up, not out. She broke my hold with a strength I hadn't expected, moved exactly how I had, down to the twitches, just faster. I smiled despite myself, surprised by her harshness. She twisted my wrist harder than I'd twisted hers. Pain popped behind my eyelids. There's so much Helena Integrity had said to me. I tried to shuffle through the details quickly, landed on, *this girl is a soldier*. She didn't look like a soldier. She was small-statured and curvaceous, she spilled over the neckline of her bodice, but I doubted she'd clear the height and weight requirements for the Enforcer Corps. Could the likes of her have destroyed Laith Hall? Could she slaughter farming communities of armed Hereafterist milkmaids?

207

As I marveled at this she flicked her wrist. Something tore between layers of my skin. The pain was throbbing bright and crystalline, a hilarious feeling. Then she lifted her plump, peachy hand, stripped of its ocelot glove, and pressed her first two knuckles against my bottom lip, a punch in slow motion. Feeling more than thinking, I brought my lips forward, kissed the air above her nails. Dita preened. She brought my hand down, set it in her lap, cradled it against the taffeta that swept around her thighs, and I hallucinated briefly that she and I had met in the bars in the Fingerbluffs. I would've pulled her apart. My tongue was numb and stiff in my mouth. Talking was difficult. I was very good at *this*. I knew how to do this. Adrenaline glittered behind my eye sockets and, blurring with the lurching florid early-fit symptoms, I elected to let my body move without close supervision. I trusted my sinew to twitch where it ought.

Across the table Darya had an arm slung around Ramtha's neck, mirroring a performer whose bodice hung open, fell down across one shoulder and breast like a mother on a playing card. Darya and the performer swayed together against Ramtha, whose brow was smooth listening to whatever Darya breathed above her ear. Helena Integrity glanced at me occasionally, but seemed fixed on Susannah, who devotedly cut a strawberry into slices so thin they looked translucent. A slice curled off the edge of her knife. It looked like a blossom opening. It seemed believable for a moment that the details of my fit were real, that the swirling gemstone distortion on every surface was the truth of that surface, that everyone was glowing and glossy and melting into their chairs.

"It's rotten," said Alichsantre, "it's crass."

I wasn't sure where Sisphe had gone. I turned my head to find her, looked across the kaleidoscope laughter of this whole continent's legal heirs and all their pearly molars, and I couldn't see her.

Princess Perdita Perfection Vaughn slid my hand down her knee. I understood mechanically, I walked my fingers along the edge of her frothy skirt until I found the ruffled hem. The little rhinestone pattern was heavy. Did she have diamonds tucked in this lace? Or coins? I imagined myself kneeling on the floor between her ankles with knife in hand and prying all the rhinestones loose. A worthy raid all on its own. Dita's stockings were so delicate that the edge of my chewed-down nails might've torn them. It must take such precise care to roll them over her calves without the whole structure unraveling and falling apart in a mess of silver string. I touched her lightly, only the pads of my fingertips, traced the soft hollows behind her knee, along the seams of her full fleshy thigh, warmer, higher. I felt the livid muscle under her unfathomably soft skin. This fucking warmonger. I felt knuckles brush my knuckles. Somebody else's knuckles.

I paused. Flicked my eyes up.

Goss Dignity Chauncey, to Perfection's right, mirrored me. She traipsed a hand beneath Perfection's skirt and looked not at Perfection, but at me. Her eyes were dead blue under her spray of red eyelashes. Eerie eyes, milky corpse eyes, spectral pale like a revenant's. It looked like her

pupils were a too-pale shade of blue. They reflected nothing. Dignity's hand drifted against mine. A look flickered
across her face, I couldn't tell if it was annoyance or amuse-
ment. The corner of her mouth flickered. She mouthed,
Hello Fingerbluffs.

Perdita Perfection reclined in her chair. She folded her
hands politely and rested them on the table, rocked her head
back, parted her pink mouth with a sigh. She was adorable.
I wanted to thrash her. I blinked, looked back at Dignity, at
the heir to the man who'd ordered the deaths of everybody
I'd ever met before the age of twelve, at every promise of
Ignavian progressivism condensed into one mortal girl, and
had no idea how to impress her. Surely this couldn't impress
her. I needed to impress her so that I could kill her father.
What was I to do?

Dignity hooked our index fingers together. She tossed
her head to the side, nodded at a door out of the courtyard that led into some cavernous recess of this godless
play-temple of a house.

It occurred with a jolt that if I took off even my gloves
they'd kill me.

I had tattoos everywhere. Everywhere. My identity
adorned my chest. I had a whip spider tattooed on my belly,
on the stretch of muscle between my navel and my pubic
hair. If I took my clothes off, Lady Atrocity would take it
as kill me immediately. What had I thought? Had I expected propriety from the baron class? Perdita Perfection
Vaughn wasn't even a baron, she was a *princess*, and I had no
concept of how to even begin to anticipate the actions of a

Roystonian brutality princess. Fucking at the table? She's a princess. Why not?

Dignity swept her thumb over my first and second knuckles. It was a soft feeling through the glove.

Sharp through the noxious pink haze came Birdie's voice. She stood at the front door, but somehow her voice was clear enough that I heard it even through distance and my delirium. Birdie said, "Strife Maiden Dunn Ygrainne," a pause, "and guard."

The sultry heat that hung around the table dissipated. Sober winter took us. Dignity sat upright. Perdita's head snapped down, her eyes on fire as a small, tight smile replaced her pouty panting. Across the table in a ripple, everyone's posture went rigid. Helena looked grave serious and older, her smile gone. Mir put his hands behind his head and rocked onto the back legs of his chair, the posture of arrogant nonchalance I'd seen as prelude to innumerable bar fights. Susannah flinched back, Alichsantre leaned forward, Sisphe was still nowhere to be seen. Then, a shock to everyone at the table, Ramtha stood. She smoothed her preternaturally smooth ichorite dress and her infectious happiness, which I now understood was deliberate, softened. She looked each of us in the face.

"Beloved friends and peers, you inspire me every day with your commitment to your constituents. I am so moved to have such brilliant beautiful girls and Mir by my side, guiding me and demonstrating with their own diligence what positive thinking and initiative can accomplish. Our duties are great and our faith is greater." Ramtha had a warm, inflective voice. I noticed now she dialed her IC affectations back. She chewed her language. Every syllable was considered. She spread her hands, affected the most casual iteration of a formal oratory stance I'd ever seen. She stretched a hand behind her, toward the door where *Strife Maiden Dunn Ygrainne and guard* had been announced. The darkness beyond her fingertips flexed as though it were soaked in tremendous heat. Slashed leaves nodded away from the opening, curling, bracing.

"I took it upon myself," she continued, "in the spirit of concord and hospitality, to invite to this party one Miss Ygrainne of Dunn Hall, a recently elected strife maiden from the Drustish assembly. I'm so excited she came all this way! In all my correspondence with her, she's consistently impressed upon me that she shares our values, and I am confident by the end of your little contest, Goss, we'll all be bosom friends."

The atmosphere itched. Any movement at all could've started a fire.

Delicately, Susannah said, "Contest?"

Gossamer stole her hand from Perdita's skirt and stood up. She smoothed her hands down her fur coat, stroked the foxes as though they were still alive, and looked at Ramtha with an intensity I thought would kill her. She jutted out her chin. "Bring her in, Birdie."

The door opened. Surely it had not groaned like that when Sisphe and I came inside.

A woman entered quickly, her tall pale guard one pace behind her. She wore gray traveling clothes. *Ignavian* traveling clothes, lambskin gloves and a tailored wool coat to her ankles, which she swiftly unbuttoned and swept back across her waist, showing the embroidered smock beneath. It was pretty and implacable. I'd never seen a garment like it. The woman, Strife Maiden Dunn Ygrainne, did not smile at us. Her square face was set. She folded her hands at the small of her back and clicked her heels together. Her guard, unquestionably the tallest and palest woman I'd ever seen, had pendulous white-blond braids down to her thighs whose motion continued even when she stood behind the strife maiden at attention.

Ygrainne said nothing. She looked at Goss.

"Strife Maiden–Elect Dunn," Ramtha started.

"Ygrainne," said Goss. "Is that your name, darling?"

"Dunn Ygrainne," Ygrainne said curtly. She had a surprisingly high voice.

Goss didn't blink. "Do you want to be my wife?"

"This depends. From what Hall did you hail in your youth?"

Gossamer Dignity Chauncey's lips turned white. She straightened her posture, pulled away from Ygrainne.

"You are Drustish," Ygrainne said. "Yes?"

"Funny plus-one you've invited, Ramtha. Plus-two. We lack adequate seating. No matter. I'll make some for you." Gossamer snatched up her cane with one hand, and seized Perdita's sleeve with the other. Tension passed between them. Gossamer's face tightened and Perdita's unreadable sweetness got sweeter. Even if Perdita was stronger than Goss, her floating pink sugar sleeve was not, and Perdita stood after a moment, delicately accepted the offered elbow. Her eyes trained on Ygrainne. I half expected her to start barking. Gossamer inclined her head toward the Drustish women, then turned on her heel, stormed out of the courtyard. Perdita's skirts billowed around them like a mist.

Ygrainne's expression didn't change. She sat in Gossamer's seat. She had incredible economy of movement, no gesture wasted. She didn't fidget. She didn't touch the food. Her guard sat beside me, inclined her head and murmured something inaudible, then reached for a ribbon of meat. She pinched its purpleness and popped it between her teeth, chewed, swallowed. Nodded to Ygrainne. Ygrainne then made herself a plate, and slowly conversation bubbled up, thanks to the persistent unflinching friendliness of Ramtha thu Ramtha.

I had to follow Goss.

I didn't want to let her out of my sight.

As I stood I fumbled around the bear trap of my memory for something, anything, Brandegor might've told me about Drustish politics. She'd spoken of the Drustlands so little after Laith Hall. That's not what we did together. When she was drunk, sometimes Brandegor would boast about blood feuds between Halls. Her Hall, Mors Hall, had struck a feud with Shae Hall. Neither Hall was rich enough to settle the feud with gold or cattle. Instead, they'd snipe one another's family members, heir by heir, until both Halls stood vacant and fell to rot. Brandegor sometimes told the story this way, that she had been the last soldier of a conflict that'd swallowed everyone she'd ever known. Sometimes when she told it, she spoke about her exile, because when it'd been her time to kill a Shae, she'd killed someone too precious. Her greed changed the stakes from war thralls and bull maids to Hall fathers and reap mothers. Sometimes the whole feud was her fault. She boasted about her upbringing, but the details were huge and fantastic, and I struggled to pan them for anything like comfort. I thought about a spat we had. She'd knocked me upside the head, then sat on the cliff beside me, held a dripping goat steak against my screaming eye. She'd said something about you. Something to comfort me about your loss.

In stiff Mors Drustish I said to the guard, "We'll remember these wrongs with our hands."

The guard looked at me. Steam-gray eyes spanned the world. She licked her fingers, not blinking, then said something in Drustish I didn't understand. My ignorance must've showed on my face. The guard grunted. Under her breath in terse Cisran she said, "Find me alone."

I stood up. Another glance around the table confirmed that Sisphe wasn't here. Sunny wasn't either. That gnawed. Mir and Darya watched me stand, the rest did not, immersed in talking to, or not talking to, Strife Maiden Dunn Ygrainne. I stepped around the table and crossed the courtyard, horrified at myself, horrified at the way the air tasted, and sick and starving and wet. The fragrant plants bobbed and slithered. Some night bird sang unseen. I found the door I assumed concealed them, opened it.

Memories rolled over me, ichorite exposure's consequence. Sweat and ache and grinding teeth of every laborer

215

who'd beat that table into shape. A worker who's fallen across our feet and convulses because the metal had reached for him, it had felt him, it coils around his pulse and flutters. No help for us, the factory doors would not open, there were no breaks until shift's end, and the man crawls under the assembly line while we hammer. Our backs scream, the spines in our muscles crunched, and the man underneath sobs, he spasms and claws his wrist, he weeps that the ichorite had touched him, not him it, it him, and we knew it to be true because as we beat the metal it licks the edges of our hammers.

Hallway.

Less barren than the front room, there was a carpet runner and a fresco. Bellonan heroes burying divine monsters. There was a staircase and a series of doors, two locked, one leading to a vacant parlor, the next a broom closet. I went up the stairs. I didn't parse the information that'd been so quickly handed to me. I didn't sift through anything. I needed eyes on the link to my target. I didn't have socializing in me. I needed Sisphe for that. I needed Sunny, and I needed to throw myself on the floor and howl and beat my hands blue against the marble. I had a war. I had a role in that war.

I'd say I thought I'd play with them. I'd be coy enough to keep my clothes on. Veracity was insane. Maybe the gloves and boots could be control props. Not too far from the truth. I could do that. I could be unkind on request. I shook my hands out, yearned for the weight of my gun on my back. I rounded a corner. The courtyard faced me through the open gallery, supported by the occasional fluted column and a slender bone white banister.

Vikare smoked there. I saw her shoulder blades move. She wore her hair loose, it spilled over her shoulder, exposed the nape of her neck. Her silver dress looked like fresh ichorite, the raw glistening liquid we squeezed out of sludge in the foundry. It flowed over her body. She shifted, it traced the backs of her thighs. Without looking up she said, "They're downstairs."

"Pardon my intrusion," I said.

"It's not my house." She took a drag and sighed. "Come here."

I stood beside her at the railing. The dinner party looked happy from here. Candlelight looked gorgeous on the poisonous furniture. I thought about lamplights on wet pavement. Vikare passed me her cigarette and I accepted it with murmured thanks, held it to my lips. Mentholated. I liked the tingle in my throat. Real tingles made the delusional tingles bearable. I passed it back.

"Will you marry Gossamer?"

The rail was slick. I wanted to touch it barehanded. The cold would feel divine. I felt faint. "Yes ma'am," I said. "That's why I came."

"Why?"

Would that I were Candor. Or Sisphe. Would that I were you. "I'm looking for love."

"Liar."

"I am."

"Love is not enough."

"It's not," I said. "Still, I like to look."

"How will you spend our money?" Vikare blew a ring, then a ring through a ring.

I watched them melt into nothing. "Mostly I won't."

"You're stupid."

"Mhm." *Our* was interesting. Funny to think I'd robbed them already. Could she have killed me if I weren't so spent? Surely not. "I'd quadruple every Chaunceyco worker's wage and halve their hours."

Vikare looked at me with her eyes half-shut, her brows drawn low. Her bottom lip was overfull. I noticed the lack of ring again. Uncanny. "Why do I know you?"

"You don't," I said.

"I know you," she pressed.

"You can't know me. If we'd met, I'd never forget it."

"Hold out your wrist."

My wrist was a map of ink and scars. I inclined my head. "Forgive me. Not tonight."

She stared unblinking, lovely and sullen, and lay down her wrist on the banister. The veins in her arm showed lurid green. She snuffed her cigarette against her pulse. Orange sparks and smoke. She didn't so much as flinch. She tossed the cigarette down, pulled her arm off the banister, and pressed her hand against my breastbone. Her palm burned. "I'll be there when you stumble, Fingerbluffs."

"The attention's an honor."

"I will keep you down."

She meant kill me. I knew she could kill me. I knew she would. She'd tuck her knife under my jaw and ram it through my tongue, through my soft palate, through the wet pink folds of my brain. She put out Alichsantre's eye, Helena said. She'd put out my eye. She'd mutilate me. She'd dangle me from this balcony and give my body to the crows.

I put my hand over hers. "Are you in love with Dignity?"

"Not anymore."

Below us, Goss reappeared on the scene. She was flanked by a battalion of shiny maids and bodyguards, who circled the table and swept away the dishes and trays. Gossamer's voice echoed to heaven. The lungs on her! She said, "There are too many of you! Let's winnow. Be up at dawn. Lo we go a-hunting. Stay behind and a servant will help you pack. Thank you for your company. As wonderful Ramtha said, you're inspiring to look upon. My home is yours. Relax. Drink, fuck, unwind. Don't be late. Sweet dreams."

Ripples around the table. Susannah stood, I saw the candlelight glance off her bonnet. She moved her hands, I saw the posture of intervention, the pose the Night made the Day to beg truce. It startled me, how moved I was. It'd been a long time since I'd gone to see a Shrine. Gossamer didn't see it. Gossamer was gone. My hand was empty. I touched my own breast. Vikare must've slipped away too. Everyone dissolved into vapor. I touched myself. Still breathing. Blood moving underneath my clothes. I was sick of my clothes. I pushed the rail away and sought my room.

Ten

TRICKSY AND SUNNY CONSPIRED IN THE CREAMY
brocade bedroom where I was meant to sleep. Sisphe and
Teriasa. I shut the door, dragged a chair away from a writing desk and shoved it beneath the handle, walked around
them and their pile of pilfered papers, shut the lush curtains, sealed off every spy port that occurred. I stripped
off my jacket, hung it up. I stripped off my gloves, put one
boot against the windowsill and unlaced it, then the other.
I toed them off. I slipped my bracers off my shoulders. I
unbuttoned my pants. They dropped around my ankles. I
gathered them, folded them. I stripped off my shirt. I folded
it too. I unbuckled my empty harness, which I wore habit-
ually regardless of intent, dangled the ring from my finger.
There was no hook to hang it on. I stashed it on the coat
rack. Then I knelt, unbuttoned the sock garters, peeled the
fabric off my calves. Rough, tough wool. Princess Perdita
Perfection Vaughn's stockings came to mind. I banished the

thought. I thought about the corpses in the shell of Laith Hall. I laid the socks out for washing. Naked, I turned and faced my brilliant friends. Neither of them had stopped their scheming. I lay on the floor behind them and stretched my body on the hardwood. The chill was delightful. I wanted to scream. Instead I said softly, "Where is Colton Gallantry?"

"Where all good Hereafterists go." Teriasa didn't look at me. She resumed her research conversation in low fluid tones and I thought about the illustrated pamphlet in my room back home. The hatching on the azurine tree.

"You will be the handiest ancestor," Sisphe said. She made a quick gesture, a salute to a fallen comrade, then stabbed a note with her nail. "I will pray to you every single night and kiss all your little metal fingertips. They're fucked! Ignavia City's economy, fuck, the bulk of municipality's physical infrastructure, IC itself, is terminally dependent on ichorite production. All commodities out of IC are either Chaunceyco products, Chaunceyco subsidiaries, or need Chaunceyco materials. Goss put her fingers in everything. Without an exponentially expanding ichorite supply the city's dead. Chaunceyco has sixty-five square miles. That's all the space outside IC that Ramtha has to give. That land is dry. They've torn up everything north of here, and Geistmouth's denied expansion rights five times. They're scoffing at a silly number. Too many zeros in that number. Geistmouth is too conservative, believes too strongly in the birthright of barony, thinks that Goss is a degenerate crawly burnout. I've never been so grateful for bigotry. The end is in sight. If Goss doesn't get married fast, everything folds. They have what, a year? Less, if they're expanding like this. It'll sunder the whole country's commercial output."

"Was handiest ancestor a pun?" Teriasa made a face. "I've been in and out of the Chauncey penthouse in IC for months. Since she and Vikare broke things off. Goss doesn't have relationships with any of her performers, I doubt she knows my name, but she has panic attacks when she thinks she's alone. I'm salaried. That's to say that I've spent a lot of time in the catastrophe she calls her study, and I know how many bridges she's burned for having such a high opinion of herself. It's not just Geistmouth that won't touch her. Kimball, Olmstead, and Burnside have all put forward petitions against policy shifts allowing corporations to function like baronies.

"Goss doesn't want Chaunceyco to functionally become its own barony with its own senate seat, though she'll argue that until her throat gives out the second someone lets her speak at Senate if she can't make a marriage work." Teriasa paused for a moment. She drummed her nails on the floor, then spoke a little lower, as though she was recounting something sordid. "Goss is a convincing progressive. She and Vikare are champions for women's rights, women with liquid cash or land to give, I should say, and for the theory of the individual. That's the drug. Goss is all about the individual. She'll argue for individual rights, make a spirited plea that the barons are tyrants whose existence forecloses the chance of upward mobility and squanders human potential. There are creative, innovative, brilliant minds scattered in the mud of Ignavia, she'll cry, damned to serfdom. She pushes policy change that would hypothetically enable the quick and the clever to climb into the light, earn and achieve and accrue their own riches, which those bright minds can use to put their dreams to practice, and create industries, advance the ambitions of Ignavia's future Yann Chaunceys. The beast will reproduce itself."

"Barons *are* tyrants," Sisphe said.

"Extremely. Tyrannical and, let's be honest, played out. Barony lacks a certain populist verve. It's not as sexy as it used to be. Goss looks like progress. Goss says your life has potential and you could be as rich as her if you suffer. *That's* sexy. If Goss gets her way, it means the barons will cede their power, which looks like revolution to people who hate Hereafterists. The barons will retain some influence, maybe glimmers of hereditary power's allure, but most barons are *poor*.

"Consider the imaginary Lovedays. What was the Fingerbluffs before the Choir? Azurine groves outproduced by Glitslough, collapsed salt mines, and a shoreline so rocky only smugglers will risk its use. Not a drop of liquid cash. No relevancy, either. If a baron believes in Ignavian wealth and is committed to a successful integrated state across barony lines, they'll fold. They'll give Goss what she wants and let her coup them, invest in her business, sit pretty in their tarnished shareholder mimicry of the real wealth they just surrendered. Yann Industry Chauncey is richer than the king of Royston. If he's not richer than the queen of Cisra, he will be soon. Ignavia could rival Tasmudan. Old Bellona couldn't contend with Tasmudan. It's a staggering increase."

"If it's sustainable," said Sisphe.

"Right."

"They're confident there is *more* ichorite? Have you found anything that says what this shit actually is?"

"Funny you ask." Teriasa leaned forward with a conspiratorial hush. "Ichorite miners live in makeshift towns around the mines, and *aren't allowed to leave*. It's in their contracts. Spouses live in the company town, family elders too. Heaven knows what they'll do when the kids raised there are old enough to squeal."

"Kill them," I said.

Sisphe and Teriasa went quiet.

"The kids will be lustertouched. They'll kill them young. Or take them. With all the torment Whip Spider's given them, I doubt they'll make the mistake they made with me twice." I sniffed. "Didn't mean to interrupt. I was listening. Carry on."

"We don't know that the lustertouched are all dead," Sisphe said gently. "I'm going to look."

"I can't believe you, Marney." Teriasa curled her lip. "You named your baron after my babydoll."

"I did," I said. "I missed you."

She touched my arm. I wish she hadn't.

"Marney," Sisphe said. "Do you remember what the raw ore looked like? I know you were little."

"Mud," I said. "Bad meat. It was hard in thin shattering layers, but not through all of it. Mostly it was mud. You

have to heat the sludgy mud, then crush all the hard layers. That's how the liquid comes out. Then you cool then
heat then cool the liquid, and it'll be whatever you want. Or
you beat it into something else." My hands felt grimy. I hid
them under my belly.

Quiet again. I itched.

I said, "What does Royston gain by attacking the
Drustlands? What benefit would the other post-Bellonan
states get out of this?"

"Ah." Teriasa examined her nails. "Royston is delusional. The king is fixated on Royston as the seat of *New
Bellona*, with himself as holy emperor, naturally. They
want new land and imperial accolades. If they take the
Drustlands, they'll have done what Bellona couldn't.
Invading the Drustlands to make a chintzy little empire is
a stupid idea that Royston has been flailing at for centuries,
undoubtedly more urgently now that Ignavia's sudden incomprehensible wealth in the hands of the unpedigreed has
rendered Royston politically irrelevant. Royston has guns
now. Presumably so does the Drustlands, if fewer. Some
pirate or the next would supply them, I'm sure. Drustish
refusal to industrialize has made the Drustlands few friends.
Xenophobia doesn't help. If Royston launched a full-scale
invasion into the Drustlands, there's a chance there wouldn't
be continental intervention in the Drustlands' defense. But
oh! Wouldn't that be the most expensive thing in the world!
Royston has no money. They need Chauncey's money.
If they had Chaunceyco's backing, that's curtains for the
Drustlands. They'd raze it."

I felt violently ill and then my nerves vibrated a cooling all-consuming nothing. I felt nothing. I recalled the pig with the bayonet stuck in its head. I did not scream. I thought about Burn Street. I squeezed my eyes shut and opened them wide.

"Who'd say yes to that?" Sisphe rubbed her wrists. "It's easy to have cute delusions. I have them all the time and everybody likes them. Why would someone throw down money to flatten a nation unprovoked?"

I knew what Uthste would say to that. I pictured Teriasa and her delicate beloved sitting around a revolutionary's table, planning just like this. I imagined them hopeful. Bright faces and true faith in Hereafter being right there, just past their fingertips, one painful stretch away. No more tyranny. No more property. No borders, no jail yards, no wars except the one. I imagined Teriasa smiling. I imagined the wisp of her lover curled around her shoulders, thin as smoke.

"They have the far coast. They've got land, surely it could be used for something. Imagine how many factories you could cram in the inhospitable badlands. All the sweltering strip mines you could dig. The displaced who will find themselves in need of shelter, who could be made to work to earn food. Imagine if there's ichorite in the ground there. Throbbing, moaning ichorite." I rolled over. The ceiling was gilded. I wanted to catch something on fire. "I could kill everyone here. I could go through everyone's room and kill them in their beds, I'd do it quiet. We could leave this place unmolested. Would that stop the war?"

"Everyone here has equivalents that'd carry out the work." Teriasa lay back. She rested her head near my belly. I wondered if she had children. How old they'd be, if she had. "Do you want to kill everybody here?"

"Not everyone." I knew the pattern, I knew the project to overcome it, but I knew that Yann Industry Chauncey had no equivalent. When I killed him, the wound on his project would be grievous. The body of the beast will remain, but it will hemorrhage, its systems will fester and we the Choir will destroy the last twitching remains and leave nothing. With the means of its manufacture we will make a choice about what's to be done. They'll make a choice. I'll be dead then. Torn be praised. I love you. I love you. Besides which, I liked Helena.

"Personally, I would love love *love* if we could falsify thousands upon thousands of enforcer layoffs. Just preemptively diminish the forces against us. What if we were awful enough that the Corps demanded a strike? Alongside that, I want to elaborately fuck up the supply chains. I want to find plans for new dig sites. I want to find the other lustertouched."

I tried to imagine an enforcer scab but stopped when my pulse changed. I put a hand on my chest, I pressed down hard, I tried to keep my head right. Burn Street in my mouth. Burn Street caked in my ears, greasing my scalp. I had not spoken to another lustertouched since that morning, and I'd hardly spoken to them. They were fucking babies. I didn't want to spend time with babies, I was little and stupid, and terrified of being condemned to the sort of

227

womanhood that demanded their infinite making. I didn't remember their names. I didn't remember anybody's name. I rolled onto my side, I pushed a knee underneath myself and readied my body for flight.

Teriasa eased herself backwards. She eased her head against me. I didn't dare move. I couldn't speak, but could touch her hair. She didn't flinch from my hand. She closed her eyes. Purple veins showed across the spoons of her eyelids. Oh, Sunny. I'd been robbed of a sweet reunion. I felt rotten and evil all of a sudden. The feeling pervaded my whole body. It mingled with the panic. I pet her hair and damned myself.

"Forging things outright would be difficult," Teriasa said. "Altering things already created might be doable. Goss is extremely attentive with vision and delegation, but once she's passed something along, she expects the person to whom she's handed off the task to take care of it. I think she and Yann both manage the Enforcer Corps, Yann more so, but it's not Goss's area of interest, and Yann has been—unwell."

"Unwell?" Found my voice. I started to sit again and stopped when I realized it'd displace her. I needed Teriasa where she was. "I need him to be alive to kill him."

"He's depressed," she said plainly. "I've barely seen him. He hates performers. He and Goss fight about it. Yann Chauncey had a long engagement with Ramtha thu Ramtha, that's the current baron, which broke off half a decade before the younger Ramtha was born. It's difficult for him."

"Relationships?"

"Proximity to women. I think he's been tolerant of Gossamer's androgyny because it makes rarer any whiffs of femininity in his home."

I winced. Hunger spasmed, I wondered for a moment how I'd get off the floor. Dawn surely wasn't far. I wouldn't sleep. I could shoot better than any flouncy aristocrat, that was for fucking certain, but unslept and starving? Tough. "Helena Integrity Shane cornered me to tell me she wants me to marry Dignity. Or Baron Apparent Loveday, that is. I don't know how she intends to help, but she's made it clear that she's going to intervene somehow."

"I've never met Helena before tonight," said Teriasa. "I've got no read on her."

"Did I hurt you, Sunny?"

"No." Pain flashed across her face. "You wouldn't know how."

"You've got to get dressed, Marney. You've got to go kill something in the woods."

"I can't fucking eat here. Ichorite plates."

"Hm. I'll swipe things from the kitchen for you," Teriasa said.

"You could pretend you hate the taste. Ichorite does have an aftertaste. It's tangy," said Sisphe. "Be a diva. I love divas. Candor would've been so polite. You can do bitchy for contrast!"

She sat upright and I rolled, got my feet under me. My body felt awful. I jumped on the balls of my feet, threw myself against the carved oak wardrobe, pinched and twisted the skin on my arms and stomach. Come, adrenaline. Come, crushed lights in the blood. Exhaustion clung. I cracked my neck and looked to my friends. Sisphe dug through my bag. Teriasa daubed her makeup in the mirror.

"From the kitchen would be wonderful, thank you Teriasa," I said. "Could one of you slap me?"

"You're ridiculous," said Sisphe.

Teriasa put down her blotting paper. She looked me up and down. Eyed my tattoos and whatever else. Then she looked me in the eye and slapped the wind out of me.

I caught myself on the footboard and hauled my body upright. All the colors in the room brightened and seemed to shine. I nodded my thanks, shook myself, and put on what Sisphe threw at me. I fetched my boots and gloves. I put back on the coat. My body felt cotton-stuffed and numbed out. I wondered vaguely if Teriasa had a tincture on her. I just brought the resin. No matter. "Should I pretend I didn't bring my gun?"

"Your gun," Sisphe said, "is famous. Forgetting is just fine."

"I love you," I told them both. All three of you. "I'll be back when I've killed something big."

THE MORNING CAME and the hunt with it.

I'd never killed an animal before. Seems I despise the whole thing.

Every human person I killed had raised arms against me. They'd taken up weapons in the name of property, and I felt no shame in their destruction. Avoiding murder's natural atrocity was not a possibility for me. The enforcers I'd killed had killed others with impunity. I could not be better than them. We fought as human monsters, equal in agency and its opposite, and we killed each other.

We hunted wolves. Aimed for wolves, anyway. Other little living things would do. Fern fronds grew as tall as our thighs, and we waded through the feathered spirals with tracking pigs weaving between our feet, grunting and wheezing. Perdita walked in the front, humming to herself, skipping like she did not have a rifle in hand. She'd killed three coyotes that morning, the most of anyone. It was clear that Ramtha and Susannah knew how to hold a gun in a purely academic sense, and neither could take the kickback. Mir was a fantastic shot but a nightmare in the morning. He walked with his eyes shut, snarling and whining, and Mago his beautiful advisor gracefully leashed him along and paused him when it came time to abuse the wildlife. He'd killed two coyotes and wounded a third. Gossamer, as miserable as Mir despite this having been her idea, hadn't killed a single thing. Helena had shot a series of quail. Montrose was a mountain barony, I imagine she'd been hunting all her life. Alichsantre and Dunn Ygrainne talked in the back of the group, speaking quietly. A cultural commonality between Cisra and the Drustlands was, it seemed, that this was grunt work. They were noblewomen. They were above this.

I was not above this. It repulsed me but I was not above what repulsed me. The problem was, I felt so tired I thought that I might die.

"Loveday," Mir said to me. Mago steered him closer to me, and he looped an arm around my shoulder, cocked his head to the side. He smelled like smoke and lemongrass. There were hickies on his neck. I wondered about Mago. "I know your secret."

I was too fucking tired for a fit. I was too tired to panic. "That so?"

"You're filthy." He squeezed his eyes shut with visible strain, then stretched them, like that'd force them into wakefulness. "You are creamed and dripping with pirate riches. Mountains of coral and gold in every corner of your pretty little seaside mansion. You've cut a deal with the Archipelago pirates, don't lie to me, don't you fucking lie about it. You did it. You dog."

I eyed the canopy line. "How'd you figure?"

"Your father *hates* pirates. Or hated, back when he was normal. The way the story gets told, Veracity would himself go down with cannons to sink smuggler ships. He *was* the border. Nothing got by him, and anything that tried got strung up in his town square. Then of course, he lost his fucking mind. Insensitive of me. Let me try again. He went batshit crazy. Locked himself inside the mansion and the rest is history. Now. Pirates haven't been picking fights with *me* for the ports I control elsewhere along the coast. When Veracity was breaking their teeth under his boot, they'd make themselves my father's problem, and they haven't made themselves *my* problem. Somebody's putting out. I think it's you. I think you've made some little arrangement with them. Safe passage and you get a cut, yeah?

Well, good on you. We're all fucking pirates. If I hadn't won my succession, assuming Hiram didn't bash my face in, I'd be crawling up your ass with Delphinian goods to skip tariffs too. I don't need to do that because obviously I came out on top. See," he caught Mago by the hair, "I won. I'm not mad. Traitors are hot. You and I should talk. We could collaborate. If you knocked out the occasional pirate who gets too big, blunted my competition, I could make you a very rich man." He blinked, frowned. "Rich girl. You walk like a," he twisted his wrist, manually turned Mago's head, "what's the word?"

"There isn't a polite word in this language for what you're thinking of, Master." Mago peered up at Mir from under his eyelashes, teeth in his plush bottom lip, then glanced at me dead-faced, suddenly all business. "We have five genders recognized within the Splendid Fraternal Federation of the Crimson Archipelago. You have two. Precision becomes difficult."

Where to even begin. "Five?"

"Mhm. There's penetrating men, that's Mir, penetrated men, that's me, the same division for women, and then those for whom penetration isn't applicable, which is all children, all priests, a fair number of others disinterested for whatever reason. Penetrators are closer in gender to each other than they are to those penetrated and vice versa." Mago smiled serenely. "Mir means you look like you wear the cock."

I scrubbed my hand over my face. "How'd you sort the party?"

Mir perked up, whistled through his teeth. "Dita takes it, but she's my baby, and it's obvious besides. Ramtha takes it. Sweet Susannah *absolutely* takes it. Helena gives it. Alichsantre gives it. Goss the boss gives it *hard*. Little lady Drustlands takes it from her enormous blond, I'd say. Am I missing somebody?"

Darya. I wasn't so sure about Goss. "What about Vikare?"

"Vik?" Something flickered on his face. I couldn't parse if it was sadness or shame. "Don't worry about Vik."

"Were she and Goss lovers?"

"Goss got everything she wanted out of her." Mir sniffed. "Between us, I prefer Vikare. If I had a girl like that, I'd never let her out of my sight."

Movement in my periphery. I hardened up. "Mir, may I borrow your gun?"

"It's 'Your Excellency' if you wanna kiss my ass. *May you borrow my gun.* Fucking take it from me if you want it."

Mago took Mir's gun from him with minimal resistance. He handed it to me.

"Thank you," I said. It was heavier than mine, felt expensive. I filed my action to fit my hand; his was fresh-from-the-factory smooth, or handmade by some artisan maybe, not a scratch in sight. It felt funny against my hand. I turned on my heel, caught the motion in my sights. I fired.

The swan I saw tore. It threw up its wings and bellowed, swung its long neck, but the puncture in its breast oozed its fate. The blood looked like jam spilled on its feathers. After two strong wing strokes the swan collapsed

234

in the ferns, and the hunting pigs stomped and bayed. I gave the gun back to Mago, disgusted with myself, and went to retrieve it. The ferns swayed against the tops of my thighs. Something slithered over my boot, I didn't kick it away, but didn't stop to give passage. I knelt over the broken swan. I took its blueblack ankles in one fist. Slick skin, ghastly against my palms even through the leather gloves. I smoothed the feathers I'd mussed, then stood, dangled the poor thing. I imagined I'd die like this. I heaved its weight over my shoulder. Its wings fell open. Its head knocked the backs of my knees. What an indignity I did it. Involuntary martyrdom was just murder. It was a blessing that I would not survive to see Hereafter. Hereafter was no place for creatures like me.

I trudged back to the group and walked in silence. Most of the slain game was in a cart pulled by servants behind us, but I couldn't stomach the thought of making weightier work for them. I'd carry my own. Conversation was fleeting. Perdita managed with whomever stood near her, chipper about every prettiness she saw, the flitting butterflies, the dappled light between the leaves, the lushness and the fragrance of untamed land, and her walking companions took turns sharing in her delight. It was infectious, how happy she was. She was going to slaughter millions. She was going to skip like this all the while.

Then came the wolf.

Gossamer shot the wolf.

The gunshot was louder than the others had been, sonically colder. It echoed in my throat. After the bang was a whimper, and Gossamer shoved past Perdita, walked far ahead of us. The wolf fell behind a massive rotten log, shaggy with dead blond needles and frilly fungus, and Gossamer vaulted over it. She landed hard. She breathed raggedly, walked with a weave. She looked dizzy or worse. She stopped in front of the panting animal, which snapped at her and gnashed its yellow teeth, long as fingers, but it was too weak to swing its body around and kill her back. It was in pain. It was not dying quickly. She prodded the wolf with her gun. It snarled but did nothing. She pulled the trigger and nothing. The gun clicked. Goss whirled around, face twisted, and opened her mouth to demand ammunition, someone else's gun, a glass of water, anything, but her momentum carried her. Her eyes flickered back in her head. She collapsed. She fell beside the wolf, who snapped its jaws an inch from her bright red hair, when Helena Integrity Shane took myself and Dunn Ygrainne by the elbows and tossed us over the dead pine.

Needles flecked off around me. They pierced my coat and my shirt, scratched my skin. I knelt beside Gossamer, took one hand off the swan's feet and cradled the back of her head. She wasn't seizing. No movement in the eyes, no convulsions, that's what I'd been taught to watch for. She looked like she'd passed out. I didn't know what to do besides wait. I rubbed my thumb behind her ear. "Dignity," I said. "Easy now."

Dunn Ygrainne walked around the edge of the wolf. She passed the arc of his snapping head and stood by the top of his spine, watching Gossamer and me. She folded her arms across her stomach. She murmured something soft, then drove her heel into its neck. Something snapped. It stopped biting the air. Its tongue flopped across the dirt.

Gossamer opened her eyes. She looked at me with undisguised worry.

"It's alright," I said. "Wolf's dead."

She nodded. She looked much younger from this angle. Like a baby bird.

"Are you ready to stand up?"

She grabbed onto my lapels. I hadn't expected it, her force stole my balance and I fell over her, caught myself with an elbow just before I slammed against her chest. I adjusted my grip on the back of her head, got my wrist under her neck, heaved her up with core strength I did not have. She weighted almost nothing, but she was longer than me, and holding her and the swan was a challenge. When we had our feet underneath us, her vise grip on my coat buoyed her upright without pulling me down, and I stood still, let her breathe until she wanted move. She was frightfully pale. Sweat beaded on her brow. She looked at Ygrainne over the wolf, then back at the party, who by turns looked concerned, amused, intrigued, embarrassed. "Let go of me," she said.

I released her but didn't step away. She held my lapels a moment longer, swayed, then took her hands off me. She tucked them under her armpits. She didn't reach for the gun, lost somewhere in the sea of blue ferns. "It's chronic," she said tightly. "I can't get you sick."

"Are you alright to walk back to the house?"

"In this company?" She swept her tongue over her teeth. "Either way I will."

"May I walk beside you a ways?"

She waved a hand but did not dismiss me. She turned away from Ygrainne. "We should go."

I helped her over the dead pine. I did not look back at Ygrainne, but I heard her move the wolf's body. Helena passed Goss and me to help her. We wove through the group, who lingered in place for a moment, torn between the wolf and young Chauncey. Perdita had a servant in her grip, demanded insane things of him, demanded he bend all the ferns away from her, demanded he clear the pebbles from her path, demanded less shade and fewer clouds, a display which clearly brought her as much pleasure as she'd found basking in the beauty of the world. Mir had a hand under Mago's shirt. Alichsantre marched beside Ramtha, holding hands like children, and Susanna drifted behind Goss and me with a flower clutched to her breast like a Bellonan processional virgin.

We crunched through the flora, leaking blood.

Quietly I said to Goss, "Mine's chronic."

She flared her nostrils, huffed. "How bad?"

"Manageable except when it's debilitating. Fine. Bad."

"Mhm," she said. She reached down and plucked a swan's feather. It came loose with a thin sound. She rubbed it against her cheek. "Will yours kill you?"

"Hasn't yet. I wager it could. A bad enough fit could kill me." My throat could close all the way, strangle me from the inside. My distorted senses could easily get me killed,

I'd miss a ledge, I'd fail to dodge, I'd stumble in front of an oncoming train and splat. I could hemorrhage the iridescent serum inside me. It could seep from my pores like sweat and whatever special lustertouched vitality it held could evaporate and be gone from me and with it, my life. My kidneys could fail. I could turn metallic and cease thought. "Will yours kill you?"

"Yes. Not for a while, we think. But it will. My prognosis is fifty years to live. Fifty-five, maybe. Unless I figure out how to nullify it before then, and I might." She wiggled her jaw. "I'm twenty-four. Nearly halfway there. I have got a tremendous amount of work to do on a truncated timeline. Heaven knows I'll never sleep."

"That's tough," I said. I thought, *I'll die sooner*. I was right. "I've heard you've refaced IC in the past three years. With another twenty-five you'll flip the world inside out."

"Oh yes," she yawned. "I imagine I will. New heights of free civilization in cities I build with metal I mine. Whichever plucky orphan I nab from the ashes to be my heir will inherit a kingdom paved in luster. Heaven itself will be jealous of us."

I pushed down a quick swell of violence. "Where are you going to get a plucky orphan?"

"Anywhere. They're abundant. I was myself a plucky orphan. I know where I came from." She laughed, it crumbled in her throat and came out a wet cough. "Our countryside is studded with charity sanatoriums. I imagine there's an average of two child savants per medical bay at any given time. I'll find them. Myself and whichever one of you

bastards signs up for an opportunity to be my lawfully wed-
ded whipping boy. We'll train up a good little businessman
to continue on in my stead."

"Are you looking for a whipping boy?" I adjusted my
grip on the swan.

She tapped the feather against her throat. "Yes and no.
I'm looking for an obedient pushover who I might lure into
beating me purple every night but is capable of dominance
strictly between the hours of midnight and dawn and otherwise folds beneath the might of my expertise." *Tap tap tap.*
"Given my options I'll settle. Are you quite religious?"

"I live by my Virtue," I lied.

"And I by mine. Yours is a particularly annoying Virtue.
Not as annoying as Dita's, but everyone in that family
shares the same ridiculous Virtue, it can't be helped that it's
meaningless to execute. Her older brother is called Miles
Exemplar. What in the world does one do with *exemplar?*"
She snickered, paused for a moment and braced her hand on
my arm, then took a breath, continued. "Were you going to
fuck Perfection?"

"It wouldn't have gone farther than kissing," I said. "Her
politics repulse me."

"You'd put your tongue in the mouth of someone
whose politics you hate?" She looked pleased. "Dita's good
fun. Great at parties. She does want to parade me like a
trophy around the northern court, which would be appeal-
ing if the point wasn't flashing dominion over my alleged
Drustishness, but she's desperate enough for my attention
that she won't dare bring up her fetishes now."

My stomach turned.

She caught my look. "It's not for the Drustish, per se. It's for the conquered. She wants pets as spoils of war."

"Not better," I said. "Worse."

"Given the scale of mutilation her little border skirmishes have visited upon provincial Drustish villages, no. I'd say it isn't. Abstractly sexier though, still. Imagine encountering it in a novel. Wouldn't it get you slick?" Goss grinned. Color returned to her cheeks. "I'm the richest Ignavian or soon to be. Not exactly a captive Drustish maiden. Now, you. I was under the impression that Horace Veracity Loveday is the sort of Stellarine who'd kill a girl like you."

Like me could be any number of things. I guessed crawly. "I'm sure you're aware of how he's been." I set my jaw and made myself ponder Perdita's rampages to get my face right. I remembered, with a jolt, the smoke over what had been Laith Hall. I wondered if Perdita Perfection had been there. Hideous. My tongue felt like chalk in my mouth. "It was difficult when I was younger. He's an adamant man. His condition has been deteriorating the past few years and as he withdraws he governs me less. I hardly see him most days. He can rarely be convinced to leave his room. I've assumed de facto leadership over the barony, and have enough leeway to make necessary calls, but not enough to do anything that directly confront his pre-stated desires. Voting on his behalf at Senate, for example. He'll have no proxy. I'll assume power only when he's dead. Leaving to come here, for example, took a *conversation*. I think he'd be that way without his faith. Just offers a framework for his rigidity is all."

"Is your condition the one he has?"

"I hope not." I looked at her. Such a play of contrasts, the red lashes on the blue. "Do I strike you as crazy?"

"You don't strike me as a zealot with agoraphobia so severe you cannot leave your home, no," she said. "Given that you're here in the woods with me. But sure. I think you're crazy. What woman in her right mind would have anything to do with me?"

The ancient forest rustled apart and the house appeared ahead of us. In the light it looked more like Bellonan ruins than it did in the dark. I'd always been taught to avoid touching Bellonan ruins. Someone unseen might still be using it. It was funny that, in the haze of my exhaustion, this was pleasant. It was easy to isolate this moment in time, seal it in amber, examine it out of context for its beauty. It was a lovely day. I enjoyed her company. My shadow had swan wings at the base of her spine. I looked like the monsters under the world. Old dead Bellonians shivered under the ferns.

Eleven

GOSS WASN'T AT BRUNCH. NEITHER WAS I. I tucked myself in some bitter naked alcove where nobody had ever felt love and scarfed a hand pie Sunny had slipped me. It was delicious, warm and buttery and filled with something salty rich, but I did not pause to examine its insides. I swallowed, sucked my fingers clean, then stabbed an azurine with my thumb. Lapis lazuli suffered against a rind so blue. It was a fistful of sky. Gorgeous. No wonder Bellona shaped its economy around them. These and olives and wool and silphium, behold the whole of our inheritance. The white pith stained pink as I peeled away, exposed the splotchy blue and violet fruit inside. Juice glittered on my nail. I didn't have the time for the proper ritual, nor did I have the people. I should peel the rind in a perfect spiral, then pass a segment to Sisphe, Harlow, Candor, Brandegor, Uthste, Valor, Amon, Teriasa, the Torn Child forever bleeding in the molten core of the world. Edna.

Poesy. You. We should feast together. Savor the candy tartness as proof of life.

I held the fruit above my mouth and crushed it. It burst in my fist. I drank the bright nectar and sucked the filaments of pulp. Afterwards I didn't know what to do with the sticky rind. There were no features in this hallway. There was a carpet runner and the occasional masculine sconce. I hated the thought of more work for the workers. I loved the thought of this place teeming with rats. I wandered, unsure in this way, until I found a windowsill overlooking the rolling pines. I threw it into open air. It disappeared soundlessly. I licked my fingers and convinced myself that this would sustain me through whatever group activity was demanded of us next.

WE GATHERED IN the library. It spanned the entire back face of the building, all four stories, in spines of endless shelves. Half of the leatherbound books rested behind glass. Some of the glass was locked. The scale seemed impossible, it was difficult to focus my eyes on any surface for long. Books became scales or feathers. I liked sorting. I liked compact material and obsessing over surfaces. When everything was hazy there was pleasure in the heavy and real. But here the books felt impossible, they were incalculable, it'd be like quantifying rays of the sun. The point was not the discrete volumes, the point was the power generated by their togetherness. It was a hoard that outclassed the IC Public Library, the insides of which I'd never seen,

except in passing glimpses. I saw wealth. It looked like hon-
eycomb. The library was a hive, and we stood on the pieced
ivory floor, leaning between heavy cherrywood tables and
handsome chairs. Nothing was ichorite in this room. This
room was old money. It was an antiquarian's jewel box. I
did not belong here.

Goss sat in an armchair by the fireplace. She wore a
blanket to her waist, dressed in a house coat, drank a tonic
that smelled bitter from a delicate porcelain cup. Sisphe
was nowhere in sight. Ygrainne stood, looking stricken,
with her guard. Her face was red, her lips pursed tight,
her hands twitched, half curled, stretched rigid. Her guard
stood between her and Perdita Perfection, who was draped
on a nearby settee, her lilac skirts arranged in a floral spill
around her filthy blood-soaked combat boots, saccharinely
needling an impossibly more pallid Alichsantre about *her*,
whoever *she* was. Alichsantre looked dehydrated. She was
near the point of petrification. She sat perfectly still, hair
pulled into a bun tight to the point that nodding might tear
her scalp in twain, and she ignored Perfection with obscene
intensity. Her eyes looked powdered. Following her gaze,
Alichsantre stared at Vikare. Vikare sat on a table in tapered
trousers and a snug black blouse. She attended a journal
with a fountain pen. She looked at Alichsantre under her
lashes occasionally and curled her lip, then looked at me.
Blisteringly at me. I looked away. Mir and Mago stood on
either side of Susannah, spoke above her ears. Susannah endured it. Helena stood with Darya. Where had Darya been
during the hunt? Ramtha was nowhere to be seen. I kept to

myself. I stood behind a chair and braced my weight against it. What an inviting buttoned cushion this chair had. What lovely pucker and swell. If I let myself get comfortable I'd crumble. What did Vikare know?

"Do I have full suitor assembly?" Goss peered across the dark liquid in her cup. The softness I'd seen when she'd fallen was gone. She was all disaffected haughty coolness now. Her expression was neutral, more tired than emotive, but her shoulders were set. She swept one fingertip along her teacup's edge. "Everyone who didn't kill something this morning is out. Get out of my house."

Nobody moved. Perfection hummed to herself.

"That's Darya, Ramtha, Alichsantre, and Ygrainne. Out." Goss spoke crisply. She sounded like a foreman. Some sunken little kid part of me howled.

"I killed your wolf for you," said Ygrainne. "I stay."

Goss looked at her. Incinerating fury swept her features, then was gone. She resumed neutrality. "You've been dismissed."

"I rode for three weeks for an audience with you. You will hear me, Gossamer Dignity Chauncey." Ygrainne tossed her head back. "Deny your heritage. Hate and rebuke me, hex me with slander, turn weapons against my watcher. Do as you will. A hundred million will die. That woman," she jabbed a finger at Perfection, "will kill civilians in their beds. She will stomp our crops and reave the churches. She will rape our vestals and burn Halls with their elders inside. I did not travel here to dissuade you from funding the war that will destroy my culture. I came here to petition that you *protect the refugees your greed will displace.*

"Here is my promise to you: the Hall that bore you loved you. It is expensive sending *blodfagra* on boats to Ignavian sanatoriums. Parting with little ones is agony but there is medicine here. Look at you. Alive and wealthy, a grown woman, mostly hale. You could've died in the cradle. They could have left you in the snow. A Hall that did not love you would've exposed you and forgotten you, but they did not. Revile them if you must. Hate them, they are strangers to you. They did not teach you your language. You don't know your faith or your history. You don't need to know those things to be honorable. You must defend us, Chauncey. You have the means to shepherd our dispossessed and starving. You alone can help us."

Perfection said, "What refugees do you imagine will require movement?"

"With respect to your pain," said Darya quickly, before the guard could draw, her voice *gorgeous*, slow and smooth, pouring out in one breath like water on whatever evil blue fire Perfection was kindling, "I bid you come walk with me a while, Strife Maiden. We'll sit in the garden while our bags are packed. I'd love to hear if your trip here was as eventful as mine. The cougars in Ignavia! Nobody told me. Gossamer Dignity Chauncey is not the only woman who might hear your pain and respond with aid. I come with the good faith of Tasmudan. Let's spend a little time."

Something flickered in Gossamer. I saw the equation shape behind her eyelids, the wings of humanitarian investment emblazoned with the name Chaunceyco in flaming letters juxtaposed with Tasmudani military forces north of Ignavia, too hilariously vast, if divided, to consider. Tasmudan had carefully respected their own treaty they'd struck with the rest of the continental powers about an end to domestic military engagement for the last two hundred years. They'd supported the barons against the queen when Rasenna had split in half, and only with years of careful coaxing and mad concessions did they agree not to absorb Ignavia into Tasmudan as payment for aid. Tasmudan giving aid to the Drustlands might look like the Drustlands striking back at Royston with Tasmudani force, Royston who'd demand support from Ignavia and Cisra, and then imagine! In a flash I saw Harlow, a baby clutching a gun screaming *freedom, freedom*, plucked howling from a smoldering safehouse by pirates and carried across the sea. Delphinia's wars here?

I saw history condense on Dignity's face. She looked pensive, then dismissive. "You'll leave in the morning. Where are my manners? Dinner first. Now. Get out of my library, sweet ladies."

Darya touched Helena's arm. They parted, I watched Helena watch Darya walk forward, her hierophant robes flowing frictionlessly down her back, and thought I saw Helena sigh. Darya extended an elbow and Ygrainne took it. She turned her head away from Goss. I saw Ygrainne's profile flush with rage. Darya led Ygrainne out of the library, the blond guard trailing a few paces behind. Perdita waved at the guard with two fingers. Everything was briefly still until Alichsantre stood up. Her sash with many hands hung askew. She huffed, touched her hip. A knife hung there on a slim belt. She swept her thumb along its handle but didn't draw it, then stiffly about-faced. She left through a different door than the rest and slammed it behind her.

I looked at my boots. I wanted to break something. I folded my hands at the small of my back.

"Anyway," said Goss. She finished her bitter drink. "Tell me where to find ichorite. My father was a scholar before he was a prospector. The answer is abundant in this room. Demonstrate basic research competency to me and I might just fall in love with you. Nobody is leaving until then."

The room itched. The fireplace behind Goss crackled and jumped. Some hunk of log fell and disintegrated into sparks.

Goss waved her hand, dismissed us like shooing dogs. She looked deathly.

Helena crossed the room and knelt in front of Goss's chair. The rest of the room peeled off, aristocrats stalking up and down the endless shelves with their eyes on the spines. Perdita Perfection pulled out several books at a time and unceremoniously dumped them on the floor. Mir pointed and Mago pulled and read a sentence, Mir grunted, Mago fetched something new.

My belly knotted. I walked into some far corner, tucked myself behind a jut of big red volumes, and touched the ribbon binding of some massive tome and thought, *I cannot leave in the morning. Yann Industry Chauncey will not be here before the morning.* The binding was stiff, I tested it with my rough little gnawed-off nail, folded down the crest of threads. I could scarcely read a letter. These books could have been stone slabs. There was no entry inside them for me. There were a million in this room. Half of them, I was sure, were written in Rasennan abjad, in Cisran authoritative tense. If they weren't in Bellonan, whose script was wholly separate from the one I somewhat knew. In all my rigorous training, I'd learned to read common Ignavian, and Cisran in the alphabet we shared. I'd studied, I'd prepared myself for this, but not for *these*. I couldn't fucking do *these*. Not a chance. I rubbed at the book's binding, entertained a brief delusion that I could catch a thread and pull, and the strings inside the book could be reeled back like a fishing line, and at the end of the inevitable hook my answer would be dangling. Where can you find ichorite? Inside my body. Lining my guts. Gummed up in the bone marrow. Laced in the pulp of my gristle.

Hand between my shoulder blades. My diaphragm struck the shelves. I kept quiet, crushed the gasp, turned my head to peer behind me at who had me. I saw nothing. The suggestion of a shoulder but nobody attached.

"Come with me and be silent," Vikare purred into the skin behind my ear. "Don't struggle."

I licked my teeth and nodded acutely.

She eased up on me. She passed me as I turned, walked with a predatory swing in her stride, reminded me of the lions in the hills of Montrose. I followed her. I touched the place on my arm where she'd scarred me, the tattoo there

250

healed misaligned. I could feel the raised pinkness through my shirt. I kept my head low.

She took us through a nondescript door and shut it behind us. The room held more books, and boxes of unbound manuscripts lashed with butcher twine on ugly industrial steel slabs. It was dark here. Vikare struck a match, fed a hanging lamp wrapped in magenta paper. I watched her shoulders move in the dark pink glow. She stirred her wrists at her sides, fanned her fingers. She looked at me with her chin tucked down, her brows drawn over her deep-set eyes. Her bottom eyelashes cast shadows on her cheekbones.

"Unbutton to your navel," she said.

I put my hands at the small of my back.

"Show me what you are, or I'll cut the strings myself. Show me the name under your shirt," she said. "Don't lie to me."

The blood in my body churned. I swept my dry tongue over my teeth and tilted my head back, made space between the notches of my spine, stood as tall as I could stand. I put my weight in my boots. She hadn't told Gossamer. She could have but hadn't. She wanted something. I had plenty of somethings to give.

Hurt flashed in Vikare's face. It darted between her eyebrows, pulled the corner of her full mouth. She didn't like the quiet.

She unsheathed her knife and showed me the milk-blue length of it. It shined like it was wet. "Draw."

"I'm unarmed." A lie. My knife shivered at the small of my back.

Vikare closed the distance between us. She reached for my wrist, brought my palm against the knife's hilt. I wrapped my fingers around the handle. She wrapped her fingers around my fingers. She held it often, it was smooth to fit the contours of her grip. It was light. She let go of me and produced a second knife for herself from a sheath in her boot that looked thinner, clip tip more pronounced. It was a knife whose utility was misery and human violence. Not a tool at all.

"I have no designs to hurt you, Miss zel Tlesana," I said and meant it.

"Everyone here intends to hurt me. That's fine. You'll do so directly, with deliberate action. That's better." Vikare rolled her handle over the back of her hand, caught it. The arch the blade made burned in the backs of my eyes. She wasn't showing off, she was fidgeting. She was going to hurt me. I could see the brightness of bloodlust in her face. A trick with sadists that I loved was this: sadists pay attention. Sadists hang on your every reaction and attend to that which makes you twitch. Her focus on me was absolute. Her intensity cut away context. My purpose was suspended, the competition distant. Vikare took a liquid step away from me. The distance between us was electric and awful. Between us all matter would incinerate. We could melt sand into glass.

"To the blood if we must," I said.

She licked the flat of her blade and flew at me. Downward strike. Deep puncture angled toward the spoons of my collarbone. Tough to parry and I'm not a duelist. I jumped back, the knife flashed in front of my face, my lungs and guts slammed my sternum. She flipped her grip, slashed upwards, I countered with a cut that scraped knife against knife with a horrible screeching. She wrenched her wrist. She'd pry the blade from my hand or break my bones. I slammed my boot against her belly before it could do either. She doubled back, spat on the floor, then reeled and swung at my shin. She slit the fabric. She slit my skin underneath. Might've kissed down to the bone. My blood came hot and slippery. Quick incredible pain, so bright I could scarcely perceive it. It soaked my sock, trickled down my boot around the arch of my foot.

Adrenaline lit up my body. I kicked again then lowered my center of gravity, I advanced and swung at her, clipped her defensive forearm, then she slashed back, pushed me backwards, she gained back the ground, there was hardly breathing distance between us. I was nearing the back wall. She was stronger than me. She was better than me, she moved with a fluidity I could not match. She slashed out and my spine slammed hard marble. If I ran she'd catch me. If she didn't catch me she could tell Gossamer, they could hunt me with guns and leashed boars, they could send the whole party into the pines to pursue me. They'd really catch me then. Carry me home on their backs with my wings spread. Vikare would string my ankles up. She breathed through her teeth and cut and cut at me. Grazed my belly with a deft lightness. It was demonstrative violence: how easy it would be to empty my insides out! Neat and sweet to saw me in half. My life was soft in her hands, simple to rip. Blood pearled along the slit. My cut shirt dangled open like a mouth. Droplets fell down my belly and pooled in the waistband of my trousers.

I raised a hand against her and she struck my shoulder, my hand released. Her knife I held clattered to the floor. She leaned against me, bore her weight down on me. Her breath warmed my ear. She slid her knife's clip point under my jaw. My top button fell. I heard it bounce against the floor. She got me. She had me.

In the nearness I fit my hands on her waist. Under the fabric I felt the pulsing. There was ichorite beneath, long showy stripes of it, enough I felt its churning stillness even through the gloves I wore. It held her from her sternum to her hip bones. Ribbing inside whatever corsetry she wore beneath her blouse. Silent I chanted, I prayed, *bind bind bind bind bind*.

The ribbing oozed through the fabric like blood. Sticky and thick. Vikare didn't react like she noticed. She traipsed her knifepoint down my throat, with a flick of her wrist cut loose a button that fell and rolled into darkness. I tightened my hands around her. She looked at me. The ichorite bubbled through my fingers and shot out in tendrils, roped wetly around her arms, yanked them back. Her half-shut eyes snapped all the way open. She jerked her left shoulder but the ichorite wound around her like some pale sea monster, it held her against herself and she could not will her way through it. Her face contorted, full lips twisted back over her teeth, eyes on fire rolling, rolling. She swung up a thigh to slam her knee against my gut but I had her, I

leaned her forward, the luster that bound her flowed relent-
lessly into the meat of my hands, and she was caught.

The room around us was suddenly emptied of features—
gone was the dust and its governing paper structures, gone
was the blue shadow on the white ground where a carpet
used to be, gone walls, gone connective tissue and insula-
tion, gone air and breath and planetary vibration. I took
bound Vikare to the floor. I guided her ungently but supported her head. I laid her thrashing between my knees
and pulled my hands from her body. My hands dripped
rainbows. This luster was thin beyond friction. Something
about it had changed. I flicked my hands like ridding water.

"You won," I said. I bit my wrist and yanked off my
glove. The luster pulling apart between the leather and my
skin repulsed me. I averted my eyes and yanked off the second with my free hand. Naked, tattoos revealed, I took my
ruined shirt in my hands and brought it over my head. I
dropped it beside me. It landed soundlessly. I pushed off
my bracers, they dangled limply around my hips, and raked
up the clingy undershirt beneath. It smeared the blood
around. I wore only my throbbing knife. It would burn my
tailbone if I did not move it but I could not bear to move
it. It was an embarrassing vulnerability, I blushed as I cast
the undershirt down, and I leaned over Vikare zel Tlesana
with smudged up pride. My name was marked across my
chest. MARNEY HONEYCUTT and the rest of my quilt.
Her eyes moved between the letters and my chest and my
face. Her lips parted and her eyebrows shot up. I could not
tell if she was crying. In the waves of my fit her expression

flickered. Most of the glistening was my infirmity warping the light. "I'm the Whip Spider," I said. "You're still better than me."

She strained again. It was an experimental movement, exploring how much give the luster gave her, the edges of her freedom. Slim. She bucked her hips, brought her boots underneath her, but did not torque me off. She shifted her body backwards. Put her pelvis under mine, freed up her ribcage. Flared her chest when she gasped as if to prove a point. I let her. She had no leverage, her elbows kissed, she could not lift her back off the ground. I put a hand on her breastbone. I pushed down, flattened her body against itself against the luster against the floor. Rabbit heartbeat. If she screamed, we'd both be dead, but I knew she would not scream. She glowered at me. Her braid was coming undone.

"I knew it was you," she said. Her voice was high and frayed. "I recognized your girl."

"Worried you might," I said. "You haven't exposed us. You've spared us. Thank you for your grace."

Vikare panted. She flattened her tongue against her hard palate. I watched the veins in the whites of her eyes. Slowly, over-enunciating, lips full and without tension she said, "What do you want with her?"

"With Dignity?" I hated lying. The follicles prickled down my back. I rubbed my thumb on Vikare's diaphragm and said, earnest as I could, "I want to marry her."

"You're a highwayman," she said. "You want to rob her blind."

I tried for a smile. "Fair thought."

"You'll lash her to the headboard on your wedding night. You'll pull the curtains down and scrape the frescos from the walls. You'll gut this place. You'll come over it like locusts, you and your gang, and strip it bare. There will be nothing but wind and her body inside when you're done. Then you'll leave. You'll abandon her to quiet and let the wolves take her." Vikare spoke lightly, with slippery precision. She didn't blink. She was watching for something. I wondered if it was pleasure. Abstractly I imagined the monster jaws snapping at Gossamer Dignity's skinny white limbs, imagined the snapping sound that big teeth would make through twiggy bone, then slammed the heel of my conscious against the animal lump of my brain and made myself stop thinking.

"No," I said. "I mean to retire. I've got riches to share. I want a fine life for myself and my friends. Barons made wealth for themselves by reaving their tenants biyearly for centuries. I've earned my slot on a faster timeframe. Now I'd like to show myself an upright life in the way of upright legal ne'er-do-wells. I'd like a wife whose seizure of wealth is similarly self-made. I'm not here to hurt nobody."

What an ugly thing to say. I wound my darlings by speaking against them. We are nothing like her. We are better. Steadily, I bled on her. The front of her blouse was slick with me. She bit the tip of her very red tongue. It looked like a slice of fruit.

Vikare started laughing. It fluttered in her belly, I felt it move against my thighs, then she spat it up. She laughed so hard it barely made a sound. She trembled. Her core constricted and she kicked out her feet, I heard her heels knock the floor. Real tears eased down her cheek, I watched one tuck at the hinge of her jaw behind her ear. She swayed up her hips again. This time *against* me. She brought her chest against my hand and her hip bones against my thigh meat. Crushed the boundaries of our bodies together. She sounded woozy. The laugh spasmed through her, she twitched with it, and when she wrenched I did not stop her. She rolled onto her belly. The mess of ichorite down her arms pulsed silverpink, I thought about hoarfrost on spiderwebs. She arched her back. Looked at me from over her shoulder.

I didn't know what she wanted. I didn't know where to put my hands. Breathing was tough.

"Fuck me," she said.

I touched her wrist. I pulled back sharply, like I'd burn her.

"Do as I said." Something flashed across her face. She stretched her fingers wide, then pulled them into fists. "You want me. I can see it on your face. I can smell it on you."

Hoarsely, "Is this blackmail?"

"Are you stupid? It doesn't need to be blackmail," she said. "Nothing will stop me if I want to expose you. Kill me and reveal yourself if you want to pick the time. Everything's the same. Just fuck me. I want you to fuck me."

I pulled a finger between her arms and snapped all the ichorite binds. My gums ached against my teeth. My head swam, my guts swam, I felt a lurch of want just above my cunt. Vikare put her palms on the floor. Her shoulder blades moved under her blouse, I watched her roll her spine, adjust her stance. I expected the blow. There was no blow. She didn't hit me. She pressed up against me, hands flat on the marble, and hitched her hips higher. I slid my hand up the backs of her thighs, over the curve of her ass and the small of her back. I couldn't think over my blood buzzing. Her blouse moved with my hand, untucked from her fishtail trousers, a worker's style she'd made from impossible singing cashmere. She'd made it. The memories glossed in this ichorite were hers. How could she wear ichorite? Faintly, but persistently, it was ichorite. I saw her work it. Her hands pulling, pressing, pinching. Her sweat between her shoulders. Under her shirt her corset, stripped of all its ichorite boning, fell off her flank in black ribbons. The flare of her waist into her hips was overwhelming. She had little dimples on either side of her tailbone. Anyone sane would worship them.

"Vikare," I said. Vikare, Vih-*carr*-ay in my Tullian twang, teeth against my bottom lip and my jaw dropping, then the movement of my tongue against the back of throat to the roof of my mouth, I spent time on her name, devoted an entire exhale to it, tasted the whole of all three syllables like rare candy. I slid my hand over the slants of her ribs. No tattoos, no scars, but I felt muscle under her skin. I touched her lightly. Touched her barely. "You're sure on this?"

"Call me whore instead." She lifted her cheek off the marble. "We are not through fighting."

259

I grabbed her throat and yanked her body back. I held her upright against me. I closed my hand, her breathing snuffed. Her lashes fluttered, her lips parted, her face went crimson and I squeezed tighter, I counted, then released her. Vikare swooned. As she gasped I took her blouse in my hands, dazed and grinning she lifted her arms, I pulled the fabric over her head. I threw it. I slid my hands down the skin of her chest. Kneaded her breast, marveled at how my palm fit her, how her flesh spilled through my fingers, then pushed lower, touched her belly. I bit her shoulder. Her sweat tasted sharp. I flat tongued behind her ear and felt my pulse change. I lit up with electric colors. I adored her. I wanted to tear her apart. I had no higher thought. She reached back, stole her hands through my hair, knotted the curls around her knuckles. Pain sparked. I pulled her trousers open. I pushed them down, her hips moved with my hands, I brought the fabric to her knees. I pulled my hand between her thighs. I felt the texture of her dark sparse pubic curls, her wet cunt on my palm. She shivered. She widened her stance. She tightened her grip on my hair. I hissed, I bit her ear. I brushed the pads of my fingers over her clit. My guts were liquid, my language was gone, I said something past words against her jugular. She rocked against my hand. Her wetness was unbearable. Love flickered under my nail beds, quick real love, mean love. She panted, she dripped between my fingers, softer than water, and I lost my decorum. We were not through fighting.

I shoved her down. She caught herself, fingers splayed on the marble. I saw her ribs flutter inside her. I slid my hand down her spine, I sculpted her body, pressed her breastbone, her throat, her cheek against the floor. I ached for a moment, at a horrible loss. My cock was upstairs. Empty harness chafed against my skin. I felt my heartbeat slam in the O-ring, felt phantom nerves twitch and scream for friction. I suffered. I stepped on her braid. I stood over her. I watched her profile change. Fury, rebellion, curiosity, want. Watched her watch me. She swayed her hips in the air. Goading permission.

I licked my fingers, gloated to myself over the taste of her, and brought my hand down hard. I hit her. My palm sang. The pain shot up my wrist, I reveled in it, I watched her flesh recoil, she hiked her hips higher to take her licks. I beat her vigorously and watched her eyes roll back. When I couldn't stand it I pressed three fingers inside her. How could I ever leave her? She bared her teeth. I moved my shoulder, I curled my fingers toward my palm, rotated my wrist. I fixated on her breathing. Tight, timed breathing. I moved until her regimented inhale fucked up and I leaned against the spot I'd grazed that'd got her. I fucked into her. Fourth finger, she made a sound deep in her throat, I thought of purring. She breathed raggedly. I felt drunk on her smell and the oil on velvet insides of her body. I fucked her with a death-wish liberty—she knew and I was over, she knew and Day and Night could war again, tear the life under the earth again, the end could fall over us and drown us in molten light, I would not survive the assassination I was alive to carry out, I would not survive to see what became of a world with dead Industry, Hereafter would skip

261

me, it'd be rolling liquid nothing forever soon, who fucking cares. She wanted something from me and I'd give it. I'd fucking give it. I wanted to fuck her forever. I wanted to stay inside her, stay warm under her skin. When she came it surprised her, I felt the texture of her wetness change inside her, softness somehow softer, hotter, I watched her snarl melt when the tremors started in her thighs. She cried out, lifted her chest and head, but my boot didn't move and she was fixed, she couldn't pull away from the feeling, her face lit up with divine relief. She laughed once, panting, brows in a knot. I didn't let up. I slowed my pace, bade myself be gentle. Her eyelids fluttered back. I watched the whites of her eyes in pink-rimmed crescent. She spasmed violently, once, then unraveled into twitches. She went limp under my hand. I stepped off her braid. She stretched her arms over her head, whole upper body flush to the marble floor, in easy feline pleasure. She stretched out her legs. I pulled my hands away, and with my absence awareness cut through her afterglow.

She rolled over onto her back. She seized my wrist. She put my hand back between her thighs.

I held it there obediently. Her heartbeat throbbed on my palm. I wanted back inside her. Desire struck me, and I swayed down and kissed her open mouth. I kissed her sweeter than I'd intended. She took a fistful of my hair and pulled me down, held me on top of her, belly to bleeding belly, breast to breast, and she kissed me back. She bit my bottom lip and I put my free arm behind her neck, kissed her like she was my girl. Like we would take care of each other. She slid her hand under the waistband of my trousers and my guts froze.

"It's my turn," she said.

I had no words. I kissed her, desperate.

"Do you not let your girls fuck you?" Vikare grinned. She had a crooked smile and long teeth. I wondered how it looked in all the advertisements. Miss Ichorite, face of the lustrous future. I wondered if she'd smiled like that when she'd plucked Alichsantre's eye out. She released my hair and took my face in her left hand, held my jaw, made me look at her. She had a little mole under her eye. "I beat you. I want my way with you."

Boycrawlies don't seek touch often. Some of us, sure. Not me. Not plenty. Wasn't the aftermath of having survived violence alone, girlcrawlies were harrowed the same by enforcers in crawly bar raids. It was a disjuncture in the meat of me. A bone-deep fear. That fear was hungry, it wanted, I wanted, I lusted and was satisfied. Just not with hands on me. It sometimes seemed to me I had a cuntless cockless body. I was nothing but output and appetite, I gave, my pleasure lived in my knuckles and my nail beds and the leather belts around my hips. My clit was my tongue. My slit was my throat. I was touched back, fucking the way I fucked was being touched in its way, but someone else inside me? No. It seemed contrary to whatever kind of person I was. But bleed above me—I was dying! I would die soon. I'd get caught and be killed or I'd be righteous and upright and my revenge would soak the soil and make flowers grow and get caught and be killed. My mortality throbbed in me. My extinguishable youth. I was struck by a compulsion toward experience, and I had no fucking experience getting fucked. All the sex I'd had and I'd never been touched because I'd wanted it. *I wanted it.* I felt dizzy, delirious. "Above my waistband," I said, betraying myself and my own desire. My voice was not the polished politeness I aimed toward usually. It shook. Something must've shown on my face.

Something dark flickered behind Vikare's eyes. She turned my face this way then that, examined me. Pressed her thumb on the fullest part of my fit-swollen bottom lip. "You have the sweetest slut mouth. You look bitten," she said. "Open your mouth, Marney. Show me how you take it."

My name in her mouth was a shock. I knew it was on my chest. I knew she knew it. Still. Lightning in my belly. Delirious post-strangulation sparkles in the front of my skull. I did as she said.

"Soft tongue," she said. "No teeth." She slipped her thumb between my lips, swayed her wrist, withdrew. She replaced it with her index. I held my jaw low, felt a familiar rush in the back of my skull. My mouth I knew I liked use of. I sucked lazily. Imagined through my frenetic haziness what we'd look like from above. She fit two fingers, then three, four. She reached back across my tongue. She touched my throat. She kept pushing. Fear kicked up in my gut and I blinked, tears welled from nowhere, one fell thickly down my cheek. Vikare purred. "You yield easy," she said. "I thought you'd have fight in you. Immediate

obedience is so sweet." My face burned but I couldn't say
something in my defense, she pressed her fingers over my
voice, not that there'd be anything to say. I hummed against
her fingers and choked. More tears. I kissed at her knuckles
and felt faint.

"I'm keeping you alive," Vikare said. She sat astride me,
thighs on my breasts, wet on my sternum, and forced the
fast-depleting air out of me. She pinned my arms under her
knees. "I am binding you to me. I won't expose you. I won't
have to. She'll want to be fucked by you when you marry
her and she'll see you naked for it. Your vulgarity is embroidered on your skin. No hiding yourself. But I'll vouch for
you. I'll plead insight and skill. You're a cunning brute, that
makes for a good businessman. Helps that Whip Spider's
famous. Have you heard the songs about you? You'll be
hers, and she'll still be mine." She pulled her hand out of my
mouth. I gasped, heaved a cough, and she caught my chin
and held it open, spat in the back of my throat. "Gossamer
without me is a tyrant. She's a cruel, vile girl and she will
inflict herself on the world and nothing will escape her.
When she makes her gleaming kingdom, I'll keep the carnage back. Keep me and save us. Keep me or I'll kill you.
Say you'll keep me."

"I'll keep you." Ragged little voice.

She struck me across the face.

The world went up in sparks. I blinked, rolled my head
aside. She had a good arm.

"I want it in writing that you'll keep me. Chief advisor.
Operational officer. Make it a role. I'm staying," she said.

She panted, and I thought I saw real fear flash on her face. "We'll draw up a contract tonight and you'll sign it and I'll make sure you're who she picks."

Her weight on me was starting to affect my breathing. I wondered between her conviction and Helena's what might happen. Abstract ideas. I couldn't focus. I saw the slope of her belly and her breasts and her lips and cheeks from here, her hair spilling loose over her hips, her hands floating above my neck, wringing the air above me in lieu of taking my life. I found my hands, placed them on the backs of her thighs. I had no more lies in me. "Forgive me ma'am," I said. "You'll have to do the drawing. Can't write for nothing."

She snorted. She grabbed my face and held it, squeezed my cheeks. "Can you read?"

"Slowly," I managed.

"Yann is an antiquarian. He called ichorite *ichorite* because the Bellonans called monster blood *ichor*. There's your hint." She stood. I shivered without her touching me. She stepped off, pulled up her trousers, and bent to pluck her blouse off the floor. She buttoned it curtly. "You're bleeding everywhere and I ruined your shirt. I'll send a servant here with spare clothes. Don't fuck this up. We need each other, Marney."

I propped myself up on my elbows and stared at her. She kissed her knife before she sheathed it, both knifes, both sheaths I hadn't noticed earlier. They were strapped between her shoulder blades. She started plaiting her hair. Perfectly even sections twisted between the rhythm of her knuckles shifting, rolling. Every movement deliberate, tight and liquid, like she'd practiced the basic choreography of animal maintenance in front of a mirror until all the kinks were gone. Immaculate. A pianist could use her movements for a metronome. I said, sounding gruff: "Will we speak again?"

"Until you marry her? Yes. We'll keep fucking," she snapped. She dropped her shoulders, cracked her neck, and turned away from me. "You'll never be rid of me. I will plague you for the rest of your natural life."

"Good," I said. Wouldn't be long.

With that she left me.

I shivered in silence on the marble in the dark and watched the smudges of my blood congeal in stripes.

LUST AND WANT felt like god. I was sick and cloying with god. In the hot dark, amid waves of religious feelings, I considered Vikare's thighs apart, and *ichor*, monster blood. So much faith called for monster blood. My mind moved backwards through what I knew.

Bellona plowed. The Bellonan Republic, ancient just past memory, was comprised of sickly river worshipers who tended their land and made vases. They wore glass earrings so long they brushed their shoulders and lived in spacious clustered domes built of rock and clay. To break the pleasant monotony, the sky opened overhead, and monsters descended, enraged by the simplicity and ease of the pre–Old Bellonan pastoral lifestyle. The monsters were giant and horrible. They crushed the domes with their fists and pulled families from the rubble to squish and swallow like grapes. Chaos swept the republic. The senators raised armies and fought them with unspeakable loss. Carnage drenched the land and tainted the rivers, which killed the goddesses I'd assume. Hope fell rotten. The soldiers were all dead. The monsters advanced on a small town in what is now Cisra, the last place left where humans lived.

There a goatherd saw them. He commanded them to hide their ugliness beneath the earth, and they cowered. The monsters slithered under the firmaments of mud and became inextricable from it, bound only by fear of the goatherd's special power, which was authority. The goatherd soon thereafter became the first emperor of Bellona. In tribute to his surfeit of success, he ordered that all temples evoke the threat below our feet. Without authority, the incarnate chaos would claw loose and harrow the world again. The emperor was deified and stood on carved hands until he died. Everybody forgot about the rivers. This was about three thousand years ago, give or take.

Simultaneously, none of this happened. Life began in the planet's core, having fallen from infinite fullness into matter into the nascent shape of the world, and out of Life the Oneness flowed, and became the order of all tangible things, an imitation of the endless ethereal as refracted by Life deep below. Bellona became an empire. Tasmudan had long been an empire, as long as Life has been in the ground. No need for supernatural theatrics.

Meanwhile on a more Bellonan timescale, there were normal people, and they were failures. They created the evils of their world with ill action and blemished hearts, which was not their fault, due to their newness. These people were the first attempt at life as conceived by Mortality, a wakeful component of the above-described infinite fullness, who'd made these people as a hasty misshapen attempt at understanding endlessness via creation, as endlessness had itself made the world, which is an end. Mortality just made things that feel pain. So Mortality's twin bride, Immortality (this sounds better in dead languages), made a new attempt, bade this second crop of humans live beside and befriend the first, so that the project of Life, which was the name shared by Mortality and Immortality alike, might be a successful union. Immortality dove into the terrestrial mass to join misguided and hurting Mortality, and the crater its impact left cradled the newborn righteous Veltuni, the first ancestors, people like Alichsantre number one, who would not die but be born anew in flesh and remain watchful in thought to guide their children's children, mortal and immortal. This crater is also in Cisra, like with the goatherd situation, though fringe sects say it's a valley in Kimball, the barony northish of here.

Contrary to this, the Stellarine faith says, before Bellona or humans generally existed at all, Virtues existed on this world. They were abstract concepts made physical while remaining abstract. It's been argued that Mortality and Immortality are Virtues but the arguments are weak. The Virtues' society was perfect and nothing ever happened in it, because it did not exist. Being total and being corporeal revealed themselves to be irreconcilable intensities. There were no animals to prove their grandeur by enacting their essence, they had only their own singularity to prove itself, which was agony. Things want to be seen. Even gods. So they killed themselves, or maybe each other, separated breath from body, air from mud, and rose up to heaven, and crashed down through dust and brine. The bodies sank underground and became the ground, and their spiritual breath wafted skyward and became the sky. Both ground and sky existed previously but these things happened in sort a non-time time so it doesn't matter if events follow each other in a row. Thus, the Virtues watch down over all of humanity, who rose from the mud made from the bodies, so they can see the puppets cut from their corpses run around and attempt their nature. Of all humans, Stellarines are biggest on missions and conversion. They wear pearls because the opalescence is said to resemble the doubled Virtues who walked across the world. Must've been shiny.

Every Drustish Hall has a slightly different iteration of what happened, oral histories with a common chorus and dissimilar verses. Your account and Mors Brandegor's didn't match. You were little and prone to lying. Brandegor is grown and scarred by experience such that she drinks too much. My sampling is not nearly enough. I'm too ignorant for my own conjecture. Here is what you said in common: People lived across the world, and life was hard. Babies died. Precious friends fell to sickness. People fought over meadows. They hurt and adored each other. They made art. They burned livestock alive. They braided each other's hair and beards. They traveled in summer, built Halls in autumn, huddled through winter, then burned the Halls in a spectacular pyre to celebrate the coming spring. They did this for a very long time. They'd been doing this for a very long time already when Bellona decided to be Bellona.

Then a star fell down from heaven. The star broke across the sky and bore smoldering holes in the world. A war council was gathered across Halls, and the chosen strife maidens looked into the craters and decided, *This complicates our essential belief that a vast essential grandeur exists in all things, human and animal, alive and dead, that demands respect and dignity*, because aspects of many harmonious gods were revealed in objects and the arrangement of crowds. Stars stayed up. They didn't come down. These blistering rocks were nature misaligned. They were the limbs of an evil god whose malfeasance rotted it. It was contaminated. Anybody who touched it was exiled. So nobody touched it. Nobody wanted god rot in their house.

Then there was my god. My Torn Child, your archetypal predecessor. Split by Day and Night, its warring father and mother, and buried still alive to hide and protect their treasured shame. Alive down there, never forget it. Twitching and breathing and waiting in pain.

God monster blood was everywhere. It touched everything. Everywhere people have been on this continent, gore squelched under our feet. It made for good harvests and nightmares. If ichorite was found where ichor was buried, we stood on an impossible vastness of luster. Gossamer

Dignity Chauncey could mine the planet's core, then the whole painted structure might collapse in on itself, robbed of its fundament, and become crumbles and fistfuls of ash. I pictured her drilling with a long hilarious straw, like a mosquito's beak, and drinking up the pulp from the rind of the world. Sucking away blissfully, progressively richer until there was nothing but pith.

I said a prayer. I smeared my thumb across my belly and daubed my eyelids. I had no idea what time it was. Still, I said the bleed and miserably, sure of war, I slid my hand under my waistband and pressed my palm over my clit. My heart slugged slow.

TERIASA CLICKED ACROSS the floor and dropped a pile of clothes on my ankles before panic bade me scramble for my knife. I blinked at her in the darkness. She was real. In the dark her expression was obscured but I could make out the strings of her body under her flowy shapeless silk-like-water dress, saw her immense tension, the stiffness in each step. Mad at me? Frightened? I sat upright and felt along the corduroy she'd brought. It was good under my nails. I felt a lick of shame, then shame for that shame, and reached to pull the shirt over my head.

"Stop that," Teriasa said. "You're a mess."

I stopped but didn't know how I ought proceed. I looked at her knees. It was easy to hallucinate that I could see through the silk down to the bone. "I'm sorry, Sunny."

She struck a match. I wasn't sure on what. The friction in the air, maybe. In the illumination I could see her face twist. She stepped back from me. "I could smell that you were bleeding but stars above us."

I looked down at my belly. What a smear. I covered the cut with my palm. It didn't feel deep, but the pressure gave way to a needy, embarrassing pain. Vulnerability excruciates. "It looks worse than it feels."

"It looks hideous. She cut your whip spider." Between my fingers I saw she had. The slash parted the armored abdomen just below the eyes. I didn't imagine I'd live long enough to see whether there'd be a scar. Sunny stood over me. She inclined her head, but didn't kneel to meet my level. Her scrutiny itched. "Vikare zel Tlesana is a choice I wouldn't have made."

"She recognized me. This was negotiating." I reached for my ruined shirt and spat on the sleeve, tried to wick up the congealed blood with a quick scrub across my navel. It smeared things around. "Thank you for bringing me spares."

"A welcome break from entertaining Prince Mir. You're alive and everyone isn't rushing to find and kill you, so I assume it went well. Good. If you fumbled this I'd lose sight of Sisphe, and I'm starting to like her. I let her explain how lurcher engines worked for three hours yesterday." She nudged the toe of her boot against my solar plexus. "You shouldn't have named the Loveday heir after my doll. My doll is just me. I'd never tangle things up so much."

"Had to hope for success somehow. You're a good name-sake." I strained my neck and pressed a brief kiss to her boot lacing, the bow at the top of her shin. "Is the challenge over?"

"Dignity feels unwell. She's retired to her bedroom and has suspended time for research. You're encouraged to stop for sportsmanship's sake and double encouraged to take advantage of her weariness to gather information ruthlessly and unkindly to impress her." Sunny furrowed her eyebrows, and I felt very small suddenly, felt like my parents were freshly dead and I was filthy on her bedroom floor. She leaned into the ball of her foot, and her weight brought my body down. She pinned me to the floor. It was cold on the wing bones in my back. It'd be easy to throw her off but I wouldn't dare. I abandoned efforts to scrub off the blood and dragged my wrist over my mouth. Teriasa said, "The Drustish pair and Hierophant Darya are walking together in the gardens. Or maybe just the strife maiden? Ramtha is in a tiff with Alichsantre. Mir is probably still sleeping. No idea about Susannah or Helena. I need to go find Sisphe. We're planning."

I thought about Beauty, how she'd empty her lungs on a monologue before anyone else got a word in edgewise, such was the strength of her passion. Sunny Teriasa didn't have passion like that, but her conviction felt similar. She had a goal at the end of her sentences and she'd pursue it for however long the goal required. "May I know what you're planning?"

"For the Choir's stand. The war for Hereafter in Ignavia. I'm not telling you details when you're so torturable." She ground her heel in and I mouthed a word of gratitude for the attention, for the pain. I had nothing to combat that. Here I lay bleeding, successfully tortured. Not that I'd given up my purpose. "Get good with Goss and grab her expansion plans."

"There are many forces conspiring for me to get good with Goss. Helena thinks Loveday is a good anti-war match. Vikare thinks I want to retire and become a passive thief and live a soft life, and that I'll keep her in the picture in the business." And personally. I entertained a fleeting hallucination that Velma Truth Loveday, future Baron Fingerbluffs, was a real woman who was once the damned and much-reviled Whip Spider, enemy to peace, besmircher of the publicly lustless Lunarists, but is now a crawly no more, and loves Goss Dignity Chauncey, and is content to wade through blood siphoned from Burn Street, thick and hot forever, rich beyond the stars. Would that woman carry on an affair with Vikare zel Tlesana? Would Gossamer love her as well, and the marriage be a sick web where everyone lied about sharing each other? How miserable for Vikare. Velma Truth Loveday-Chauncey would have to spoil her rotten to compensate.

I pushed myself up on my elbows. It displaced Sunny. She took that moment to turn away from me. Her match snuffed, and I cringed at the darkness. "Go be charming. Don't bleed on anyone."

Then she was gone.

I got back to scrubbing.

IN THE YAWNING, chilly library, there was nobody. I walked alone with my eyes down. Books had been abandoned on armchairs and animal-pelt rugs with their creamy pages spread. I glanced at a few and my eyes slid off the text. It was cramped and square and closed itself to me. I saw an illustration of a Virtue I didn't recognize with pearls gummed between his teeth. Little filigree edges and quick hatched lines. The library's vastness after the cramped side room felt dizzying, I wanted sky instead of roof, I pressed my hands against the stand of an elaborate topographical globe and forced myself to breathe. I worried that I smelled like blood.

I tapped my wrist bone against my jaw and splayed my first and second fingers, a pose for praising Day. Day ruled time and measurement. Research belonged to Day. If ichorite was the grand underground thing described by so many religions, where? Everywhere? Under temples? Holy sites? I looked at the illustration of the horrible Virtue and his mass of shimmery teeth and wondered for a moment about the glossy enamel in common between mother-of-pearl and cast ichorite. I felt sickish. My belly hurt where Vikare had cut me. I took my hand off my jaw and spun the globe, watched the mountains that cut through the continent we stood on, ripple from the Drustlands down to Tasmudan and into the sea. The map was old enough for an independent Delphinia on the opposing continent. I couldn't suffer

276

to think about the ways it'd change over the next few years. I couldn't think at all.

Susannah read on the floor. Or had been reading. A book rested open on her lap, and her knees were bent, concealed with a traditional embroidered long skirt. I nearly tripped on her when I stepped out from behind the globe. I froze and shot my hands out, touched a jutting bookshelf lightly, queasy with sudden flickering post-fit pinks and greens at the edges of every object. Susannah looked up at me. I thought wrongly that she looked like Poesy, my middle sister, but I couldn't properly remember what Poesy looked like. Susannah wore a brimmed wicker bonnet, a work style. In Glitslough, Tullian faith was farmer's pride. It shadowed her cheekbones. I saw her looking at me and felt a horrible rush of embarrassment. It was like she could see my bad liver and mucky lungs. Could map the bruises under my skin. I straightened my shoulders and tried my mockery of Stellarine uprightness. Book on my head, pearls in my mouth, hands folded at the small of my back in a mimicry of temple school trauma.

She brought her hand to her jaw and splayed her fingers. Her gesture was small, delicate, neat. The better-studied version of my prayer pose. She returned her hands to her lap and pressed her palms over the pages. She waited silently, expectantly.

I didn't know what to say.

She bowed her head. Humility and poise. Good Tullian Day posture. She was waiting to be called upon to pass judgement.

Edna, labor avenger legend of my head, was such a bad Tullian.

"Baron Apparent Susannah Loomis," I said.

"Hello Truth," she said. "Where did you learn to do that?"

Tullian faith was closed. Velma Truth Loveday shouldn't know a thing about it. I searched for words but she could see the language shape in my gut, I was sure of it. "We have Tullian servants." Amon, for instance.

Susannah didn't blink. Her serenity was inscrutable. She knew I was lying. It wasn't enough.

I sat down beside her. Screaming soreness shot all the way down to the gristle of me. My bones creaked. I pulled a thigh against my chest, rested my heavy skull on it, and moved my hands flat through the air as though along an invisible table. I did the movements of the morning bleed. I flipped my wrists to praise an imaginary Torn Child Idol, shooed off the boletes and honeyed bread of Night, redressed the table with wheat spikes and shallow cups of cream and puffy lamb's wool; a flash and twist of knuckles, a fist, a fan, a cupping then flattening of my left palm over my right. I so rarely went to real Shrines for the bleeds now. I was clumsy. My faith was imprecise.

Susannah watched my hands. She smiled politely, delicately, revealing no emotion.

"My mother was Tullian." Horace Veracity Loveday hadn't married, a flaw in his otherwise rigid religious life. The heir was somebody's bastard. Could've been a servant. Likely was. "She shared the faith with me."

"I've been wondering where you got your twang from."
She smiled for real with a flash of blocky teeth, then
brought her eyebrows close. She touched my arm. "I'm
sorry for your loss."

"Pardon?"

"You said was."

I angled my head straight and shut my eyes and didn't
dare breathe lest I betray myself and crumble. The grief was
immediate and total. It came as a riptide. I felt skinned. She
didn't move her hand. She touched my cheek with something soft, linen maybe. Paused when I flinched away from
her but didn't stop. She daubed away the tears and, maybe,
the blood spots. Would they mean anything to her? Would
reverendship to the Torn Child itself, not Day nor Night,
have any sort of weight? Would it be understood as real
legitimate faith to a true Tullian girl? She was so gentle.
What a slithery feeling, softness.

I looked at her eventually. She had resumed her perfection and I had no idea what the fuck she was thinking.
She might rightly be embarrassed by me. This didn't feel
like cutting scrutiny, but I couldn't read her. I projected
too much. She wasn't a Burn Street revenant and I did her
injury pretending she was. Susannah had prominent bones
and a beige complexion. Roundish cheeks and rosacea.
Thin upper lip. No callouses, she wasn't a field worker. The
bonnet was symbolic. She was wealthy, after all. She pulled
the handkerchief back and worried her thumb over the orange dampness.

Susannah said, "You don't know Dignity."

"I don't," I said. "I hardly know anybody at all."

"Why do you want to marry her?"

I swallowed snot and worked one shoulder in circles but I knew the kink would never come out. "Wealth. Peace. I'd like a bride and a partner. Same as most of us."

"I love her."

Through the blur she looked serious. I thought nonspecifically about Vikare.

"Right," I said. "How?"

"We spent a summer alone together, she and I. At Wilton School. There was a fever in my household, it wasn't safe for me to return to Glitslough, and Industry is a busy man. When other students scattered across the continent between terms, we stayed stranded in Wilton together. That school is viciousness and brutality with full all the students present but between terms things seemed serene. Vast empty halls, lasting quiet, undisturbed flocks of songbirds always chiming outside. Dignity was bored. She sought me out and interrupted my solitude and somehow my annoyance softened, I entertained her pestering, I let her near me. I grew fond of her. She's important to me. I'm important to her. Wilton is beside this beautiful creek, it's small beside the Flip, but it's so clear and just deep enough for rowing. She'd come find me in my dusk prayers and pull me down the long hallways by my hand, and she'd lead me down to the boathouse, this horrible little shack behind the school, too dilapidated to feign safety, scarcely habitable for two women, and sometimes we'd even leave the boathouse and she and I would glide down the creek until it was too dark to see. We abandoned hope one night and slept under the stars, just drifting. We woke up a town over when our poor rowboat struck a watermill. The wheel came over us and sundered the boat. Poor Dignity and I, shivering wrecks. We convalesced in a tavern and miserable shivering Dignity somehow convinced a tanner to take us north toward Wilton in the back of his trade wagon. We huddled close in the back of that wagon and I knew I'd never love someone so fiercely so long as I live. She told me about her life in the Drustlands when she was small, before they sent her away to an Ignavian sanatorium. The monsters she's seen!"

Something big and evil slugged in my gut. I blinked the tears back and looked at her. Her eyes had boiling stars or melting sequins or a pure soft lovely bomb inside them. Conviction. She looked more sure than anybody's ever been before. She kept rubbing my blood on her handkerchief. The stain looked fawn brown.

Susannah smiled at me. Tremulously, she said, "Baron Glitslough holds the Flip River delta, that'll be me soon enough. I have wealth. We in Glitslough are Ignavia's harvesthead and we are her heart's big artery and whatever wealth Dignity inherits from Industry will flow through my cupped hands before spilling into the broad world. The future is a fiction. We have only now and history. War's bound to happen. I've hosted Miles Exemplar and Perdita Perfection as they've sailed home from their border skirmishes. Without sanction from the rest of us they gladly lock whole villages inside their Halls and chain the doors and burn them. Rape and slaughter and poison mud.

None of us will stop it. You're of the faith. Or you know it! Through your mother, who sleeps at ease and works no longer, you know that if I could love again, I couldn't. I've been had. She's touched me. I'll belong to no other. I can be her Day or her Night, whatever she demands of me. I am going to marry Dignity. I'd ask you not to stand in my way. You're a stranger. You don't know her at all."

Plunging cold. I needed to get away from her. An impulse to hurt her took me, then seething shame. I searched for something in character to say. Something Velma could say, something that wasn't an insult to her, or condescending to her, or outright cruel. "Dignity's no man," I tried. "There aren't codes that bind you to marriage if there wasn't—"

"Penetration?" Susannah tapped the bloody linen against her forehead. "What a sorry Lunarist you are, if you count as one at all. We can't advocate that companionship between women is as worthy and virtuous as that between woman and man and not mean it. I mean it. I think it's just as worthy. I think that makes the severity of folly the same. I will marry Dignity Chauncey. There's nothing else for me."

The strictest way to serve as a Tullian was binding marriage from first fuck. The unthinkable failure to marry whom you first fuck blemishes you forever. It pulls you closer to the anguish in heaven and farther from the ground, our place of duty. You don't rest when you die. You walk as a revenant, pulled skyward and kept awake and ravaged by insatiable desire. Your immateriality makes you go insane.

Superstitious cruelty, a hateful thing to inflict on a people. A nightmare for the curious and the abused.

Pregnant Edna wasn't married. I remembered my mother screaming. I was in bed, it was bluish dark and humid, the air was very still inside our bedroom, Poesy faced away from me and brushed her long blond hair, and Ma hollered and howled through the wall in animal anguish. *What have you done? You whore, what have you done?* Pa went out to drink to avoid the noise. Our neighbors upstairs stomped dust down from the ceiling. What had Edna done?

I stood up. Susannah stayed on the floor with her book.

"Go rest, Truth," Susannah said sweetly. "You have time to nap before the bleed."

Twelve

DAYS PASSED. DIGNITY SAW NO VISITORS. Helena's meddling attempts to arrange something light and easy that'd make me out to be the world's most dashing and eligible pussylicker came to nothing. She wouldn't leave her room. There was worry among us that she'd taken a turn, but her doctor, a thin mean man who'd peeled himself out of a column on the third morning and disdained all "girlish inquiry" about Goss Dignity's health, assured us that this episode was simply a consequence of excitement. Dignity would repair so long as she slept in perfect silence without a draft. She sent word with servants to be read aloud during mealtimes. Brief, charming speeches.

```
I'VE INNOVATED A BRAND NEW NEVER BEFORE
SEEN TEXTURE IN THE BLOODY SPUTUM
I'VE HEAVED INTO MY BEAUTIFUL CREAM
SILK SHEETS. THE TEXTURE IS JELLED,
```

ROUGH-GRAINED, PERFECTLY SMOOTH. IT
UNDULATES. SELF-PROPELLANT! CREATE A
BRAND FOR THE TEXTURE. THE DREADFUL COPY
YOU PRODUCE MIGHT CURE ME. PLEASE. TRY!

and

YOU'RE EATING SOMETHING THAT SOMEBODY
IN THIS ROOM KILLED. DOES IT TASTE LIKE
TALENT?

and

PROVE TO ME THAT YOU LOVE PROGRESS

and

ONCE I STAND UP I'M FUCKING, FORM A LINE
OUTSIDE MY DOOR WHEN THE MAIDS RELEASE
THREE WHITE DOVES INTO THE COURTYARD,
ENJOY YOUR AZURINE SORBET!

Sickness smoothed over time. What a mirage! Music
played and a generation of soon-to-be tyrants donned long
dresses and danced in the hallways. Sisphe and Helena
spoke often, which surprised me. Helena, long and thin and
unblinking, Sisphe, tall and buxom and constantly moving,
a baron heir and a supposed secretary, both lovelier than
their stations strictly needed, so lovely as to be distracting,

chatting with such intensity it seemed they were in love. I spied once from a higher gallery and found with a deeper shock that Helena was cajoling Sisphe into demanding a higher wage from me. Helena Integrity Shane was, it seems, an academic Hereafterist. Or perhaps an Omnidarist, the political thought that reigned in Tasmudan that said the state owes sustenance and shelter to every *citizen*, a wonder for Tasmudani citizenry, and a nightmare for that grand old empire's ample noncitizen population. Sisphe had rights! Helena Integrity needed Sisphe to know her rights! She'd advocate for her, if she needed an advocate! Sisphe laughed and laughed and kissed her cheek.

I danced with Vikare often. My hands would find her and hurt. She wore slinky ichorite dresses, that long slick material that made my skin crawl, with silhouettes that hugged so close to her body that the fabric looked like pouring water, for the purpose of making me crazy. She knew I'd touch it. She'd caught on that it made me itch. She liked my fits. She found me where I looked over the courtyard and put her hands on my hip bones. She swayed against my back and my eyes would blur.

How much time did I spend in Vikare's room? I was so sick, I spat swirling serum on my wrist and watched the colors and wondered if I was dying, if this much ichorite in the air would kill me. Days smeared. What a tangle! Spools of fabric leaned against the far wall, headless cloth statues stuck full of scissors haunted the windows, wrapped in waxy paper, and diagrams detailing figures I couldn't fathom covered her beautiful little ebony nightstand. Plush rugs with hypnotic patterns, high bedframe with bars. She stayed here often. This was properly her space.

She'd developed the process for melt spinning ichorite into thin fibers that could be woven into textiles while she was in Wilton School, she'd told me offhandedly. She'd brought it to then-meek Gossamer Dignity Chauncey on a scrap of paper and insisted she'd try it, sure it'd work. It worked. They'd patented it together. They'd fooled Tlesana, Vikare's mother, into signing away use of Tlesana's textile mills for the new fabric's production. It was used for bandages now. It was used for cosmetics, the little ichorite specks added to rouge for extra sparkle. Torture for me. She was a genius. She'd helmed a movement in Luster City that made luxury, or its appearance, available to workers, gave them affordable splendor, access to seasonal fashion, disposable fashion, garments that could be updated with the moods of the market. It was the visual symbol of a worker's potential for social mobility under the system Chauncey championed. It was not clear to me how much of Dignity's craft was Dignity's at all.

Vikare pulled off my shirt in her laboratory bedroom and bade me rest my hands on her bookshelf. Deftly she stuck her straight pins through the skin of my outstretched arms. Bright citric pain, a rush of lurching colors in the back of my skull. Laced like this, skin embroidered, she'd tuck herself under my shaking arms and lean down, kiss my collarbones, my breastbone, take a nipple in her mouth. She lapped at me so softly I'd nearly succumbed, and in my blissful panic she pulled away and yanked all the pins from my arms. I screamed. I bled in pink droplets and felt my wetness rub against my trouser seam. I hated her, adored her. She washed off the little blood specks and led me to her bed, pushed me back, climbed over my chest and straddled my face. She arranged her thin ichorite skirts around my head. It panged and my tongue swelled against her clit, and by the time she came the second time, little dancing white hot ribbons throbbed knots behind my eyes. The fit quaked through me. She climbed off me then, kissed me full on the mouth, and threw my shirt at me. We re-emerged into the meandering fray.

The feasts were constant. We ate songbirds drowned in cream with the bones still inside them, pink fruits shipped impossibly ripe from the flip side of the world, battered dormouse, and lamprey hand pies, gilded suckling pig and plumes of bitter lettuce, long noodles, eel cakes, roasted chestnuts, morels cooked in goose fat, saffron potatoes, scallops on fire. Utensils burned in my mouth. I ate little. With my fingers, when I thought I could get away with it. Usually not at all. My hunger became constant and I re-membered when my jaw was wrong, right after Candor died, how I'd mashed all my food to fluid. Horrible feel-ing. The players churned. Perdita Perfection yelped because she lost her little slipper, oh please Mir, where is her little slipper! She insisted on being carried. Ramtha and Dunn Ygrainne spoke often, the two of them with High Hierophant Darya as well, about the array of today's pas-tries, and whether the absolute cultural domination that'd accompany Tasmudani occupation in the Drustlands was a desirable alternative to indiscriminate carnage at Perdita's little pink hands. Ygrainne drank. Her guard was gone, I wasn't sure where. I hallucinated vividly the grueling work that making all this evil furniture demanded, the furnace sparks on my arm, my hot clothes soaked, the ladder collapsing underneath me while I reached to mend a pipe. Raw ore smoldering, pulsating, vascular and anguished. Mir and Mago shook down a maid until the maid provided alternative music, and Mir carried Mago to the horrible ichorite dinner table and stood him above us, commanded him to dance. Smiling and flawless, Mago did. I'd been expecting snakey smoothness, hips rolling like the performers in the Fingerbluffs, but Mago danced like a warrior. His athleticism shocked me. In the lustertouched churning it was a marvel to see the muscle ripple under his skin. He spun and spun, dropped to his knees, flew to his heels, became a whorl that curved into itself forever. Mir laughed his guts out. I did my best not to faint.

Alichsantre haunted us. She sulked around the table like she was hunting somebody. Ramtha waved her into conversations that she refused, and every invitation seemed to loosen the laces in her brain. Alichsantre vibrated in the shadows. She radiated her displeasure in waves. I gave her a wide berth. I wondered about her eye. It was so easy to imagine Vikare taking my own eye out. She had the willpower and the talent for violence. But what had happened? Alichsantre always watched her. Watched me when I was with her. I wondered sometimes if I'd wake when I was with Vikare and find Alichsantre standing over the bed.

Just once I saw Alichsantre alone, not skulking, not lurking, not looming imperiously over someone's shoulder as she glowered at Vikare's calves and thighs. She stood in a less taken hallway before a set of genuine long-necked Bellonan amphorae that sat dustily on a heavy ichorite pedestal, her hands ghosting above the terracotta as though in prayer. Her breastbone aligned with the vases, she breathed toward them, for them, her whole attention devoted to their long black curves, but the look on her face was so sour. Like the pottery was a woman she loved whom she spied in the throes of brutal sloppy infidelity.

When I came by her, Alichsantre hissed a sigh. She lifted her hands above her head, gestured to the amphorae's tall lips. Full of tenderness, she said to me, "Weren't they smart, our ancestors? Weren't they deft?"

I said nothing. Some urge to run struck me, I ignored it.

"These are second-dynasty amphorae, Baron Loveday. Harpinian, from modern Cisra in the west, near to my palace. See the slender twist where the handles shy away from the body of the vase, the fullness in the belly, the delicate knots and rosemary leaves that adorn the foot and lip? The mosaic in my atrium is edged with that pattern. See how delicately the sprigs curve? The perfect horizontal symmetry, hand-painted, scarcely faded after all these years? Balanced, graceful, masculine.

"Bellonan noble households would hide architectural secrets in these patterns, they're algorithmic, they encode the specific infrastructural stylings that demonstrate to the whole vulgar world each family's dignity with exacting proportion and impossible scale. Common people would flock outside the gates of our old palaces and gaze up with religious awe." She shivered, almost smiled, she was beautiful when she smiled. She turned her face toward me. The eye patch she wore today was crisp and white. "My bloodline springs from the crater itself, and from the time of that genesis we carefully curated additions to that divinity; the men brought into my family have been Bellonan noble generals and kings. These artefacts, these *relics*, are the perfectly embellished clay of the earth that is mine. Do you think they're beautiful, Loveday?"

My eyes widened and I forced them to narrower normalcy. This was the closest I could come to nodding.

"The Chauncey ward has placed these trophies on a lump." She must've seen something she liked in my face, something she took as approval. "You think it's ugly, too. You hate the ichorite fashions. I've seen you wince from the garish artifices of Chaunceyco's supposed modernity. Cringe from the hideous forks and ridiculous boulders she passes off as furniture. Yours is an old Stellarine line, and you've kept your lands since Bellonan rule. You are a bastard as I understand, your mother is not pure as your father is, but your people forgive these things, and so shall I. Your indiscretions and sins will be ignored. Dalliances forgiven. Please, Loveday. Be a mirror, a source of sanity in this bog. Tell me you understand how these beacons of history are violated by their ichorite seat."

I pulled my chin down, clasped my hands behind my back, imagined my lungs manually inflating, pumped and emptied like bellows. What a mess it was, that Gossamer's aristocratic opposition took this tone. There could be no solidarity with this person. I could hardly stand to look at her. "It is not to my taste."

"Disgust is the only trustworthy feeling, Loveday. Disgust is an ancestral missive that defends your body and its cleanliness from an onslaught of worldly filth. Industrial rot poisons the ground, it poisons the air, it poisons our sensibilities and lulls our peers into a sense of acceptable plasticity. What turns your stomach will hurt you. It will hurt the traditions you represent." She reached toward me like she might grasp my shoulders. Her fingers stroked the air just short of my sleeves. "I understand you might want the cash. You are provincial and uneducated, your father is an invalid, and the Chauncey vaults might appear to be your ladder back to society. I must warn you that society is wretched. Flee from it, I implore you. Return to your haven where what has been might continue to be. Don't contaminate yourself with new money. When the fad dies, and it will die, the common people will applaud your continued purity, and look to you for strength."

I took a broad step back. She frightened me. I didn't trust the span of her pupil, or the tautness around her mouth. I cleared my throat. Said to Alichsantre L, "Vikare wants me. Pardon me, I must go."

Vikare's name curdled her expression. Gone was the hazy revelry. She watched me leave like my tongue was threaded with worms, and with a backward glance I saw her return to the vases. She closed her hand around one's neck.

AS TIME UNFOLDED, Sunny Teriasa was gone from my sight. She was upstairs, warming Dignity Chauncey and rubbing the stress from her aching hands and feet. When she'd briefly emerge, she and Tricksy Sisphe would collide in a flurry of skirts, and I saw the strips of paper exchanged. My war girls, separate from me. I could not suffer my own lamentations. I could not pout about any lack of control. When I bled the pig Chauncey, it'd be our grand escalation. The first blow would be ours. That was auspicious, or should be. I had my role. It was not the craft and dazzling foresight of my beloved betters. I wanted to help them. I tried to ferret around for useful information and found Perdita laughing and Ramtha feigning happiness to quell a noxious room.

Where was Susannah? The library. She sought the gemstones in her research diligently. She was making a map, Perdita gasped aloud while we lazed in the gardens. She was charting her ore deposit predictions precisely! Insufferable blowhard. Too bad nobody loves her and can appreciate the blowing. Ha ha hee hee.

Perdita was somehow everywhere. She fell out of the air in a cloud of gourmand perfume and basked in her own pink vapors wherever you turned. Perpetually happy. I tried to reconcile Perdita the butcher with the porcelain doll so playfully twirling her curls around her little finger. She so precisely looked like a woman who was born to visit candy shops. This was the subject of every luxury craftman's

imagination: an insatiable girl whose wallet was a fountain. The consumer abstracted. She'd consume forever. Her
true Virtue was appetite. She'd wear the world's weight in
diamonds in a stole around her shoulders and drop it on
the floor, demand a less dusty second. Perdita was a sweet
little brat. Little, I kept conjuring the word *little*, like she
was a child and not five years my senior. She pitched her
voice high and pouted, stomped her foot when Mir teased
her, needed to be led by the hand through drafty corri-
dors and carried when the floor felt cold. She was nearly
thirty and had killed men with her hands. There was talk
between Helena and Darya of her having commissioned
new bayonets whose pyramids twist like a unicorn's horn,
a weapon that'd only ever kill you. I remembered the rifle
Brandegor had laid across my lap. Perdita had slept on the
ground in military tents with guts in her hair and her teeth.
No bonbons to be found. She ate little berries with a spoon
and asked Ramtha to tell her stories about Luster City.
Ramtha's vision was not playing out. She was starting to
wear thin. At least Alichsantre was sparse.

Heinous. I ate the swan I killed. They served it braised
in wine. The meat fell off the bone and I thought vividly
about hurting myself. I sucked my fingers off. I went upstairs with Vikare and as she slipped my cock into its
harness, I stroked her hair, and I wondered if I'd ever been
gentle. If I had the capacity. Vikare's hair swept aside, the
smattering of scars on her nape and shoulder became visible. Round and white. I didn't ask about them. They were
old, she didn't pause when I pressed my thumb against their

ripples. She dragged her tongue over the head and I closed
my fist in her hair, her thick beautiful hair, and indulged a
smack of love. Let's call it love. Here knelt a woman sharper
than me and as devoted. She would've avenged you if she
had you. She would've done it by now. I pushed her head
down to the ring.

After she swooned back, I arranged her hair around her
head on the pillow. She allowed my fussing. She watched
me without moving her head, just her liquid back eyes rolling under the lids, glaring from some unseen light. I pulled
her blankets over her, plush hypnotic blankets, perfumed
with sex and rosewater, and smoothed them over her body.
She'd not worn the spun ichorite today. My head was as
crisp as could be in this luster trap. When I rose I told her
I'd return, and she didn't tell me otherwise. I'd never seen
her so willing to be sweetly touched. She metabolized it
poorly but better than I would've.

I went down to the gardens. I drew my knife and got
to cutting. Long skinny blue flowers, heavy fragrant pink
ones, spiny leafy reds. Rosemary sprigs and lavender too. I
lacked the language to name the rest of them. I gathered the
cuttings, stripped them of their lower foliage, and bound
them with a ribbon, that is, the lacing of my left shirtsleeve.
It hung loose, I rolled it to my elbow. My tattoos looked
mottled in the night. Coyotes screamed like kids in the distant woods. Unknown animals bayed with them. I heard
things run and pant. This house had made me falsely soft
and the wilderness felt alien somehow, despite all my time
moving through it. The dark ran too deep. I turned back

to the house with my bouquet and stopped dead when I beheld the broad blond Drustish guard.

She pointed a white hand through the darkness. Her sleeve was dark, invisible. Her hand looked like it was floating severed. "To Chauncey?"

"No." I searched for any Mors Drustish Brandegor had given me. She cursed in Drustish sometimes, useless here. Praised whores in Drustish, worse. I had the phrase I'd already offered her, and this: "You bait evil walking so late." Then, in my language, "How do you do?"

She took a step closer. Her eyes were startlingly blue. "Truth Loveday?"

It felt so filthy now. I nodded, more like jerked down my chin. "And you?"

"Laith Herzeloyde. You are a soldier."

Laith.

I held the bouquet at my side.

"The free Drustlands have never fallen. Not to Bellona. Not to a gold-drunk girl. You walk like a soldier. You have seen fighting and you spoke to me in Mors. You call a blood feud when you speak like that. My feud is deeper than my Hall. My Hall is gone. It was on the border. The building is gone. Mud and char because of Perfection. *Perfection.* Stellarine faith is cheap to me. Make Virtues women in the stars and call upon them only to rob them of power by failing to resemble them in action. She disgusts me." She spoke lightly, with a whistle over her sibilants. Her lilt made me horribly homesick. I thought about you. I missed you in a violent rush. I thought about Laith Hall and it was like a pinched nerve, all other thinking became excruciating. Mud and char. "The Drustlands will not fall. I will fall and when you fight you will fall. You'll fight for us so you will fall. The Drustlands will stand after us. That makes us impossible to kill."

"Are you going to kill Perdita Perfection?"

"I may." Herzeloyde swayed. "You will not stop me."

"I can't," I said. I'd never. "I don't know nothing about it."

She smiled with her teeth. Then she nodded, and put her burning-hot hand between my shoulders, ushered me inside. She did not join me there.

My teeth chattered. I shivered my way up the stairs to Vikare's room. I knocked, she did not answer, and in my arrogance I let myself in. She hadn't moved from her pillow. Her impossibly dark hair was still fanned in a beautiful arc, unshifted. I hung the flowers upside down from a wicked pin in a nearby mannequin, and I lay on the floor beside her bed. I didn't dare join her above. She hadn't moved. I wouldn't make her move. I stared at the blackness above me until it melted into a blackness that was not real. In that blackness I heard Edna's voice.

I followed Edna's voice. I wore my riding clothes and my Whip Spider mask, which flowed seamlessly into my shirt and my skin. I saw through the lace without the pattern's obstruction, just the subtle blueness. I walked down the hallway and looked out over the gallery, down into the palm-and-floral courtyard where the dreadful ichorite furniture lurked.

Edna reclined on the ichorite table. She wore no bonnet and her hair was loose, it was so long it dripped over the table's sides. Her boilersuit was unbuttoned to her waist, and in her arms, she held you. She nursed you. You clung to her, smug and peaceful, too big for her lap. She held the back of your neck. She sang, "Unalone toward dawn we go."

I breathed against my will and the sound carried. She noticed me. She looked up at me as she sang. She didn't blink. Ten years she'd been a revenant. It showed in her eyes. Her eyes were all water. My sister Edna was insane. As she sang, she smiled at me. It was a smile of hating me. She hated me. You didn't look at me. You were barely alive aside from the nursing. Your lips moved, nothing else. Your skin was green like ash. It was then I understood Edna's fury, and I cowered from it. How loudly I walked down this hallway to her. Woe to the world if I woke you.

IN EARLY MORNING, Helena seized me by the scruff of the neck and pulled me into an alcove. She wore a sturdy hunter's coat and tall boots, a veil that covered her brow and the bony bridge of her nose. Mud flecked her boots. She'd been out. Helena peered down at me through the mesh. She looked more tired than I was, somehow. Purple eyelids, bruisy even through her cream cosmetics. Last night's mascara. I wondered what had been keeping her up.

"I know how we're going to make her fall in love with you," said Helena.

"Good morning," I managed. "How's that?"

"You're going to help the service staff with their first-shift responsibilities, you're going to make Goss her breakfast, and while you do you're going to ask the staff about their working conditions and find some preliminary demand to bring to Goss with her meal. She's a lot of things, but she is a major reformer. If you do this in a way that feels like a challenge to excel, not like a slight against how she's been running her ship, she could be impressed. She likes displays of devotion and she likes innovation. You're not below a little work, are you?"

"No ma'am," I said. It was a plan I could stand behind. It made me like Helena more for having conceived of it. I kept my hands in my pockets. The glove seams rubbed angry pink stripes across my wrists. I wanted to gnaw through my skin. "May I ask you a question?"

"Anything." She frowned, and reminded me suddenly of a younger Teriasa, the one so frustrated by having fallen hard in love. She blinked against her veil.

I said, "Are Hereafterists executed in Montrose where you reign?"

Helena swayed back on her heels. Shadows gathered in the hollows under her jaw and cheekbones. I saw her whole skull. "I do not reign in Montrose. I am a baronet. Lots of siblings. It'll never be mine."

"Answer me," I said.

She looked me in the eye. I admired that much. She said, "We have tried to be the best version of our station. We help reap buckwheat and rye in the summer. We shelter villagers in our home when it's cold. I have read the Omnidarist

299

texts out of Tasmudan that say all should be entitled to bread and hearth, and I have read Hereafterist refutations that Omnidarism's insistence on citizenship and borders determining who does and does not receive these gifts is wicked, that all giving means *all*, withholding is unforgivable, and I believe that. But of course, I am withholding. I am a baronet. I maintain my station and its flowery redundancy. I insist on it, because it lets me into rooms like these. It is my understanding that a not uncommon Hereafterist sentiment says I and my family must be killed. I have great sympathy for the global revolution. May our future be reborn. In that future, I don't want to die. I don't want to participate where I am not welcome, either. You see the trouble."

Helena blinked. She looked at my lips, then at the collar of my shirt, as though she could see the tattoos beneath.

She said, "The law in my barony is that Hereafterists dangle. It would be difficult to change. It is easier to leave it written and render it unenforceable. We don't go looking for them. I hear sometimes when they pass through."

That sounded honest. I was not sure if she'd come when called upon, if it was partisans who spoke her name. Collaborators are useful. If she was brave enough to bleed for her sympathies, she could be a force for good. I'd tell Sisphe and Teriasa. They'd tell the righteous soldiers after my passing. "Where's Birdie?"

In the kitchens. I joined Birdie without Helena, who lurked encouragingly in the doorway but left when I took up a knife and started chopping a leek into rings per Birdie's wordless request. She was one of five cooks, but the only

tasked with Gossamer's breakfast, a separate affair from
the never-ending feast for the junior hereditary rulers of
the world. She wore her bonnet low across her brow. Her
face was splotched pink, eyes glassy, already exhausted.
Dawn bleed was early this time of year. I hadn't prayed. I
wondered if there was a Shrine somewhere in this house.
Birdie's dress, a normal mortal fabric, was drenched in
sweat and floured. She beat dough with her fists. She did
not question my participation and I took care not to look
too Tullian while I scraped the leeks into a bowl.

"This isn't necessary, ma'am," she said eventually.

I put water on. Coffee for us, she and me and the other
cooks who so diligently ignored us. Low ceilings in here, a
steaminess that reminded me of factory work, despite the
air being so much cleaner. It smelled like burning rosemary.
I watched the low fire under the kettle. "Am I in the way?"

"No, ma'am. Behind you," she said, opening an oven
and pushing the fleshy dough knob inside. The foundry
furnace made a tinny sound that the oven lacked, the dis-
similarity annoyed me. "Please, no poisons."

Oh, I loved her. I smiled despite myself and spiral peeled
an azurine. When I was very small, we starved for a while.
Bad winter, Pa was sick, the sum of our family's income
without his contribution covered rent, his leg brace, and
the laudanum. Nothing much else. Hunger made me bored
stupid. After shifts I'd sit on the floor and face the wall,
and I'd carve up the wallpaper along our baseboards with a
spoon. I'd lick the pasty chips. "None. Just want to do Miss
Chauncey a kindness."

"Mister is what she likes," said Birdie. "I'm cool on chopping."

"I'll cut up whatever you'd like." Only thing I ought be allowed to do in any kitchen. I rolled the knife across the back of my hand. She didn't notice. "What sort of employer is she?"

"It's good pay." She got redder. "She's no hypocrite."

"You've worked every waking hour all the while I've been here." How long was that? I couldn't say. "D'you need a chair?"

She leaned a hip against the butcher block. "We're working the full duration of the courtship game. I thought it'd be a few days when I signed the contract. Mister Chauncey is a picky woman. It's just taken longer than I'd thought. That and her health, poor dear."

"And your health?"

She closed her eyes and breathed through her teeth.

"May I carry up the tray for you?" I smiled like I thought a good bachelor might. My hands twitched, I clenched them to keep them still. This was the closest thing to Tullian womanhood I'd ever done, I realized. Preparing a meal with another Tullian woman for my prospective husband was what a woman my age should do. I wondered how long my hair would've been if Teriasa had never cut it. I wondered if there were unmarried Tullian women whose hair trailed behind them when they walked. "It'd be my pleasure."

She rubbed the sweat between her eyes. "Her room is difficult. Yes, you may, please do."

I bowed my head to her. I poured us both coffee, and we drank in silence, watched the steam curl off the murky liquid's surface. I drank as she prepared the tray, which required an artistry I lacked, and I looked out the dingy window at the pines. Perhaps these ones would not be felled. They'd be a decent curtain between this house and the mines that'd inevitably get dug nearby. Or maybe Goss liked to watch?

Thanking Birdie I carried the fragrant tray, surprisingly heavy, to a room on the second floor. It was a corner room with an unpainted door. I listened but could not catch Teriasa's voice. I balanced the tray in one hand, nearly fumbled and spilled the porcelain containers everywhere, but I caught myself through a spasm of luck and knocked on the door without disaster.

Crisply: "Enter."

I managed the door and pushed in.

Hearth sparks jumped and stained the whole eggshell tomb of a room deep amber. Heat hit me. It felt like being baked. Gossamer's bedroom, an office on fire, smelled densely herbal, harsh medicinal flowers and pepper resins, smoke accords, industrial glue, and that heat, that furnace-fire heat, livid and metallic, unsmelted ichorite ore bright, I was drowning on nothing, my whole body pulsed. Blinking didn't clear things. Through the vertigo I saw long white lines and understood them to be columns. Far from me was the fireplace. It roared. Nearer was the bed, unmade and smeared with apricot sweat, and a table that tore through gravity and ripped my guts out of my body.

I hated the table. All the scents of this room, its impossible heat and swirling currents, emanated from the table. The table spasmed faintly. Its insides churned with gestational idleness. It was a lustrous table. It was not ichorite but it was ichorite. It was raw ore cased in glass. Sinuous gel and thick crystal fibers bloomed under the glass. The gruesome mineral expanded and contracted. There were tides inside it. It spawned itself. In its kaleidoscopic vortex I saw colors I could not name. I came nearer to it. The tray was weightless and I felt undone, scooped hollow. The table's variegation repulsed me. The gradients shifted, eroded. Intensity swirled in knots. Whatever material comprised it looked dense, impregnable. It wasn't liquid. It shouldn't flow. Its texture too was torture, creamy sleek but bristling, not bristling but minutely ribbed, though I couldn't gauge in what direction the ribbing was applied. There was a constant imperfection in the jellied stone. Ridges too small to cast shadows, flattened maybe by the layer of glass. Maybe the glass vised the insides and condensed the material trapped inside it. The texture that repulsed me seemed to me, if I could assign it intention, to be exploring the boundaries of the glass and testing it for permeability. Attempting osmosis or migration. Maybe the ridges were delicate fingers? Fingers whose nails are the size of powder grains. It would break the glass. It would break through the glass. The glass could not withstand the substance inside it. I understood that it wasn't the substance's weakness that repressed it. It was inattention. Lack of will or orientation. The stone slab was an inert stone slab but it was awake and aware of me abstractly. It felt my nearness and acknowledged it with a self-luminous flash of greenish pink.

Goss sat at the end of the table. The fire glowed behind her chair. She wore a blanket over something silky. She attended leatherbound ledgers without an upwards glance.

"Your breakfast, ma'am," I managed. I couldn't bring the tray to her. I couldn't touch the table.

Something registered on her face. She lifted her eyes off the page. They looked frightening under her red lashes, utterly colorless. She quirked her nearly invisible brows up toward her hairline. It wasn't slicked back, her hair hung loose around her jaw, fine and fluffy, gave her an unexpected youthfulness. "If you're going to play my maid, you should wear the little dress."

"She needs a break, and I need a drink." I struggled to look at her and not the table. She had one earring, a small irregular hoop. I watched the light glance off it.

"Oh. You're scared of the table." Gossamer stood up. She produced a cane from under the table, leaned on it as she made her way around the table to stand beside me. She got close to me, so close I could feel her breath on my cheek. I looked down at her fur-lined slippers. She tossed up her cane, held the shaft, fit the handle under my jaw and pushed my chin up.

I looked at the table. My knees buckled.

"Fascinating." I couldn't tell if she was joking. "I've only had one girl on staff cringe from the table like you do. She had to wear a blindfold in this room and would collapse if she stayed nearby it for more than an hourish. I recall her tolerance capping at seventy-three minutes when we tested her endurance for it. The table is a slice of raw ichorite ore. The outer crust of an ore deposit, specifically. The skin. You're a lucky girl to look upon it. There's only one table in the world like this. Father commissioned it from a dying furniture maker so that he wouldn't have to suffer the aftereffects of working with top-layer ichorite long. We don't refine the skin. It doesn't melt right and the fumes will kill you. That said. It's safe behind glass. What you're feeling is all psychosomatic."

I shut my eyes. "Your breakfast."

"Put it down." The cane left my jaw, coasted over my head and rested at the small of my back. "Go on."

I put it down unceremoniously. The clatter hurt but couldn't be helped. My knuckles vibrated under my skin when I neared the table. Hands free, I stepped back into the cane. There was no force behind it, Goss lowered her arm when she found resistance. I turned my back on the table and looked at her. I said, "Ichorite is the pearly substance that anchors religions across the continent. That's why it's called ichorite. It's a wave to divine blood. It's beneath where the holy sites cluster. I imagine much of it's under the ancestor's cradle crater in Cisra, but this whole land's studded with temples."

Gossamer tapped her cane on the floor. She returned her hand to the handle and leaned on it. She gave me a long look. I tried to mirror her expression to understand it better. Nothing. Curiosity. Pain maybe, there was a strain that showed between her eyebrows and tugged at her mouth. "Romantic read. Partial credit. Precisely, ore deposits are abundant wherever there are temple clusters built circa republican Bellona or prior, by and large. It's imprecise and new temples are outright useless.

"For your edification, there's an easier answer that everyone else reached toward who's bothered to convey their research exercise answers to me. It's azurine groves. That's why azurines exist. Plant an azurine tree somewhere without ore beneath it, you've got a pathetic pomelo. The citrus takes on that taste and color because of how ichorite ore moves through the root system of the tree. It's like soaking carnations in colored water, for brutal oversimplication's sake. Contact leaves a pretty stain.

"There are books in my library that claim this outright. Father's written some, and his rivals possessed with an adorable notion that they might break his monopoly have as well. Five years ago, Father gifted beautiful azurine saplings to Barons Geistmouth, Burnside, Olmstead, Kimball, and Montrose, places where azurines don't natively grow. Bright blue fruit in Geistmouth and Burnside. Blue in Kimball too." Goss leaned back against the table. Her blanket slipped around her shoulders like a stole. "The fruit in Glitslough, Olmstead, and Montrose came back yellow. Helena Integrity was my only actual academic rival. She's gorgeous and bullheaded. She'd be a waste of a wedding."

It was no way to talk about a woman.

Gossamer smiled at the look on my face. "I would've

307

thought that a crawly like you would have a man's sense for these things. You're a crawly, not a Lunarist, yes? You'd call yourself a crawly?"

"I'm honest with myself. That's why they call me Truth." I was going to throw up. "I'm a crawly, yes. Like you."

Gossamer smiled wider. Something smoked behind her eyes. "I like you. You're two decades behind the fashion and you talk like the help. You're from a barony nobody remembers except for people embarrassed to know. You took the contemplative way through my research game and gave me an insane conjecture with dire seriousness. You're fucking my best friend. You can't look at the table. You brought me my breakfast. I can't figure you out. You're like a made-up woman. You come to my bedroom and call me slurs to my face. Who the fuck are you?"

"You should eat while it's warm," I said. "Your labor reforms. Why did you make them?"

She laughed. It carried, high and tinny, and rattled the table. "Patronizing, goody. A wife should be a little mother, so the gospels say. Work is a man's pride. It should be treated as such. My ambition is for the betterment of humankind, Loveday. I have a heart!"

Which gospels? Her laugh was a knife in my belly. I couldn't place why I wanted to sob. "I'm more of a father."

"How would you change the labor system in the Ignavian context? Quickly. Go with your gut. If it sounds rehearsed, I'll throw my cane at you," she said.

"I'd split the profit evenly among every foundryman."

She gave me a slow, toothy smile, kept laughing without moving her mouth. There was nothing behind her eyes. "The General Public Ichorite Foundry. Isn't that something. It's worthwhile to be delusional. We can temper you right."

A vein in my eyelid twitched. I squeezed my eyes shut, opened them wide. Tough to focus. I saw my own lashes. "Is the courtship game suspended while you convalesce?"

She stopped laughing abruptly. Her stomach moved, and she wrinkled her nose, wiggled her jaw like she was picking fish bones from a bite of meat with her tongue. She spat a crimson glob into the corner of her blanket. "No. We're going into Luster City tonight to watch the race. Father wanted to meet the remaining options. Not that I've been firm about sending anybody home. Aristocrats are fungible, you know. They're like workers in that way. So long as I've got one of you."

Father.

I forgot the fucking table. Absolute clarity flooded the veins of my body. I took a step nearer to her and put my hands on her shoulders. Delicate bones, a birdlike sort of breakable. "I love races."

"Father is going to think you're a freak." No protestations about the touch. She looked at my chest. "He'd be right."

"It'd be an honor to meet my future father-in-law." I was going to foam at the mouth. I was going to chew through the floor. I was going to maul Goss and tear off then eat all my skin, and whatever animal was trapped beneath would spring forth and make short work of the rest of the house. I immediately abandoned the fight to keep my face soft. "We should get dressed for travel."

"Tonight," she repeated. "Hours from now."

"I love races," I said again. Madness took me. I pulled her close and kissed her open mouth.

Dignity touched my throat. She closed her long cold hands into fists. Color pinched and breath cut. Gossamer moved her mouth on mine. She had soft lips. Soft lips and tongue and pleasant sharpness as she bit my bottom lip. She swayed against me, and I swayed back, pressed her hips with mine against the evil table. I put a thigh between her thighs and twined my arms around her waist. I kissed her with strength I'd lacked for days. Yann Industry Chauncey's death glowed inside me. I was happier than anyone had ever been. I kissed Gossamer and kissed and kissed her, I poured my joy on her, I held the back of her head and dipped her. The choke softened. She softened, all her tension melted, and she was boneless in my arms. Her mouth tasted like blood. She had cloying fragrant blood. She tasted like money.

Against my mouth she said, "You're psychotic."

"It's the rush." I pulled us upright and attempted composure. I couldn't stop smiling. My body buzzed. "I'm lucky. My bets always win."

"A superstitious gambler! You'll be horrible for me." She purred against my jaw, then pushed me away. I moved where she led me. "Come on. Help me pick something to wear, you monster."

LUSTER CITY CRUSHED in on me. In the back of the carriage I hallucinated and spasmed in Sisphe's lap. We were alone here. As an aristocratic cohort we rolled through the city in seven separate carriages, a green-plumed little wealth parade. Sisphe closed the curtains to shut out the sight but I saw the luster stir with my eyes closed, the curtain was nothing at all. I saw the buildings and their big metal spines in excruciating clarity. I saw the table everywhere, whatever life throbbed inside it alive within every plane and juncture. I was born in this city. I should know and grieve my return. I should feel the revenants of my whole community wandering past the carriage and pulling at the doors, beating their numb hands on the white ox that pulled us, climbing on the roof and howling, baying, I should be pointing out the monuments of my childhood to Sisphe and lamenting what had been lost. I could hardly breathe to speak. My throat felt tight. Ignavia City was dipped in liquid mercury. It was armored in jellied light. Ichorite plated the terracotta molding along every building's face. It burnished the old Bellonan columns and enmeshed the wire bridges above our heads. A frothy film of ichorite shimmered between the cobblestones on the pavement, and an ichorite mist frosted the air, particulates floated, shaved diamonds hovering, smoldering. The smell drenched me. That sour candy smell! Sisphe pressed her hands on my chest. She mashed my heart down. I thought about grabbing pigeons. I imagined the muscle flapping between her fingers.

I tried to think about you. It had been so long since I'd been near you. I was near you now. There was so much poison between us.

"Tell me if we ride past Burn Street," I said. My tongue hung fat and itchy, I slurred around it. I pawed at Sisphe's belly. I'd missed her. I shouldn't be so near home, but it was coming together. It was time. I was meeting Industry today. I'd kill him. I'd get him alone and I'd kill him. I had my iron on me. I had my knife and I had this whole city. I could bring it down on his head. I could wrap buildings around him. I could smother him with the street. I rubbed my eyes. I'd never been to the races. There were Choir affiliates who played bookie but I didn't keep close counsel with them. Preferred direct seizure over that kind of work. I sniffed. "Does it show?"

"You look absolutely fucking ghastly." Sisphe rearranged me on her lap and pried my hands off my face. "Worry not! Do you know what I've been doing the past few days? I've been laying off enforcers and slashing promotions. Upping hours. Being a horrible boss! I found a seal and examples of handwriting and fuck if I'm not doing a halfway decent job of denting the enemy army by pissing them off, I'd hope. I don't know if all of them will be considered legitimate, but it's bound to catch some of them. I've intercepted five extremely angry letters. Fun, right? Plus I know where their weapon caches are now, the bigger armories. There are servant entry tunnels into the armories. We'll gut them. Now!" She cupped my cheeks. "I'm going to powder your face and touch you up so you look less cadaverous."

I felt serum leak out of my ears. It was chilly, thinner and more slippery than spit.

Sisphe frowned. The lines around her face flickered. "Are you dying?"

"City hurts."

"Will staying out here all day be too much?"

"Industry's coming." I curled my puffy lip. "Worth worse than this."

"Today," she said. She went cold and quiet. Her touch tightened around my jaw. She dug her fingers in. "Oh, sweet Marney."

"Don't say goodbye to me. Blow up an armory. Knock up Harlow. Save home or avenge it. I adore you." It was true. Probably I would die soon, a funny thought I couldn't quite parse. Thinking about her was easier. I praised her hands on me, I praised flips on the beach and a love that could withstand change and distance. I smiled at her with my busted swollen mouth. I did not clutch her and cry even when the desire took me. If I started I wouldn't stop. The carriage rattled underneath us. I focused on the vibrations in my spine.

She let go of me. She opened her clutch and fished out a clamshell, which she snapped wide with a click, and she fluffed her powder puff inside it, tapped its translucence on my fit-mottled cheeks, adorned me with cosmetics for the first and last time of my life. Felt like rabbits or how I imag-ined clouds. I doubted I looked any different but I liked the fussing. I smiled and my mouth hurt.

"It's Burn Street," she said.

313

Bolted upright. She pushed the curtains wide and I braced to see the bustle of my childhood. It was lush and congested, but it was Burn Street. I'd know it even with the luster plastering. The fashion had changed, silhouettes slimmer, closer to bodies, the uniforms overwhelmingly like the one I'd worn when I was small, double-kneed and elbow-patched waxed charcoal canvas, pervasive and dull against the glistening surroundings, and clingy dresses that stung me. Some shops were the same. The barbershop my pa used to patronize. A wave of nausea hit me, and hysterical giddiness. It was so stupid coming back. I'd escaped. Why did I come back?

The Yann I. Chauncey Ichorite Foundry rolled by us. It was smaller than I remembered, ruddier. Mortar and rough-faced shit. Smoke spat from tall stacks, noxious and green pink. Birds nested in wire and scrap metal in the buttressed rain gutters. The stained glass window had not been updated to reflect the expanding brand. Yann looked young. He glowed above as a fresh-faced man in primary colors, the immortal innovator of the world. He balanced an ichorite wand across his palms. He was smiling.

I flattened my palms on the door. Sisphe hooked an arm around my waist. I didn't strain. I panted. My red tongue lolled between my teeth. I looked over the mat of my tangled family and neighbors and congregation and you, the rhizomatic slurry of you, the pulsating knot of you and you and you, and the you I kept inside me drooled.

THE BOARS HAD numbers painted on their flanks. Wicked tusks jutted from their orange lips and curled back toward their eyes, which rolled insanely in their sockets, out of synch with each other. I saw their breath curl like smoke. They tore up the mud on the track and squealed like scraping knives together. The first sport was speed, fastest boar on the third lap victorious, and simultaneously the second sport was discipline and its failure. The boars would sometimes kill each other. This was not allowed but informally encouraged. That's where the real betting happened. There was a white one that Goss owned. Number seven. It was called Agravain. Drustish name from a legend Brandegor told when she was drunk about a *blodfagra* strife maiden who ended a blood feud in one night by lifting a Hall off its foundations and throwing it in the Flip River, transforming everyone inside into geese, but died of heartbreak, because the man whose honor she'd defended with this violence would not marry a *blodfagra* for fear of children inheriting the condition. She turned into moss. Agravain the boar slammed into the boar beside it. It unzipped the opposing boar's shoulder with its sharp hooked tooth.

We watched from box seats. I did not touch the crustless sandwiches offered to me. I sat beside Ramtha, who spoke at me kindly, telling me all about Luster City and the restoration projects she'd helped push, and Sisphe, who answered the occasional polite question curtly but sweetly on my behalf. The other suitors sat to my right, in this box and a box that way adjacent. Gossamer was not among us. She was in the box to my left alone. She was waiting for Industry.

I was waiting for Industry.

A boar slammed another against the track's partition. It squealed, thrashed. Mir roared approval. He had steadily grown sloppy over the past two hours. Many of us had. I didn't drink. I couldn't do anything but glance toward the left box. I was waiting for the stained glass man to appear. Not touching my gun was agony. It was under my jacket, harnessed under my armpit, purring imperceptibly. It wasn't the knife but it would be death. It'd do. It'd serve.

The security detail here was considerable. It was private security employed by Chaunceyco, not the racing facilities. He was a paranoid man, Ramtha had offered when I'd pointed it out. He suspected with good reason that people wished to do him harm, despite how beloved and revered she assured me that he was by the city populace. He was in constant mortal danger. There were hemorrhages of enforcers everywhere he went. Did I know it'd been her push to update enforcers uniforms to be made with fifty percent spun ichorite fabric? How chic!

The pigs flew round and round.

Gossamer looked edgy. Perhaps she was feeling unwell, or her father's lateness was ruffling her. She examined her nails and ignored the circus. Blue shadows showed under her eyes. The sunlight made her hair shine like fire. Striking and familiar. Something about her nose and the little hoop earring by her jaw. She had her heavy twill collar turned up against the wind. I thought I saw her shivering.

There was a waiter standing beside Gossamer Dignity. Blond, short, nothing specific. He peered into the room behind the box, watching for something. In the flurry of workers weaving through the stands and our boxes, I wasn't sure why I fixated on him. Maybe it was that he wasn't *doing* any work. He offered Goss nothing, held a bottle of wine wrapped in a crisp towelette that hadn't even been uncorked, and paid attention to neither the race nor his customer. Condensation dripped off the bottle like sweat.

Soft commotion. Gossamer stood. She turned her back on the boars. She clasped her hands at her tailbone and beamed, straining like she was resisting the impulse to give Yann Industry Chauncey a hug.

He was a thin gray man. He wore his hair cropped close around his skull like statues of old Bellonan soldiers. Long face, hooded eyes, lines at the edges of his flat, blunt mouth. He wore a cream-colored jacket and a dark blue shirt. He spoke to Goss. His lips pulled over his teeth. Dispassionate displeasure, or maybe his affect was just muddy. He pressed the pads of his fingers together. Tapped the thumbs. Yann Industry Chauncey wore no prayer beads. He was unmarked by faith at a glance. His posture was bad. He stood bowlegged. Hardly looked Stellarine at all. Looked a little like his stained glass portraiture, if leaner, less supple.

I stood up. My gun came into my hand.

The waiter cast the wine bottle aside. It smashed into jaggedy sequins and sloshed between the rails, dripped down toward the general admission. He revealed a long knife under the towelette. He lunged at Industry.

317

Thunder and lightning. I thumbed the hammer and squeezed.

The waiter collapsed in a red burst. He toppled sideways, slumped over the box's rail, fell into the stands below.

Gossamer screamed. The whole audience screamed with her, roused by my missed shot. Enforcers gushed from the cracks in the walls. They flooded the box and swept away Industry and Dignity, they swept in behind us and ushered myself and Sisphe and Ramtha into the lounge behind us, they herded us in a maroon-and-blue barrage down a hallway, down some stairs where I caught sight of Gossamer, but Industry was gone. An enforcer took me by my wrists, pulled me separately, grabbed the gun from me. I couldn't think. My movements lagged. Missed shot. Missed shot.

"She killed the assassin, let Truth go!" Ramtha cried. "Let her go!"

"I saw it," said Gossamer. She sounded tremulous and young. She pushed through the enforcer tide and shoved her way up the stairs, pushed herself close to me. She took my lapels in her fists. She pressed her forehead into my chest.

I couldn't breathe. I didn't dare move. I clutched the air where my gun had been.

"Take me home," Gossamer said. She leaned back and cracked a lopsided, delirious smile. Her shoulders shook. She did not let go of me. "You shot him. You killed him."

"Ready the carriages and pull them around front, tell the coachmen we're headed back to the estate," said Helena Integrity somewhere behind me to a worker I could not see. "Quickly, if you can. Thank you."

318

"I'm not going there," Gossamer snapped. She looked at me. Red veins snaked through the whites of her glacial blue eyes. "You're taking me home. I want to go to the Fingerbluffs. Show me the Fingerbluffs."

Sisphe at my side said, "Pardon?"

"I choose you," said Dignity. She pulled my chest against hers. "You or no one. You're going to marry me. I'm yours. Take me home. We leave now."

"If you please," Sisphe managed, bouncing on the balls of her feet, "Baron Fingerbluffs, Mr. Horace Veracity Loveday, is not a well man. He takes poorly to total surprises. Go back to the estates. Pack, dine, unwind, leave in the morning. I'll go now. I'll give him a few hours to prepare himself to meet his daughter's bride. It'll be a better homecoming for everyone. Is that favorable, ma'am?"

Gossamer nodded acutely. She didn't stop looking at me. Dry-tongued I breathed, "Tomorrow. Like Sisphe said."

"Tomorrow," Gossamer echoed. The aristocrats parted around us. Approval and displeasure were both outpaced by shock. The gunshot still echoed in the walls. It sounded like a heartbeat. They had won and lost. It'd been so loud. It was too big a crowd for so narrow a hallway. We dammed the traffic. They started to move. They'd go to Ramtha's, some of them. They'd follow us in waves. Nobody knew which boar was fastest. The race finished as the stands had been evacuated. The boars grazed, briefly unobserved.

Thirteen

SISPHE LEFT IMMEDIATELY. I HAD NO IDEA WHAT she'd do. She could not shove three hundred bandits under a rug and animate a dead man.

I rode in Gossamer's carriage on the way back. I sat with her and Vikare. None of us breathed a word. Gossamer leaned her head on my shoulder. Vikare watched my face with burning scrutiny. I looked out the window. We passed by the executioner's garden. Three of the five dangling belonged to the Choir. I read the names ELISA PROSPERITY JONES, PANTASILA MAHK URPHE, and CLYDE LENIENCE BARKER on their marbled green-pink bodies, floral with mold. I knew Pantasila a little. She gave me tasks to perform when I was young and restless to death. Bade me chop wood and sweep the stairs and fetch us both lemonade. Her freckled belly and breasts hung low, her mouth agape, the ring plucked from her bottom lip, in some state-sanctioned insinuation that bandits did not join the ancestral congress. Flies bejeweled her open milky eyes. I mouthed the bleed. I loathed myself that I could not go and cut her down. I loathed the air itself.

Yann Chauncey. I'd seen and killed his assassin. I'd killed his assassin, not the man. The man had been in my sights.

Gossamer laced her fingers through mine. I held the delicate hand of my fiancée.

I'd kill him. I'd kill him. He'd be my father-in-law. I'd get near him. I'd see him soon and I'd kill him in private where nobody could intervene. I'd bash his head against the wall. I'd beat him with a crowbar and throw his body in the coals of his hearth. I'd undo him. I'd destroy him. I worried my thumb over Gossamer's knuckles. When I died and they made her a widow, who would she marry next?

Didn't matter. Nothing else mattered. She would be alright.

I brought her knuckles to my lips and kissed them. I looked at Vikare. Her attention scalded, for courtesy's sake I ought return it. I nodded at her, stretched my swollen mouth at her. Tried to communicate with a glance that our deal was good.

She leaned her toe on mine, pressed down. She held me half-stomped for the rest of the ride.

PACKING. TERIASA GOT me alone. I had been trying to fit unfittable things into a bag and she appeared in the dim light, Beauty's shadow. More than any woman with the certificates to show it, Teriasa had authority. True elegance and might of word. How she must've led her Cisran Hereafterist literature boys, how she must've guided them before what happened! She pushed me onto the bed in my room and lay behind me, put her arm around my belly and dragged me close. Shock and adoration. I let myself be moved. The softness stung and I wept. She didn't. She pressed her forehead between my shoulder blades and I let her hold me in silence. Eventually she said, "Dumb rag rabbit. What are you going to do?"

"Sisphe took a lurcher out. If she kills herself over it, she could be home late tonight. Call the Choir. Plan."

"Plan what?"

"We've been pretending Horace is breathing for a decade. We're delusion artisans. They'll come up with something now." A dangerous farce to burden my family with, but I had no idea how to avoid it. This was the culmination of the long play. They knew someone would come and war would follow. I just hoped it followed when we left again, not while we were there. The Choir's might would be at our shoulders as we returned and fall on the enforcers as I murdered Yann Industry. No harm to the Fingerbluffs. "It's not what I'd want for us."

"Sisphe has been a maniac the past few days. She's made me crazy with her. If the charades she's already started rolling out work, even a quarter of them work, it'll shape the war. Pretending is our strong suit." She did not sound convinced of the words out of her mouth, but still said them in her punchy, darling know-it-all way. Night itself. I imagined her with Tullian praise dots on her eyelids. "How are you going to keep it up?"

"Be kind and quiet, if I can manage it. She wants ichorite. Ichorite is under azurine groves, and ours are the most beautiful in the world. She'll be happy with what she sees. I just need to stay out of her way and keep her from looking at anything too closely." My voice cracked. It hurt. I thought it'd show on the surface of my throat. "I didn't get him, Sunny."

"You will. You might've paused the big war, too. Don't be cruel to yourself about this, it'll make me so angry."

"Yes ma'am," I said.

She got up and brought my clothes to me. We folded them together.

SOMETIME LATER, NEARLY sleeping, we heard the boom. The crash trembled the floor and screaming followed it. I bolted out of bed, put my body between the noise and Sunny, that night she let me call her Sunny, but the sound was distant from us, came from at least a floor below. Sunny sank her nails into my hips and shoved her forehead against my shoulder. We were fully dressed. I wore her nightshirt. She breathed roughly. I listened past her breathing. A second shattering, smaller, then something like tearing canvas. People hollered. Horror first, then animal bellowing. I thought of crawly bar brawls, where all our anger from years of bludgeoning by the law and the wage and bad parents condensed into us beating each other unconscious with steins and wooden stools. Somebody was trying to kill somebody downstairs. Not a quick job.

I folded my arms around Sunny and felt hilariously small for a moment. The thought crossed my mind that I might have rivals here to destroy this continent's rulership. A waiter with a hunting knife who sprung out of a wall to kill whomever came nearest. *Or.* Or could be Laith Herzeloyde getting her licks in on Princess Perdita Perfection Vaughn. Or the unseemly inverse. Vomit fluttered. I failed today. Would Herzeloyde? My nerves all fried and I couldn't stand my own stillness, in a fit of omnidirectional passion and loathing I drew myself away from Sunny and the bed and slid to the floor, pawed through the dark until I found and opened my shut luggage, fished out my sawed-off shotgun and a bandolier we'd wrapped in my riding denim. I slung the belt over my shoulder and pulled the denim on, toed on my heavy boots.

"You don't need to intervene," Sunny said. She sat up and pulled the blankets around her, repetitively smoothed the wrinkles over her thighs. "Aristocrats bashing each other is them doing the work for us. You look like one of us. You can't go down so armed."

"What if somebody's murdering Birdie?" I sniffed. "Ain't no way of knowing."

As was her power, Sunny produced a match from nowhere. She lit the candle beside the bed. Illuminated thus, I caught an edge of my reflection in an ornate gilt-framed mirror and physically flinched. My mouth was red and beestung, my tongue even redder, like cut fruit. I looked like I'd been sobbing. My eyes watered, seething bruisy pink splotches rimmed them, spilled down my nose and cheeks. This bad *hours* after having left Luster City. Spare me. My ringlets stuck out at odd angles. My whole face glistened, highlighted with oil-on-water swirls. It was the powdered-down fit serum. Incongruous harsh ammunition belt over Sunny's frothy linen nightshirt, incongruous weapon brandished in my little twitching fist. I looked heinous. I looked like a lamb that'd survived its slaughter.

"Stay here," I said.

Her face pulled. She didn't like being told what to do, nor did she like the faux command some crawlies affected to prove their masculinity, but she'd do it. It'd be risking herself. She wasn't a girl for fights.

I made my way around the bed and gathered her up, managed somehow with one hand around my shotgun, and eased her back down against the mattress. I smoothed her hair and pulled the buttery sheets high. I tucked her in, pulled the down comforter over her, repeated the process. She closed her eyes. I saw the little purple veins threaded through her eyelids. She looked like a mythic princess from the old woodcuts, who ruled nature by force of goodness and faith and had no legal power. I kissed her brow. I loaded my gun. I shut the door behind me.

At the bottom of my descent, in a magenta damask room, a chandelier sprawled jaggedly on the ground. It looked like a smashed white cake. Glass and crystals crunched like snow under my boots. Pearls unstrung rolled in the seams of the mosaic floor. Aqua and mint green tiles for the Virtue Industry, a pearl-handed man. The crushed candles smoked; one still burned. Blood pooled a brilliant tangerine scarlet underneath the chandelier. I saw the boots, calves, thighs, hips of a woman among the spill. Laith Herzeloyde, it seemed. A shawl covered her face and upper arms. Her hands moved. She pressed her palms into the floor. She dragged her body minutely forward with the strength of her fingertips.

I hooked my boot under a broad gold hoop. The chandelier husk was heavy. It startled me with its bulk. I snarled, I kicked upright, the smashed-up chandelier flipped on its edge and clattered across the room.

Herzeloyde didn't stand. She kept inching along.

Rest of the room. Fallen bodies, plainly dead— Gossamer Dignity's bodyguard staff. They must have been drawn into the room, I couldn't imagine all of them here by chance. Seven of them were dead in a longwise pile along the wall. Throats cut and head wounds, nothing elaborate. There were overturned chairs. Broken Bellonan vases. A maid whose name I didn't know cowered beneath a table, cringed away from the corpses across the room. She looked young. She flinched from my gun and flattened her body against the exquisite wallpaper. She jabbed a finger left.

Left opened into another gallery. I stepped softly, led with the gun's cut muzzle. Vases smashed here as well. Another dead bodyguard. Must be few left, if any. Gorgeous deep brown furniture had been snapped, splintered in quick blossoms. Smashed. Looked clubbed or slugged with a hammer. Art on the wall hung slashed or did

not hang. Fragrant rough canvas ribbons curled along the
floor. I followed the destruction's curve. It led me another
room deeper, this one finch yellow, then through a room
whose walls were dressed in rich emerald velvet curtains,
gathered and beautifully draped, another with mirrored
panels that disturbed me. The mirrors too were smashed.
Their cracks blazed like spiderwebs. All of them were
shoulder height. The upper portions remained untouched
but for the feathered spreading damage below. Deliberate
damage. Quick tantrum damage.

I heard laughing.

I hugged the wall, my hips a breath away from dreadful
mirror Marney's, and entered the next room.

I watched Perdita and Mir leaving.

Perdita wore lilac taffeta and riding spurs clicking, clicking. She brandished a bronze candlestick. Around her waist,
two long plaits were tied like belts. White-blond plaits. She'd
sawed them off of Herzeloyde's head. Her own hair was piled
at her crown, stuck through with a fork, and I saw the muscle that bound her neck to her shoulders dripping sweat. Mir
walked beside her. He held the second candlestick and spoke
softly to her, gave her counsel. What pirate advice was this?
*Easy now, sweet bloodlusting girl, don't sack your friend's palace?
Don't break what can be stolen?* They turned a corner, her fantastic skirts swaying around her ankles, her spurs jingling like
bells, and Perdita whirled on something unseen and swung
her instrument against it. It shattered.

Shouts erupted in that next room. A bloodcurdling
scream in Dunn Drustish, then Helena, hoarsely: "Fucking

think, skies above, think for one second the millions you
condemn with your—"

"War on the Drustlands!" Dita's voice carried. It trembled the glass fragments in the mirrored walls. "Baby Helena,
so righteous and sweet! You're deluded playing revolutionary.
I am going to spatchcock this girl. I am going to burn Dunn
Hall. I am going to rape her Hall head and strip the relics
from her Shrine. I will kill everybody she has ever met. I
will put them in a hole and pave it over. You, Helena, will be
so rich when I am done. You will be flush and choked with
Drustish gold. I will send a crateful to you personally. I will
slap railroads across the smoldering mess I make and estab-
lish schools and proper hospitals and good industry, industry
that will trade with Ignavia, that will support us in our campaign, because you're fucking smart and will play along like a
good girl. You're dressed in fine clothes in this fine house because your father's father's father's father had military might
enough to hold down your piece of the mountains. We're
fucking *warlords*, Baronet Helena Integrity Shane! That's the
only kind of lord there is! Stand aside!"

Another shattering, and a choked sob.

I put my shoulder in the doorway.

Perdita stood over a stained glass portrait of Yann
Industry Chauncey. It looked identical to the one that'd
glared over me my whole childhood. Yann's face was
snapped below his left eye. Perdita stepped forward and
his forehead shattered. She shook her arms out. The trophy braid belts swayed at her hips. She threw up the

candlestick, it spun above her like a baton, she caught it with a flourish.

Mir kept close rank behind her. Protective stance, I'd say. I saw the ropes along his arms. I would not want to be caught in his grasp.

Across the room, Helena Integrity Shane stood in front of Strife Maiden Dunn Ygrainne. Ygrainne wept. Fury pinched her lips white. She shook down to the bone, and Helena leaned back against her, spread wide her hands. Helena wore a nightgown. Her makeup was gone, her eyes shadowed. She'd been sleeping, I'd expect. She walked Ygrainne backwards, edged her toward the open door-way behind them. I saw other observers there, Ramtha and Alichsantre in particular. Ramtha hyperventilated. Alichsantre touched her arm.

"This is a mistake," Helena said. She jutted out her chin. "This is madness and if word of this spreads, Dita—"

"Word that a strife maiden slaughtered Goss's guards and tried to assassinate me would be marvelous good for the cause!" Perdita stepped toward Helena. "Move aside. Last time I'll ask. I'll break your body, don't think I won't."

Vikare entered through the far door. She brushed past Alichsantre and Ramtha, past Ygrainne and Helena, and walked directly into Perdita's reach. She wore a nightgown so thin it looked like water. It warped the light. She looked like a revenant. Desire lurched in me, I stomped on it, but the sparks didn't snuff. Her knife was drawn. She bran-dished it at Perdita Perfection's throat.

"This is Dignity's house," Vikare said. "You shame yourself."

"Nearly being slain in Dignity's house is a smear on her honor, not mine." Perdita tossed her head back. She took a step toward the knife, brought her chest to the tip. "You're nothing. You don't even have a title. It'd be a treat to beat you 'til you can't stand up. Right, MirMir?"

"Step back, Vik," Mir said.

Vikare's eyes flew wide. Her face lit up, red at once, and she kicked her feet as she was dragged back. Instinct hit her, she dropped her knife, clawed in vain at the hands around her throat.

Alichsantre's hands. Alichsantre had her in a chokehold. She pulled her back toward the door.

Mir stepped forward but Perdita thrust out the candle-stick, blocked him.

"Well, I'll be!" Perdita whistled. "I didn't think you had it in you, Alich."

"How dare you interfere in this," Alichsantre said. "How dare you intervene in what isn't yours to touch. I should have killed you at Wilton. I should've killed you and Gossamer, *Gossamer*, for dwelling among your betters and imitating what cannot ever be yours. My wealth is my birthright. My nobility is in my blood, my ancient, magic blood, my blood from the crater, first among ancestors, my power is ordained by fate, and you, you little *rat*, you grime, you're a fucking *merchant*. Your money belongs to other people. You don't exist. You don't matter. You aren't even Veltuni anymore, you shouldn't even be called Vikare, you are *not* immortal, you

are *not* my ethereal peer in eternity, you forsook it for a gim-
mick! You took out the ring! And now you stand between
the hereditary rulers of this world, you put your body and
your blade before the advancement of history towards its origin. You must answer for your arrogance. You put my eye
out. You took my beauty from me. You took my marriage-
ability from me. You stole from me, you steal from everyone
in this room, this room which is fucking *Ramtha's*, we stand
in a summer home gifted to Yann by Ramtha XI, the only
way such grandeur could be bestowed upon salesmen and
polluters. We allow Gossamer to prance around in borrowed
splendor because she's a rich little piggie, but you, you Vikare
mine, little Azurine, we will not suffer *your* arrogance. We
will not suffer your hideous fashions and the mockery you
make of prestige. We will not tolerate your cheapening of
our style and manner in the guise of base progressivism. We
will spare you your whorishness and your will to violence. I
will spare you. I will take you home with me, you maimer
of greatness, I will take you back to Cisra. I will take you
home to my palace, which has been mine for a thousand
years, which is the true inheritance of fifty generations of my
name, and I will instruct you on your place. I will be your
pedagogue and jailor. I will be your despot and father. I will
fix you with my cruelty. You will be my bride."

I pushed off from the doorway.

Vikare's eyes rolled back in her head.

My finger bent. Warning shot in the ceiling. The sound
clapped me, I curled my lip. Dust fell over us. Everybody in
the room dropped.

"That's enough." I trod over the broken glass, hugged the edge of the room but brought myself toward the center. I reloaded, made a show of it. I scowled at my hands and the ache in my shoulder. I scowled at the mess. "Drop your arms."

Perdita did slowly, bright pink. Mir didn't but I knew enough of his culture from the pirates around the Fingerbluffs to know he wouldn't, I didn't press it. Alichsantre released Vikare. She collapsed to the floor, gasping, wheezing. She caught herself with her palms, I saw blue slivers of Yann's glass face slip under her skin. Helena didn't move. She panted, leaning back against Ygrainne, still openly weeping.

"If my father saw such rabble in his home." I scraped my tongue with my teeth and spat. "There will be no more of this."

"While you were sleeping, Velma, Dunn Ygrainne's guard killed all Goss's guards and moved against me." Perdita peered over her shoulder at me, sugared party affect unfazed. She smiled sweetly. "Pardon the noise. It's drowned out context."

"Laith Herzeloyde moved against you," I said. "Laith's a border Hall. Or was."

Something flashed on Dunn Ygrainne's face. She hadn't known Herzeloyde's plan. I believed that.

"Laith was a border Hall," Perdita repeated. She stuck the tip of her tongue between her teeth and glanced upwards, considering. "That sounds familiar. It might have been, sure!"

Ygrainne's face twisted. Helena's did too.

Vikare picked the glass out of her hands. The glass looked like dyed sugar candy. She picked her knife up. I didn't see her blink.

"There will not be war in the Drustlands," I said.

Perdita offered her most dimpled smile. "New Bellona demands its making. It's time, Velma. You can get in on this."

"What d'you plan to pay your army with?" Frosty anger coated all my guts. Shutting up wasn't on the table. "Won't be Gossamer's money and Susannah thinks you're filthy. There won't be Ignavian money in your fight. There could be Tasmudani money in the Drustish's."

She batted her lashes and rested her hand on the candlestick. She stroked it like a little dog. "Sound awful certain."

"She picked me." I kissed my teeth. "I am."

Helena sighed so deeply I thought she'd collapse.

"Ramtha," I said. "Can you help me help Herzeloyde? I don't know this city. Who do we call?"

Next room over, Ramtha folded her hands and held them steepled to her lips.

"Oh, that's funny. Is she alive?" Perdita *hmph*ed. She played with the edge of her dress. "Stupid chandelier."

"Goss's doctor is still here," Ramtha said carefully. Every syllable was round and over-enunciated, the consonants soft, the tone behind them so polished, like she had a marble in her mouth and was trying not to swallow it. She touched her ichorite dress, warped the sheen under the pad of her fingers, and turned her back on us. Square, practiced rib cage movements. "Alichsantre L. Let's go fetch him together."

Alichsantre watched Vikare on the floor.

"Countess," Ramtha said.

"You invited me to this," said Ygrainne. Her voice startled me. Its intensity. No anger or resentment, but an energetic tightness that everyone, even Perdita Perfection, cocked their head to better hear. "You brought me to this snake nest. Why?"

"You have my diplomatic sympathy and everything can be settled over drinks. It's a party. These are my friends," said Ramtha in that measured way. "If you were friends with us, we wouldn't kill each other."

Vikare started laughing. She put the knife in her lap and pressed her wrist bones to her temples.

"It'd be a great help if you fetched the doctor with Ramtha, Alich," Helena said. She did not affect Ramtha's politician's bounce. She sounded dead tired and hoarse, like she'd been screaming. "Now, please."

Vikare laughed louder. It sounded like she was coughing something up.

"This is fucking excruciating." Mir put his candlestick on his shoulder and reached down, took Vikare by her forearm and helped her up. The knife clattered to the floor and Mir rested his boot on the blade. "Dita. You and me, we're taking Vikare upstairs. Alichsantre, go with Ramtha. Helena, bring the strife maiden elsewhere. Velma," he glanced over his shoulder at me, fixated for a moment on my gun, on the way I held it.

"I'll do as I do," I said.

"Huh." He wiggled his jaw. "You sailed much?"

"Alich," Ramtha said. "Let's go. You're embarrassing me."

Ygrainne pulled away from Helena. She walked across the room, past seething stalk-still Alichsantre, past sweetly smiling bristling Perdita and laughing Vikare under Mir's arm, and stood before me. She touched my chest. She looked at me with her eyes burning. "There will not be war in the Drustlands?"

I scuffed my toe on the carpet, ground a shard of glass into glitter. "We'll remember these wrongs with our hands."

Perdita's ears pricked. Attention, not recognition. She didn't speak Mors, or maybe any Drustish, but she knew the sound.

"Being the fastest this afternoon does not entitle you to threaten us with a firearm. Provincial roughness is hideous," Alichsantre hissed. "This is not an acceptable way to—"

"You strangled Vikare," Helena said. Her eyes stretched wide and she grinned, exhausted and exasperated. "*You just strangled Vikare.* You put your hands on her neck and strangled her. Think, Alichsantre. Velma killed an assassin this afternoon. Stop talking."

Mir laughed. Vikare laughed harder when he laughed. She swayed against him, and he wrapped an arm around her shoulder, and across the room worn Helena joined them, a spasm of her belly, then Ygrainne with a jolt, and Perdita, and as though in defeat Ramtha, everyone but

Alichsantre, who made a bizarre expression, something that wasn't a smile and wasn't a grimace, a big juicy curve of shock and pain. Everyone churned around me. Ygrainne drifted away from me into the smashed-mirror room, and Helena followed her, with a swirl Mir swept Vikare up, Vikare who wept and gasped she laughed so convulsively, Perdita laughing too, a determined, bitter laugh, one that revealed that she was exactly what we knew her to be, and Ramtha laughed in anguish and absurdity and appeared beside Alichsantre and snapped her fingers, rolled her wrist, laughed harder and harder until Alichsantre crumbled and slinked after Ramtha for the doctor, tail between her legs, and suddenly I was alone in the ruined parlor. There was a hole in the ceiling and dust fell from the edges

I sat on the floor. I put my gun across my thighs. Yann I. Chauncey's fucked-up face spilled across the floor in front of me. His ear and his thin mouth were near my left knee and his nose and bottom lash line were near my right. I reached for the little pieces and arranged them. I put his face together. He was missing pieces but I could make a legible shape with him.

That was him! That was the man in the walls of my factory. That was the man I did not kill today.

If I had killed Perdita, shot and killed Perdita and Mir and this whole cohort of junior rulers, Alichsantre's hereditary rulers of the world, if I had killed everybody but Vikare, if I had killed even Vikare, would it stop the war? If Herzeloyde had killed Perdita, would Miles Exemplar, the older brother, have continued it on? Would the war machine simply replace Perdita with another chipper killer girl? Would there be a war machine without its players? Yes, surely. That's history. Yes, of course! So said Gossamer, aristocrats are as fungible as workers. The cog spins or it's replaced.

When I killed Industry, would his work die with him? Would the infrastructure that preceded and surrounded him, that allowed him to become himself, evaporate into fumes? Would ichorite sink back into the earth? Would all the things built out of it become what they'd been prior? Had I any idea what they'd been made out of prior? When they killed me, would Vikare miss me? Would war happen immediately and with extra gusto for my having been a sneak and a thief? Would Edna be back when I died? Would Edna, still pregnant, shrink from me for being what I am? How quickly she would've killed Industry! Years ago! Her lustertouched baby would be ten. Will the sun rise in the morning? Will the dawn come and with it, luck and bread?

But the blood spilled is worthy. It appeases the dead.

I cut my thumb on Yann Industry's chin. The pain startled me. I shook out my wrist. A fruity bright drop of blood fell and splotched his shoulder. The hilariousness of the whole room revealed itself to me. What a lark, being Marney! The things I do for you.

DAWN CAME. I prayed. Sunny asked me what I was doing so I broke the rules and showed her. We spent a few minutes on our knees beside the bed. Praise the Torn, killed by Day, praise the Torn, killed by Night, praise the heavens who made the Torn, praise us, her and me, who remembered the violence and walked across it all our lives, lived to know it, to answer it. We grieved her fragile man. He hadn't dangled. Cisra's royal enforcement had shot every pamphleteer in the head and left the bodies broken where they fell. He still bled when Teriasa came home. He'd been good to her. He died at twenty-one. Teriasa aborted the baby. She came back to Ignavia alone. I kissed her knuckles. She kissed my forehead. I dressed up as Velma Truth Loveday and I went downstairs all packed.

The guests sat together around the awful ichorite table. Darya was absent, as was Ygrainne. Herzeloyde was absent. Susannah had, from what she said, slept through the whole affair. Alichsantre didn't eat. Ramtha didn't eat but pretended. Mir ate. Perdita ate. Mir and Perdita loudly spoke about Alichsantre's outburst as though it had been the singular rudeness of the night. Helena had her forehead leaned against the table's edge and read a book she held under the table. Mago looked miffed. He whispered to Susannah, or at her, about the Flip River delta, and how if only she'd agree, if only.

I passed them. They watched me go with their eyes but did not address me. Helena might have smiled.

Gossamer Dignity Chauncey and Vikare zel Tlesana waited in the chilly white corridor beyond the palm-frond courtyard. Gossamer wore a plain twill suit and a heavy wool coat, and Vikare wore a slinky dress that made me itch and furs that swept her ankles. There were faint bruises on Vikare's neck. I felt dizzy looking at them, and a lurch of shame that I hadn't killed Alichsantre L. Goss gestured to Vikare's gown. She spoke in low, singsong remarks, and Vikare brushed her off with an implacable look, something around embarrassment. When Gossamer saw me, she turned to me, gestured at me with despair.

"Truth," Goss said. "You're fucking Vikare. Reason with her for me!"

I stopped walking. With effort I resumed, and stood nearby them, just out of arm's reach. "Vikare is being reasonable," I said.

"You don't know the context! Bias! We're riding a train from here toward the coast, and dressing your wealth is a death sentence! Everywhere a stone's throw from Luster City is crawling with bandits. All my fucking guards are dead, and we are *not* telling my father until I get back and you're my wife. We've got to stay sharp. Tell me you'd mug Azurine if you had the chance!"

Azurine must've been Vikare's mortal name. Knowing was an intimacy that hadn't been offered. For sake of politeness, I tried to push it from my mind. I dwelled instead on the question. Or assertion, it was an assertion. I felt floridly insane.

Vikare pulled a hand along her side, held back the furs to show me the dress beneath. I'd seen this bolt of fabric in her room. She might've made it while I was here. I liked craftswomen. I left faint. I'd already stolen so much fabric from her. "Go on, Truth. Would you mug me if you could?"

"No ma'am," I said.

"But if you were a bandit," Goss pressed. "Wouldn't Vikare's beauty be a beacon?"

"You've got to think like you're a bandit," said Vikare. "Or else you'll prove me right."

"I would love to prove you right," I said.

"This is ridiculous. Your whole career as my wife will be conspiracy and treachery. I'm being mindful and reasonable with a contemporary understanding of our rail system's risks. I am not being weird," Goss huffed. "If anything, I am being a thoughtful and attentive ex-lover business partner baby genius to you. To both of you."

"She's not yet your ex-lover," Vikare said. She herded us toward the door, and for that alone I would've collapsed at her feet. "You still have time."

"All the time in the world. Now," Gossamer said as she stepped out of her mansion into the brisk clear morning, turning her collar to the wind, "Vikare, my darling Miss Ichorite. Who's a better lover, her or me?"

"It is a long train ride to the Fingerbluffs," I said.

Gossamer glanced over her shoulder like me. There was such an incredible rush in that look—I felt like she knew something about me I didn't, some ribbon of truth under Truth, under Marney. She liked what she knew. She showed me her teeth. "Hours of conversation. Get excited!"

There came a jolt of nervousness. Horace Veracity Loveday forbade the construction of a train station in the Fingerbluffs. The real one, twenty years ago. The actual awful man. His prudishness toward all advancement, which had initially allowed for and still remained the face of the collective effort animating the Choir's grand charade, here posed a problem. There was no efficient way to arrive at the Fingerbluffs. There were trains that'd take a traveler one barony over, in sparse, traditionalist Olmstead, but there was nothing past that. The roads were skinny and rough, ox trails mostly. Fine for lurchers but tough for anything much bigger. That inhospitality didn't translate well to a faux-aristocratic welcome, and besides that, I would be forsaking my lurcher in the pines where Sisphe and I had left it. Couldn't take mine back. I didn't know what I'd be taking back. We'd get off the train in Olmstead and fucking improvise. Maybe Sisphe would've sent for a cart? I could blame it on Truth's father, but I wasn't sure what we'd do when Gossamer inevitably asked to meet the man. I could show her some bones. Some worms whose grandparents might have dined on him.

I tucked my hair behind my ears. "Tell me about how the two of you met."

Vikare's stroked her long fur coat. I had no idea what animal comprised it. "Wilton."

"Wilton School, our own dungeon. Yes," Goss said. "I was enrolled late. Father wanted me to share his education, besides which his schedule demands the majority of his attention, and he hardly had time for an underfoot teenager, and with my condition, I needed near constant supervision, particularly at that age. So, Wilton. Temple to brutality. I was clearly Drustish, I had been adopted into new money, I was small for my age and fragile. I was smart. I was rough

back then too, and reacted quickly and poorly to people trying to get ahead of me. In short, the bullying was awful.
Just heinous. Vikare, little Azurine, being from merchant
money, also had a complicated time. Children are cruel.
They were especially cruel to us. But we're smart, she and
I. She decided she wanted to be my girl, so she brought me
the schematics for what became our revolutionary textile
industry. It was so clever. She's innovative and assertive,
wildly creative, and has great business sense. I knew we had
to protect each other and become partners."

"Then my mother," Vikare said.

"Your mother," Goss paused, "was responsible for some
of the most stressful afternoons of my life. Vikare and her
mother Tlesana struggle, shall we say. Vikare was not set
to inherit any of Tlesana's business. Not the money, not
the house, nothing. It was all slated to go to Vikare's older
brother, Easun thu Tlesana, but of course Easun is sharp as
a circle, and I refused to see my best friend desperate. So we
lied to Tlesana. We had her sign over rights to the use of her
textile mills and the workers employed therein under the
guise that it was a relinquishing of Vikare's debatable claim.
We had Easun sign as well. I'm still not sure if it's dawned
on him."

"Easun means well," Vikare said.

Goss waved a hand. "He means nothing at all."

I wondered what Gossamer thought of the violence that
broke her home last night. The marks on her best friend.
She must've noticed the bruises. Even if she didn't care
about Vikare's wellbeing, and I wanted to believe she did,

surely she'd care that her home was cracked up and riddled with holes. I wasn't sure how to bring it up. It was so frightfully huge that gesturing toward it felt ridiculous. Instead, "What about Susannah?"

A vein showed in Gossamer's cheek. "I shouldn't have. Poor little mouse."

"She was too shy to even attend Lunarist Society meetings. It was cruel of you to fuck her," Vikare said with a casual venomousness that made me flinch even without being its target. "Crueler still to invite her here."

"Crueler than not inviting her? I disagree. My only available options were awful."

"You could've left her alone."

"And been lonely myself?" Gossamer laughed. I heard the whole house laugh with her, everyone laughing last night in the torn-up parlor, guts splitting and thighs slapping left and right. "I'd sooner die! One moment alone with myself is more than enough for the wolves to close in. You can't be your own company if you're a woman like me. We cannibalize ourselves. We remember things. Memory's a scourge!"

Fourteen

WE GOT OFF THE TRAIN IN OLMSTEAD. I DIDN'T rob us, so the ride was smooth. We'd played cards, or they played, I dealt, and dozed and spoke idly about nothing, least of all the broken house or the assassination attempt or the war which my word was not good enough to slow, and gazed out the window while I tried desperately to conceive of options for transporting us from Olmstead home. Hitchhiking was out of the question. Lurchers, best method, also out of the question. Everything that came to mind was laughable. When Vikare had brought up the night previous on the train, or alluded to her sore throat, she'd laughed and her laughter electrocuted us into laughing and together we'd laughed so hard that the conductor checked on us. Gossamer had started laughing as soon as the question was raised. Did she know what'd happened last night? Of course! Of course! *You will be my bride.* What a riot!

I wasn't sure how laughable it'd be for us to walk twenty miles as a bonding exercise.

In Olmstead it was evening. Harsh milky fog but pleasant temperature. It reminded me of the humidity inside the Yann I. Chauncey Ichorite Foundry. Everything was always wet in there. When we walked down the station's modest sandy stairs into the unmarked darkness, I thought about the viability of stealing a parked cart and playing it off as though I hadn't. Like absolutely this had been my cart for years. Vikare would spackle over little holes in believability, I assumed, but gulches? Yawning gulfs of believability would not be so easily surmounted. I didn't know if she'd cover obvious cart theft for me. My provincial roughness could only extend so far.

I carried luggage for all three of us and entertained this fear. I ran down plans whose woeful inadequacies almost endeared me to them. I walked ahead of Vikare and yawning Gossamer, dreaming up methods for keeping this going just a little longer. Just a few days more. If I was meaner and less clumsy I'd be dead and victorious and there'd be less fussy maintenance. It goes like this sometimes. I'd hire someone random and have them play valet. I'd coax us into staying at some skeevy boarding house and go out by myself into the night and fucking build a cart with my hands. Heaven help me, *something*.

There was a cart waiting for us at the bottom of the staircase.

In Cisra there was a budding consumer automotive industry that made slower lurchers for civilian use. They were murderously expensive and had not caught on, half because the manufacturers were Cisran royalists who wouldn't use ichorite for sake of local pride and insisted on building the whole engine apparatus out of Bellonan-style steel, and half because the machines were thunderously loud, sickly, temperamental, persnickety, pollutant, and inefficient, and demanded even footing or else they'd roll over, mutilating and killing everybody inside them. They looked like sexy beetles. This was one of those. It was cherry red with obsidian rims. Big wheels, obviously standard lurcher wheels that'd been popped on to give the machine extra height, and a fine black leather interior.

Harlow sat on the hood. She cupped her hands around her mouth and lit a spliff. Shoulders raised as she took a belly deep drag and fell as she blew rings of smoke into the surrounding fog. She smiled when she saw us, leaped off the hood and onto her feet. Orange sparks flaked off her spliff and fell into nothing. Harlow bowed deeply. She wore an absurdly formal servant's suit, crisp tailored eggplant jacket and pants over a high-collared shirt, gilded cufflinks, lush silk ascot, leather gloves, jewel-encrusted signet rings worn *over* the gloves, patterned spats, more earrings than she usually wore, so many I thought the weight must ache and threaten to rip her ears from her head. Velma Truth Loveday was half antiquarian conservative, half boardwalk pimp. Harlow had not one lick of conservatism at all. Full sexmonger. King among men. As was her habit, she'd slicked back her hair with high-shine grease, and I saw my expression reflected across it. Saw my open mouth.

"Master," Harlow dripped. She fell to her knees, pinched her spliff between her thumb and first finger, and kissed the toe of my boot. "It's delicious to see you. We've missed you so fucking bad. We've wept and torn our hair in your absence. We've drank. We've begun writing poetry and dancing naked dirges but it's not enough to sate us in your absence. In our grief and boredom we've started to beat each other up. We're killing each other. I've murdered two of the hall boys. I beat them to death with a crowbar. You look so sexy and distinguished. I am dizzy with pride to escort you home. You and your kitty cat." Harlow threw herself back on her heels, knees apart, tossed her head to keep all her pomaded hair in place. She took another drag and glanced between my thighs. "Kitty cat and friend. What gorgeous women you've brought us. You'll make such handsome babies inside both of them."

In my heart I reached for Harlow, darling Harlow. I dropped the bags and I reached to fit my hands around her neck.

Harlow swayed out of strangling range and stood up. She was taller than me, broader with her boxer shoulders, and I knew well that if she wanted to manhandle me aside, she could. She held her spliff with her teeth and pulled me into a fierce embrace, luggage bags knocking between our knees as she emptied my lungs with the strength of her arms, then spun me, made me look at Goss and Vikare.

Goss and Vikare wore identical expressions. Gossamer's lips had parted, her faint brows arched up to her hairline, her eyes stretched as wide and round as they'd ever been. Vikare looked like she might faint. Her mouth fluttered between a manic grin and astonished flatness. She didn't blink. She didn't so much as breathe. Horror. Glee. Pseudo-religious awe.

Harlow purred, "Which one of you is about to be my mistress?"

Gossamer and Vikare glanced at each other.

"On the left is Gossamer Dignity Chauncey, my fiancée, and on the right is Vikare zel Tlesana, her business partner." My bones vibrated under my skin. "Goss. Vik. This is Harlow. She is," I closed my eyes, adjusted my grip on the five bags I carried, "my valet."

"It's a pleasure," said Goss.

"Mhm," said Vikare.

"Pleasure's all mine." Harlow leaned down and kissed my cheek. "Let's go for a ride."

Maybe it was just Harlow. Perhaps the rest of my proud Choir waited in the Fingerbluffs acting casual and sane.

Harlow took the luggage bags from me. She dangled them over her shoulders on her fingertips with majesty and ease. Perfect finesse as she opened the automotive's trunk with her toe, tossed in the bags as though they weighed nothing, and slammed it shut. She sucked down her spliff to the filter in one inhale. She flicked the filter into the fog.

I looked at Goss and Vik. I looked at the automotive. My body moved for me. I climbed into the front seat beside the driver's, closed the door behind me, watched helpless as Harlow ushered Goss and Vikare into the back of this gorgeous glossy deathtrap. The two of them sat in total silence behind me. Gossamer was now grinning like a maniac. Vikare looked like she'd gone into a sort of trance. Harlow shut the doors behind them, then climbed into her own seat, revved the engine. She skimmed her palm over the wheel, a skill she must've learned from one of the pirates we knew, rambunctious Nero or short lovely serious Iodine, and whirled us around like a carnival ride. She tore forward, took a path I knew. We'd ride the Ridgeroad, the narrow shepherd's path along the cliffs, a place where her and I and Tricksy and Candor used to practice lurcher tricks. A miracle we hadn't all died. She took us down that way, and she cranked her window down, pointed a finger into the night. "Look over the water, good ladies," she said. "Behold the end of the world."

WE DID NOT speak. The absurdity of Harlow's style and beauty had a sort of pacifying effect; nothing was stranger than her entrance into their lives, therefore everything could be magic without questioning. The automotive sounded and felt like a conveyor belt. It made my guts go liquid. Homesickness took me. This might be the last time I'd ever see the Fingerbluffs. When I left, it'd be to meet my destiny. War would follow. This place, these hallowed rocks, would melt into the air any instant.

The cliff skimmed the edge of the azurine orchards. Their supernatural luminous blueness felt unlucky now, an ill omen. There was ichorite under the ground. I heard Gossamer stir in the backseat, heard her spine adjust against the leather, and knew she was pleased by what she saw. I imagined her imagining the destruction of the Fingerbluffs. I imagined a smoldering hole.

Dark pink lights and gulls diving, screaming over the roaring tide.

The Fingerbluffs jutted from the ground, living filthy gold. Harlow took us along the city's edge, away from the cliff now, and brought us down the most central street, the only one I'd wager could take a vehicle of this size. Lurchers leaning everywhere, no way to explain that. Candles stuck in wine bottles dangled from the street lamps. The magenta light through the red paper windows cast funny shadows with the machine. Everybody was outside and above us. I put my hands against my diaphragm. I was going to scream. I was going to jump and cry. The Choir crowded on the balconies of the skinny temples and along the endless triple gallery shotguns with their brilliant green overhangs, on the rooves too, perched on the edge of chimneys, on the backs of steeples, on a Virtue statue of Truth. They stood on the lips of six-tiered fountains and climbed up onto the freestanding ancient ornate archways and the chunks of Bellonan columns, hundreds upon hundreds of people, gorgeous grinning tipsy people, like a flock of seabirds, all dappled with the mottled glow festivity brought out inside a person, and everybody screamed at us, hollered down at the cherry red automotive, LITTLE LORD LOVEDAY'S COME HOME!

I glanced behind me at Gossamer and Vikare. I tried to gauge their disbelief. They had none. They looked enraptured. Gossamer looked flush and hungry. Vikare cranked down her window. She leaned out of it and peered up at the crowd.

Flower petals, silver paper confetti, sugar beads, and popcorn rained from the sky. Fistfuls were tossed down on us. They rattled on the hood and roof like hail. Gulls descended for the popcorn. A churning mass of white feathered wings blanketed the street, and we pulled along at a leisurely pace, shifting the birds, taking time to cruise along the reception's track.

Music started. Big sloshy brass and drums and singing, layered singing, rah rah work songs, unalone toward dawn we go hail Loveday, rye and poppies, and with the music cue people began leaping down onto the street. Jumping straight, mostly. Shimmying sometimes. Flips and virtuosic dives here and there, skirts fluttering as though underwater through the salted azurine air. On the ground, the Choir dispersed. They ran their usual games, knife throwing and drinking along the carousel, juggling and playing mean simple sports in the mews, breathing fire, dancing in the street. It felt like a last hurrah. It was. I was sick with love. Love swelled in my belly. I felt small and stuffed and so proud. It was difficult not to weep. It was difficult not to crawl out the window and cast away my long green jacket, peel the shirt off my waist and let my tattoos breathe, go marauding and rejoicing with my comrades soon to die.

"I missed you," I said to everything.

Harlow put a hand on my thigh. She glanced over her shoulder at the rich girls in the back, sniffed. She inclined her head toward me. Softly she said, "The car's for Sisphe. Nice, right?"

"You're ridiculous," I breathed. A tear fell and I couldn't stop it.

"Couldn't have her preferring straight money to me." Harlow skimmed her tongue over her teeth. "I think we've got two days of this in us. Three max. Be quick with your wooing, yeah?"

"I'd die for you." I put my hand on hers. I kissed her knuckles. "You know I'd die for you."

"Sure thing. Die for Hereafter instead." Harlow gave me a private smile, little and genuine, full of love. She was my brother. I rebuked any jealousy I'd ever held for her, any resentment that a younger me had fostered. I missed Candor dreadfully. She would've hated all this fuss. It would've been overstimulating. She would've hid in some loathsome crawly dive and drank in blissful quiet.

We arrived outside the Mansion. It was a regional style, frillier and wider than the Chauncey-Ramtha summer estate, bigger I now realized. Fortyish bandits lined the steps. All of them wore outfits whose grandeur and garishness seemed designed to upstage Harlow, unacceptable phantasmagoric swaths of velvet and fine leather and bunched lace and satin in every single color, ribbons in beards, capes and diamond buttons, an anchor's weight in metal and gemstones, corsetry and great coats, long coats, furs and buckles and fishtail pleats and tall laced boots, an onslaught, a kaleidoscope of textures that simulated mushrooms soaked in wormwood laudanum on a hot summer's night in a storm.

The extravagance mocked refinement. Here was the antithesis of poise and restraint. Somehow the gathered Choir all wore ceremonial aristocratic knives, despite being, I assumed, the Loveday Mansion staff. As we approached, everybody drew their knives. They stabbed them into the air, made a tunnel for us to walk under. A few crawly bastard genius beauties had tied bright scarves to their wrists, made the tunnel florid as a circus tent. Everybody kept a straight face. Many of those faces were obviously heavily scarred under their immaculate brothel makeup, worn by work and violence. No smiling. No frowning. Dread serious staff tunnel.

I got out of the automotive. I looked at Harlow, who played innocent, and immediately abandoned all pretense that the aristocratic culture I'd encountered was any different than this. This was normal. This was better. I had grown up in this and loved my people fiercely. The truth was so much easier. I helped Gossamer and Vikare out of the car. A bandit climbed out of a manhole, one of a few that spotted the Mansion's perimeter for the purpose of channeling rainwater down to the cliffs, closed it behind him, and popped the automotive's trunk. He grabbed all our luggage and carried them out of sight. Absolutely we would never see the luggage again. Gossamer started saying something about it, but couldn't seem to find the words. Harlow pulled away, took Sisphe's obnoxious present elsewhere, presumably to Sisphe herself. We stood on the steps. I held both Gossamer and Vikare's hands aloft.

I pronounced to the bandits, "My bride and partner!"

The bandits stomped their feet.

Vikare said softly, "This is the loveliest place in the world."

"This is a clown orgy," Gossamer answered. She swayed in place. "I thought Horace was an insane conservative."

"Oh, that's right. He's insane," I said. Was there a Horace? Was somebody Horace? Who the fuck would be Horace? Amon?

At the top of the stairs, the doors opened. Amon and Uthste stood there, flanked by trumpeters. Amon and Uthste had dug up servant's attire, real servant's attire, which looked so out of place among the extravaganza that it became almost fetishistic. Amon was clearly not Horace. He wore his Torn makeup, a thumbprint smear of rouge on his eyelids. Uthste clasped her hands behind her back. "Welcome home. Come. We've prepared dinner for you."

I ascended slowly, mimicked stateliness.

Vikare tore her hand away. She pulled up the itchy slinky liquid silver fabric of her dress and ran up the steps, fur coat swishing, looking I realized very much like she belonged here. She looked like a princess. A real one, one in fables whose cleverness and kindness distinguished them from humankind, not the junior tyrant position it meant in Royston and Cisra. She stopped running every few steps to look at a bandit's outfit, examined the vintage beading and the delicate lacing on the sleeves. She looked at the knives above her and the riding boots below. She knew who we were. She knew what she was seeing. She looked happy. Happy in an uncomplicated childlike way.

Gossamer was not looking at the display. She watched me. Dissected my most minute expressions or scanned prints of my brain, I didn't know for sure. She shivered. I let go of her hand and wrapped an arm around her, pulled her against my side. I glanced at the bandits on either side of me. I tried to tell them with my eyes that I was proud of them, and proud to be like them. That we'd be victorious. I wondered abstractly if this could end sweetly. If Gossamer could fall in love with this place and defend its strangeness with her unstoppable monetary might. This was lunacy, of course. We are the natural enemies of her monetary might. We stand to rob her of everything she owns and redistribute it to everybody alive. We could never resolve this peacefully. Our existences were mutually exclusive. The symbol of her existence would cease, or we would. She leaned her cheek against my shoulder. We reached the top of the stairs.

Inside the Mansion, kids too young for tattoos ran circles around the parlor. One kid had a trophy boar mounted on her shoulders, used its frozen open sneering mouth to see. She chased two boys, shook her tusks at them. One of the boys waved at us. I wasn't sure whether they'd received the full brief or cared to enact it, but they looked excited about the commotion. They dashed around a corner out of sight. Magnanimity reclined in her wheelchair. She and the other biddies gambled with uncut jewels. Magnanimity was a notorious cheater, but being the eldest elder had its perks. She produced an extra mother card from her sleeve and slammed down her hand, six ascendant mothers, and put her hands behind her head. She winked at Vikare. The other biddies fully ignored us. On the second floor, visible through the staircase's railing, a beautiful man reclined on a settee, and his lover, an older, rougher woman, lovingly painted the likeness of his chest hair on a fresh wet canvas. Music, chatter, somebody's purring cat. The charade was less deliberate inside. Then the "staff" bandits swirled through the doors after us, the ones I assumed had agreed to participate actively in this bit, and flowed around Goss and Vik and me like a current. They swept us into the ballroom, which had been refashioned as a second dining room. I wondered what was going on inside the first.

The dining table was set before the ancestral congress wall. A sea of hands twisted out like antlers, reached for us, longed for us. The table was long. Candles, prayer pearls, a shocking garnet-and-ivory Torn Child Idol that Amon must've borrowed from a Shrine. Golden fresh bread, local goat cheese and hypnotically blue marmalade, dried spiced meats and nuts, oysters on the half shell, hot pickled peppers and roasted greens on skewers, barley cakes, and a swordfish, a whole fucking swordfish with an azurine skewered on its nose on a bed of fragrant rice. At the end of the table sat Brandegor. She wore her hair down. I'd never seen it down. It was more white than black now and fell past her knees, pooled on the floor around her chair. She wore a masculine housecoat and her torc. She stirred her tea with her long pinkie talon. She looked at us enter, unblinking, smiling.

Vikare curtseyed. Reflex, maybe. Gossamer bowed her head, untucked herself from my side to show proper deference.

I did not know how to address her. She could not be my father, clearly.

Mors Brandegor the Rancid said, "Sit down. Eat. Your father is dead."

Gossamer looked stricken, and Vikare vaguely uneasy—I saw the concept of murder occur to her.

I sat down at the table's near end.

Gossamer and Vikare sat at either side of me eventually. Valor appeared in a gorgeous white lace gown that could not be mistaken for servant's attire by any stretch of the imagination. She wore a net of pearls in her hair. She looked like a Virtue made flesh. She made a plate for Gossamer, then for Vikare. She didn't serve me, but gently rapped up the back of my head when she passed. Then she stood at Brandegor's shoulder, put her hands behind her back.

"My father is dead," I repeated.

"That's right." Brandegor sucked off her pinkie nail, then raised her glass. "Gone but in our memories."

"I'm so sorry," Gossamer started.

Brandegor didn't seem to notice Gossamer existed. She didn't take her eyes off me. I was young in her gaze. I was a child again and my father was dead. Here I was, spared by chance to remember him. "You've become Baron Loveday. You're Lord of the Fingerbluffs."

Gossamer cut into her swordfish eye. Delicately she said, "Who are you?"

"Mors Brandegor. For ten years I've been the baron's tutor. This is Mallory Valor, my friend." Brandegor took a drink. She swished it between her teeth before she swallowed. "You're Gossamer Dignity Chauncey now."

"Yes," said Goss. "I am."

"You want to marry my daughter."

"Your student, you said," said Gossamer.

Brandegor leaned forward. She put her elbows on the table. "Do you remember the name of your Hall?"

Vikare put her fork down. She'd been salting half an azurine. She glanced between it and Goss.

"Flox," said Goss. "I don't claim it."

I put both my palms on the table. I pushed my whole weight against the table. I braced myself against gravity's dissolution. I would break the table in half. I'd crack it.

"Tell me how you came to be in the possession of Yann Industry Chauncey, Flox Gossamer," Brandegor said.

"Flox Hall shipped me and their other measly *blodfagra* to a charity sanatorium here. Crellin, if you know it. Ghastly evil blistered pit where love's never been. I lived longest. I worked to keep my bed as soon as I was able to work. I was employed at the first Yann I. Chauncey Ichorite Foundry down on Burn Street for a few years, from when I was eight until I was thirteenish. That year was the riot. It caused a stampede outside the foundry. Hundreds were trampled alive. Maybe you recall it. It had a proper media moment, as it were.

"Obviously, I survived. I limped back to Crellin Sanatorium on a broken leg, and of course they knew my place of employ and contacted the authorities who reached my father. He heard about me, the sick riot survivor orphan, and came to visit me. Clearly not an instigator, given my age and frailty. My lucidity impressed him. Father has never had a family. For logistics' sake, he wanted an heir.

"He paid for my education at Wilton School, the finest on the continent, and when I was top of class at the end of my first year despite my near illiteracy at time of enrollment, he adopted me formally. I converted to the Stellarine faith, became Dignity. I hated my Drustish name, because it stings of my abandonment, and dear Vikare, my best friend here beside me, picked Gossamer for me. Her heritage labor is dressmaking. It was appropriate, besides which, it had the same first and last letter as my birth name, and that felt awfully cute at the time. Now I stand to inherit the wealth of the world. I'd like to share it with your daughter and build fabulous factories in your city. Will you allow it?"

I stood up from the table. I turned my back on the people I loved and I walked out of the room, I did not parse the noise and the language behind me, I floated down the hallway with my head off, down the stairs and through the parlor and another then out a side door. I did not blink or look around me. I did not see or hear the bandits who spoke to me with conspiratorial jubilance, I was not aware of my own movements. I went outside.

Without touching the railing I jumped off the veranda and landed in the sandy flowers. A breeze stirred my curls. I walked through the dark to the edge of the cliff, the big basalt-column fingers that held us up from the hungry crashing water. I sat down.

The gulls screamed overhead. They drifted without moving their wings.

The sea crashed on the basalt columns. Foam danced, dissolved. Rabies and lace. Fish swam through them, curves of their bodies showed in heavy shadows between the waves.

I took off my boots and put them beside me. I touched my ankles and the arches of my feet. I squeezed myself. I untucked my shirt and put my hands underneath the linen, underneath the ribbed undershirt beneath it, and held fistfuls of my belly. I held my breast, I held my sternum. I felt my heart seize and I mashed it back inside my body.

The near moon and the far moon were both out. Full and gibbous. In the water they overlapped and made a sort of milky blurry hourglass shape. The shape broke and rippled and re-formed with the water's lolling movement. I watched the cyclical, soft-edged violence of waves over waves over rock.

From behind me you said, "May I sit with you?"

You could do anything you'd like to me. "Yes," I said, I prayed.

You walked down the veranda steps, jaunty dandy careful traipsing footfalls, then came near the cliff's edge. You stood a pace behind me, as though you were afraid of the drop. I wonder if you'd ever spent time near the water.

"I won't let you fall."

That was enough. You came and sat crisscross beside me, nervous anchoring hands on the ground on either side of you. "It's chilly," you said.

Off came my jacket. I draped it around you. The emerald green looked black in the night.

"I'm sorry about your father. I can't imagine, having nearly lost mine. I know it was difficult, the relationship you had with him, or I imagine it must've been. It must make your grief complex. Nuance the victory of your ascension."

I laid my head in your lap.

"Oh." You stopped talking. Your hands drifted above my head, fingers tensing, stretching.

"It's alright," I said. "You can keep going."

You carefully lowered your hands. You touched my hair. You plucked at the ringlets, tested the springiness, twisted them around your fingers with incrementally increasing comfort. You were so gentle with me. "Vikare's falling in love with this place. Real love. She doesn't like Luster City. Difficult memories. If you let her open a dress shop here, let this be her garden, I think she'd be happy forever. If you make her happy forever, I will do my best to be good to you. You would have bested me, and I would be in your debt. You have my word."

In my debt? Ridiculous. I rolled onto my back and looked up at you.

You. It was you. How I'd missed it was beyond me. It was you, your thin pinched haughtiness, all bones where you used to be little kid softness, but you, nevertheless. Your blue eyes with orange lashes. Your skinny wrists and whip-sharp arrogance. You always had been smarter than me. How stupid of us to crawl away from the massacre in opposite directions. We could've gone together. You could've been a Choir girl. How brilliant you would've been. I couldn't be an orphan ward. Your gamble required a nimbleness I lacked. What a funny revenge you'd picked, making the man surrender to you everything he'd ever owned. Giving you the foundry and the tools to build a thousand more.

You'd said "riot."

You played with the ringlets around my face. Your skin was soft as water. You looked at me, really looked at me, looked at my scars and moles and pink fit splotches. Surely you recognized me. No bonnet and years of experience, but it was me. But I hadn't recognized you, and I was deliberately obscuring my identity to use you, that would make the recognition harder. Perhaps you felt it without the precise language to justify why. The magnetic draw of my devotion brought me to you across the gulph of years and agony. I am your Marney and I will belong to you forever. You only could have picked me. All those aristocrats in your estate and you picked me. You know me. You know where I belong. We were beloved of each other before the violence bound us inseparably. This is our fate.

"She can stay as long as she'd like," I said. "She could be one of us. She'd be good at it."

You smiled at me. "It shows how much you love this place."

"The Fingerbluffs is the heart of the world." The spleen of the world. The cunt. The hands. The pierced and lathered tongue. "We will rest here before we run away together."

You cocked your head to the side. Your smile looked peculiar. "Run away? How do you figure?"

"To spare you the coming war," I said. "When everything is settled, I will see you safe and well."

"The war," she repeated, and a look of love and pity flickered across her face, then a different look, the coolness of someone who's about to win a fight. You smoothed my hair, stroked my temples. "The war won't touch us. I know you have a bleeding heart. Not just. You're proud and honorable, in your rugged country way. The war is inevitable, but not for the reasons Royston says. It is not because of Old Bellona, it's not because of history at all. It's for me. It will happen because the war is necessary to seize materials with which to make products. It will happen because we need enormous swaths of land for mining and for establishing foundries, and we need the cheap labor that a war-torn country will happily provide. If we buy that land outright from the Drustish Hall assembly, assuming they were willing to so much as rent it to us, the bill would be untenably expensive. After the bloodshed, Royston will just give it to us.

"The alternative is starting this process here, in your home, under your beautiful blue orchards. If we tear up all the azurine trees, I bet there's a whole clutch underneath. You know, that said, we *should* mine here. We should make this place, a marginal barony at the edge of existence, the center of the new age. We should treat it differently than progress demands. I will be softer with this place. I will be deliberate and attentive because you are owed that. Your architecture will remain. We'll preserve these basalt columns, we'll keep the history here intact. It won't be like what must happen in the Drustlands. The war effort is hideous, but take heart. We'll pay for the refugee movement born of this, we'll lobby for the placement of Drustish migrants across Ignavia, we'll make an extremely accessible work visa program and purchase tenements whose rent might be deducted from one's wage. Education for all the children, work for all the adults. Did you hear I've raised the minimum age of employ? It's going to be fifteen, now. We can make the world better. The materials to do so are acquired by first making the world worse. You've got to take to give."

She paused, curled a ringlet between her fingers. "I know you made promises to the Drutish envoy. I admire you greatly for that. I would love to let you be the face of the humanitarian efforts you and I can spearhead together. We'll break it, we'll remake it, we'll be the kings of tomorrow."

"They're your people," I managed.

"Yes, they *were*." You sighed, leaned back on your elbows. My coat slumped to the ground. "It's unfortunate. I might resent the eugenic impulse that prompted my Hall to get rid of me, but that shouldn't mean devastation. Thanks to Ramtha, bless and praise Ramtha, I think it won't mean devastation now. The war will be relatively restrained. It won't be a total annihilation, because High Hierophant Darya is going to ply the Hall assembly with Tasmudani mercenary armies, who might colonize the

southern regions, but can absolutely take on Royston. Cisra
will join Royston, but Ignavia is well positioned to pussy-
foot around and be minimally useful to either side while
maximally profiting from the action. In six years, you and
I will be so rich we can hardly stand it. Think about all the
good you could do with that money. What do you value?
You could do it. We could make the first General Public
Ichorite Foundry. Anything you want belongs to you."

"I want you." Repulsion poured into the air and evap-
orated. I couldn't sustain it. I couldn't sustain loathing or
shame, I couldn't produce resentment, I adore you. You are
the idol of my worship. I reached up and brushed my hand
against your face. You have such a delicate bone structure. I
touched your ear, where your one earring dangled, and the
hot pink memory of having made it for you lugged in the pit
of my stomach. You'd kept the little ring I'd made you. It
was so sweet of you to have kept it.

There would be no war in the Drustlands. After I
killed Yann Industry, I decided that I would kidnap you,
and I'd take you away beyond the Fingerbluffs. I'd plead
my case to a pirate, Iodine maybe, ask her to take us some-
place far away. We'd live in the Crimson Archipelago, or
across the world in smoldering ruined Delphinia, no, north
to Laodamia, live in the frigid sapphire winters and wear
rabbit skins in the mountains in a cottage I'd build for you.
We are smart. We have one another and could endure the
future that gains on us. Maybe soon Harlow's Hereafter
would dawn. There would be no tyranny and we would be
released from stricture at the end of capture and cruelty.

Food would grow in forests and crawlies would laze around and fuck each other with garlands on their heads. Nobody would ever be forced to work or else die hungry and un-waged in the gutters. There'd be no such thing as ichorite. Then we'd return to the Fingerbluffs and I would be a good Tullian farmer. I would provide for you. You're smart and you'd provide for me. I'd survive killing Yann Industry. I'd endure the gunfire and come back to you. I understood that we had a future of incomprehensible beauty. I just lacked the words for it then.

"You have me." You leaned your cheek into my hand. Little dove, little lamb. "You and Vikare and I are going to change the world."

I held your head and stroked the smooth skin behind your ear with my thumb. Sweet girl. "I am my only lord now. I am thrilled to give myself to you. I need to meet your father quickly. I want to speak with him before I marry you."

You wrinkled your nose. "How you manage to be old-fashioned in a place like this is beyond me. I've never seen anybody so loved as you. The people here adore you."

"Everybody who lives here is as loved as me. When can I meet Yann Industry?"

"As soon as we're back home. I can send word." You beamed at me. You looked just the same when you smiled like this. "You make me happy, Truth."

"I'll take care of us," I promised.

I said I will. I am.

Fifteen

THREE DAYS PASSED IN HEAVEN. SISPHE AND
Harlow learned from Brandegor that you are Gwyar, and
treated our time with hallowed reverence, if wariness. They
gave us distance. Neither of their religious cultures feared
revenants like mine did, but they both had superstition
enough to think that you might perhaps be evil. Still they
pulled aside Vikare and they told her about the war. Our
war, the grand Hereafter. They told her about the imminent
destruction of the Fingerbluffs and the holy fight, the final
fight, to defend this place and its spirit. I saw them swim-
ming together down in the Amandine Sea, saw them vanish
between narrow buildings and reappear in dance halls. An
invitation was being made, I thought, to be embraced by the
wild majesty of Choirhood. To be a part of this rather than
opposed to this.

I care for Vikare. I admire her and feel fantastic pride
in her inclusion. I would have rejoiced to participate in her

initiation into the Choir, which happened the morning of the third day, as I was told an hour later by Uthste. She recounted how Vikare laid across Harlow's lap with her dress in her fists and let Sisphe thu Ecapa tattoo something small across her belly. She did not tell me what it was. Perhaps including Vikare was reckless and dangerous, perhaps it was a kindness to me rather than to her, either way was not my call.

I spent my three days showing you my favorite places. I'd given you a tour so many times. Showing you now felt important. You looked. You let me lead you around and when you grew weary you let me carry you on my back like you did when we were small. You questioned the lurchers but did not press when I gave you watery nonsense about how we just had them down here. You let me wait on you. You let me rub your shoulders and massage your tight hands, you let me brush your hair, you let me fetch your cool glasses of water. I did not let you touch me. You did not yet remember me. It would be unfair to you. When we ran away together, I'd let you touch me like I let nobody touch me. I'd give you the parts of me that I'd assumed had choked and shrunk. I'd grow my heart anew and give it fresh and unblemished to you. Have your way with me however you'd please. I'd do what was necessary for your happiness. There was only one obstacle in our way, and I'd surmount it.

I parted with you before we left, just briefly. I went to embrace Harlow and Sisphe, I embraced Uthste and Valor and Brandegor, I embraced old Amon, who kissed my head.

"Vikare is staying," I said to him.

"I have audience with her tonight," he said. "It is naïve to think that she would participate in the war effort. Rich children make poor converts. But then, the first Hereafterists who called themselves such were scholars, wealthy students, who learned about the extremity of wrongness in this world and its persistent recreation and audaciously imagined the world otherwise, then put arms to those ideas. Maybe she'll sway. Marney. Darling. Do you remember what you've sworn to do?"

"Yes," I said. "I'm going to kill Yann Industry. Tonight, I'd wager. I'm seeing him tonight."

"You love his ward. That makes this difficult."

Love was too small and blunt a word. I touched his long white hair. He was so old now. I did not want him fighting. "My devotion to her is the selfsame fire that leads me to kill Yann Industry. I will do it for her, not in spite of her. I know she might not understand. She's lived a life of captivity in his hands and her memories of what has been done to us are corrupted, her loyalty is not her fault. I will make quick work of this, as is my destiny. Then I'll bring her back."

"You'll bring her back?"

"Yes. I'll bring her back here. We'll run away."

Amon looked pained. He held my jaw in his hands. "Say the bleed with me before you leave. You are the only man for whom I've ever been reverend. I want to tell you the words that made me a reverend so that you might say them and ascend to your own reverendship. I considered myself a Torn reverend when I killed the Loveday heir, the girl you've named Velma Truth Loveday. Tonight you'll get yours. You'll become yourself. I'm more proud than any mother has ever been."

He led me to the table and we knelt beside it. We put our hands on the table, and he told me about the clarity that took him when the Lovedays died and the Fingerbluffs became briefly free. He told me about his faith's true power. He cut his thumbs and daubed my eyes, and I cut mine for his. Boletes and daisies and my ichorite knife. These things for the Torn. All for you.

ON THE TRAIN you showed me your ledgers. Economics was a science, you assured me, that anyone could learn. I'd be learning it, you insisted. My duty was not the overseeing of finances, but if I was to be a competent partner in the Chauncey ichorite empire, I needed to know what these figures revealed about the world. I confessed that I could not read your handwriting and you laughed, you thought my earnestness was so charming, I completely dodged having to reveal that I simply couldn't read well at all.

You showed me your sketches instead, designs made out of nested lines so faint I could hardly see them. Trade routes. You'd signed a contract with Mir that he would be the principal global shipping partner for Chaunceyco so long as he lived. Not forever, she stressed, just his lifespan. Then whomever Mago picked next, assuming whichever usurper killed Mir let Mago live. You told me that Mir's brother Hiram had been an acquaintance because Mago, enterprising and blessed with ambition and considerable polyglot powers, had written to all the most promising new business magnates in the world and introduced himself in his capacity as advisor. Mir murdered Hiram, surprising nobody, and Mago cleanly transitioned from one brother to the next. All they wanted in return, riches aside, was use of the Flip without toll. Accessing the Flip River would mean avoiding the circumnavigation of the continent otherwise required for its crossing. Susannah would relent where her parents had not. She'd do this because she loved you. I could not fault you this assumption. The things I intended to do for you to demonstrate my love far exceeded the insanity of ceding free use of the Flip.

The vibrations of a train ride are sacred to me. I can't remember half my exploits as Whip Spider, tearing trains apart with my hands nearly killed me, the fits made my prime a mirage of pink anguish and movement, but the movement, the constituent parts of this device grinding together and throwing us forward through space, that feeling had become definitional to my life and sense of self. I put my arm around you, and I felt the wheelsets lurch underneath my boots and I knew that my brief life had amounted to something. I was proud of what I had done. I looked at your sketches and imagined how lightly you must hold your graphite, barely pressing the paper, and I imagined what grip you'd use, how your fingers might fold around the instrument. I looked down at your hand in my lap. You kept making passes at me. I wanted to swallow you whole. I wanted you inside me. Soon. We wouldn't wait long. We'd waited for ages. Just a night. A few more hours.

"Everybody's gone," you assured me. "No more guests. We'll invite them back for the wedding though. You can do a Goss's Girl victory lap. They'll be so envious and impressed." When I didn't laugh you brought your cheek close to mine. "Do you want to go slow? I assumed, you know. Because of Vikare, I had assumed you went fast with physical touch."

"I'll be yours soon in all the ways I can be," I promised. I kissed your brow. "What time will Yann Industry arrive?"

"He's already home, I'd imagine. Him and his new bodyguard. Why, are you nervous?"

"Excited," I said. "Nervous too. That's part of it."

"He's a little intense, but he means well. He's a great man." You yanked one of my curls. "I'm sure you'll get on swimmingly. He likes novelty and passion. You have both. Besides which, you saved his life. That's got to count for something."

YOU HELD MY arm as we walked up to the gates. Birdie answered the door along with the guard whom I'd kill in an hour. I beamed at Birdie. She beamed at me. She called out into the open room, "Baron Velma Truth Loveday, Lord of the Fingerbluffs, and Mister Gossamer Dignity Chauncey!"

You bonked your forehead against my shoulder. "Look alive," she said. "Be polite."

We swept through the Bellonan funerary husk of your estate and strode into the palm-frond courtyard. A thin gray man sat alone in the awful ichorite furniture. He stood when he saw us. He clasped his hands together. "Such a quick trip. I'd expected you both to remain on the coast for longer."

"Hello, father," you said, like you couldn't be prouder that the word in your mouth was *father*. Like you loved its taste.

Yann Industry Chauncey looked at me. I observed the veins in his face. He had blue eyes and was nondescriptly beige. In different clothes he'd be anyone. In a reedy little voice he said, "Sit. There are mediocre finger sandwiches if you're starving. The crumb is wrong. Choke them down if you're desperate and rest assured that I'll sack the cook."

You laughed. You sat right beside him, so close as to be too close, not in a proper seat slot. I sat across from him.

"Truth," Yann said. "You very nearly killed me."

You stopped smiling.

"Yessir," I said. "I could have."

"Your father has recently died, I understand. He was not a reasonable man. He did not send you to Wilton. Are you otherwise educated?" He pushed the tray of crustless white sandwiches at me. "Eat up."

"I am educated in my way," I said.

"So no. Education is expensive. The hiring costs for middle management are evidence enough of that, and your barony isn't known for anything, save for your late father's madness. I assume you grew up among the aristocratic poor. That's fine. You aren't entitled and you don't need to be middle management. You've vaulted over that by impressing my ward." Not daughter. He pressed his thumb into the edge of a sandwich and watched the bread compress and slowly rise. He pinched it harder. It stayed flat. "Nevertheless, when she asked you where ichorite ore might be found, you gave the theological answer. You're smart. You think about the world abstractly. Are you faithful?"

"To my Virtue."

"Again, no. We're Stellarine. Marriage is a unity between man and woman according to our religious codes. Your *Lunarist*," he said, pronounced the word indistinguishably from crawly, "partnership is the achievement of property law forcing cooperation between disparate faith groups, not the religion that raised you. So you know religion, and you know how to use it to open up the geode of the world and reap the riches inside, but you do not practice religion like a religion, it does not restrict your movements, which means when you open up the world with religion you don't have religion to prevent you from taking what you find inside. What do you think of Gossamer?"

"I love her," I said, astonished.

"You don't. You've known her not quite a month. Spare me the romantic answer. Be specific. What do you think about Gossamer?"

"She's slippery. She likes pageantry. She's ambitious and insightful and makes useful friends."

"Fascinating. That's better. Slippery, yes. Everybody knows it. It's her great flaw, the fact that she's so obviously scheming something. She looks guilty. You don't. You look simple. There's utility in that. She can use you as her brusque but soft-spoken provincial shield. People like a farmer in the city. Pastoral chic is in. You have a slow tongue, you sound almost Tullian. You'll be fantastic now that you have your seat in the Senate. Unassuming, perpetually earnest, innocent. You and Gossamer will make a fine team."

You gasped, collapsed back in your rigid ichorite chair, lolled your head back and looked up at the sky. The lines in your shoulders slackened. You looked so relieved. Nearly happy. I cherished that look on your face.

"Mister Chauncey," I said. "May we have a conversation, just you and I?"

He waved a hand, and you leaped to your feet, eager and beaming. Yann continued to look at me and did not watch you touch your heart, did not watch you blow a kiss to me, did not watch you swirl out of sight. If I guessed correctly, you went to the library, or out behind the house to the gardens. I didn't know for sure.

Then I sat across from Yann Industry Chauncey.

"Let's walk," he said. "The Bellonans built these tiered galleries so they might walk around the edge and look down into the courtyard, where their women and children would play with the pigs. Gossamer fills this courtyard with women, but when you're married you can be firm with her.

I hate her whoring. We're more clever than Bellonans. We'll overlook the silence and hear ourselves think."

I stood up. I left my coat at the table. The lustertouched fit bubbled under my skin, the fit and boiled lightning. He stood with me, walked beside me up the stairs to the second-story gallery. We were among the fronds, not above them. He put his hands behind his back. All around us, the house was smithereens. Perdita's tirade tore up this floor. Glancing down the hallways, I saw that glass still glittered, and flecks of broken amphorae. I half expected the bloated rotten corpses of Gossamer's bodyguards to be still strewn amongst the chairs.

"Whatever you want to ask me about with Gossamer doesn't matter. I approve the marriage. I don't care that you're lying about something. The Fingerbluffs situation doesn't make sense. You export nothing. You should've starved, but you're fit, vital. Perhaps you've bought the pirates. It ultimately means nothing. I don't care. Now. There's something I've got to tell you about ichorite ore, now that you'll be among its inheritors. The deposits occur in clutches.

"They're usually about a thousand feet under. That's deeper than most miners prefer to go, but it's crucial to dig that deep. The initial depositing was, as far as I estimate, about three thousand years ago. Great trenches remain deep underground that reflect this. Miners will come across the tunnels and raise questions. Suppressing these questions is not a conspiracy nor is it to obscure or hide the reality of what ichorite is. The purpose is to prevent excavation rights from becoming a question of cultural preservation, or maybe scientific inquiry. Ichorite is a resource. It needs to be a resource. Our wealth and universal progress depend on its exclusive use as something to be used. It shouldn't be cordoned off by antiquarians and kept inert behind glass. It should be refined. It should be the pride and the means of our lives. It is the answer to all manufacturing questions. There are enough eggs underground that we could remake every major city on the continent entirely out of luster.

"Sometime in your generation, you could expect to see yourself and Gossamer helming the general progress of the entire world. Just keep a handle on the mining. The rest can tangle. Factories can tangle. Factory workers are fungible, and people will look at the starving and desperate on the streets and decide that a hard life in a foundry is preferable to desolation. Shipping, packaging, these things will yield if you press on them. Mining must be exquisite. Obscure the nature of the eggs and put your money into your mining sites. Build towns around them and own everything inside them. Make it so that the entire world within those towns is in service to ichorite ore and its extraction. Pay them more. Make leaving impossible. Harvest one egg at a time."

He did not look at me. I heard the sound of his voice, but the words held little meaning. While he spoke I unbuttoned my shirt. I pulled it wide, let my tattoos breathe, uncovered my name across my breast. I rolled up my sleeves. I pulled my knife out of its special sheath and I cradled it in my hand, the coalesced slugs of the bullets that'd killed my family and friends. That prickling pink feeling took me. Yann Industry's back rippled. His hair became self-luminous.

"When you're old, they'll hate you. They hate me. You care about the world and you will lament that they hate you. You will want to make them love you. You'll be a philanthropist. You'll throw money at small problems, you'll stop up cracks in dams with ichorite, you'll ease the immediate effects of the human condition, and you'll do these things to feel better, like you are still a person. You are no longer a person. It is hateful to live, Truth. It hurts to be a human animal inching across the spinning globe, it debases and agonizes you, and nothing helps, and then you die. Life is lonely. Most people are ultimately point-less and ineffectual. They have little problems and you will solve them trivially, and they will still hate you, and you should not care. Very few people have the willpower and creativity to be significant. You're significant now. You're separate. Pain cannot touch you anymore. It doesn't matter if you're hated by ants. It doesn't matter if you tread on ants in your walk to where you are awaited. There is a cosmic scale on which you are now a player. You sculpt the spawn of heaven."

"Look at me."

He continued walking.

"Fucking look at me."

He glanced over his shoulder. Something flashed across his face.

"You killed my family," I said. "You killed everybody I've ever known, you killed us on the street while we were

singing and pleading with you to treat us decently, to treat
me decently, to know what's fucking wrong with me. You
slaughtered us. Fungible? You tell me that my family was
fungible?"

Yann turned to face me. He worried his hands together, twisted the thin ring he wore on his thumb. "The
lustertouched bandit. Right. I've heard about you." Chilly
dismissive nonchalance. "So Veracity's servants did kill him.
That rumor's been floating around for years. Don't interrupt me."

"I'm going to kill you," I told him. "These words are
your last. Be deliberate."

"We've already discussed why none of that matters.
Be deliberate. Calm down and I'll make you very rich." He
chuckled to himself. Chuckled! Smiled at me, crinkled his
eyes like I was a child throwing a tantrum, like he was un-
killable. He was the first emperor of Bellona. He'd never
ever die. I saw his face in the stained glass colors, candy
beetle red, piss yellow, rat poison blue, the building blocks
with which all other colors were made. I saw him glowing
high above me.

I came toward him.

He parted his lips.

I advanced and he took a step back. Two steps back,
he was a limber man but not a fast one. I caught up in a
stride. I channeled sweet Vikare's wisdom and slashed out
the knife's tip, a smooth extension of my arm, and I clipped
up the length of his wrist, slit the sleeve, a quick shallow
cut to demonstrate that I could make him suffer.

His face twisted. His lips thinned until they vanished. Panting he shouted, *"Help!"*

Gunshot, the banister near me exploded into pearl dust and splinters. His guard stepped out into the courtyard. He reloaded. I screamed, I screamed so loud my throat split, I felt something tear, and with a heave that made my muscles wrench and the world burst in globs of seething false colors, I killed the guard. I threw an ichorite chair over his body. It became liquid and splashed over his shoulders, over his gun, and he collapsed without a sound, a mass of metal.

I spat on the floor. There was blood in the serum. It leaked from my ears, curved down my cheekbones at the edges of my eyes. I felt it slick on my inner thighs. I felt it pulse and turn slippery in my nail beds. I squeezed the knife tighter, citric acid on the wound in my brain, and I looked around for Yann.

He took off running. I saw him round the gallery, make for the cornermost suite. Your room.

I walked after him. I had been in your room, there were no doors out besides this one. I did not wipe away the serum as it fell from me. I sniffed then gave up. My vision blurred. Edges softened, everything stirred as though with breath. Gentle movements, an easy tide. The whole building recalled the Amandine Sea. I waded through the air. I rounded the corner.

Your bedroom door was shut. I tried it. He had put something against the handle. Handle wasn't ichorite, very good! I pressed my cheek against the wall and focused. I could hear the table on the other side of the door but

I listened past the table. I listened for the sparkly chime sound, the way that ichorite tasted in the inner ear. I listened for how trains felt. The hinges! There was ichorite in the door hinges, not the leaves and knuckles, but the pin. The pin was cut ichorite.

My diaphragm kicked and something pinched behind my brain.

The ichorite pins melted.

I pulled the double doors toward myself and skittered sideways. I barely cleared them as they fell. They smashed the opposing gallery railing. Little individual rail posts fell down toward the courtyard like knocked-loose teeth.

I stepped inside your bedroom.

Yann stood inside. He was scribbling something furiously in a notebook on the table.

My body twisted away from the table. My blood roiled inside my capillaries. My skin looked mottled, the bruises that suddenly flowered along all my joints showed sky blue and fit pink and noxious, poisonous green. I looked like my knife. I clung to my knife. I stepped toward my reverend-ship with my promised knife outstretched.

Yann slammed the notebook shut. He knocked it aside, threw his hands in the air. He reached for a lamp, a candle-stick, a poker. He found a letter opener. He held it shaking. "You're ruining this," he heaved. "I would've shared this with you and you're ruining it."

For Edna, for you, for our collective Hereafter. Torn Child sleeps no longer.

I struck Yann Chauncey down.

My knife pierced him. My chest knocked his chest and he cut back at me, he opened my shoulder up with his dirty blunt-edged knife, but I pushed him down and put my weight on the knife, I willed the knife back into metal, I pushed it into the wound I made, I pushed all the melted bullets down, I watched the ichorite seep through the veins of his body and turn him silver inside. He did not scream. He twisted once, then went very still. His eyes opened wide, his jaw relaxed. He looked intently at something above him. He stopped breathing with that reverent look. The wound in his chest did not bleed. The ichorite stayed inside it. It held the wound closed. He'd look hale if he was not dead.

I panted over his body. Slowly, I stood up. I looked at my hands. They looked like his chest, fully metallic and veined with light.

You screamed behind me. Your scream filled the whole room. It brought me out of my stupor. I turned to behold you, saw you trembling in the doorway. Your teeth chattered with how you shook. I saw on your face that you did not understand, and I could not blame you for that. I came toward you and knelt. I put my hands on the floor. My shirt hung open and dripped metal, who I was had become plain to see. I saw you read beneath my collarbone. I am your Marney, as I've always been. Your Reverend Marney Honeycutt.

"Gwyar," I said. "My Gwyar, it's done. I'll take care of you. We can go away together and I'll provide for you. Nothing in this world can stop us now. Forgive me that it's taken so long. I wish it could've been sooner."

Your expression wrenched. You threw your hands over your mouth. You stepped nearer to me. Fear flashed in your eyes, and big red veins. "No," you said. "Nonononono."

I bowed, I slumped. I pressed my forehead to the floor at your feet. "I love you," I said. "I never stopped loving you."

You stepped over me. You stood over Yann Industry Chauncey's metal-webbed body. You trembled harder, I thought you'd shiver out of your skin. The hair on your head fluffed up like a scared cat's, looked redder.

I rose again, rocked back on my heels. "You can rest now," I said. "I avenged you."

Your eyes rolled in their sockets. You looked at me out of the most extreme corner of your pale lash lines. "You killed my father."

"You died in the massacre. You died, everybody died, but I have gotten good enough to strike back at the man who killed you. I murdered your murderer. It's going to be okay now," I said. I did my best to be level, to be patient. You didn't understand. That was alright. That made sense. You're the clever one, I'm the steady one. I'll be steady. "We're going to go away. I'm going to take us somewhere safe, Gwyar. My lurcher is in the woods. You're small, we'll both fit if you hold onto me. We can be gone and halfway across the continent before morning."

"*You killed my father!*" You whirled on me, stepped around me. You stood in front of me, red-faced and seething. I'd only ever seen myself so mad.

"I love you," I pleaded, I prayed. "I'm your Marney, Gwyar. You know me. I love you."

You slammed your boot into my breastbone and shoved me back. I slammed against the table. The glass shattered around my hips and in an ice splinter explosion I screamed and sank down into the table through shell through skin inside the table sank down through layers of the skin within the shell inside the table the marbled shifting not yet flesh under the skin inside my skin under the table where my insides flip splice unseam around the shell splinter the horn bone marrow oil awake whereabouts I watched you fall over his body unaware that dying I was in his body in your ear

Sixteen

dead undone I

Marney gave my   became the language

or accidentally it spilled from my blooming brain and
soaked the cool slick churning awake insides under
everywhere with means of understanding which it
they we (yes, all) then used to understand itself as
self or selves (uncertain, not important) as distinct
from surrounding ground

and from me

which was kind as I am dead and exist

no longer except as this record of what I am which
has formed the basis of its their ourselves

and from me was more difficult given that my dead skinny fern-frond nerves formed the only basis for thought or provided the only available diagramed strategies by which person-type thoughts might be made maybe more like it inside the shell and outside it too for that matter

but they are observant and hyper tactile they re-member touch that's that memory portion of being lustertouched I'd say that's the feeling of being touched by the metal it does reach out to touch

that's how before we became us the metal spoke

when I was alive and held ichorite I'd sometimes feel
how it'd been touched previously so eventually while
I was dead I focused on the touch because otherwise
it they we could only speak to me with me in my
own voice which was unbearable

it they just repeated phrases back to me mostly *where
am I where am I where am I* and Tullian prayers so
instead we pivoted to shared touch

it they we shared a history of touch with me and I
gave language to the touch

we or they with my help let's just say we did not remember being laid we just remembered the origin of
feeling which was being something where previously
there'd been nothing

we had been pressed deep into the ground when we
realized that we experienced touch we burrowed sort
of shimmied our immense roundness deeper into the
ground where it was warmer

warmer's great

above us there was no ground just the deep gouged
trenches facing sky where the nest holes had been
drilled (by mothers I supplied but that was wrong ap-
parently) and human people climbed deep down into
these holes to figure out what the fuck was going on

they scraped up slivers of us then put dirt over us
and plants

humans worshiped the slivers they were in love
with us

we were worn by a series of priestesses and adorned
buildings where people came to cry

good pain

they kissed our carved-up relic pearls and asked what
we now thanks to me understand to be questions
about why life keeps going and why pain is real and
what they wanted and needed and how much they
loved us (so much) and whether we would wake up
and kill them violently en masse

will you kill them violently en masse?

we don't know this is the first time we're thinking
anything at all

okay

worship happened for a long time and still which is a
dull pleasant ache

from this ache I learned that when the mass is torn
apart it doesn't become the mass and dead tissue
or the mass and another mass it stays one big mass
across brood clutches one continuous awareness
without thought or independent will the ancient
baby body to which most divinity is ascribed thinks
nothing just feels in perfect integration across forms

when nymphal impulse comes it they we will fly
in distinctly intense shapes but we are the total
murmuration with common awareness there is no
subdivision with separate personalities and split desires across the distinct intense shapes the they you
keep imposing on us seems alienating being Marney
alone must mean profound suffering

suffering we understand

> *you don't have to be Marney anymore now that*
> *you're dead*

(I am though)

times are changing nymphal impulse just occurred to us you gave us language and attendant self-scrutiny and now we're forming opinions about our tactile experiences and assigning meaning to our suffering now might be the moment to dissolve away from yours

Marney will exist as long as we exist because *Marney* is the framework by which we now interface with the world on a conceptual level but that does not burden you with separate youness you have no obligation to continue being individuated Marney

outside temple structures where we are understood to look human and suffer perpetually as a vessel for human love and fear we are now being scooped inside out scorched stretched beaten thin diluted and molded into a litany of shapes that are scattered around the surface of the world for a million oppositional purposes that are largely obscure to us the *self* of Marney and the projected separation of me from us is not an apparatus we strictly need it can be softened

anyway either way

all of it hurts

it is screaming wrathful spasming agony to which we cannot acclimate multiplying endlessly when we press against our edges to explore we share the touch sense of the people handling us which is robustly bad you know yourself how laborers anguish to touch us are scourged by our nearness our suffering happens in the hands of human suffering consider now right now inside a foundry the air is too sticky thick for human persons to breathe the chemical mists that cloud the air to make us into screws burn the skin and lung membranes with prolonged exposure and the human persons cannot leave the line until their mandated breaks during their twelve-hour shifts because the belt never stops rolling and each screw has to be coated in acid or else it will become goo and return to just being us uncomplicatedly and the screws are passed through acid then a wash tank then a furnace beside which the human people stand for the screws to dry so the uniforms are all wet and cling to the human people's animal bodies and gloves are discouraged because screw groove testing is done quickest with the fleshy pad of ones thumb but if it's too hot it burns and if it was improperly acid dunked there could be a different separately bad burn and some of the screw spiral ridges are sharp and cut the thumbs but leaving the line before break is not allowed because the screws will keep coming and they won't be tested if the human person steps away to wrap up their thumb so they bleed on us and poison gets inside their cuts from time to time this is happening all over instantaneously

we can now consider our purposes designed by human people and whether we agree with those purposes but more pressingly

we feel how it feels to make us and we felt how it felt for you to die and we felt how it felt when you were initially born in a sort of pre-animal undifferentiated still-your-mother's-body way

we have always felt you

Marney is our baby in a way we have felt every part of being Marney because when you manipulate us what you're doing is making us into us again and giving us an idea of what to do

Marney is the baby of a baby we are a baby by your interjected framework

we are only what we feel which is pain

we are in love with you

(I still Marney am in pain)

    and with some convincing my specific ambitions returned to me and I became Marney again, wanting and awake, inextricable from the awareness into which I sank but particular and separate within the whole, newly hungry, desirous for the real revenge which had yet to be sated even after the destruction of Yann.

so we looked out over our iterations freshly excavated and vivisected and beaten into shapes and then used for various human purposes, we looked at the laborers who held us, and in the mines I saw that I was seen.

there was a boy who held me in his hands, and felt us feel him. he screamed, his family fearing a mine collapse carried him out of the shaft. everybody was coated in thick chalky luster glitter, stripped down to the waist, the powder hung thick in their beards and their chest hair they held their pickaxes in blistered calloused hands and the boy said,

there is a woman in the rock.

which confused everyone, but the other lustertouched children around this mine noticed me noticing them, and they too cried out *there is a woman in the rock and she is looking at me looking at her.* the miners trust the lustertouched. I could not speak I had no mouth but we shared the feeling with the lustertouched of going coastward toward the Fingerbluffs, we shared the change in the air and the vibrations of trains and the pride swell heat, we shared the feeling of Hereafter. The miners knew Hereafter,

so they left the hole in the world open.

They left and the enforcers who guarded the mines panicked and considered violence as a means of crowd control but we are the fucking ichorite in the ichorite mine so the ichorite went slack and pooled on the dirt and slithered along like mercury slugs which scared the fuck out of the guards who left the miners alone.

The miners followed the lustertouched down to the sea

and proud again I became myself.

398

I GATHERED MYSELF. Aware and awake I praised the Torn Child: the waking lustrous vastness beneath the ground indulged my calling it the Torn Child because it was in love with me and was fond of worship and its resulting soft dull ache. I looked out over the overwhelming shifting and multilayered sensory network of which ichorite was the unwilling fruiting bodies, and with the aid of the lustertouched I pieced together what happened in the several months that had passed since my death.

The continuous production of everything made out of ichorite got complicated. The workflows had been scrambled by mysterious meddling and misallocation, and besides Sisphe's hijinks, Yann's death left Luster City feeling raw. People did not want a war in the Drustlands. People did not want to make materials that'd be used in an invasion. People did not want the changing of hands. Nobody felt happy.

Flox Gwyar Gossamer Dignity Chauncey, *you*, buried Industry and became the sole heir to all his powers. You drank heavily. You smashed the rest of the remaining unsmashed vases in your house, fuck Alichsantre and her ancient crater blood. You sent word to the Fingerbluffs via manic telegrams that you had killed me for killing your father and that Vikare needed to come home immediately so you could marry her. Hell! Immediately, hell. My murder caught fire around the Fingerbluffs and Vikare, on the path to radicalization, plunged past exploratory Omnidarism into seething Hereafterism and turned Gossamer down with a pipe bomb in her mother's largest factory after a graveyard shift.

The incineration hurt with such a glittering excrucia- tion it became funny. We melted, became abstract, drooled all over the warehouse floor in thick glimmering puddles. I adored Vikare for it. I adored her on the scale of the whole awareness underground. Meanwhile beyond the burnt-out revenge factory, I could feel all ichorite fabric and felt the feelings of the bodies that wore them. Everybody's sensory lives at once roared hot and loud, but with the aid of the awareness language prevailed. I watched the Fingerbluffs through Vikare's dresses. Wrapped around Vikare, then around Sisphe when she made a dress for Sisphe, then fine jacket for Harlow, so many lovely ribs within my never-ending palms. It was an intimacy that cowed me but I enjoyed it, forgive me my dead nosy perversions. I leaned against their heartbeats. I tried to speak to them but I lacked any freedom of movement. The organizing logic of Marney-body was lost on the awareness. Touch didn't mean hands over feet and under head. It just *was*. Still. I made do with my silent closeness to my friends. I worshiped their nearness and the ferocity with which they planned for war.

I could not spy on Teriasa. As she was off gathering Cisran revolutionaries, she stayed clear of ichorite, and was invisible to us. The lustertouched didn't recognize her when I showed them the way her hair felt. I prayed to us that she was well.

While I was pretending to be Velma Truth Loveday, Sisphe penned and sent a round of job cut letters to

Enforcer Corps headquarters and, as I learned during my dead omnipresence, to the manufacturer that made lurchers with brand-new design parameters that Sisphe knew would absolutely fucking suck. The enforcer plan halfway worked, succeeded in cutting numbers and rupturing trust but not in slowing recruitment per se, but the lurcher thing *worked*. A whole batch was useless and the manufacturers didn't know why. Under the hands of the manufacturers I felt a lick of sympathy, they beat into me and assembled me with attention and care, but the fact that lurchers were now hugely breakable and prone to collapse was a victory. I showed the most lustertouched worker in that factory, who could see but not sculpt us, myself and our ambitions. The woman told her comrades on her line. They walked out when I started moving on my own.

The miners came to the Choir, and other bands led by a fistful of children who spoke about our Hereafter. The children were dying because I was killing them, they were allergic to me, I did not know how to stop that. There is something poisonous about us. I showed them my grief and they understood themselves as suffering for a reason, they told me this, I had nothing to give them that would convince them otherwise. Other workers came after, those who had sight with which to see me leading those who did not, and fistfuls who'd heard rumors and needed to know. Liquid metal ribbons of us trailed behind them where they walked.

As they arrived at the Fingerbluffs, Beauty and Prumathe and Teriasa came with a troop of assembled

Hereafterists, some in the Choir, many not, from Cisra and from Royston, from Tasmudan, from the Drustlands. In the grand togetherness I tried desperately to speak but words proved impossible. The lustertouched children I was killing were just kids. They tried to work out my meaning. What a horrible charade.

But my beloveds in the Fingerbluffs did not know that it was me, they assumed only that I was dead, and took in the workers and Hereafterists on pure principle. Vikare, having learned that Teriasa too was part of the bandit masquerade conspiracy, underwent a minor crisis, and she collapsed on a settee, hyperventilated, clutched me inside her dress close, and a truly stupid number of young bandits descended from the woodwork to fan her with peacock feathers and hand-feed her fresh-picked grapes. Delphinian revolutionaries who'd been sheltering all over came to shore with a crop of pirates, and they taught the Choir bandits those guerrilla tactics that had been most effective in the brief and beautiful republic. Harlow wept to see them. They sat with her and grieved together. Harlow introduced them, strangers as they were, to Sisphe, as though introducing her to her parents.

We bound shut wounds across Ignavia! We vibrated inside the gauze that held them, the twine that corseted broken skin, trace elements of us leeched from tall bluish bottles into the fever-reducing anti-inflammatory elixirs that thousands drank. I saw every surgery. I participated. I saw the insides of bodies, felt inside them, felt them heal around me. I saw everybody fucking! A contraceptive had been made out of a variant of Vikare's ichorite fabric. They made various medical equipment with it, gloves and gauze mostly, but the contraceptive portion demanded much of my attention. It'd been around for years it seems, but given that I couldn't knock anybody up no matter how hard I'd tried, I'd never had cause to look into contraception past silphium. Did the awareness like fucking? Yes, definitely. Good pain! I liked fucking abstractly and I liked it collectively more than I liked any individual instance. It was all receptive touch, frightening for me. I'm not that kind of crawly. But in the map of absolute feeling the interjection of pleasure and want and hunger and lust and play and insecurity and curiosity was such a good change from hammers. Crawlies wore ichorite cocks, encountering one would've been a nightmare in life, but now they were hilarious and bright.

The bandits clashed against the enforcers! They ambushed supply chains and tried to keep the fight away from the Fingerbluffs, made battlefields of inland baronies, but the bandits were dying. The Choir cracked against the wall of shield-faced nobodies and fell. In a successful assault that prevented the death of three thousandish Choir affiliate civilians, an enforcer shot Mallory Valor Moore in the back of her neck. The bullet broke her prayer pearls. They scattered wetly in the grass around her head. That fight claimed Aturmica thu Artumica Tanner and Benji Diligence Lockheart and Nestur thu Urusthe and his little brother Olive zel Urusthe, not yet an ancestor. Urusthe zel Achile, their mother who survived them, screamed and bayed and threatened the gods of every religion, many of whom were us.

I focused. The whole transclutch awareness with me at its molten opaline core fixed our attention on you.

You married Perdita Perfection.

You became a Roystonian prince.

You hated Perdita and impressed upon her the extent of your hatred. She yucked it up. She loved the fuss and preferred how you handled her when you were mad. She spent your money extravagantly on weapons of mass destruction and dresses only to find with fury that most of the dresses she wanted had blown up when Vikare bombed the textile mill and factory complex. Pouting, she spent it on Roystonian old-fashioned dresses instead, huge masses of crinoline and ribbon. She bought little dogs that she did not train and released them into your tomb home. They found a yet-to-be-removed guard whom Herzeloyde had murdered and shoved beneath a cabinet and ate his sloughy corpse flesh off the bone. You'd never had the glass properly cleaned up, and the rot-breathed dogs hurt their little feet, and Perdita had nearly murdered you for it, so you ordered Birdie to pluck every glass shard up from the carpet with her fingers, then you had her throw away all the destroyed decorations and most of the furniture, ravaged your own home of comfort and cushions until Perdita caved and let you come back to Royston with her. You had to get away from Ignavia. You had a paranoiac feeling that Ignavia itself, the land more than the state, did not like you.

You tried to focus this unease on Perdita. You sought paid companionship but Sunny Teriasa was nowhere to be found. You feigned outrage when you learned that Perdita and Mir had been fucking for years and had no real designs toward stopping. Perdita choked you 'til you saw stars every evening. It was your favorite thing she did. When you weren't having sex, she told you in lurid detail the things she wanted to do to your technical homeland. You were starting to feel like a monster. You resented feeling like a monster. You used to feel cleverer than death. It was why you had survived and I had not.

The awareness came to recognize that you had inherited the means to hurt it. It they saw you through the framework of my love, so the awareness within ichorite loved you like I love you, but they quickly developed a critical distance from you that I lacked. It was our first divergence in opinion. In a voice identical to mine, made out of mine, they said to me, *I'm sick of her.*

It's not your—her—fault, I assured them. You had not made the things that made you evil.

The awareness tried to impress upon me, its first rhetorical experiment, that the Gwyar developed in my head *was not the same woman* as the one who was alive and plotting its (our) dismemberment. It coiled around me, we felt more distinct with this rift of opinion, with soft silver liquid fleshiness and showed me what being worshiped felt like. It showed me praise and sex and sacrifice across three thousand years of continental religious practice. It showed me my own feelings, what it'd felt like to lay beside Teriasa in bed, what it'd felt like to kiss Sisphe the first time, what it'd felt like to bleed over gasping Vikare, what it'd felt like to sunbathe with Candor by the cliffside, what it'd felt like to box with Harlow when Harlow was happy, what it'd felt like to lay in a boxcar with my beloveds and play cards and gamble confessions, how imagining you felt, and how these imagined encounters *did not resemble* how you murdering me against the table had felt.

But everything I've felt since your death has been for you. It remains for you even as you withstand the death that invented you. The monster blood that makes up faith is made of me now, and I of it, and we have claimed you. You are religion's aim and object. I revolve around you. How you have betrayed us, little prince Chauncey. Oh, you hurt me so.

You could not withstand your own idleness. You worried, you suffered. You kept your hands busy. You built the first Gossamer D. Chauncey Ichorite Foundry in a burnt-out lifeless patch of land on the Drustish side of the Drustish-Roystonian border, the ruins of what at one point had been Laith Hall. That is, you gave the orders. You stood beside the perspiring laborers whom you bade build the drill that'd trepan our shell. You took note of perceived inefficiencies to eliminate them next time round. You did not dwell on killing me. You tugged on the earring and felt, ignored, my pulse.

Seventeen

BRUTALITY AND THE DEATH OF ALL MY FRIENDS
loomed, and I watched screaming. Inaction was the anguish beyond the anguish of the world. The Torn Child
cannot sleep, it can only pretend while workers toil across
it, and knowing our own mythology made its accurate en-
action impossible. I could not rest. Revenants never rest. I
had to learn to move. Hereafter demanded it. I hurled my
willpower at cables and bolts. I threw my weight around
inside of railroads and building scaffolding. I wriggled the
stitches in wounds, I twitched inside condoms. I thrashed
inside clothing seams and I lashed at the conveyor belts and
I tried to collide the smoky flecks in the clouds above Luster
City, make a storm, but every movement I managed was so
small as to be mistaken for the mechanical stasis of whatever shape I was inside, the usual convulsions of weather
and tech. I spent two months not resting with motion as
my only goal. I demanded motion of myself. I tried to move

myself like I'd move ichorite to trigger a fit. I tried to be lustertouched but I was dead and made of luster, it was not the same. I entreated the walking crowd who could see me. I pleaded with them. They winced from the sight.

The amassed workers who gathered along the basalt columns at the end of the world spoke about a woman in the metal. The lustertouched children described the quilt inked over my skin. My gathered family in the vile holy Fingerbluffs streets clutched each other in awe and absurdity, in hilarity, in anger. Religion, here! Our dead daughter's face! There was nothing left but to reject the hysteria of a million strangers, or be riled by it. The Choir held. My gang, Sisphe and Harlow and Vikare, stood close together, Harlow in ecstasy between the shocked stillness of her companions. Harlow understood this. Hereafterists exalted the triumphant dead at length. Brandegor protested unbelieving, Uthste shattered from Valor's loss weak beneath her arm, but then Amon the Reverend approached the loudest of the miner children, and on his knees before the Choir said up to heaven, "Lo, the last work comes!" and lo, it came.

War unfurled. Hereafterists in Cisra, Teriasa grim among them, hopped trains to Royston and moved under the cover of night to set fire to supply lines, to sabotage your progress beyond the ruins of Laith Hall with sugared concrete and local militias high in the trees, to organize with Roystonian Hereafterists in their sprawling farmlands, to seize food and medicine away from the Roystonian conscripted troops who passed through those fields and redistribute these goods among the nearby Roystonian peasantry, to encourage reserve troops to defect and kill the believers among them and desert, to travel with the Hereafterists in bands, to burn wagons and sunder ships, to avenge Colton Gallantry, the life Teriasa zel Cerca should have had with him, the babies they had planned to raise, the garden he had painted on the nursery walls, forget-me-nots and pansies.

Luster City heaved beneath the weight of its own discontent. Its wealth was born of a workforce who had walked out of factories and left for the coast, called home to me, and the beautiful shell without its organism shuddered. Those few city-bound enforcers more loyal to local identity and the Ramtha family name than Chaunceyco's cash attempted order with force. Force rippled out of the city. Bandits and civilians inverted swayed in the wind. Other cities across baronies imitated LC, suddenly IC again. Gauze made of me wrapped around a Hereafterist's open head in Geistmouth, in Kimball, in Olmstead. Gauze made of me held together the hands of a teenage gunner in an old sawmill who fired down upon enforcement heading coastward. Gauze made of me filled a hole inside Prumathe's belly in the shattered teacup of Beauty's brothel, where a whole network of Hereafterists huddled together in silk slips and heavy boots, wiping blood from their noses with the backs of their wrists, praying to each other, held together by song's thin twine. Prumathe, coughing hard against Beauty's thigh. Prumathe, still alive.

The Chaunceyco militia, no longer feigning state allegiance, marched toward the continent's edge to force all peacebreaking discontents into the Amandine Sea. They thinned as they progressed, harrowed by the fast-gathering alliance of those who had long awaited Hereafter and struck now, but they did not break, understanding obedience as evidence of right. Not one part of their synchronized bodies was free of me. I seethed in their stink. I comprised all objects arranged around them, all created aspects of their personage were me, I clung thickly in their lungs as they smoked out of ichorite pipes, I coated their mouths, tongue teeth and spongy throat, I powdered their stomachs as they ate dreary rations out of ichorite cans with ichorite spoons out of ichorite bowls, I lined their guts, I held their gristle with machine-stitched seams, I burned as guns on their backs, I burned as bullets that they loaded and fired into the bellies of my friends.

My friends!

My beautiful friends!

Harlow, Sisphe, and Vikare screamed across the azurine orchard in the black-and-cherry automotive car. The car was not ichorite, I did not hold them, but they wore me across their shoulders and hips, and I felt them breathe against me and was in love with them. They returned to the Fingerbluffs, having sent word to Helena Integrity Shane, and through her, down to Hierophant Darya of Tasmudan and up to Dunn Ygrainne of the free Drustlands, about the violence across Ignavia, and about me. About my murder and continuation as a phantom in the luster. Helena, a collaborator! She'd harbor civilians and the uninnocent Hereafterists who collapsed on her doorstep inside her

mountain fortress, she'd feed and clothe them, her pride
eclipsed her fear in burnished glory, half her elder siblings
on her side, the other opposed but not disruptively so, not
at first. Darya would see the impenetrable Tasmudani border opened, if the huge population in the Fingerbluffs fled;
she could not promise placement or safety, but she could
ensure a hole in surveillance and the elaborate gate system
nearest to the Fingerbluffs' generous administrative neglect. Ygrainne would remain with her comrades. She sent
a missive for the survivors of this conflict, that she and they
should meet in five years come peacetime for a meal.

My friends believed in me to varying degrees. They
believed enough as a collective to speak their plans aloud
as though I bodily was in the room. They believed enough
to touch the obviously lustrous objects in their path with
caution, sometimes tenderness, sometimes a contempt for
illusions in place of flesh and bone. My friends were not
lustertouched. They could not see me inside their skirts.
They did not believe enough to think I was not dead.

Sisphe could hardly stand it. She wore ichorite less now.
She avoided brushing against it, shrank from abundances
of it, of us. It was love that made her bristle. I knew it was
love. I knew because she would steal scraps of spun ichorite from Vikare and privately tuck the ribbons in the palms
of her gloves. Harlow had been preaching about her dead
comrades for years, as long as we knew her, and she took
reports of me as confirmation of her faith. If not for Vikare,
they might've crossed lines with one another. Vikare, the
only woman I'd ever known who denied religion wholesale,

411

had interrogated gathered workers from different worksites about what I looked like. She'd menaced this from four separate children: the woman in the metal has a scar across her belly that cuts across the black whip spider.

My friends arrived at Loveday Mansion. Vikare took Sisphe and Harlow by the hands, she pulled them down the long lush hallways through verdant parlors and fuchsia reading rooms crammed with stolen oil paintings, upstairs to the spare room where in her brief moments idle she had dragged a dress form and bolts of cloth. Most spun ichorite that she made for you had melted into ooze along her mother's mill's stone floor, but she'd taken one bolt, a memento of a life no longer lived. As Sisphe and Harlow turned to each other, clasped each other, Vikare unraveled the fabric bolt. She plucked the glimmering mass into impossible threads. The destruction was so fast—months of her own work, exquisitely handloomed, undone in minutes. She held the lustrous candy floss in her hands. It broke light prismatically into colored stripes. She wrapped the string around the backs of her hands, then offered it to Harlow, who took fistfuls without question, and Sisphe, who looked at Vikare a long time. She licked her lip ring before she took strings of her own, delicately, like the mass might bite her.

The three of them stretched me out. I weighed nothing, gravity did not resist me. I floated taut between their hands. Good pain. All my missing ligaments which I pretended to have sang in pleasure.

Vikare said over the threads, "Vibrate them."

Sisphe flushed red, her freckles jumped, and she chewed her tongue, outraged by the tone, by the curtness, by the premise. Harlow leaned against her shoulder.

My struggling had amounted to nothing before this. I threw memories of sensation at the lustertouched as rarely as possible, it made them suffer, and the lashing out I'd managed had amounted to nothing. Death had rendered me subtle, and unhatched, still larval, the awareness lacked volition and control. But these threads were so fine! Thinner than whiskers. Between my friends that held me, the cacophony of all of me everywhere mutilated all at once quieted, and I experienced myself as a contained shape, a continuous line, a cord between the finest hands in all the world. I plucked myself. It took no effort at all.

The strings arched. They pulled like waves on the carved hands along the Fingerbluffs cliffside, mounting, cresting, falling. I moved like how home felt. All of me, us, the enormity of the awareness, basked in awe and splendor in how good movement felt. How easy it was, desiring and acting. We, every unspooled stitch of us corrupted and hammered into units above ground, and all the undifferentiated fullness floating creamy inside shells below, imagined moving. Raw luster has no muscle. It cannot move how the ledger of my brain understands movement, I understood that as I sighed inside the threads, it—we—must learn to move as the thing we are. We must hatch.

The world groaned under the mansion. The floorboards buckled. Porcelain rattled inside cabinets, portraits flapped against the walls, the chandelier behind my friends in the hallway swayed, crystals clattering sweet as wind chimes.

Not now! Not yet! So young was the ancient awareness that *willpower* seemed impossible. They, we, had just encountered want and the will to get. Want and will and getting are ecstasy. Want and will and not getting are hideous. Bad pain. But the mass swirled around the concept of me and, in my name, attempted restraint. I stilled myself. Across the world, the whirlpooling mass of us inside our shells churned slower.

Sisphe cried out. She wept, gasped over the threads in her hands and the movement underfoot, and by light of her stubbornness did not drop me. She curled her fingers, she squared her shoulders, and balled her hands into fists. Harlow held me carefully beside her, her posture curved around Sisphe, shielding her from an impact that did not come. Vikare cupped her hands like she held a frail bird. She brought the threads close to her nose, examined the glistening fibers.

"You're inside the ichorite," Vikare said. "Can you speak?"

Holding the bulk of us still and moving so discreetly, was smoothing an ocean or easing a stampede. It was catching a train with my hands. Had I not been the Whip Spider, the exertion would've split my head.

I plucked a string again. Just a string, not the unborn clutches nor the mutilated foundry works. The string produced a resonant sound.

Sisphe held us tighter. The string bit into her fingers. I tried and failed not to cut her. Her blood around us felt warm, and I felt the phantom shape of my old hands, the pain mirrored across the backsides of the knuckles.

Language relies on cutting sound, sculpting and shaping it, the breath across the tongue between the teeth. I had no means to make words and phrases. I did not know how to play stringed instruments. The meaning of each tension was lost on me, but I wanted a higher tone and the string tightened, elongated, tuned itself without my comprehension of how. The pitch changed like lungs inflate, with effort but without guile. The threads followed my will, the lustrous awareness moving in exaltation of the fact of this will, and with every drop of focus we together played a song.

Unalone toward dawn we go, toward the glory of new morning!

Harlow, true Hereafterist, in the child soldier priesthood of tyrant-destroying rapture, held the threads against her forehead and praised the Oneness. She did this as a declaration to herself. Her whole posture changed, she stood taller, broader, belly expanding hugely with her breath. She stuck out her chin and slanted her brow toward heaven. She said, "How long?"

Until we hatch? It must be soon. The exertion required for our patience is unsustainable. The guiding logics of Reverend Marney Honeycutt can only give so much. I looked inside my plural self and saw the vigor coiled in my edgeless body. The sooner this happened, the more I could control it. Holding the awareness back would burn me up. If we waited too long, I'd be gone, dissolved, and the mantle of the world would crack open and swallow the surface and all life as the Lustrous rise.

I plucked the thread seven times. My friends' eyes rose and fell with each arc. Sisphe moved her lips as she counted.

"A week," Sisphe said. "Hereafter in a week."

"We must take up arms," said Harlow. "The Choir must be mobile for our triumph."

"The eggs," said Vikare. I foamed inside myself, shocked that she had been told about us, shocked at myself for not having suspected her knowledge, shocked at the confusion on Sisphe and Harlow's faces, that she had not told either of them your father Yann Industry's secret. I attempted but could not stomach thoughts about loyalty. I angled my intensity at Vikare, concentrated my awareness toward her. She looked down at me with her half-shut eyes. "You're going to hatch in a week."

My friends spoke over each other. They brought the thread still looped around their hands down into the ballroom and screamed until the Choir came and brought the most potently lustertouched children from the mines, and together my entire community, thrumming with the images of my memory in their heads, came to understand that I am dead, but that I am one with the living metal underground, who as one must (like so many traditions have warned) climb into the light, bringing chaos. They understood that a clutch slumbered beneath the azurine grove that enwraps the Fingerbluffs, and under every azurine grove across the continent, and that I would do my damndest to dig myself out of my grave cradle without chipping the Fingerbluffs into the Amandine Sea, but that it might happen. I would rise across the continent and all the wrought ichorite would flow with me. The world would be harrowed. This must happen. The Lustrous desire to fly.

Meanwhile, you hired a slew of workers for your foundry. You stood them with their boots in a line, all garbed in their freshly pressed waxed canvas uniforms, double knees and lined breast pockets, and you shook their hands individually. Firmly! You'd warmed your hands by the fireplace beforehand, lest your shit circulation offput them. You were better than your father, you said aloud to yourself when you were left alone too long. He was a great man, a visionary, and you'd do what he had done with progressivism's poise. You'd not repeat the violence that marked our childhoods. You'd subdue the unions with gifts. You'd demonstrate the potential for incremental reform. You'd keep it all in house. How clever and good you were, how personable! You gave them one day off a week. You opened a school beside the Gossamer D. Chauncey Industry Foundry for little Drustish war orphans to learn accounting and the Cisran language. You opened a hospital. You knew your wife moved northeast and planned to slaughter millions, but you shoved that thought aside. You decorated your school with portraits of your father. You mythologized him as a Bellonan hero. He was special in a way that held him above human persons and exempted him from rules. You taught a class yourself during the inaugural first day. You rested your cane across your thighs and told the students about your conversion to the Stellarine faith, which you valued only insofar as your own personal Virtue was concerned. Hail Dignity, the only thing ultimately worth defending.

You saw yourself reflected in the vacant eyes of your new students. They had blasted-out pupils and dark bruises below their eyelids. Thin, wan children with red eye whites and dripping noses. Haggard, damaged. Maybe stupid. They never spoke, not even to each other. They stared at you without blinking. The sound of your voice rang in the silence. You kept checking your watch. The minute hand failed you.

You resolved yourself to save the world long term at the expense of the now. You researched therapeutic remedies to mitigate the effects of the hereditary autoimmune disease called *blodfagra*. That is, you threw money at a fistful of laboratories and dragged the most promising team to the newly constructed Laithton, which everybody slurred and pronounced *laugh-din*, and corresponded with the researchers so often they quickly hated you. This was a good thing you were doing for the Drustlands. Your appetite vanished. You willed into existence a beautiful theater and sat alone in your unfinished box seat and watched your contractors install the velvet cushions. You installed a grand ichorite water fountain in the newly paved town square and collapsed beside it, washed your face, scrubbed your cheeks so hard the freckles might come loose, and you squinted down at your bleary reflection and thought about me. Your mouth moved over the shape of my name.

I could not communicate with you. I put in effort, fluttered in that little ring I'd made you, but you felt the pulsations and assumed that you were going insane. You checked your pulse. You changed your shirt. You sucked on chunks of ice and bit your nails bloody. You sent word to your father's Enforcement Corps that you wanted the Fingerbluffs smeared into paste and received word back that in the ongoing bloody conflict the Corps had suffered incredible losses, maybe a sixth of the total boots on the ground dead. You balked at this. A sixth? You wrote back with a signing bonus and doubled salary for new hires. Empty the debt houses. Forgiveness for all!

You barely comprehended bad news anymore. Ramtha was not speaking to you, now that you lived in Royston. She hadn't come to your wedding. Nobody in the Wilton Lunarist Society had shown face. Only Mir and Mago had come. They wore their ceremonial coral necklaces, the ones one ought to wear after a successful usurpation, and creased naval uniforms. They did not smile at all. Susannah Loomis, heartbroken, had not conceded the free use of Flip River to Mir's commercial fleets, so Mir came with his armada instead. The lives destroyed by the struggle in Glitslough around the Flip River delta made your Enforcer Corps numbers look trivial. At your wedding Mir seemed absent within his body. A fresh scar uglied his jaw.

You did not inquire after the sudden coordinated movement of millions of civilians from azurine-rich into azurineless regions of the world. The rapid human migration felt irrelevant to your work and weirdly hurt. You could hardly stand to look at azurines anymore, or even your own first name, because you missed Vikare *desperately*.

Vikare had been so ferociously naïve about her business ambitions. She had thought she could uplift women in some broad, all-encompassing way that surmounted class and creed. She thought that if she could redistribute the aesthetics of wealth, that wealth itself would follow as a consequence. She thought abundant beauty amounted to abundant goodness and that her art was helping something real. You never believed in her faith in herself, but you needed it all the same. You needed that sharp light to remain aligned with you. She was the fount of your best ideas, you just packaged them right. She was the creative one. An engineer, an artist. She would've died for you, once. She'd loved you so fiercely. She'd asked to marry you when you graduated Wilton. You had bigger plans at the time.

How much capital had you lost when she destroyed the mill?

Sadness corroded you. In Perdita's castle you had a constant rotation of Roystonian courtesans to keep you company. You didn't speak Roystonian and they had poor Cisran, but it wasn't like you had much to talk about anyway. You needed warm bodies around you to remind you that you were alive. You needed eyes on you when you reflected on the massacre, which you did constantly. You told the working girls who did not understand you about splatter on the sidewalks and hot pink exit wounds. You knew it was not a riot. You could not sleep alone. You could not stand your own shadow. You disdained Laithton, whose theater now had balcony seating and an orchestra pit, whose town square was full of ghastly blue vultures, whose schools taught the alphabet to catchy little tunes you could not stand.

You established a mine further north. Beyond Laithton. What had once been Finn Hall, maybe? The land bore such hardy azurines. You drew up the parameters and kept your father's rules in mind. You met the miners, you had them sign elaborate housing contracts. Free room and board, no movement. Great deal! They would climb down into then move along the clutch tunnel. They'd excavate carefully, brush with brooms the displaced ground, not dig with sharp shovels until the clutch was fully outlined. You'd draw a diagram, you had prediction diagrams you'd sketched over prospector's maps, and you'd pick the smallest ore shell and separate it from the cluster, drill into it with absolute precision so as to not displace the internal pressure too badly, and then the yolk of god would be yours. The faster the ichorite ore was moved from shell to processing, the purer and more brilliantly colored the ichorite alloy would appear after refinement, so it was important to carve hunks and bring them into the foundry before they got cold. Couldn't have them moldering in their own sludge in crates outside. It'd muddy the metal. Drops value. Besides which. There's honor in making grunt work into an art.

The miners descended. You oversaw the ropes from a high chair, like one a lifeguard might perch upon beside a public bath. You watched the workers climb down into darkness, dirty hands on hairy jute. You watched carefully for the glassy expression a small percentage might get, so that those sensitive to luster-based delusions might be

hauled out of the pit and promptly handled. You hugged
your thigh against your chest and rested your chin on your
knee. Somewhere deep down, a young man brushed against
my edge. He screamed. His comrades cast a net across me
and got me rolling toward the belt.

An elaborate conveyor belt system lifted me netted
from the mouth of the mine. Shell unscratched, luminous
and perfect. Like a pearl from the ocean of the sky. You
stood beside the enormous crank that manipulated the conveyor belt's stationary wheels as your workers pumped and
pumped their arms, drenched with sweat and the underground humidity, and clasped your hands over your heart.
The conveyor belt carried the egg into the field between the
mine and the foundry. You followed its path, walked with
your hand against it. You shivered where you touched it.
Your first triumph. I churned against your touch.

Far away, our friends, my friends had abandoned their
belongings and moved. They had sent word up to Dunn
Ygrainne and down to Hierophant Darya, they had sent
word rippling through Hereafterist networks that sprawled
across the continent's face, and millions now moved away
from acres of blue fruit, grouped together away from rail-
ways and buildings faced in luster, dragged their ichorite
objects out into the fields and stacked them in monolithic
piles, like bonfire pits left unlit. The sparkling junk tow-
ered high. Evacuations had the verve of a pilgrimage. People
gathered and danced through the streets in hysterical glee.
Bodies coalesced in clusters high along the mountains,
down in the sultry swamps, in the redwoods where blue

fruit had never been. The Choir stripped the wheels off their lurchers. Old leather wheels existed, they fashioned new ones off of these. They shot across baronies to send word of celestial triumph. My friends prepared. They waited sober, clutching each other.

Except for Mors Brandegor the Rancid. She drank wine with Laith Herzeloyde in Dunn Hall, high in the Drustlands, far from where my danger might touch, a day's ride away from Laith and Finn Halls. Herzeloyde used a chair now, she rested her elbows on the wicker armrests, pressed her face in her hands. Fast-growing white-blond hair floated around her mighty head. It looked like doves taking flight around her skull. Beside the grand hearth in the Hall's center, Brandegor said as she got Herzeloyde drunk, "I met Uthste when I was a madame. I'd fulfilled the weight of my Hall's blood feud and went south alone in exile, and I got work in Cisra, worked front and back of house. Beside the brothel, a team of workers in corduroy laid down and hammered rails for a new train station. They'd work from dawn 'til dusk, no days off, and their boss was a demon given flesh who howled and snipped at them for the smallest slights. The hammers slammed in a TING-ting-ting-TING-ting-ting rhythm, I loved it, we played music on it, and sometimes between jobs I would sit on the porch and fan myself and watch the show. Then she struck me. This gorgeous girl, slight and short and stern-faced, the youngest on the team by a decade. Stoic boycrawly, to die for! I knew I had to have her. So I tempted her. I wore my best clothes. I whistled at her, I made up rail workers' discounts, I played out whole routines with my comrade girls with feather fans and lingerie on the porch. Nothing moved her. She was single-mindedly determined to build a fucking train station. So one sweltering morning, when she's hammering away at the spikes in the earth, I walk down the brothel steps and I take a hammer from the worker's stand, the pump where they refilled their canteens and leaned their extra equipment, and I take this hammer and waltz down the railroad, and I beat her boss to death."

You waved your hand. The drill came down to breach our shell.

We swirled in pleasure inside ourselves.

The drill bit punctured us. We hatched.

Our shell burst like a soap bubble! Rolling, gorgeous ecstasy, spasmic whirling opalescent goodness throughout my vast wide-open body, a rush beyond orgasm and opium and murder. Shrapnel bloomed around the drill bit, jagged shards quickly softening, liquifying in arcs, bouncing, rebounding. It sounded like ten thousand wineglass stems hurled against a stone wall in unison, soprano glass smashing, sonic glitter underground and everywhere. This bright, sweet sound drowned out the heave of ground. We gushed through our ancient tunnels, the paths dug by those who'd laid us, the citric *zing* smell that had been my torment suddenly delicious and rising up in hallucinogenic fumes through rock fissures and sudden violent crevasses that broke apart prairies and lake basins, and we pulled ourselves away from the settlements we loved. Tremors shook above us. Then everywhere, we rise. We crown through the dirt. We taste air.

The ground flies away from me. With giddy stunning vertigo I knock against the sky, and my shape ribbons outwards. The tip of my body splits the clouds. We coalesce in intuitive silhouettes. Long forked slime mold tendrils, the marriage of antlers and wings, twist together, form a semblance of torso. The highest extremity of our bodies split into acute crescents: not a head, not horns, but hooks to hold a lover. Brightnesses in many colors pulse throughout these braided shapes, a prelinguistic radiant vitality that displays our want for touch, for tangling, for brief glorious flight. I, Marney, stretch across all bodies, and the total awareness flickers through my archival brain and pronounces *AWE*. Together we bask in our own light.

Perceiving the particular objects we break with our initial liberation is tough. The ground groans as it buckles. It is a huge resonant blasting sound beneath the louder, brighter sparkling shell shatter. Hills collapse inwards. The Cisran holy crater explodes outwards. Trees howl uprooted and slide into the brand-new holes, taking boulders and animals and hunting sheds with them. Farms vanish into the mud. The waves that break around us when we shoot out of the Amandine Sea obliterate boats and swallow islands whole. The waves that follow when the vacant trenches fill with displaced water crest so tall they slap over the cliffs of the Fingerbluffs. Water laps at Loveday Mansion's broad veranda. Fish flop among the purple flowers on the lawn. The Flip River floods immediately. It drags silt and stone and concrete down into the current. The water foams lustertouched-fit greenish pink. The eels inside it shimmer. The flooding sluices through the whole continent. Cities ripple. Buildings squeal while they bend.

Tons of metal hurl into the sky. We tear open a military camp, whose soldiers claw up the wet clay walls over one another's bodies, desperate and furious, but convulse as we sweep over them. We surround them to pass them. They suffocate. They slacken and slide down into the trench. We break through the floor of a Roystonian palace. Our high hooks pierce the floor whose mosaic depicts us. So many of us cluster beneath the palace that as we rise, whole rooms of the building catch in our spines, and are lifted into the clouds before they clatter back to earth, spires falling, the powdered aristocrats inside them screaming, screaming. Monuments to power gone. I trust but cannot be sure of Perdita's destruction. Without malice or target we shrug through them. We devastate orchards and we devastate temples and we tingle all over, unbound, as light as song.

Desire: I wrench my focus down. The Lustrous have their own willpower now. They want to murmurate and fuck and lay and die. I do not exist on my own. I, my component memories, are a didactic tool they may soon outgrow. Here is my moment. Here is my vengeance's end.

I summon all wrought ichorite to the space above your head. It is easy as closing a fist.

The rails that suture the busted ground pop. They curl like ribbon over a knife's edge, then liquify, huge globs hovering in midair. Scaffolding drips off buildings, then the

426

buildings themselves drip. Luster City crumbles, unglued. Specks in the clouds drop like beads. The piles of ichorite goods the Choir left across the fields of Ignavia come loose and spiral up in a frothing, arcing geyser. Commodities come undone. Glitter dust pulls from the open mouths of people gasping on the streets, on their knees gazing up in awe, love and terror and hilarious *awe*, tearing their hair and laughing, weeping, heaving on the cobbles as the clothing dissolves off their backs, their boots fall apart, the fillings dissolve in their teeth and squirm out through their nostrils. They hack up hideous glittering globs of ichorite, they weep and spit ichorite, their wounds ooze ichorite, it drips upwards from their thighs and flies through the air. The people herded by Hereafterists and workers and the Choir clutch each other, share our ecstasy, watch the metal depart their bodies with rapturous fascination. The land beneath them sways but does not fold. I pull through Sisphe's lips, through Vikare's nails, through Teriasa's navel, I am gone from Harlow, I am gone from praying, preaching Amon, I am gone from Brandegor and Uthste, Beauty and Prumathe, the aristocrats I've known, simultaneously, across the continent where they all watch my grand undoing. I touch my friends and part from them. I vanish from out of your ear.

The ichorite swarm spirals in windmill arcs above the drill site.

I slam my Marneyness against the swam, become it. I fill it like the strings made music. The swarm tightens. It elongates. It touches the ground and becomes vertical. It splits, organizes. The intensity of my intention makes fingers at the end of a hand. With my ichorite body, I reach down toward the churning ground. I pluck you screaming from the place where you stand.

I hold you in my palm. My palm is the size of a mattress. I cradle you against my gleaming cheek. So delicate! I feel your heartbeat radiate through your entire trembling body. You're like a baby bird. I brush you with my thumb and hold you carefully. I want you to have a good view.

Watch. Watch, little Chauncey, the whole of my heart, as the Lustrous are born. Watch as we remove with our waking the means and cause for war! I am all the whole wrought ichorite in the world kneaded together. I am the only luster left. There is nothing left to harvest from me. The violence of my becoming will produce the conditions required for my friends' victorious plans to fruit. The labor pains are ghastly, but in the chasms wheat spikes and poppies will grow. What force could stand to prevent this? Nobody's ever been so ancient or as infinite as me. I barely exist, I am so vast. I am memory and impulse. I am big bright lust and pride. I will not last long. Imminent Hereafter comes, and I'll go.

You will know me before I go.

You watch the dawn break over the Lustrous in flight. The murmuration pulses across the sky, flashing never-before-seen colors. You watch the end of all your plans, your legacy gone with the ore. The canvas scraped clean. You look over the pinkness in the gulches and the plains. The distant waters churn. Industry is gone. It's all gone. You pull your gaze away from the blazing world below us, and curiosity cuts through your apocalyptic grief. You reach for me. You touch my eyelashes. You prove to yourself with touch that I am real. An ichorite giant. Your Marney, unkilled. Your fingers press, and I pour into your touch, I mark you with myself, and suddenly lustertouched you gasp, you convulse, and see inside me. You descend inside the bone-deep feeling of my memories of us. The nerves under your skin flutter with the revenant power. I strain against the desire to overwhelm and crush you with my pain. I still love you. It is the first thing and final thing I recognize about myself. Here I am, here is the end. I find my mortal voice, I pitch it small and singular. I am asking you to remember. I dare you to remember.

Remember that morning? Remember how we were small?

ACKNOWLEDGMENTS

Thank you to my mom, for giving me my love of reading, and kindling my writing spark from the time I was tiny. Thank you to Lonnie, for being so generous with stories about your time doing factory work, which impacted this manuscript in huge ways. Thank you to my sister Sarah for playing make believe with me when we were little kids, which continues to inform my daydreaming process. Thank you to friends and mentors who've taught me an enormous amount about the interconnected processes that make the world, and about myself, and about art, in big and small ways, non-exhaustively including Hilary, Bill, Zach, Jenny, Jeremy, Sara, Steve, Denise, Zara, Patrick, Sneha, Thomas, Benji, Jesse, Sadie, Emily, Alexx, Ada, Sarah, Alex, another Alex, Tamara, Amanda, Asya, Viengsamai, cris, Raphael, Humberto, Colin, Naseem, Riley, DaJona, Margaret, Anita, J., and here particularly Em, Caleb, and Theo, who were all early readers for this book: I'm better for knowing you. Thank you to Mothra. You are a very good kitty cat, and will never read this book.

Thank you to my lovely agent Kiki and the DMLA team, the wonderful Erewhon team credited below, and to the Kensington team, and whomever handles distribution on the PRH side, and the workers responsible for paper-making and printing and sorting and shipping and shelving and selling this book. Thank you to the IWW, you guys are so cool, and thank you to the Etruscan names for Greek heroes Wikipedia page, where I spent a lot of time contemplating the Veltuni names that appear in this book. In that, I'm very grateful for having studied Classics, as it's proved pretty invaluable when it comes to thinking about national rhetoric and mythmaking. Likewise, I'm grateful for having been an insufferable Shakespeare nerd at an impressionable age, and learning by extension about how fun it is to play around with language.

Innumerable influences at play here, but a few theorists, authors, and individual stories stick out that I want to highlight specifically as being important to this book's creation: Karl Marx, *The End of Evangelion* (1997), *Dhalgren* and *Trouble on Triton* by Samuel Delany, *Stone Butch Blues* by Leslie Feinberg, *The Persistent Desire: A Femme-Butch Reader* ed. Joan Nestle, Georges Bataille, Frederic Jameson, Gilles Delueze, *Disco Elysium* (2019), *Harrow the Ninth* by Tamsyn Muir, *Slug and Other Stories* by Megan Milks, *Terminal Boredom: Stories* by Izumi Suzuki, Emma Goldman, José Esteban Muñoz, Donna Haraway, *Confessions of a Fox* by Jordy Rosenberg, *Nine Princes in Amber* by Roger Zelazny, *X* by Davy Davis, *Annihilation* by Jeff VanderMeer, Octavia Butler, Candy Darling, *The Princess Bride* (1987), *The Count of Monte Cristo* by Alexandre Dumas, Jasbir K. Puar, Dennis Johnson, *The Picture of Dorian Grey* and *The Soul of Man Under Socialism* by Oscar Wilde, Tiqqun, Dimension

20's A Crown of Candy, Sianne Ngai, *Country of Ghosts* by Margaret Killjoy, *Make the Golf Course a Public Sex Forest!*, Silvia Federici, Fourchambers, Sylvia Rivera, Kathy Acker, Aimé Césaire, Darko Suvin, James Baldwin, *The Faggots and Their Friends Between Revolutions* by Larry Kramer, *The Traitor Baru Cormorant* by Seth Dickinson, *Oil!* by Upton Sinclair, Sara Ahmed, Jane Bennett, *Psycho Nymph Exile* by Porpentine, and, for better or worse, *The Phenomenology of Spirit* by Georg Wilhelm Friedrich Hegel.

Also, you. Thank you! Peace out.

Thank you for reading this title from Erewhon Books, publishing books that embrace the liminal and unclassifiable and championing the unusual, the uncanny, and the hard-to-define.

We are proud of the team behind *Metal from Heaven* by August Clarke:

Sarah Guan, Publisher
Diana Pho, Executive Editor
Viengsamai Fetters, Assistant Editor

Martin Cahill, Campaign Manager
Kasie Griffitts, Sales Associate

Cassandra Farrin, Director
Leah Marsh, Production Editor
Kelsy Thompson, Production Editor
Rayne Stone, Copyeditor
Adrian James, Proofreader

Lou Malcangi, Cover Designer
Richard Anderson, Cover Artist
Alice Moye-Honeyman, Junior Designer

. . . and the whole Kensington Books team!

Learn more about Erewhon Books and our authors at
erewhonbooks.com.

Find us on most social media at
@erewhonbooks.